TUMBLEWEEDS BURNING

—— *Book 2* ——

-A Novel-

TUMBLEWEEDS BURNING

──── *Book 2* ────

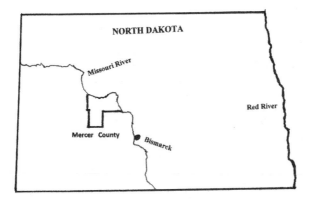

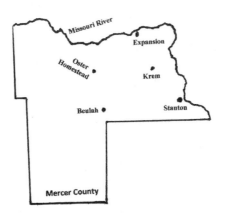

MILT OST

Library of Congress Control Number: 2014922837
ISBN: Hardcover   978-1-5035-3045-4
                  Softcover   978-1-5035-3046-1
                  eBook   978-1-5035-3044-7

Print information available on the last page.

Rev. date: 04/13/2015

To order additional copies of this book, contact:
Xlibris
1-888-795-4274
www.Xlibris.com
Orders@Xlibris.com
552728

Contents

Dedication

Sabrina, Catherine, and Deborah
who taught me so much
and fill my life with joy,
along with Delores
and all my family and friends
who have blessed me more
than words can ever tell.

Foreword

The story of a quarter-million German-Russian people is a love story untold. They loved the old country, but they loved their new land more. And more than both, they loved their God. This continues the story of one of those families, across five generations of time.

And for the Osters, what a trip it was. From being nobodies in Germany, they went to being yet smaller nobodies under the czars of Russia. From the Black Sea to the Statue of Liberty, from the bustle of Ellis Island to the raw silence of middle America they endured persecution and fear, yet gave themselves over to the strange miracle of being protected, somehow safe and finally at home.

Their beginning, in the land where they expected milk and honey, was lived out under an overturned wagon box on the buffalo grass of the Dakotas until their sod house would shelter them. Rattle snakes and coyotes were their companions, tumbleweeds and early death their nemesis, murder and black magic their unseen neighbors.

But with iron wills and stubborn determination, they turned the heartland of America into a flowing river of food production that could feed the world.

To be nourished in the bosom of this people, speak their dialect, absorb their idiosyncrasies, but most of all to be steeped in the profound hope and faith that colored every page of their life, has been a privilege indeed. It is my hope, dear reader, that as you walk these pages, your heart might experience a gentle touch of that as well.

M. Ost

Glossary

Arbusa – watermelon, sometimes called "wasser melon."

Bessarabia – province in southern Ukraine, west of Odessa and the Black Sea.

Blatchinda – pastry dough rolled out and filled with pumpkin, sugar, cinnamon, folded over and baked.

Borscht – "poor man's soup," made with cabbage, onions, carrots, potatoes, garlic, salt, pepper. Some used beets instead of cabbage (made "red soup"), and topped it off with a dollop of sour cream. Could upgrade with tomatoes and pork sausage or pork shank.

Czar – Russian equivalent of Roman "Caesar." When writer speaks it is "czar." When characters in the story speak they always make it "tsar." Czar's family is: wife – tsarina; sons – tsarevich; daughters – tsarevna. (In German, Czar becomes "Kaiser.")

Dah – Russian for "yes." (Nyet for "no.")

Dampf Nudla – yeast dough rolled out, then rolled up like cinnamon roll, put in covered pan with onions, garlic and water, and cooked.

Dessiatine – Russian land measurement, equals 2 ¼ acres.

Dorf – German for "small village."

Eggles – slang for "that's ugly, and gives me the willies."

Fleisch Kuechla – dough rolled out and filled with hamburger, onions, salt and pepper, then folded over and deep-fried in lard.

Gel – used for "right?", "correct?", "you agree?" (hard "g" as in gallon).

Gatch – slang for a person who is a "really weird duck."

Gurke – pickles.

Halupsy – cabbage leaves rolled and stuffed with onion, hamburger, rice, spices, covered with tomato sauce and baked in the oven.

Halvah – sweet confection, served as candy; made from sesame seeds, nut butter, sugar, glucose, honey. Variations could include sunflower seeds, cocoa powder, vanilla, almonds, orange concentrate, or pistachio nuts for different flavors.

Hectare – German land measurement, equals 2½ acres.

Hootzla – slang for "a big bunch of nothing."

Ja – yes, pronounced "Yah."

Jammer elend – slang expression of shock and surprise, more intense than "Ei, yei, yei." Pronounced "Yahmer ale-end." Literal translation: "misery of miseries."

Kaladyetz – head cheese, jellied dish similar to Schwarta Maga, scrap parts of pig when butchering, boiled in broth, poured into pan, layer of boiled eggs, carrots, parsley added, cooled, and sliced as luncheon meat.

Knoepfla – dumplings; flour, eggs, milk, mixed and dropped by teaspoon-size into boiling water.

Kase Knoepfla – cheese buttons; noodle dough rolled into sheets, cut, stuffed with cheese mixture, folded over and boiled in broth. Similar to manicotti or pyrogies.

Kuchen – yeast-raised pastry dough rolled out, put in pie tin, covered with half-inch layer of cooked custard, and slices of fresh or canned fruit laid in (peaches, apricots, blueberries, prunes, or rhubarb), sprinkled with cinnamon and baked in oven.

Kuechle – fry bread, flour dough fried in lard.

Kvass – low-alcohol Russian drink made by fermenting black bread in water, adding yeast, sugar, malt extract, and flavoring with mint, strawberries, apples, or raisins.

Schwarta Maga – made from pig's head, snout, ears, brains, feet, and other scrap parts, all fine-ground, broth added, cooked and poured into cleaned pig's stomach. Thin sliced and served with bread as breakfast meat.

St. John's Bread – the "locusts" John the Baptist ate in the biblical narrative. A chewy, dark-brown pod, six to ten inches long that grows in clusters on trees in the Middle East; rich in fibers, sugar, iron and calcium. Also known as carob. Its seeds are used as a chocolate substitute.

Stirrum – pancake batter stirred until it fries up like scrambled eggs, sometimes mixed with raisins, sprinkled with powdered sugar and cinnamon. Often served with lettuce-and-cream salad as a light supper.

Swabian – or Schwaebisch, German dialect spoken by German-Russians coming from Bavaria and Baden-Wuerttemberg area.

Tanta – used variously for aunt, grandmother, or honorific for older woman.

Verhuddle – a tangled mess (pronounced "fer-WHO-dle").

Verst – Russian measurement roughly equal to kilometer, or six-tenths of a mile.

Wurst – sausage; also word for measurement of one foot (Russian "fut").

Chapter 1

Wittenberg #2

Lady Liberty, standing lonely vigil in the harbor, heard a lot of languages. Were she to ask any of the Oster clan, gazing at her from on board the SS *Armenia*, these new immigrants would have been quick to reply, "We're German, that's it."

Never mind that their forebears had answered the invitations of two Russian czars to come live in that land. Never mind that they had lived in Russia for a hundred years. They were pure German and not, to their mind, some alien half-bloods.

But hope went sour in that land of czarist promise. Life became hard, burdens heavy, persecutions more bloody by the month. In the last year of the 1800s, Christian Oster and his wife, Karolina, left everything behind and set out for the land of promise. A year earlier, their daughter and husband had given in to the lure of fabled America and ended up in a German-Russian enclave in western Dakota. A hundred years their family had plowed Russian soil and eaten her harvest, but they would not adopt the Russian tongue. Then the Russian Double Eagle turned on them, and they were glad to leave it behind.

But mythical Lady Liberty would not quickly pour milk and honey for these new children at her door. They yearned her freedom, but her blessings would not come free. Filled with dreams, they would have to deal with hard realities on the wild prairie frontier to which she pointed them.

Soon two more Oster sons heard her call and would shortly follow their parents. Gottfried and his wife, Wilhelmina "Mina," along with John and his wife, Fredericka "Ricka," under life-threatening duress in that old country, fled from Russia and landed on American shores in 1902. Like the rest they also landed, strange-tongued and scared, at the foot of Lady Liberty.

After untangling themselves from the anthill of Ellis Island, they jumped to the vast grasslands of western North Dakota to join their family and put down roots. Their small farms on Dakota homestead land were immensely different from the comfortable cocoon life in the *dorfs*, little villages, of the Black Sea area they just left; but once their "soddies," sod houses, were glued onto the prairies, they were stubbornly determined to make this land their home.

White civilization had filled the Red River Valley and was creeping ever westward, across the Missouri River, around Fort Berthold Indian Reservation, and edging toward the unglaciered badlands. Buffalo wallows were swallowed up under the plow. Wild prairie roses felt their first nuzzles from cow noses.

But to be civilized meant to have schools and churches, and these German-tongued immigrants, so fiercely protective of their heritage, were just as fiercely determined to plant their offspring rich into the mainstream of their new English America.

Their school, Wittenberg #2, was to have been constructed the previous summer; but the county superintendent's office had problems, and it was delayed a year. The District #2 people were sorely disappointed, but there wasn't much they could do.

Since they themselves knew very little English, they could not homeschool their youngsters, but most of them brought a *Deutsche Fibel*, a German primer textbook for beginners, and with this they gave their children a basic start. The older students were put to work reading the Bible and learning the catechism, all in German as well.

The following year the school was finally built, located on a little rise at the edge of the valley, on land donated by Adam Keller.

The building, four steps up on a cement foundation, was twenty-two by thirty-six feet, with a six-foot entry hall on the south side running the entire width of the building. The inside wall had hooks for coats and space for overshoes. This six-by-twenty-two cramped entry area was also their "gymnasium" in inclement weather. It was all the indoor exercise space they had.

The main room had two windows on the north, four on the east, and to protect against the fierce west winds, none on the west. There were no lamps, no lights, so on cloudy days they just had to squint and keep working.

A teacher's desk stood at the front of the room, in front of it a backless recitation bench. Behind it, high on the wall, were two somber, framed color portraits: George Washington and Abraham Lincoln. To one side hung a four-foot map case with pull-down maps of the whole known world; beside the desk, a small bookshelf which held several dozen library books of interest to different ages, a set of encyclopedias, and a dictionary. The chalk tray at the bottom of the double blackboard held two erasers, four pieces of dusty white chalk, and a slim three-foot wooden pointer for map work. The forty-six-star flag waved proudly on its pole outside. These items, a potbellied stove, and twenty double desks and the Keller School was furnished to set these prairie children on the road to absorbing the wisdom of the ages—or at least a start.

There was no well and no pump, so the students had to bring their own drinking water for the day, usually a pint jar inside their Karo syrup lunch pail, together with perhaps two sandwiches, cheese, and a cookie. No water also meant no washbasin, so all wiped their hands on their bib overalls and kept going. That included the girls, for whom standard dress was overalls as well.

The one luxury of the school, which most students did not have at home, was a board floor. Rough boards to be sure, hard to sweep and cold in winter, but still a distinct novelty to the younger students.

Fifty feet from the school, a second small building was constructed, with a two-hole toilet for the girls on one end, a one-holer for the boys on the other, with a woodshed in between.

A hanging bell on the roof would have been refined, like their school in the old country, but these frugal Germans considered it a luxury here, so a six-inch bronze handbell was added as essential school equipment. It was placed on the right-hand corner of the teacher's desk for handy access, opposite the round wind-up table clock.

Twenty double desks were arranged with ten on each side, beginning with the smallest in front near the windows and getting larger toward the back. The older students would occupy the ten desks on the windowless west side.

A black, potbellied, cast-iron stove, that burned both coal and wood, sat on a tin base in the center of the room—sole defender against frost in the winter, drier of wet mittens after snowball fights at noontime.

The county superintendent of schools in Stanton hired Mr. Henke as teacher and purchased a minimal supply of textbooks. School officially started in September, with fifteen pupils showing up. Most of the students knew no English, and Mr. Henke, a young man who fortunately was himself of German-Russian descent, patiently started them at the very beginning of the ABCs and numbers.

Henke was a graduate of heavily German-Russian populated New Salem High School and went on to earn a teaching certificate after one year at Concordia College in Moorhead, Minnesota, astride the Red River of the North.

Concordia College, a scant dozen years old, was organized by a tableful of Red River Valley men of deep faith and stout character, thoroughly Lutheran and thoroughly Norwegian. And although the founding documents spoke in erudite terms of high Christian ideals and righteous goals, there were also hidden agendas to its beginnings.

"Ja, we need our own college out here then," whispered Hjalmar Olufsson, well-to-do Valley bonanza farmer to his friend in one of the early meetings. "I don't want my Leif runnin' off to St. Paul and gettin' taken in by one a' them young Irish Catholic high-steppers."

"Ja"—the friend's eyes glowed at the terrible picture—"the hot-blooded things even make him forget his good roots, like Samson and Delilah."

"For sure, then."

When young Henke arrived in that flatland Norwegian enclave, he soon discovered a cow of a different color than he had ever known. Instead of kuchen and sauerkraut, he found himself stepping into a world of lutefisk and lefsa, with customs strangely different from his own. Walking down the dormitory hallways, he had to get used to lot of "Uff das" and *Mange Takks*, many thanks."

His friends took to calling him "The Roosian" and good-naturedly teased him, "Hey, Roosian, how far can you spit them Roosian peanuts?"

"Further'n you can put 'em, Norski Buddy," was Henke's stock, smiling answer. To their surprise, after Henke offered them some sunflower seeds, they grew to like them as well for times of bull-session relaxing.

Through it all, Concordia did manage to wrangle the hissing S's from his speech, getting him to say the word "was" as "wuz" rather than "wuss," among many others.

When the Wittenberg school parents came to the new school to meet Henke, they were deeply respectful, but Henke endured awkward moments when they addressed him as "Herr Henke."

"Thank you," he responded, time after time, "but here I am *Mr.* Henke."

They knew no English to speak of, and they knew he knew what they knew, so "Ach, Ja, Meester-r Henkey it is" was their invariable response.

Since there was no convenient place to live, several Keller families living near the school decided that they would take turns boarding their new teacher, a month in each home. Although having him live with students of the school was somewhat awkward, there was no other choice, and all made the best of it.

Now as Henke started his tutelage at Wittenberg #2, he quickly discovered that even the middle students knew only scattered English words; and although they knew how to read and write German, they still had to start learning English at the very beginning as well.

The tongues of these new German immigrants had a difficult time forming some English sounds, so on the second day of school, during the instruction period for his three fifth graders, Mr. Henke picked up a piece of white chalk and walked to the spotless new blackboard. Until now it had only one sentence written on it, at the very top left-hand side: "Your teacher is Mr. Henke." Now, in the center of the shiny blackboard, he wrote a large letter *W*.

Then, while he called his fifth graders to come and sit on the recitation bench, he knew all the other students would be listening in just as intently, and he asked, "Mathilda, what is that letter called?"

"'Vay,' Herr, I mean, *Mr.* Henke," she replied, turning crimson.

"Yes, Mathilda, in German that letter would be called 'vay,' but in English it is pronounced 'double-u.' Can you all say that?"

"Dough-bel-oo."

"No, listen carefully now. It's not 'doughbel' and not 'oo,' but 'dubble' and 'you.' Say 'dubble-*you.*'"

"Dubble-*you!*" they chorused back.

"So when you see a word that begins with 'w,' it will always begin with a 'woo' sound, not a 'v' sound like you'd say it in German."

Walking back to the board, he printed, "Wash your wool in warm water."

Then, with his pointing stick touching each word, he said slowly, *"Wash . . . your wool . . . in warm . . . water.* Can you say that together?"

"Vash your vool in varm vater."

"Oh boy," he chuckled, "we have some work to do, don't we." They laughed as well, although they weren't quite sure why.

After the fourth try, they were finally getting "woo" sounds out, even though it still didn't sound right to their ears.

Next, he went back to the board and wrote the letter *V.*

"Heinrich, what is that called?"

"Fow," answered Heinrich, using his best German pronunciation.

"That's right, Heinrich, in German *v* has an *f* sound. So 'vater,' which you know is German for 'father,' would be spoken as 'fater.' You are exactly right. But now we have to throw that letter out on Keller's rock pile too and give it a new name."

When they all chuckled, picturing *V*s slamming into the rock pile close to the school ground, he continued, "From now on, when you see *v*, it will be pronounced as 'vee.' Can you all say that?"

"Wee."

"That's tricky too, isn't it. Watch me: put your top teeth against your bottom lip and see if you can make it come out as 'vee.' Try it again."

With some comical facial contortions, they began to come out with "vee."

Back at the board, Mr. Henke wrote "Victor held a vast vase" and led them all in saying it together.

After a number of twisted tries, the *V*s finally came out victorious.

Then he wrote, "Victor wore a warm vest."

That combination threw the slickest tongues into a tangle.

"Now, write all these words down, and take them home and practice them with your parents. Make sure they help you get 'em correct, all right?" With considerable effort, the words were formed in their tablets to take home.

He knew this would be a huge challenge to the parents as well, but with this one lesson, the whole neighborhood would have a leg up on riding into the wide American world in style.

Now he could begin with the ABCs, numbers, and simple words. Although the students' ages went from six to fourteen, learning had to start at the beginning for the entire group and progress from there. Their First Readers saw hard usage.

Henke also took on the challenge of getting his students to form a "th" sound in their speech, getting "the" instead of "da." And the hissing *S*s were sitting at every desk. But those things too would come in time, and the youngsters were a joy to teach, energetic and eager to get on with becoming good Americans in every way.

A number of older boys did not start for several weeks, because they were needed for threshing, but before long they too were at their desks, although in many cases they were not the most studious of pupils and were more often overly interested in the girls instead. They had worlds of catching up to do, but hopefully listening to the instruction time with the younger ones would also get them in tune with the mysteries of English, along with their personal focus on the infinite mysteries of femininity.

Recess and lunchtime were the most difficult, because Mr. Henke tried to get them to use only the new tongue, but they knew no conversational English for the playground, so his rules had to be bent and delayed until well into the year.

The students knew they were now in America, and that meant learning English in school. But somehow it seemed that when something needed to be said forcefully, saying it in German always carried more power—especially if you were angry!

Chapter 2

A Cauldron of Change

The next years were times of immense change, not only in their little corner of the world but across the civilized world as a whole.

Their little valley was now called Antelope Valley, though there were few of the fleet-footed creatures to be seen. All the land available for homesteading was taken, with soddies popping up across the entire valley, on the hills beyond, and moving ever farther west.

The Valley itself was a roiling cauldron of change.

"Have you noticed," said Ricka to her husband, John, one night after they finished supper, "nearly everybody around here is having babies?"

"Not only babies," replied John, "stock's exploding too, cattle every place you look."

"And sheep and pigs."

"More land going under the plow too."

"I even heard the neighbor's rooster crowing the other morning."

"We're not alone anymore, like when we first got here."

Though horses were still in heavy use, a few tractors—some steam, some gasoline—were rumbling and belching smoke across the fields and pulling much bigger machinery than before.

****

For the members of their new Peace Lutheran congregation, the biggest change came when their numbers had increased enough so they could raise the money to build their own church. Matt Huber donated two acres of land on the high plateau a mile south of the flowing Missouri, and here they erected their small tabernacle to the Lord. Together with a neighboring church to the west, they formed a parish to call their own pastor from the Iowa Synod's German-speaking Wartburg Seminary in Dubuque, Iowa.

During construction time, the new pastor remembered that in his student days at Wartburg Seminary, he had seen an advertisement for church bells from the McShane Bell Foundry in Baltimore, Maryland, and on a student visit to one of the larger churches in Dubuque, he had seen a McShane Bell. Now he tried to convince the members of Peace that a McShane ringing out over the prairies would be truly unique in their area. When the idea met with strong resistance, several Renner families decided they'd give the needed money in memory of their grandfather who had died in the old country before he could come here.

The special bell in its heavy wooden crate traveled the same rails they had, east to west. It silently passed, as did they, the long, malodorous miles of Chicago's stockyards, whose loud, empty-bellied cattle did not know that they were also bellowing their last as it passed by.

Compared to the mighty resonance of the symphonic bells of Notre Dame, this little bronze cone was but a tinkle in a teacup; but to these inheritors of the last virgin buffalo grasses, its brave chime was the call of heaven itself, bidding them to come eat the bread of life. They debated not for whom that bell would toll. They knew it would toll one final time for each of them, and its mournful ululation would carry them into this prairie sod, for some too soon, too soon. Already there were several graves in the cemetery.

Their church was not alone. All around their area church steeples were being raised, mostly Lutheran, one Reformed. With few roads, churches were spaced so neighborhoods could travel to worship by buggy in an hour's time or less.

One Sunday morning, as they were in the buggy, returning home from church, John mentioned, "I sure like that verse in the Psalm the pastor read today."

"What's that?" asked Ricka.

"When it said, 'Lord, I love the house in which you dwell, and the place where your glory abides.'"

"Ja, it's sure nice to finally have our own church," she added. "I feel so close to God there."

"And I like the idea that his glory is all around us, wherever we are."

"Makes our little soddy kind of special too, with the Lord being there, doesn't it?"

"Even here in this nice buggy," he said softly, smiling at her as he reached over and drew her close to snuggle on the spring-loaded seat beside him.

****

The five-year wait for citizenship flew by like a whirlwind, and the Oster clan received an invitation to come to the county courthouse in Stanton on July 3, 1910, to be sworn in, together with a large group of other settlers, as United States citizens, "along with all the rights and privileges pertaining thereto." A big picnic, flags waving, bunting fluttering, being sworn in by the district judge, stumbling through the English of the Pledge of Allegiance, this was their day. Speeches by the town mayor and by no less a personage than the Honorable Governor John Burke, who had traveled up the long dirt roads from the state capitol in Bismarck, and the day was most satisfying in almost every way.

The main speaker, Governor Burke, carried the distinction of being the very first Democratic governor ever elected in the state of North Dakota; and although they counted it an honor to hear him, many of these newish Mercer County farmers had already developed sharp leanings toward Republican ways of thinking. To them, Burke's words somehow seemed to have an elitist Eastern tilt to them, and they came away somewhat less than totally impressed.

During these years, Theodore Roosevelt and his rambunctious clan occupied the "bully pulpit White House," as he called it; and these settlers loved him because his ranching days in the nearby Badlands of Medora made him one of them. They were further impressed when they read the articles which the *Staats-Anzeiger* picked off the telegraph, telling about him busting up large, shady business monopolies and fighting rampant corruption in Washington. Power, they well knew, brought corruption, as deviously in Washington as in the royal palaces of the czar or the shadowy bureaucracies of the old European State churches; and Republican Roosevelt was their man.

As they continued to wrest a living from the prairie soils, still more things grew to have significant influence in their lives.

"You know, I think the rubber tire has changed this country more than anything else they've invented," John's brother, Gottfried, said one day when they were visiting. "Sure gets everybody around faster."

"That's for sure," John replied, "and how about windmills?"

"Ja, and even the railroads, I guess."

Windmills opened the prairies for watering ever bigger herds of beef cattle, and railroads now ran across the state, hauling the beef to the slaughterhouses of Chicago and from there to the tables of the East, and on iced ships back to the palaces and elegant dining establishments of sophisticated Europe that couldn't get enough of that splendid marbled Western beef.

Soon rumors ran rampant that the Northern Pacific Railroad was planning to run a spur line north through their area. The *Staats-Anzeiger,* their German paper, carried articles that got the businessmen of Krem enormously excited. Since Krem had become the leading commercial center of Mercer County, there was speculation that the railroad might indeed come through their town, and already the wealthier citizens were eyeing land to acquire for making a profit off the railroad. Grandpa Christ met with a number of businessmen, and they elected a delegation to visit St. Paul to talk with the rail executives.

The Northern Pacific had finished their rail line from Chicago to the Pacific Ocean barely a score of years earlier, cutting all the way across the broad southern plains of North Dakota. They spent a million dollars bridging the Missouri River at Bismarck, and for all their efforts, the US Congress rewarded them with mineral rights to forty-seven million acres of land along their railroad. They frantically pushed their Irish and Swedish crews, and in a huge party, the Golden Spike was driven in Gold Creek, Montana, on September 8, 1883, connecting Chicago and Seattle. Now the company was advertising widely throughout Europe to entice immigrants to settle along these rails for a wonderful new life.

The Krem delegation won an audience with the NP executives in St. Paul and, to their surprise, got an opportunity to meet briefly with Howard Elliott, who after some bitter in-house struggles had become the Northern Pacific president and was briefly in town for company business.

Walking into those richly appointed, sumptuous executive offices with lavish Persian rugs over decorative mosaic parquet floors and hand-rubbed paneling from exotic places in Africa and the Far East, Krem's point man, Sam Richter, softly muttered, "Liebe Zeit, O man, this ain't the barbershop in Krem!" The wide-eyed neighbor at his shoulder quietly whispered, "That desk is as big as my house!"

After pleasantries, the delegation laid out their best possible case for a spur line from Mandan up to Krem and on west, citing the huge economic benefits the rail company could reap by hauling out their millions of bushels of grain and their grass-fed beef on the hoof by the thousands. "And don't forget," added one of the men, "the tons of freight coming west to supply all the new folks moving in here every month."

"And," continued an exuberant Richter, "we think one of the truly historic opportunities of this spur line is that it would follow the famous exploration route that Lewis and Clark took across this great country just a hundred years ago."

"Yes," chimed in another delegate, "even our people in Russia heard about that, and people all over Europe."

Richter quickly pressed on, "We're sure your railroad would have a really big business taking thousands of interested new tourists with good money out to the mineral baths in the west and to the great mountains further on."

The NP executives, including Elliott, listened politely, thanked them for coming, and said they would certainly give it careful consideration.

In the meantime, James Hill had driven his Great Northern Railroad across the northern part of North Dakota, in fierce competition with the Northern Pacific line, and others were speculating that he would run a spur from Minot down to the rich Krem country to pick up their business. However, that would again mean bridging the Missouri River, and Hill had learned enough from the Northern Pacific to leave that alone. Still, tongues kept the "limitless progress" flames alive over brews in hopeful Krem.

At home, Ricka wasn't much concerned about the railroad. She had grown tired of her little one-room soddy and desperately wanted more space. With the neighbors' help, they added a second room on the east side of the sod house. John sawed a hole in the sod for a door between the rooms, and their house was now double the size. Brother Gottfried and wife, Mina, living a mile away did the same.

They sorely needed the room, because their families had also grown. Ricka's sons, Phillip and Gottfried, now had two sisters, Emilia and Martha, and two more brothers. Mina, meanwhile, had not rested on her washboard. To her two little ones, she added four more. The three Oster sisters further west continued to fill their soddies as well. Sister-in-law Katherina Baisch in Krem added six more and was still going strong, as were many of those hearty prairie tamers.

When Ricka and Mina were visiting together, Ricka took a sip of her strong coffee and looked steadily into Mina's eyes. "You know," she said, "I am really, really tired of these dirt floors we have."

"Don't think I'm not. Grandma has a wood house with a floor in Krem."

"So does Katherina."

"Even our mother back in Russia!"

"She's had it for years."

When they approached their men, both met with a cold reception.

"Wood house would sure be nice," was John's response that night at supper, "but with a new barn, we can run more cattle and make money to care for the family."

"Ach, I don't care."

"A fancy new house won't earn no money at all, you know."

"Oh, all you men can think of is making money."

"No, it means taking better care of my family," replied John.

"Well, just maybe, taking better care of your wife is important too."

With that, John got out the family Bible to read and pray, and that was that.

"For now," Ricka thought, *"for now."*

The next week John sacked up a load of wheat to haul to the elevator in Expansion. When he climbed up on the wagon and began driving away, Ricka ran outside and shouted, "I almost forgot, pick up a coupla sacks of Dakota Maid flour."

"Why?" John called back. "We already have flour for winter."

"I need some to sew underpants for the girls. Those sacks work the best."

"Women. Always something else," John muttered to himself.

When the time came for their little Phillip to start school, both he and his parents struggled. Their English was minimal at best, and like those in Wittenberg #2 before him, he had to start from the very, very beginning.

Phillip was an apt student, and every day he brought home new knowledge of English to both the parents and to his eager younger brother, Gottfried Peter, whom they called "GP" to distinguish him from John's brother, also Gottfried. GP soaked it all up and soon had both basic pronunciations and a small range of new-world vocabulary as well. When GP's turn came to start first grade, he was ready, as were his classmates who also had older siblings, to do serious learning.

Little GP, however, faced a problem of a different stripe. He was left-handed. And the new teacher would brook no left-handers. To her it was unnatural, so when she saw him pick up his pencil with his left hand, she lost no time in telling him, "GP, that's wrong. Use your right hand."

He shifted the pencil but only got scribbles. "It doesn't work with that hand."

The next day, when he still insisted on using his left hand, she walked to his desk at the front of the room, jerked the pencil from his left, and shoved it into his right hand. Again he tried with no more success. Tears came, but "the law" didn't change.

When he came home crying and told Ricka, she hugged him and let him cry it out.

"Well," she comforted him, "she's only trying to help you. Try to change."

The following day he timidly took his pencil in his left hand again, hiding his eyes from "the boss" up front. This time it was too much for the disciplinarian teacher. She picked up the heavy triangle ruler she kept on her desk and whacked him across the back of his hand with a resounding "thwack" that bit like a thousand bee stings and made the other students shudder. It hurt so badly he wanted to cry; but while tears came to his eyes, he stuck his hand under his other arm and, with chin quivering, worked to stifle any sound from escaping.

During recess, several of the older students made a point of brushing past him and patted his back, quickly trying to let him know, without offending the teacher, that they supported him.

"I hate school!" he snarled with all the venom of an angry rattlesnake. Then keeping his voice low so the teacher wouldn't hear, he added, "And I hate *her* even more!"

He felt like running away, but he knew it would only make things worse, and at home Father would probably take the strap to him on top of it for not listening to what the teacher told him to do.

Gradually, with immense effort, he learned to use his right hand. School, however, never became a joyful part of his life. He endured it and learned because he had to. No more.

In a month, life turned more pleasant when the family went bullberry picking in the ravines across the valley. The tiny red clusters of bullberries were tart as gall during the summer, but after a hard freeze they became deliciously sweet. They were favorites of the birds as well. The large black-and-white chattering magpies loved them and delighted to swoop from tree to tree, telling each other about the good berries in busy magpie-talk.

Ricka and Mina turned the berries into preserves that made one's whole mouth sparkle. When the bright-red jelly was spread on slices of heavenly smelling fresh-baked bread and dipped into rich whole cream, it became a feast for which kings would go to war and queens would change religion.

****

During this time, as full Americans, these recent immigrants discovered something totally revolutionary. "Isn't it really something," said Uncle Gottfried one day, "that we actually get to help decide who makes the laws in this country?"

"And then sees that they're carried out," John added.

They took to this new way of life like mice to peanut butter. For these first-generation Americans, coming from lands long oppressed, voting was indeed a high privilege; and they determined early on they would never miss an election.

The year 1912 was the first time these new citizens could vote for president. They were so excited that their favorite, Teddy Roosevelt, was running again, even though he had split the Republican Party and was running as a third-party candidate with the Progressive "Bull Moose" Party.

When Gottfried came home from town a week after the election, he stopped at John's and gave them the news, "Well, Roosevelt lost. That high-hat Eastern Democrat, Wilson, won."

"Country's probably gonna go down the toilet," John replied.

"He's gonna get us into the war, you just wait and see."

Before long, a series of articles in the *Staats-Anzeiger* proved terribly unsettling to the leaders of Krem. The Northern Pacific indeed decided to build a spur line out from Mandan, following the Lewis and Clark trail on the western banks of the Missouri. But at Stanton, site of the peaceful Mandan Indian nation that had befriended the explorers, they would turn west, following the Knife River, and aim for the great beef country of the Badlands. That meant Krem would be bypassed, which surely sounded the death knell for their prospering "Chicago of the North."

By 1913, the beds were graded and rails laid as far west as John and Ricka's homestead, passing just thirteen miles south of them, and the brand-new town of Beulah started slowly rising out of the waving buffalo grasses to briefly deflect the sweeping winds of the north. Where one lonely sod house braved the blizzards a short while before, now a new town lay a-borning.

On July 4, a year later, the first magical Iron Horse came thundering into town. The Northern Pacific Company took great pains to see that the day was well advertised, and it paid off as excited talk electrified the entire countryside. Wagons and buggies filled with enthusiastic families poured in from all directions. Many left home at sunrise to get to Beulah by high noon for the scheduled "History in the Making" moment, as the *Beulah Independent* proudly labeled it.

The newspaper and the new town's zealous merchants, of course, didn't miss the opportunity to combine the nation's 138th birthday bash with this memorable moment and went all-out to celebrate it.

John and Gottfried, along with the neighbors, were caught up in this once-in-a-lifetime saga and loaded their dressed-up families into wagons for the three-hour trek to their new town. Ricka and Mina had spent hours on their Singers, sewing new dresses, washing and ironing to get everyone looking properly smart and presentable, and packed large baskets of food as well.

Arriving in town, they found bedlam. Wagons and buggies seemed to be parked on top of each other, horses snorting and whinnying, youngsters shouting and running wild. The wagons churned up powdered dust that hung in a cloud and forced out handkerchiefs, big reds and fancy lace alike, to cover scratchy coughs. Here and there, men were already far into drink, getting cantankerous, talking tough.

Behind a row of wagons, four teenage English-speaking Irish Catholic boys from south of town bumped into three German-speaking Lutheran boys from north of town.

"Hey, krauts," taunted one of the Catholic boys.

"What's it to ya, fish eaters!" the Lutherans snapped back.

In a flash, fists were up, ready for mashing faces. Just then, several older men slowly walked by, stared hard at them, and drove down the spiked testosterone level. Fortunately, the two groups did not run into each other after that fiery moment.

Mina and Ricka, meanwhile, were highly excited. Like most soddy women, they spent precious little time in crowded towns and were not used to all this noisy commotion. Suddenly they felt like anxious mother hens, clucking to their little chicks to keep them all a-flock.

"Don't let go of my hand . . . stay close . . . careful that you don't fall and get run over." Those words formed a chorus as powerful as any that Handel could compose, and just as fervent. Holding hands and staying close, they elbowed their way to the newly built train depot beside the shiny iron rails.

The anticipation in the crowd was almost more than they could stand. Some were nearly paralyzed into silence, others moved to nervous chattering that would not quit. Many needed a bathroom break, and none was available. Some ducked behind wagons, between snorting horses. No one really noticed. Or cared. Women lined up at the few one-holers behind several stores.

Some boys in knickers brought pennies and laid them on the track, eager to see what the mighty steel Goliath would do to them.

Then it happened. They heard the long-awaited, great Iron Monster coming from the east, and soon it lumbered into view. The adults in the huge crowd were pleased by this momentous event, but as the great engine rumbled in on nervous rail ties, it brought back only too painfully the long days they had so recently spent on the rails coming here from New York. And the nights yet longer trying to rest on those miserably hard wooden train benches that did not adjust so much as an inch or lean back two fingers for comfort. All those memories triggered in not a few of this crowd the stench and the crowding on the ships before that.

Most parents talked to their children to prepare them for the great engine's fabled coming. Yet now the children stood with mouths agape, petrified by its sheer size and overpowering sound as it drew close.

The horses obviously could not be prepared; and when they saw the giant, unblinking eye in the middle of this monster's black head, heard its unearthly scream as it descended on them, smelled the foul breath it was shooting out its blowhole, they totally panicked. A number of them broke loose from where they were tied and thundered away, tails high, eyes glazed in terror. Some of those left hitched to wagons ran until the wagons were bounced to shattered pieces, leaving their families first searching for a ride home and then spending days looking for their much-needed horses. These were scenes of the great celebration which were not heralded by either the *Beulah Independent* or the *Northern Pacific* in its blazoned brochures.

John's team of horses, Sophie and Schwartz, who were now too old to panic and run, snorted and pulled against their halter ropes but stayed in place. They did not know that this would likely be the last time they would see this terrifying horse-that-eats-no-hay or hear its roar across the glacial valley.

The boys in knickers raced to the spot where they had laid their pennies, pumped their arms in the air, and shrieked in glee as they picked up oblong slices, thin and weightless as cigarette paper, of the smoothest, shiny copper medallions they had ever touched.

On the way home, John turned around on the wagon to talk to the children. "*Kinder,* children, this is a day you will remember as long as you live."

"We will, Papa," they replied almost in unison.

"Boy, that train was bigger," mused GP, "than I ever thought it'd be."

"And noisier too," added little Emilia.

"But it sure scared the hide off the horses," laughed older and wiser brother Phillip.

When John turned back on the seat, he took Ricka's hand and whispered, "Remember the last night we got off the train in New Salem?"

"How could I ever forget?" she replied and squeezed back.

"What a night!"

She just smiled at him, and shivers ran down her spine at the powerful memories of the night in the Empire Room of New Salem's grand Salem Hotel when first they arrived on these great prairies. The children wondered at the secrets they seemed to be enjoying so much, hoping maybe they were talking about Christmas presents or some such wonderment.

It wasn't long from that dazzling Beulah day before a host of the great steam locomotives were noisily belching black smoke as they rumbled in, their deep-throated whistles sounding an urgent call for water and coal in large amounts. They also brought more settlers, more freight to stock the voracious demands of the bourgeoning countryside; and on their return trip going east, they hauled back everything that land and shop could produce.

Enterprising merchants built stores, several grain elevators soon towered over the village, two saloons slacked the thirst of builders and workers of the land, and churches were organized, with Lutherans, Catholics, and Baptists leading the way. A doctor to heal, a bank to handle finances, a newspaper to dish data and dirt, and the timeless home of the ranging buffalo was suddenly forever gone.

Over a span of just seven hundred days, some three hundred souls gathered from the nations, determined to turn this little berg on the north bank of the Knife River into their new home. In that short time this new village grew to the same population as highly touted Krem had in over twenty years. Such was the mythic power of two bands of hardened steel stretched across the vast prairies of the heartland.

Pioneers from a host of lands were woven into the fabric of this place, but it was the Germans from Russia, blowing into town from the four winds, who colored the page that was to become Beulah.

Chapter 3

Two Little Ones Lost

When the families returned home, much of the children's play saw wooden blocks and small stones transformed into trains. At the Osters, mighty roars and whistles came from all corners of the yard, prompting Schutz to raise his ears and stop with one front paw in midair, puzzled at the wonder of all the sudden strange noises coming from the youngsters who had never made such sounds before. Even the stately roosters and aristocratic geese stopped in their tracks and cocked their heads in silent wonder. Not only humans but animals as well were suddenly aware of an extraordinary new day dawning on these windswept prairies.

The celebration of newness, however, was to be rather short lived. Just a few weeks later, an afternoon lightning strike ignited a haystack east of Gottfried's place, and the fierce north wind soon swept the flames across the long, high hills toward the south. They raced with the speed of angry, thundering buffalo, incinerating the claim shack of one of the Keller boys and took aim at the Reformed Church and its little parsonage nearby.

****

That struggling little Reformed group, surrounded by miles of Lutherans, could only pay their pastor, Reverend Ballhagen, a miserly salary. He reflected it with frayed cuffs on his black wool suit that was rarely cleaned.

Reverend Charles Wesley Ballhagen had matriculated from Wheaton College and went on to the Reformed Seminary in Grand Rapids, Michigan, finishing near the top of his class. After graduating, he married his Wheaton sweetheart and accepted his first charge in southern Minnesota. From there he was sent out to the new mission field in western North Dakota.

Ballhagen's wife, Melita, would be described as somewhat plain and shy; some would say severe and, on top of that, like her husband, rather grimly pious. She possessed a preacher's wife demeanor that rarely saw her thin lips bending into a smile, even less to laughter.

Her brown eyes were most often downcast, seldom looking at the people with whom she talked. Dark eyebrows folded into perpetual frown lines at the bridge of her nose, accented even more sharply by uncut dark-brown hair which she pulled flat back, wound into a tight bun, and stuffed under her frayed hat. She favored straight, formless dresses that flowed along the lines of her body and caused nary a jiggle on the temptation meter for any churchmen whose mind had slid from the Good Book. All of it combined to create an impression of a rather dour companion in the parsonage. But all characterizations aside, the Ballhagens were faithful shepherds of the Reformed flock, honored and dearly loved by all.

****

Now as the terrible fire roared on, impressions mattered nothing, and the neighbors sped to the little sanctuary on the hill, fighting to keep the flames away from the church. Before they could react, sparks lit the parsonage and sent the brittle wood up in an explosion of terrifying flames. The neighbors were heartsick yet relieved that the pastor and his family were not home, since the horses and buggy were gone.

As they were stirring the ashes to stop the burning fire, their shepherd and his wife came racing up in their buggy. "Who's got my babies?" the mother screamed as they came near.

"Where are the children?" Reverend Ballhagen roared as he jerked the horses to a stop and jumped off, running toward the ashes until one of the men finally grabbed his shoulders to keep him from plunging into the smoldering embers.

The neighbors were totally stunned. "We thought they were with you."

"No one came out of the house when it started to burn," said another.

"We tried to save the house, but with this awful wind, we couldn't stay ahead of the fire."

"Oh, dear God," cried the distraught mother. "Please, not my babies!"

"We left them home alone here," the shattered father mumbled incoherently, hardly able to form words at all. "They were busy playing, and we thought they'd be fine while we quick visited the Teskys."

"Maybe they ran over to the church," shrieked the mother as she raced toward the building, her eyes blinded by tears.

"No," softly replied one of the women just coming out of the church and taking her arm, "they're not in there."

"Maybe they got scared and ran down in the ravine," Mrs. Ballhagen cried, pointing and still full of hope.

Several boys were sent down to scout through the tall grass in the ravine but found nothing.

The women led the distraught mother into the church. All they could do was have her sit down, give her water, and hold her tight while she wailed her shattered soul into the sacred, smoke-filled space.

The men now attacked the smoking embers. Several tried to lead Reverend Ballhagen over to the church to be with his wife, but he twisted free and joined in pulling the charred boards out from the ashes.

After what seemed like an eternity of digging, scrabbling, pulling, shoveling in the smoldering embers, one of the men suddenly shouted, "Here!"

In the far corner of the bedroom, huddled under the springs of the burned bed frame, they found two little clumps—the children. "Here, come quick," he shouted again. Eight-year-old Emily had her arms curled around six-year-old Stephen, shielding him with her body. She was terribly charred and lifeless.

In one blur, Reverend Ballhagen was there, and when they lifted the metal bedsprings off, he bent over, trembling so violently, wailing from down so deep they were afraid he would collapse. Several men held his shoulders as he haltingly reached out toward the charred bodies.

But with his overpowering burden of instant grief, the frantic father couldn't make himself touch the seared bodies as the sickening stench wafted up and made him gag.

The whole little band of brothers huddled around him was instantly drowned in that rotten, sweet-sour stench that seared their lungs, and they couldn't cough it out.

These strong men of the plains were well accustomed to the raw realities of butchering and death, but this stretched beyond the pale for all of them. This nauseating, stomach-turning smell of burnt flesh would be forever imprinted on each one's mind, unfading as the ink on a Guttenberg Bible.

One man walked away and retched. Others barely held it in. Several of them would say later, "I still wake up with that gosh-awful stink in my dreams."

"Quick, get some blankets from the wagons," one of the men shouted. In a flash, several boys ran and rounded up half a dozen.

As they slowly peeled back Emily's body, Reverend Ballhagen, through flooding tears, had a sudden vision of an angel focusing his eyes on little Stephen's chin, and he noticed it quiver just the slightest bit.

"Oh, my dear Lord," he shouted as his knees buckled, and he sank into the ashes.

Miracle of miracles, it was not a vision.

"Reverend, look, his bottom lip's shaking," shouted one of the men.

"And his fingers just twitched."

Little Stephen's eyes were closed, and he was unconscious, but he was alive! Half his body was horribly charred, but his face and the half of his body that was shielded by his sister was blackened but unscarred.

Quickly they rolled him into a blanket and carried him up to the church.

"He's still alive!" they cried to the keening mother as they carefully laid him on her trembling lap. She peeled back the blanket and gently laid her face over his, covering forehead, eyes, nose, mouth, every spot, with wet kisses and brokenhearted tears.

"Oh my baby, my precious little darling," she cried over and over as the women held her shoulders and silently added their tears to hers.

Already several of the men were on their way to Adam Keller's to get jars of goose fat and pork lard to cover the little body. In a matter of minutes they were back with Adam's buggy and fastest team of horses, and as soon as the comatose little reed of a boy was fully slathered in grease, they rewrapped him, and Adam and another neighbor, Gottlieb Klaudt, were on the buggy at full gallop for the nearest medical help that could possibly do anything, ninety-five miles away in Bismarck. "Wait!" Mrs. Ballhagen screamed. "I gotta go along!" But the buggy was already over the hill, flying east.

Klaudt cradled the unconscious little body, trying to absorb some of the careening wagon's bone-jarring bumps. Adam kept the horses at full Pony Express gallop, mile after pounding mile. After twenty-five miles they raced into a farm that Adam knew, and as he pulled the lathered horses to a rough stop, he shouted toward the house, "We need your fastest horses." No further talk was needed.

While he and the friend quickly changed the horses, Klaudt, in a few words, explained their emergency to the wife; and they were back on the trail, now with Klaudt slapping the reins to keep the fresh horses at full gallop, and Adam holding the unmoving child.

On they raced, far into the long dark of night. The horses' mouths were foamed, flanks lathered, eyes ablaze like headlights beaming into the void. They were ready to drop but sensed that something in this cargo depended on their strength, and they held the pace. Finally Klaudt spied a lonely lamp dimly burning in a house near the worn trail.

"Whoa," he shouted to the lathered-up horses as Adam was already off the buggy and running toward the door. A startled couple already in nightclothes, ready for bed, hearing the strange voice, grabbed the kitchen lamp and peered out into the darkness. When they saw the covered little bundle in Adam's arms, it didn't take long to see what they needed. That they were total strangers didn't matter for a second.

"Quick," Adam cried, "we need your best horses to get to Bismarck. Ours are played out, and we'll never make it."

While they were throwing harnesses on the fresh horses, Klaudt told the wife, "We'll be back soon as we can and trade the horses back."

In just minutes they were again racing through the dark, trusting the horses to somehow know the way about which, in the dark, they had no clue.

By midmorning they were in Bismarck, and still at full gallop, they shouted to strangers for directions and were pointed to the hospital.

Tying their horses to a tree, they sprinted up the steps with their light bundle and through the front doors of Bismarck Hospital, shouting at a capped and starched nurse, "He's burned. Hurry!"

Within moments they had the little one on a gurney headed for what passed as the Burn Section. The doctors and nurses labored frantically over the unconscious boy with every bit of skill and knowledge they could muster. Four hours they wrestled cruel death until Death finally snapped his fingers, and with the tiniest little gasp, life was gone.

Ninety-five miles and four more hours he had survived. Now it was over.

Even the medical professionals had tears in their eyes as Keller and Klaudt carried their blanket-wrapped bundle back out of the hospital and to their waiting buggy.

By now it was midafternoon, but the exhausted men decided to try to reach the home of their borrowed horses and hopefully stay the night there. By the time they got to the area, it was already dark, and they began to feel terribly uncertain. In the state they were in when they raced through here the night before, they had paid no attention to the terrain, and now everything looked unfamiliar. Finally Adam gave the horses free rein and let them pick their own pace and direction.

It wasn't long before the horses turned off the trail and pulled up in front of a small barn. The house had a lamp in a familiar-looking window.

"Come in, come in," shouted the Man-With-No-Name as the two men got down from the buggy and asked if they could spend the night in the barn.

The couple would have none of it, and by the time the men had the horses watered and stabled, the wife had already set out a quick supper and turned their parental bed over to the two bedraggled strangers.

After introductions, Keller and Klaudt wolfed down glasses of milk and their first meal in nearly two days. Seeing the questions on their gracious hosts' faces, the men paused from eating and told the awful story of what brought them here. In that moment, the impact of the last several days finally hit them.

"I still can't believe it," Keller said, his voice a halting whisper.

"That's the awfulest thing I've ever lived through," Klaudt added through trembling lips as he looked down, hands shaking when he wiped his red handkerchief across his eyes.

Seeing the tears in Klaudt's eyes and his shaking hands, Keller suddenly coughed, pushed back his chair, and hurried toward the door. He wasn't yet outside when his whole body shook and a low guttural moan burst out of him. The stench, the fried skin, the limp little body of death, all suddenly overlaid with the image of his own children almost buckled his knees. Sobbing convulsed his body and wouldn't stop. "Oh, God, help me," he finally breathed.

By now the parents were also feeling the horrible hurt of that tragic parsonage family and at the same time trying to comfort the sobbing children who were clinging so tight it almost hurt.

When Keller finally came back inside, red-eyed and feeling embarrassed, the father nodded to him and slowly added, "We must pray." All hands clasped, and in the coughing silence he led them in a long, heartfelt prayer for strength and comfort to their night visitors, the grief-stricken Ballhagens, and all the Christian brothers and sisters in far-off Beulah land.

After a lot of nose blowing, one of the children now standing behind the father's chair leaned close to him and whispered, "Papa, I ain't never seen no dead baby. Can we go take a look?"

"No no no," the father shot back, "you stay put right here, and don't even think on it."

By sunup the men were back on the road, retracing their way for two days and another horse exchange until they finally reached home.

Mrs. Keller had taken the Ballhagens into her home during their lonely vigil of waiting. To add to their parental despair, they now had nothing left in this world but their horses and buggy, a Bible, and the clothes on their backs.

****

At night, when Ballhagen and his wife knelt down beside their bed to pray, he took Melita's hand; and with choking voice he whispered,

"Now I know how Job must have felt when all his children were killed too."

"Remember how his wife told him to curse God and die?" she softly answered. "I'm glad he didn't, and I'm glad you didn't either."

"But he did curse the day he was born, his soul was that heavy."

"Kinda like mine," she whispered, not sure she dared say that to her minister-husband.

Letting that hang, Ballhagen led into fervent prayer for their little Stephen. In bed, both stared long at the ceiling, now black in the dark of night, and finally Melita sobbed, "My soul feels as black as that ceiling."

"Mine too. And I'd be so glad to have God take my life if only he will let our precious child live."

"Oh, so would I."

****

John and Ricka and the children, along with nearly every neighbor within five miles, gathered every day at the Kellers to join the sad vigil and try to comfort the broken godly couple whose life's mission had so recently been to bring comfort to others.

Several neighbors had nailed together a small casket for Emily whose remains were now stored in the granary. Mrs. Ballhagen struggled to see her daughter, but the men held her away, knowing the bitterness of being refused would be far less damaging than the scars of seeing that horrible, ghastly sight, along with its stabbing smell.

During those long days of waiting, life was shut down as Antelope Valley lay under a blanket of death. Days were spent being packed together at the Kellers. Little was said. The women could not talk about their children for fear of setting Mrs. Ballhagen into deeper lamenting. The men gathered in the yard mostly looked at their shoes, a few spitting Copenhagen, some rolling Bull Durham to while away the hours. Even the youngsters couldn't get enthused about playing games, only too conscious and terribly curious about the burnt little body lying in the granary close by.

Reverend Ballhagen, in his smudged black wool suit, sat by himself on a wagon tongue, his heart as wooden as the tongue, accepting the believer's handshakes with a limp, lifeless grasp that was almost repelling.

Through all their deep caring, these stalwart believers had no idea of the battle that was raging in their wounded shepherd's heart. When the pastor glanced into the bright blue heavens and noticed the cloudless sky, he silently cried, *"Oh, God, how different it looks in my soul, where all is dark and hope has died, like the night of terror for Job."* In his grinding solitude, the shepherd's vacant eyes saw nothing more, and his heart sank ever lower in despair: *"Mighty God, what grievous sin have I done in thy sight that made thy fierce wrath to be kindled against me? What caused thine arrows to pierce my heart, thine eyes to turn away from me? Hear, O Lord, hear and forgive thy most wretched of all servants."* He felt like sobbing, yet in front of his men he had to somehow hold himself together. But his heart was breaking: *"Why, O God, hast thou clothed my soul with darkness and bathed my heart in tears!"* Fight as he may, his chin began to tremble, tears broke out and rolled: *"My tongue cleaves to the roof of my mouth and my lips will not shape words. O Lord, this load is too heavy to bear. Hear, my God, hear and have mercy before I sink into the pit."*

Soul-numbing guilt and grief sat on his shoulders like heavy sacks of spring wheat and left him staring at the ground, uttering only grunts in reply to the men's overtures of caring.

Finally, on the fourth day a shout went up, "They're coming."

As Keller's buggy came closer, the Ballhagens raced out to meet them. But as soon as Mrs. Ballhagen noticed that both men's arms were empty, she screamed, "Oh, God, don't let it be," and sank to her knees. The men got down and embraced both of them, but in a moment both the parents pulled free and ran to lift the little blanketed bundle from the back of the buggy.

After long minutes of brokenhearted wailing and hugging, the tightly huddled group finally loosened their embraces. An uncomfortable, drawn-out silence suddenly fell over the group as, one by one, they realized they would need to prepare for a funeral. Fearful coughs erupted out of several nervous throats, with no one finding the voice or the courage to speak the dreaded words.

Finally one of the church deacons haltingly asked, "Reverend, would tomorrow at one o'clock sound all right for the funeral?"

In that moment, the full impact of burying his own precious flesh and blood in the prairie ground struck Reverend Ballhagen, and he choked, "I-I don't know if I can do it." Mrs. Ballhagen threw herself sobbing into his arms, and several church members stepped in and wrapped both in their arms, all in tears. "Reverend, God will give you strength, and we'll be right here with you."

"It hurts too bad," he stammered in a whisper, "my heart is b-broken right now."

Since there was no other Reformed church close by, the neighbors timidly asked if perhaps Ballhagen would want them to ask their minister at Peace Lutheran to help out.

While they had theological differences, in the face of death and resurrection they stood shoulder to shoulder. Still, the despondent parents looked into each other's eyes for a long moment, and when Reverend Ballhagen saw no answer, he slowly nodded and whispered, "Well, I guess . . . maybe . . . that would work."

The next day, a great crowd drove in from all corners of the burned prairie and filled that lonely hilltop chapel to overflowing. They bravely sang the great hymns of faith together, and the pastor tried to hold up the hope of eternal life, but hope died stillborn in this awful time. The ultimate joy of resurrection could not lift the anvil of despair that lay heavy like a millstone on every shard of proclaimed victory.

Worship finished, they carried the weightless caskets, walking the short distance to the little cemetery below the crest of the hill, and gathered around the grave that had been dug wide enough to hold the two small caskets. The pallbearers placed the little coffins on canvas straps and slowly lowered them, one by one, into the waiting earth.

"Earth to earth, ashes to ashes," the pastor intoned over much soft crying, "dust to dust in sure and certain hope of everlasting life through our Lord, who shall change these mortal bodies of ours to be like his eternal body."

The *Vater Unser*, Lord's Prayer, the age-old benediction and amen, all in their German mother tongue, and words were done. In seconds, hard clods of earth struck the hollow wooden boxes, sounding terrible echoes across the blackened prairie. A dozen shovels joined in finishing the task none had wanted, and soon the work was finished. Family by family drifted off and in stifling silence slowly walked back to their buggies and wagons.

On the way back to church, Reverend Ballhagen sobbed, "I know they're with the angels, but, dear Jesus, my heart is broken. It hurts so bad."

A few steps later, Mrs. Ballhagen suddenly shot a heart-wrenching cry across the silent prairies, "Why, oh God, why did you do this to us?"

Ricka's heart reached out to the broken woman who was now no longer a mother, but across the back of her mind flicked the uncomfortable thought, *"Oh, my dear, dear sister, don't be putting all of this on God."*

It was a thought that would receive much discussion in the Valley during the weeks and months to come.

During lunch back at the Keller house, the neighbors all joined in pledging to rebuild the parsonage within a month for the Ballhagens and to furnish it with everything they needed to start over.

The crushed young ministerial couple joined hands, and both said, "Thank you. That's kind of you, but we must leave."

They finished their brief lunch, gave tearful hugs all around, mounted their buggy, and drove away, "to the East," as they said. No one ever heard from them again.

One by one the neighbor families collected their bowls and scattered back to their homes. It was a day that the settlers of Antelope Valley, both young and old, would never forget.

The tragic day did, however, come to a surprise ending.

During the night John got up to answer nature's call after drinking too much strong coffee through the day, and as he stepped outside, he was struck by the sheer majesty of the brilliant northern lights performing their own celestial concert of hope.

He walked back in and gently shook Ricka awake, and then each of the children, who were startled and suddenly more than a little scared.

"Come outside," he said softly to the sleepyheads, "you have to see this."

Rubbing the sleep out of their eyes and stumbling outside, they jerked awake: "Wow, look at that." Following John's finger pointing to the northern sky, it was as if a pair of hands divine were racing back and forth across a giant celestial keyboard, sending out living waves of light that arced across the sky, drew back and changed costumes, then shot out again in more striking hues to dance among the stars. In strobes of spring-grass greens they flashed across the heavens, then waving scarves of magenta, bolts of deepest sunset blue, flicking capes of bullfighting red, finally fading into somber shades of royal purple and dying grays. It was choreographed Mozart for the eyes.

Without even realizing it, they found themselves all with arms around each other, mouths agape in silent awe. Across John's mind scribed the words of that inspired ancient poet as he softly spoke them now: *"O Lord, our Lord, when I look at thy heavens, the moon and the stars*—and the great northern lights—*which thou hast ordained, what is man, that thou art mindful of him, and the son of man that thou visitest him? Yea, how majestic is thy name in all the earth!"*

Back in bed, dreams of caskets and ugly things chasing them gave way to mystical streams of flowing light, stretched from North Star to Raven Feather, more beautiful than anything they could remember.

Chapter 4

The Indians Are Coming

Another change slowly took shape in the Valley. Quietly, a few at a time, Indian families from Fort Berthold Reservation drove their wagons to the new town of Beulah and found trading there far superior to shopping in their other small towns of Ree or Kasmir or Krem.

The new railroad meant that more varied merchandise came into Beulah, with merchants more eager to trade. The Indians tried it. And their route, from the reservation three miles north of the Osters, followed the Valley wagon trail past the Oster farm and continued on thirteen miles south to Beulah.

One hot and windy day, Charlie Charging Bear was returning home from Beulah and slowly drove his team into the Oster yard, his wife wrapped in a blanket and sitting in the back of the wagon. Seeing them coming, and knowing that John was working out in the fields, Ricka was petrified. "The Indians are coming," she cried out and quickly ordered all the children into the house, fearing the worst but trying to be brave.

Charging Bear, as uncertain as Ricka about how they might be received in this white place, very calmly drove his wagon to the well and slowly got down off the wagon. Carefully keeping his hands in sight, he motioned toward the well. He spoke no German. Ricka spoke no Indian and very little English.

Finally he spoke a single word, "Water?"

Ricka's flock understood and quickly whispered the translation to her.

"Ja, ja," she answered, with an unconscious smile melting her relieved face.

"Yes," the Oster children chorused in turn.

Before he even thought about it, eleven-year-old Phillip dashed from behind his mother's skirt and ran to work the pump, taking the tin cup off its hook on the pump and handing it to Charging Bear. He drank a cup, then filled it again and carried it to his wife on the wagon. She smiled her gratitude and waved a timid "thank you." None of the Osters moved, but all lifted a cheerful wave back.

Phillip said a "you're welcome" not understood by the Indian couple and nodded his head in silent farewell as Charging Bear slowly climbed into his wagon and drove back out of the yard.

A fearful moment had turned into something special for all of them.

When John returned home, the children climbed all over him, all talking at once about the really nice Indian man and woman who had stopped for a drink of water and how much fun it was to wave to them.

"And we weren't scared of them at all," beamed little Emilia. John looked across at Ricka and raised his eyebrows, not sure what to make of all this. She just winked and returned to her cooking. *Yes, nothing to worry about. Everything's fine.*

Several weeks later, the Charging Bears stopped again. This time no questions were needed as the children raced out to pump water before Charging Bear was off the wagon. Ricka had a plate of oatmeal-raisin cookies, and as soon as she came out the door, GP snatched the plate and ran to give them to the Indian couple, whose smiles lit up the whole yard.

Some weeks after that, the Charging Bears drove into the yard again. This time Mrs. Charging Bear held out a package for the eager children. Opening it, they found a large venison roast and a handful of beautiful small pendants she hand-beaded for each of the children, with a striking beaded necklace for Ricka. The children squealed with delight and climbed up the wagon wheel to hug Mrs. Charging Bear's round smiling face.

This time, with John home, Ricka motioned for them to come into the house; but the couple was not ready for such overt friendship and motioned a polite "no, thank you." Ricka quickly brought out a jar of chokecherry jelly and gave it to them in thanks for their generosity, and they were off, back to the reservation.

Over time, others timidly stopped in. The Enemy Hearts, the Lockwoods, the Little Soldiers, and the Straight Arrows all became familiar figures. They gradually came to know the John Osters as a place where they could stop for a drink without asking, even if no one was home, and a place where they would be well treated, with children who smiled an honest welcome to them.

As John and the family were gathered around the table one evening, Ricka mentioned this development about their new guests of the pump.

"I think they feel safe here," she said, passing some delicious garlic-spiced venison stew around the table.

"I like them," little Emilia piped up, smiling as she dipped a thick slice of Ricka's fresh-baked bread into a bowl of cream.

"They're fun," GP put in, thinking of several times when Indian children had bashfully gotten off the wagon and the Oster children engaged them in a game of tag around the yard, with Schutz chasing red and white alike, barking his heart out at all the new excitement.

Many a time the sudden guests left a chunk of venison or dried jerky at the front door, and often Ricka had her famous cookies to feed their sweet tooth in return. Red man and white had quietly overcome long-standing warring bitterness and forged a pacific bond around a water pump.

Still, life for the Native Americans on Fort Berthold Reservation, as on all the lands which were euphemistically "reserved" for them by the Great White Father, was not that romantic interlude so beautifully portrayed some fifty years earlier by Henry Wadsworth Longfellow when he penned his hymnodic, flowing "Song of Hiawatha."

Longfellow's twenty-two majestic strophes portrayed a world where "by the shores of Gitche Gumee/Stood the wigwam of Nokomis" and held up a resplendent young Hiawatha. He stood hero of all that is good and clean and noble in the natural world, living in symbiotic harmony with all creation, blessed with his beloved Minnehaha (*Laughing Waters*) who would be "the starlight, moonlight, firelight, the sunlight of my people."

Minnehaha would bring the Ojibwa and Dacotah people together. But, alas, for the four tribes on Fort Berthold—Mandan and Hidatsa, Arikara and Lakota Sioux—whose lives were twisted together by the schemes of treaties they did not know and authorities they did not want, such romanticism was continents away from the life they were forced to live.

Their existence hung on a much thinner thread, more bleak and destitute, more hemmed in than Hiawatha could ever imagine.

The Charging Bears would not have recognized Hiawatha as kinsman at their powwow. Nor he them.

Chapter 5

Almost an Adoption

The Charging Bears gradually began to feel more comfortable at the Oster house and, finally, one day, very bashfully accepted an invitation to come inside. Though they could not understand much of each other's language, both Native American and immigrant did a lot of talking, and what they couldn't understand they made up for in hand gestures and broad smiles.

Ricka flew to get a link of smoked pork sausage on the stove and, with quickly fried potatoes, pickles, and fresh-baked bread soon had a delicious lunch set for them.

The Charging Bears had so deeply wanted children, and none came. Now the Oster brood crowding around Mrs. Charging Bear soon brought out every ounce of mothering instinct in her heart. She was a large woman, and barely had she gotten her plate clean when all the children swarmed around her, trying to get a share of her ample lap.

In that playful moment, Charlie Charging Bear reached out and, catching GP by the shoulders, lifted the little one up on his lap. Little GP seemed to enjoy the moment as much as the older man and without flinching threw his arms around Charlie's neck and buried his face in Charging Bear's long black hair. Everyone was laughing and chattering, while Ricka, with a big smile, stood near the stove thinking, *"If this isn't the most precious moment I've ever witnessed in my whole life."*

When John came in from the field, he hardly had the horses pulled up to the barn when he was mobbed by six tongues all competing to tell him the full version of what had happened in their soddy that day. John couldn't absorb all of that at once, and when they finally all chattered and danced their way to the house with him, he cast a look of lost despair at Ricka, who just smiled and mouthed, *"I'll tell you later."*

Little Emilia stopped the conversation when she piped up, "That lady sure kinda smells different than we do, doesn't she?" The rest looked at each other and drifted away.

Several more times the Charging Bears stopped in, and each visit turned into a kind of picnic that everyone looked forward to. On one of these times, Anna Charging Bear had a bundle under her arm. She handed it to Ricka, who spread it out across the table and was utterly amazed at what she saw. It was a handwoven woolen blanket, in a double-sided light beige color with absolutely beautiful geometric designs of stars, triangles, and parallelograms in several brilliant shades of red, orange, and flaming yellow, along with blacks, browns, and buffalo-grass greens. The entire border was knotted with perfectly spaced string-yarn fringes. Tears welled up in Ricka's eyes as she soaked in the richness of this gift of love, and she walked over and held Anna in a long, warm embrace to show her affection for this friend from an entirely other world than hers. That blanket would become a rich heirloom in their family for a long time to come.

In a short while, the visits ended, the Charging Bears in hibernation. The fierce Canadian winds of November drove dark masses of formless clouds scudding across the heavens, and Bauer's lignite coal barely kept the soddy warm as the smoke rising out of the stubby chimney was whipped out level with the roof and blown down to the snow-covered ground.

The grip of bitter cold would not let up, and for days John hitched up the sled to give his little scholars a ride to school, nestled way down and buried in a box full of last fall's best wheat straw. When the two Oster clans visited back and forth in the cold dark of winter's night, sometimes only the horses knew the way home, and the little ones never got out of the straw until they arrived at their own soddy.

Soon the dark-breasted winds of December came sweeping down from the frozen tundra of the North and made the days even shorter and yet harsher. The cattle wouldn't go out of the barns except for a quick swallow of water. The horses had to haul straw in and manure out in the freezing cold but were quick to head for the barn. Once inside, as soon as John pulled the harnesses off, they shuddered to fluff their thick winter coats and shake off the ice. The wind cried through the night, an unearthly, spectral wail that delivered fearful shivers up the spine if one couldn't somehow, deep down in the soul, manage to translate it into some kind of slightly worried angelic music, even in its piercing minor key.

Most certainly it was no time to be sick, for this wind carried to fevered minds the shrieking calls of a thousand winged, malevolent spirits come to carry one's soul away to places it didn't want to go. It was a time to make peace with yourself. A time to pray. *That* these prairie families learned to do, early and often.

During the Advent Sundays of those dark days, the pastor proclaimed in church, "The Messiah will come to lighten the darkness of this world. And that little child, born under a special star and laid in a manger full of straw, will keep the light of eternity shining in your heart."

The pastor's face was ever stern, as was the custom of the day, but his voice bore a warmth loved by the hearts in the straight-backed wooden chairs. While the little ones on the backless benches in front of him pictured cows and straw and babies, the pastor went on, "That great Messiah will wrap his mighty arms around you and hold you tight until you are done with this weary world! He will not give you up!"

Soon the arctic winds were defeated. Spring came. The ice melted. Crocuses popped out of the earth. Meadowlarks returned and sang their cheery melodies once more.

The Charging Bears, too, came out of their winter hibernation. One day they stopped at John's place, and this time they had a tall young man along with them, August Little Soldier. Ricka invited them inside, and Anna, with her biggest smile, accepted, but Charlie nodded his head for John to join him at the wagon.

Since Charging Bear's English was limited, he asked Little Soldier to translate: "Oster, you are such a lucky man."

"Ja, that I am," John replied, wondering what was coming next.

"You know we have no children," Charlie continued.

"I wish you could. You'd make good parents."

"And you have a house full of nice children."

"God has blessed us," John responded.

"Well, Oster, we've looked around and there are no Indian children for us. And this is maybe kinda strange, but my Anna and I prayed and talked about it a lot, and we are wondering if you would, ah-h," and he stopped, shifting from leg to leg, fingers twitching, suddenly afraid and unsure if he would dare to speak his heart to this white man whom he thought he knew. The words seemed to stick to the roof of his mouth, but finally he was able to continue, "If you would, ah-h, think about letting us, um-m, adopt your little Gottfried."

John was stunned. "But, but we can't do that," he answered.

"But you have plenty more. And it would make us happier than anything in the Great Spirit's world could ever do."

"I know you'd be good to him, but we can't give up any of our children," John replied, gently trying to soften his "no" as much as he could.

"Listen, my brother. I'll give you two cows and two hundred diamond-willow fence posts for that little boy. He'll make my old age rich and fill my Anna's days with joy like nothing else could do."

It was a princely offer, both in the giving and the receiving, and one not lightly made.

"I don't want to hurt you, my friend, but we can't give up any of our kids," John said again.

"Why not?" asked Charging Bear.

"Because in our religion, children are a gift from God and can't be traded away," John responded, now beginning to grow rather anxious over the direction this new friendship was taking.

"Yes, the Great Spirit gives every child as a gift to his parents. But they're also gifts to the tribe and have many parents," Charlie answered. "They can go from home to home and still be your children."

"We've grown to like you and always like having you stop to visit, but we just can't do that."

"Too bad. It makes my heart heavy to hear that. I am very sad."

Charlie's shoulders sagged as he and his young translator turned to walk to the house to get Anna. Sensing his pain, John's heart sank as well. He knew the awful hurt that Charging Bear was feeling right now and the embarrassment of making an offer that was turned down by this white brother whom he trusted enough to open his heart, trusted to bring him joy. John knew as well the even deeper pain that Anna Charging Bear would feel at being turned down.

The Charging Bears got on their wagon and left in silence, a silence so deep, so heavy-laden that it seemed the heavens themselves were rent with tears. As they drove out of the yard, they both turned and waved, but the wave seemed a lifeless wagging of the hand, fronting a terribly heavy heart.

When John got back into the house, his face was so grim that a shocked Ricka asked, "John, what happened?"

John told her the distressing conversation that happened outside, and in that instant Ricka also felt the stab of pain that this refusal must have torn into Anna's heart. Words left her, and she ran to John, sobbing.

"Oh, Johnny, isn't there something we can do?"

The children listened in mute astonishment, stunned at what could happen to any of them in the coming days.

"I guess the only thing that would help is to give them our boy," John answered, gathering GP into his arms and squeezing him so tightly it almost took the little one's breath away. "But that's never going to happen."

Then looking deeply into GP's eyes, he continued, "*Verstescht du, Jung.* Do you understand, son, never?"

"Yes, Father," GP mumbled back, now also crying.

"Never!"

Chapter 6

Chilling Howl in the Night

That night, after the Charging Bears' visit, every bed jiggled as restless family members turned from side to side with jumbled thoughts racing through their minds, picturing their family from so many different angles, even living on the reservation.

Suddenly a jarring sound shattered the silence, sending shivers up every spine. It was the long, deeply unsettling howl of a strong gray wolf. In the shrouded darkness, they couldn't really tell distance nor direction.

The children had never heard the sound before, and all bolted upright as one in their beds.

"Papa, Mamma, what was that?" they chorused in fear.

Little Emilia jumped out of her bed and streaked under her parents' covers, huddling tight into Mamma's protective arms.

To John and Ricka, there was no mistaking that sound.

"It was a wolf," John answered in the dark, trying to sound calm.

"Will it come into the house?"

"No, children, stay in bed. It won't hurt us."

Outside, old Schutz, now too arthritic to give chase, sent out a few timid barks, to worry the strong gray cousin if not frighten him away.

John got out of bed and took the shotgun down off its hook on the wall. He pulled three shells out of the bullet belt, loaded one into the chamber, and, cocking his gun, stepped into the darkness outside the door. None of the animals in the yard or in the barns seemed to be stirring, telling him the wolf was not close by. In his mind, John wondered, *"Is he alone, or is there a pack of them out there? Is he hungry? Hunting? Looking for a mate? Ach, I sure wish the moon was out right now."*

John's mouth hung agape, with short breaths coming through open lips, but there was absolutely no hint of sound anywhere. It seemed as if Nature herself were holding her breath, anxious over this strong gray child of hers who had for whatever reason decided to run the risk of ranging far beyond his wonted hunting grounds.

For long minutes, John stood in the unnerving silence, suddenly back on night guard duty in the Russian Second Army, every nerve on full alert, slowly surveying every foot of earth as far as he could see in the dim, starlit night. Schutz came and snuggled tight against his leg, ears up, nose sniffing the air, softly panting with tongue dangling, then totally still.

"Schutz, is he close to us?"

Schutz cocked his head, ears straight up at full power, and looked up at his master but made no sound. He hadn't ever heard this bone-jarring howl before either and hoped it would go away before he would be called to duty.

Then suddenly, a second long-drawn-out howl, mournful and searching. It sliced the dark veil of prairie stillness like a bronze arrow but with the jarring effect of the cry put out by the inhuman Iron Horse. It was a sound that pierced the soul, at once so mystic and so stretched-out haunting that, once heard, is burned into the neurons of memory until all breath is gone.

The hair on every neck, inside the house and out, stood straight up; pulses throbbed hard in every eardrum, the fearful sound now seeming a whole lot closer than before.

Hardly had the haunting sound died down when Ricka was back to an evening in Russia, sitting with Mina and their two new Oster boyfriends on a bench in front of her parents' house, and a wolf's howl rent the Klostitz night air. For a moment she felt the goose bumps on her forearms and her strong Johnny holding her tight. "So long ago" suddenly escaped her lips, with the shocked children calling back, "No, Mamma, just now." Their voices brought her back to this house and this wolf, and she stammered, "Yes, children, Johnny—Father will take care of him."

More long, endless frightening minutes and there was no further howl nor any stirring among the yard animals. John finally pointed his shotgun skyward and fired a shot, hopefully sending a warning to the fearsome intruder. The chickens in the coop fluttered and squawked for a moment, and then all again was silent. John patted Schutz's head and slowly, carefully, went back inside, hoping the animals would sound warning if the intruder came closer.

"Papa, did you get him?" piped a thin, frightened voice.

"No, I shot in the air, and he left, so we can go back to sleep."

He carried Emilia back into her bed, and as he nestled in beside Ricka, he said, loudly enough so the rest could hear, "He's gone. He couldn't find a wife, so he went away."

With that there was a smile in every bed, and all tried to go to sleep, but sleep didn't come for a terribly long time.

When things had settled down, several of the boys had to go to the toilet, but there was no way they were going to make brave and walk to the outhouse in that spooky dark, and they felt themselves too big to use the chamber pot in the corner. It turned into a stressful, everlasting night.

In the coming days, there was much talk in the Valley about the gray wolf's howling that had been heard by a number of other families as well. Guns were loaded and kept by the door.

"You know that wolves always travel in a pack," someone opined.

"Yeah, that one was just a scout."

"You wait. There's an invasion of wolves coming," went the talk.

There was talk of a valley-wide hunting party.

But others were reticent, afraid that the Reservation Indians might misinterpret it and use it as an excuse to go back on the warpath.

"You just can't trust an Indian, you know," said one.

"Ja, the only good Indian is a dead Indian," a second chimed in.

"Aw, come on, they just want to live," added a timid voice, "just like we do."

Meanwhile, John and Gottfried rode over to Walter Keller, and along with his brother, they all teamed up and took his five greyhounds out to track the wolf. Two days they crisscrossed the hills in every direction, with much yipping and yowling by the greyhounds and several other dogs, but found no trace of the fearsome creature that stirred such deep emotions.

The bone-chilling howl of the gray wolf was not to be heard again in the Valley, though many wondered when the savage night hunters would return.

"I don't know," Athias Renner said to a group of men, "but I think one of these nights they're gonna be back, and we'll pay the price."

"We better be ready."

"Stay on your toes. You never know."

Chapter 7

Running with the Big Bulls

Time drifted along, and both Ricka and Mina grew impatient. Both of them were frustrated by having to care for their growing families in soddies with dirt floors. When they drove to Krem and Beulah and saw more and more attractive wooden houses going up— and painted, no less—they grew increasingly fretful with their lot. Especially seeing Grandma Karolina in Krem, now already grown old in her own little wood-frame house, made them more restive than ever.

One noon, while serving dinner, Ricka announced, "We're going to build a new house."

"Well, yes, but . . .," stammered John.

"No 'but.' Now!" Ricka cut in. "We're going to build a new house now!"

She looked at him with such fire in her eyes that when John noticed her rigid back as she turned to face the cookstove, with hands planted on her hips, he knew talk was over.

When he visited Gottfried several days later and learned that a similar scene had played out with Mina, he knew it was doubly over.

The women had their day. And their ways.

Within weeks, John and Gottfried both secured the services of a carpenter from Krem, whom Grandpa Christ recommended, and construction of their modest, new, story-and-a-half wood-frame houses was under way. Now they would have two bedrooms in the attic, one for the boys, one for the girls, with the parents' bedroom on the ground level, and wood floors throughout!

Ricka wanted no more of the plastered blueing colors around. She painted the kitchen a pale yellow and oiled the wide floorboards to a sheen.

She had some further ideas of what she wanted in her new house, and now she needed to get to town. She steered John straight for Bacal and Son's General Store on Main Street. Jacob Bacal, the lone Jewish merchant in Beulah, had with his family followed these

German settlers out from the iron fist of the czar to the New World's promised land of flowing milk and sweetest honey.

Settling in Beulah, he felt at home among people who had experienced the old country with him. He paid his dues to the newly organized Chamber of Commerce but rarely attended meetings and never spoke. When they asked him a question at the meetings, his usual reply was "Fine." Remembering too well the persecutions of the czar's regime, he worked hard to avoid attracting any unwanted attention here.

There was, of course, no synagogue for the Bacals to worship, and the closest rabbi was in distant Bismarck, but on occasion the family got together with another Jewish family from Hazen or one from Hebron to celebrate Passover and a few other Jewish high holy days. Observing the Saturday Sabbath was obviously out of the question, since that was by far the biggest business day, so Friday night around their kitchen table became their worship time.

The Bacal children were excellent students, but after school they returned to the store or to their studies. No one ever thought of asking them to participate in music or athletic programs. At the store, they became early adults, and the German customers enjoyed bantering with them and engaging them in conversations where they showed a delightful maturity. When they finished school in Beulah, they were sent to college in New York and never returned.

This lone Jewish family was well respected by their Gentile neighbors, with no outward acts of ethnic prejudice, but at the same time they were left out of the fabric of community life. No one consciously spoke of excluding them; they were simply never thought of. When they were out of sight, they evaporated from Gentile minds. They were thoughtlessly left out of community functions and social gatherings, and to some people, proud Jacob Bacal had no other name than "Da Jud, the Jew." Yet he was still a well-respected member of the Beulah business community, and Ricka deeply appreciated his knowledge of the day's merchandise and his caring attitude toward his customers.

Today, as John and Ricka entered the Bacal store, Ricka was again struck by Mr. Bacal's appearance. His soft hands and dulcet baritone voice, combined with immaculately starched white shirt, light maroon cravat, faux diamond-studded tie, and matching armbands seemed to achieve the desired result on his lady customers. Neatly coiffed dark hair and a subtle touch of musk cologne didn't hurt customer relations either. And his full command of Yiddish-German further helped cement many a good sale.

Browsing through his treasure trove of catalogues, Ricka selected for the new living room an ivory-colored wallpaper with embossed vines sprouting velvety purple blossoms, and for the bedroom a pattern of lightest mint green with petite soft-pink roses.

When Bacal finished writing up that order, Ricka mentioned furniture.

"*Ach, meine liebe Frau Oster,* My dear Mrs. Oster," Jacob quickly responded, looking first at John to make sure he wasn't crossing any lines, "let me show you the very newest thing from New York."

John broke out sweating but knew that in this moment he had better keep quiet.

Bacal reached under his counter and produced his most recent knock-out-the-customer-and-make-a-sure-sale catalogue with colored pictures. Finding the page he wanted, he turned the magic book to Ricka, showing her a striking three-cushioned davenport, cream colored with large, raised, plush red roses and dark mahogany wooden arms.

"This is what the nicest houses in New York and St. Paul are getting this year," he said in a soft, suggestive whisper.

"Yes, I like that," Ricka answered after a short pause, looking for approval from John, and at least not getting a scowl. "Please order it for us."

While she continued looking through the books, Bacal engaged John in conversation. "I'm so glad to have my own store here, and a house of our own," Jacob went on. "You know, in Russia, our Jewish people couldn't own any kind of property."

"I never knew that."

"And every so often soldiers came through and just stole the few things we did have. Life back there was awfully tough."

"I'm glad," John replied, "that you could get out and make it to this country like we did."

Meanwhile, Ricka selected two rocking chairs and a real factory-made table with two extra leaves and eight chairs to feed her growing brood.

John was dying a slow death, but he knew better than to raise any kind of protest. As they left the store, he shook hands with a grateful Bacal and Mrs. Bacal, but his smile was weak, his handshake limp. The wagon ride home was solemnly quiet: John upset with all the money foolishly spent, Ricka in total delight, picturing her new castle and how her life had magically changed this day.

When the house was almost finished, Ricka walked in one morning and was struck by how bright the rooms were. There was a window in every room, two each in their corner bedroom and in the living room. With the everlasting winds whistling around the corners, she knew it was not heaven, but she smiled to herself and couldn't help musing, *"Ja, this is my little Eden. And with no Tree of Temptation to spoil it."*

The day the furniture finally arrived and was put into place, Ricka stood in her kitchen and, with hands on hips, announced with an impish smile, "When Tsarina Katherina comes to visit, she'll be most pleased."

"Oh, Mother," groaned Emilia while the rest rolled their eyes and joined her groan.

Now Ricka felt like she was back in civilization, ready to entertain the governor himself, should he ever venture into these prairie parts.

When the Charging Bears next visited, after the house was completed, they felt as if they were suddenly in the domicile of the Great White Father and delighted in the sunshine of this sparkling new farm home. "How blessed you are," Mrs. Charging Bear said, still pining for her dreamed-of child, and now especially aware of how different this house was from her own dire dwelling place.

Moving out of the little sod house was bittersweet. Ricka and the children were glad to be out of its musty smell and dirt floors, but it had surely become home in these years too, and they knew every lump in the walls and every drafty spot on the floor. They left the old cookstove and rough kitchen table in the soddy, which would now be converted into the *Sommer Kueche*, a summer kitchen. It would now be the cool place for canning, for butchering, for baking bread and kuchen in the summertime, so the big house could be kept clean and cool. It would also become the playhouse for the children and their recreation center when company came. Here they could make all the youthful noise and commotion they wanted without disturbing the adults in the big house.

A change was also coming over John in these days. Although he had the boys working with him all day, he talked less with them. He laughed less. The daily hustle and bustle of a big family interacting together seemed to irritate him. And the day after they moved into the new house, he laid down a new order.

"From now on," he announced loudly to Ricka as they sat at supper, "I'm going to eat first at the table, before the rest of you."

When she and the children looked at him in minor shock, he added for emphasis, "And by myself."

Seeing the set of his jaw, she knew there was no further discussion; and from then on, that was the custom. Ricka dished up the meal, and John ate, pushed away from the table, and walked away. After that, the rest of the family ate their meal together. It was not what Ricka or the children wanted, but that's how it would be.

Not long afterward, a family several miles to the east announced that they were having an auction. They began to feel too hemmed in, the country getting too crowded, the taxes too high, so they were moving west to Montana. At the auction, an expensive 1897 Winchester twelve-gauge pump shotgun came up for sale.

"Does it shoot true?" someone in the crowd teasingly shouted.

"See if it'll hit this," shouted another, pulling off his new leather dress cap and waving it in the air as others guffawed at the idea.

"Give me the gun," John suddenly spoke up from the back of the crowd.

He made his way through the crowd; the auctioneer handed it to him. For an instant, John was back in the Russian army again, holding his Berdanka and looking for his target. He was amazed at how much lighter this Winchester felt in his hands. Just then the auctioneer fumbled in a box and offered him a lone shell.

John slipped the shell into the magazine, pumped it to chamber the shell, and, raising the Winchester to his shoulder, challenged the leather-capped blowhard, "Let 'er fly."

As the cap sailed in a high arc over the crowd, John pulled the trigger and shot the shiny black cap into a thousand leathery pieces.

There was a stunned silence, no one knowing quite what to expect from any of the parties involved.

Finally the auctioneer took the shotgun back, announcing, "Well, I guess she shoots pretty true," and asked for an opening bid on the gun.

As John made his way back through the crowd, someone nearby said quietly, "Ei, yei, yei, there's sure nothing *schusslich,* clumsy, about that Oster when he takes aim."

"Ja, and for sure that city slicker with the cap is gonna have *strublich*, messy, hair in the wind going home," answered a man next to him.

People around them laughed at the needed humor, and John smiled inwardly, delighted that his Russian army marksmanship was still very much intact.

****

The auction marked a watershed. America was undergoing deep changes in these years. And so were these great prairie plains, as some settlers were already leaving, while more new immigrants and new machines were arriving with every passing month.

When John and Ricka and their family traveled to Beulah, they began to notice a growing number of the new growling Model T horseless carriages that were coming off Henry Ford's production lines. The dirt of the city streets was already ground into fine powder by shod hooves and wagon wheels. It was by turns choking dust or ankle-deep mud that sucked at one's feet, but the high-wheeled, black Model T's had a way of navigating through it that appealed to John, and even more to the boys.

****

Meanwhile, during these years, John and Ricka had two more daughters, rounding out their family at seven—four boys and three girls—when Ricka's child-bearing years were over. In between they laid a precious daughter and two more sons into the hard prairie sod of Peace Lutheran cemetery. Each brought a brutal, agonizing hurt that grew more intense with every little casket and would never go completely away. And each also hammered home a reminder to the other children that life on these prairies was constantly hanging by a very slender thread indeed.

Brother Gottfried and Mina would finish their family with six, while sister Katherine and husband Adam in Krem would bring an even dozen new Baisches into this world. The three sisters further west would add more Dschaaks and Stohlers to the burgeoning Oster tree of descendants as well.

So with growing sons finding their flight feathers maturing and tail feathers itching, John decided that a Model T was definitely in their future, even at the outlandish cost of $550. Another reason was the declining health of their seventyish grandparents in Krem.

Grandmother Karolina had grown heavier and considerably slower, feeling the crippling effect of arthritis in her fingers, wrists, shoulders, and nearly every joint in her body. She lost several teeth and had trouble chewing. Cataracts clouded her vision. Her three-cornered *deechle,* head scarf, rarely came off, and housework was becoming a burden.

Grandfather Christian was also suffering from knees and hips that ached without end. His back, which had too long stooped over his leather-working tools, now protested all movement. A cane helped but didn't ease the pains.

Watching them slowly hobble around, John told Ricka, "We gotta get over there more and help out."

"Ja, they really need somebody around."

So a Model T it was. The Valley road was still a series of trails, as was the road to Krem, and automobile travel was a lot bumpier than Henry Ford's slick posters or the local dealer had presented it, but it still cut travel time by two-thirds and brought the family together more regularly.

Learning to drive the magic mobile was, however, quite another matter. The three pedals on the floor—left pedal for low, neutral, and high gear; middle for reverse; and right for brake—with throttle lever on the steering column and emergency brake lever coming up from the floor beside the driver's left knee took dedicated practice and time to master. Between father and two oldest sons, Phillip and GP, there was many a close scrape as they practiced driving around the yard and down their farm trail to the Valley road. Many a wrist was sore bruised from hand-cranking the engine when it kicked back and spun the crank in reverse. Getting the spark set right didn't help for that.

"We can sure run with the big bulls now," the boys shouted as they flew by the house.

The geese were terrified by this black monster that roared down on them with the speed of a famished coyote and the sound of rumbling thunder, and then suddenly it would sit totally still beside the shed without even breathing. Many a chicken and goose had to flee for its life as the car careened around in mad circles, with rookie driver's feet hitting wrong pedals. But gradually all three became decently skilled at handling the Model T and could navigate the tricky prairie trails to drive the family wherever they wanted to go. This whole new thing was outdoors, and outdoors was a thing for the men. Whatever the women felt or thought, they could only watch.

Another skill the men hadn't anticipated, but quickly had to master, was the art of patching tires, or more properly, pneumatic tubes. The tubes were notorious for blowing out from running over sharp rocks or hard dirt clumps or just normal wear. Many a trip involved a stop alongside the road, jacking up the car and putting on the spare tire. And too often the spare would blow out, meaning an extended stop while they wrestled the tire off the rim, took out the tube, scuffed around the hole in the tube with the abrasive cap from the repair kit, applied the glue, and put on the rubber patch. Then they had to heat it with several farmer-stick matches, hoping the wind didn't blow the matches out, and wait for it to dry before wrestling it back into the tire and starting the car again.

"Driving isn't just turning the steering wheel," the salesman had warned them. They had no idea how true his words would be.

****

The single thing that touched more lives during these years than any other across all of rural America was the Rural Free Delivery Act to bring free mail service to every farm home that erected a mailbox. Begun in the Eastern states at the turn of the century, by 1914 it reached Beulah, and now every Valley family had mail delivered six days a week, rain, shine, or snowstorm. Now a company in Chicago could touch every family in the Valley with one single mailing, and all received it on the same day. A hundred new things entered daily conversation.

Before that time, mail was delivered to Krem by steamboat or stagecoach, and they had to pick it up whenever they went there, often not for weeks, or when a neighbor went and dropped it off. But now with rural delivery, Ricka and Mina could write their county relatives and have an answer back within the week, and even write their parents in Russia and have a reply within a month or two, all delivered right to their mailbox on the Valley road.

Their *Staats-Anzeiger* and *Beulah Independent* papers now arrived the same day every week and kept them abreast of developments both local and worldwide. Friday evenings, after the paper arrived and work was done, soon became holy times as adults settled down to catch up on all the latest and the children learned to stay out of their hair.

Best of all, anything Ricka ordered from the latest eleven-hundred-page Sears & Roebuck catalogue, or Wards or Gurney's Seed and others, would be delivered right to their mailbox. Anything from farm tools to chewing tobacco and peeping baby chicks, kitchen utensils to dresses, overshoes to underwear, was now only an order blank and a check away. Add a one-cent stamp and Ben Franklin would transport them to undreamed-of wonders.

And, adding to these treasures to which not even the tsar had access, was the further wonder of the Christmas catalogues which all the companies put out, eagerly awaited by every child with visions of heavenly bliss in glory land.

Ricka's children, like most others, nearly came to blows for several days in early fall when the Christmas catalogues, with pages and pages of entrancing colored wonders, first hit the mailboxes.

"I'm the oldest," insisted Phillip, "and I should get first looks."

"But I'm the oldest girl," Emilia shouted, grabbing it away from him, "and girls have more things to look over, so we need more time!"

Fred hit her arm, knocking the catalogue out of her hand, and ran upstairs with it, quickly bringing the rest to angry shouts and tangled scuffles.

Ricka finally went into mother-command mode and ordered little Fred to hand it over. Then quietly sitting down on the rocking chair, she slowly turned the pages while the children crowded behind and around her, silently mesmerized by such unimaginable abundance.

Another sure sign of a new day dawning in the Valley and beyond was the presence of a McCormick grain binder in nearly every farmyard. Other grain binders had come on the scene, but all needed extra men to ride on the side platform and hand-tie the grain into bundles. Different manufacturers developed a knotter that used wire to tie the bundles, but the wire got into threshing machines, feeding troughs, and cattle's feet, so it proved more nuisance than help.

Finally, after years of research and experimentation, Cyrus McCormick and his teams came up with a knotter that used twine and would hold up in the dusty fields. Now, with an eight-foot sickle blade on the binder, the grain could be cut, measured and tied into bundles, and carried in a bundle carrier to be dropped into neat rows for shocking. So John, alone, with three horses could now harvest a full acre of wheat in just one round, going once up and down a half-mile field of grain.

"I can do more now by myself," marveled John in talking to Ricka one evening, "than twenty men could before this."

"You're just a big man," she teased. He didn't see the humor in it.

"That binder has really changed things," he insisted.

The McCormick grain binder indeed brought an immense explosion in agriculture not only in the Valley but across the entire Midwest and multiplied food production across the civilized world. Perhaps more than any other, this single invention took agriculture to a whole new level.

Unfortunately, the downside of all these advances was that a host of farmers saw profits writ large in the air and put the plow to huge plots of marginal land for more crops. A few county agents tried to sound a warning, but the desire to make big money ran deep in the soul.

"Lotta grass on a lotta hills being turned over around here for more crops," said Eisenbeiss one day as the men were gathered before church.

"And a lot of them alkali flats shoulda never been plowed up," added Hank Renner. "One day that stuff is gonna blow somethin' awful, wait 'n' see."

"Hey, you're making money like the rest of us," someone laughed, "so what'r you bellyachin' about?"

Chapter 8

Weltschmerz

The tranquility of life in the Valley was about to be sorely tested. In the teens of the 1900s, there would be pain not only at home but *Weltschmerz*—worldwide pain.

For Valley dwellers, the news began on the pages of the *Staats-Anzeiger,* stating that their homeland of Germany was engaged in another war on the European continent. By August of 1914, country after country was getting dragged into the conflict.

The papers carried articles dripping with blood as they described battles in which many thousands were slaughtered by ever-larger howitzers, dreaded poison gases, and now by explosives dropped from the sky by the recently invented aeroplanes that rained destruction from high in the air. With evermore lethal weapons being devised, and the will to use them strong, the monstrous war was devouring millions of souls, and the price in suffering stretched beyond calculation. In this conflict, the winds of war were wafting viruses that ate at the brains of politicians and generals alike.

John read the papers with a growing sense of *angst*—dread. When neighbors visited and the adults talked in urgent tones, even the children sensed the deepening concern.

"*Ich weiss nicht mehr,* I don't know anymore," John said late one evening to a neighbor as they were visiting, "but from the newspapers it looks like the whole world is getting into this war."

Phillip and GP, kneeling and listening by the heating grate in the upstairs floor, picked up the gravity in the voices below and felt their stomachs tighten.

"Our president Wilson said he'd keep America out of it," replied the neighbor, "but a lot of people are talking about us getting into the war too."

"Ja, and now Russia's in it."

"And they're talking about drafting soldiers here, just in case."

When the neighbors left, John confided to Ricka, "It's making me nervous, you know?"

"What do you mean?"

"Well, since I was in the Russian army, could our government trace it and draft me into the army here too?"

"Oh, John, it couldn't happen, could it?"

"Don't know, sure hope not."

But when they were in bed, the thought left both of them tossing a long time without sleep that night.

Then, one week in '17, the *Staats-Anzeiger* was emblazoned with the dreaded headline: AMERICA ENTERS WAR.

John took one glance at the frightful words and put the paper down. He grabbed his cap and stalked outside. *"Now it'll happen,"* he said to himself. *"I'll be torn from my family and hauled off to die in some godforsaken trench in France or someplace."*

In darker moments, his mind pictured the dreaded Russian Secret Police reaching across the ocean and snatching him back into the Russian army.

"Lieber Gott. Dear God, be my help," he silently prayed, "and don't let me lose my mind in fear."

As the weeks dragged by, time sat on his shoulders with awful agony, but no draft notice came. It did come, however, for one of the young neighborhood men, Albert Keller. A month after he arrived in the frontline trenches of France, his unit was surprised by an early dawn attack of poison mustard gas. Together with most of the unit, he was blinded and slumped to the bottom of the snaking trench, helpless until another unit came by and led them back behind the lines to waiting ambulances.

He spent weeks in crowded military hospitals in France and more months in stateside treatment after being shipped back.

When he finally arrived back in the Valley to a big "Welcome Home" party, everyone wanted to know all the sordid details, but he replied, "There's nothing to talk about," and cut off the conversation.

Only years later, during threshing, did he tell the neighborhood men a little of what had happened. As they were lunching their cheese kuchen and hot coffee in the shade of a loaded bundle rack, something triggered a set of memories in him and words began tumbling out.

Keller's voice turned strangely distant, like an alien in a faraway land, and instantly froze every tongue in the circle.

"We could see a strange-colored cloud coming toward us," he said with voice so soft they could hardly hear, "and all of a sudden my eyes started to burn. Before I could even reach up to rub my eyes, everything went black. I opened my eyes wide, but everything was gone. In one second, I was blind as a newborn skunk."

He stared at his shoes, a little stream of tears rolling down his cheeks.

His lips quivered, "You wanna know scared? That's scared."

After a long silence, he continued, reliving once again the terror of that awful time. His words came in short bursts, like machine-gun bullets from the trenches.

"That crap burned my face. My hands were burned. My armpits. My chest. My crotch. Wherever there was any moisture, it turned raw with pus and blisters.

"I puked until it was nothing but watery blood."

His face turned ashen, and he quivered as all the suffering and helplessness swept over him remembering the moment when he didn't know if he would ever again see anything in the world, whether he would live or vomit out his life in that muddy trench.

"War is hell," he finally said softly, unconsciously rubbing his eyes, "total hell," and stopped. Finally, after a painful silence, "I'm just glad I can see again."

None of the men around him could talk. Their voices were gone after these pictures of their brother going through such agony on their behalf. One by one, the men got up and walked over to Albert, silently clasping his shoulder with grips of steel that said, in their own way, *"I'm sorry, and I love you, dear brother."*

That talk never went beyond the wheat field, nor was the subject ever brought up again. The men present that day would keep those blistering words in their hearts to the day they joined Albert in the grass of Peace Lutheran. One alone told the story after Albert's death.

Albert never complained, though his scars, more inside than out, bore silent witness to his valiant efforts to help "end all wars" and from henceforth colored his life with more somber hues than ever in earlier days.

****

Shortly before America joined the war, another cataclysm was shaking the other side of the world. After three hundred years of rule by the imperial Romanov dynasty, Great Mother Russia was hemorrhaging, convulsing in bloody revolution. With things going badly in the war and severe hardships at home, a rabid group called Bolsheviks, headed by Vladimir Illyich Lenin, forced Czar Nicholas II to abdicate the throne. It left the country in an ugly leadership vacuum.

Since most of the *Staats-Anzeiger*'s readers had recently come out of Russia, that news was devoured as intently as the results of battles in places they had never heard of and could not wrap their German tongues around. Brief news articles reported that the czar and his family were being held under house arrest and moved from place to place, most recently to the East side of the distant Ural Mountains, in a city called Yekaterinburg.

Then one evening in August of 1918, John had just settled down to read the *Staats-Anzeiger* when he suddenly shouted, "Oh no, God help us all!"

Ricka was immediately alarmed at his tone and, wiping her hands on her apron, turned to see his face suddenly taut and ashen colored.

"Johnny, what's the matter? Are you sick?" she asked.

"They've murdered the tsar."

"They what?"

"And it says here they shot his whole family, too, just a month ago."

"All five of the children?"

"All of 'em."

"Even the sick little tsarovich, Alexie?"

"Yes, and Tsarina Alexandrova and all four girls."

"There must be some mistake."

"And even shot their doctor and some servants, all of them together at one time."

"But why?"

"Because the Bolsheviks are crazy, that's why. They took 'em all down in somebody's basement and lined 'em up and shot 'em, all in one horrible pile, like a bunch of pigs!"

"What kind of monsters would kill a whole family with innocent children?"

"*Die sind vom Teufel geschickt*, they were sent by the devil!"

"That's just awful."

"Ei, my heart just hurts. Ei, yei, yei."

Clapping her hands over her cheeks, Ricka cried, "I can't believe it. What do you think will happen now?"

"I don't know. I'm just glad we're out of there!"

The next day the whole Valley, along with the thousands who had so recently fled Russia, were totally stunned at this turn of events. The tsarist regime was not their favorite thing in the world, and other assassinations had happened, but no one could have anticipated this shocking development, and they worried for relatives and friends still back there.

Ricka and Mina got together and quickly wrote a letter to their Boeshans parents in Klostitz, hoping against hope that order would not completely collapse in the old country and that their elderly parents would somehow be all right.

After long weeks they had a reply. The parents had the usual complaints of old age, but otherwise they were fine and told the daughters not to worry.

Throughout this time, there had been reports from around America of German people being confronted and abused, with people questioning their loyalty to America through all these events. Numbers of Germans changed their names to avoid unpleasantries, and a goodly number of churches that used the German language in worship services stopped doing so.

But in the environs of the Valley, this never became a concern. German continued to be the language of the streets and in the stores, and worship services continued in Deutsch as before, with no discussion or debate, nor any questions of loyalty to their new homeland.

Shortly, they had word that Sister Katherine in Krem received a letter from sister-in-law Natasha in Klostitz, thanking all of them for their continued gifts of food and money to keep her family together. But she was seriously worried about the German armies warring toward them and wondering how it would go for both Germans and Russians in the *dorfs* if they advanced that far.

"And," she wrote, **"the tsar and his men have renamed a lot of our dorfs. Klostitz is no more. It is now called 'Weselaya Dolina.' You remember, in Russian that means 'Happy Valley.'"**

Yes, happy indeed, thought the Oster relatives.

****

As if all this news of upheaval and war were not enough, now the newspapers were also carrying reports about a terrible flu that was sweeping the country. Influenza, some were naming it.

"Listen to this," John reported, looking up from his paper, "they say people are getting so sick they're dying from it."

"Where's it happening?" Ricka wanted to know.

"Well, they think maybe it started at an army base in Kansas, but it's already spread all the way to Europe."

"Hope it doesn't come here."

But hope was in vain. Within weeks people were going down like ripe wheat in a bad summer storm. Deaths were happening faster than caskets could be supplied. Several elderly people in the area and several children in the Valley came down with it, and in a matter of days they were dead. There seemed to be no cure.

People became so terrified that no one wanted to leave home, and they were afraid to help sick neighbors or even attend funerals of those who died.

Soon the news in the *Staats-Anzeiger* turned even more disturbing.

"Says here," John read out loud, "that millions of people have died from this thing, and it's spreading to every corner of the world."

"I think God is trying to tell us something, and we'd better start listening," replied Ricka, "don't you think?"

"Ja, there's plenty of sin in the world, and I wouldn't blame God if he brought back a whole bunch of Sodom and Gomorrahs."

That night around the table, they prayed particularly earnestly for forgiveness and for God's strong hand to stretch forth over the earth with healing as mighty as in Moses's time, as powerful as in the days of the great prophets of old. Nor were they alone. Preachers proclaimed judgment, even the apocalypse, and around the world people of faith joined in raising prayers for forgiveness. For healing. For peace.

Fortunately, the Osters were spared.

Whether heaven heard and responded was hotly debated in many an elite theological forum and many a humble living room, but gradually the terrifying influenza seemed to gorge on flesh no more.

Then in November the papers ran banner headlines that all the world was desperate to hear.

"Oh, thank God," John shouted to the family as he opened the paper, "the war is over."

"Who won?" young Phillip asked.

"I guess we did, and they're calling it an armistice," John replied.

"What's an armourstiss?" the children wanted to know.

"Well, I don't know, but anyway, it's over."

That night there was rejoicing worldwide, and the next day at noon church bells rang in every town in the land. The following Sunday, houses of worship the world over reverberated with great choruses of thanksgiving, much dabbing of tears, and many throats choked with emotion. Never had so many people given so much thanks for so many things.

Chapter 9

Flying the Nest

The Oster boys were growing up, soon ready to fly the nest. Phillip had finished seventh grade and gone through two summers of month-long confirmation instruction at church.

Confirmation instruction, which the pastor conducted in German, was painful through all the work of memorizing catechism, Bible history, and hymns; but it was also a special time for the teens of the church to form deep relationships in the safe cocoon of faith. A number of these would eventually lead to marriage and new families in their tight-knit community.

One burr under Phillip's confirmation saddle, however, was Emil Wiedeman. A head taller than the other boys, he turned into the class bully. His favorite gimmick was to pick up Phillip's wire-handled syrup-can lunch bucket and stuff the sandwiches in his mouth before Phillip could stop him. Beating him was risky, because he was strong as an ox; but because of his rapid growth, he was a shade slow and uncoordinated, so their tussles rarely got beyond a cut lip or bruised cheek that both could usually explain away to mothers at home. But despite the Wiedeman factor, Phillip was confirmed and now considered part of the adult community.

In the middle of the extended confirmation sermon, his father, John, suddenly found himself standing again in the aisle of the majestic St. Paul's Church in the old country's Odessa. The magnificent baroque altar of white marble stood tall before him; he turned and there was the great rococo organ with its thousands of pipes, beside him the glorious stained-glass windows stretching in regal glory to the high vaulted arches. And all just yesterday. *"How different from all that splendor to this little Bethel"* flashed across his mind. And just that quick, his heart was flooded with the awful terror of running with his brother from the secret police after fleeing the czar's army. Tears welled up in his eyes, and his chin refused to quit trembling. Without knowing it, his hands clasped: *"Oh, precious Lord Jesus, you delivered us from the lion's mouth, from threat to body and soul.*

How can I ever thank you for holy freedom so big that you gave us in this little place!" A cough choked his throat; and, embarrassed, he looked around, hoping no one had noticed him fidgeting in his chair. The men around him looked, well, composed—he thought—and he was back at his son's special day.

After Confirmation Sunday, the John Hubers visited John and Ricka and asked for Phillip to come live with them and work as a full-time hand on their farm.

Hardly was that settled when the Baisches sent word that Grandma Karolina was gravely ill and asked all the family to come to Krem as soon as they could. They dropped everything, and John got the Model T ready while Ricka got the little ones ready to travel and stay a few days if need be.

They sent GP on horseback to ride to the Hubers and tell Phillip to ride west and tell the three Oster sisters, with instructions that when he returned he and GP and cousin Wilhelm were to handle the two farmsteads, milking, feeding pigs and chickens, making sure the livestock had water.

Johns and Gottfrieds arrived in Krem to bad news. Mother Karolina was hardly breathing, and though she moved her eyes and seemed to recognize the family, she was unable to talk. Several times she mouthed words, but no one could make them out. Finally, all that was left was to give her a few sips of water and hold her hands. She wrinkled her forehead, seemingly in pain, but said no more.

Blessed Karolina: the eyes of faith were filled with the brilliant light of sunrise, but the eyes of flesh were grown sadly dim and rheumy with age, limbs weary, dreadfully heavy and filled with aching pain.

After a while, their pastor arrived, quietly walked to Karolina's bed, and took her hand. After looking at her carefully for a moment, he bent over her so she could see his face and spoke, "*Geliebte Grossmutter,* my dear Grandmother, I've come to prepare you to go home to the Lord who's calling you. Are you ready?"

She looked intently into his eyes and mouthed a silent yes, and he continued, "I've brought Holy Communion along, for God to forgive you all your sins and cleanse your soul, so you'll be ready to meet the Lord in heaven."

When she slowly blinked her eyes, he turned and opened the little black box he had also brought along. From this he carefully took out a small silver ciborium (wafer holder) filled with round, half-dollar-sized, thin white wafers; a tiny glass bottle filled with grape wine; a miniature silver paten (plate); and several mini silver chalices that each held one swallow of wine, setting them all on the wooden nightstand beside the bed. Next he tipped the ciborium to shake out one wafer that he placed on the paten, and finally he poured a swallow of wine into a mini chalice, also setting it on the paten. Slowly he opened his small Special Services Book and led the group in a prayer of confession and absolution.

This he followed with the words, spoken by Jesus to His disciples at His Last Supper, telling them, "Do this in remembrance of me." The pastor continued with the Lord's Prayer, which all in the room prayed together, many with tears flowing down their cheeks.

Sensing that Grandma Karolina probably couldn't swallow a whole Communion wafer, he broke the wafer in two and touched the sliver against her lip with the words, "This is my body, given for you." Next he held the chalice to her lips, slowly trickling a small swallow down her throat. When she swallowed and relaxed, he spoke those familiar words she had heard so many hundreds of times in church, "Now the body of our Lord Jesus Christ and his precious blood strengthen and preserve thee unto everlasting life. Amen."

After several more minutes of silence, he placed his hand on her forehead and pronounced, "Go forth in peace, thou blessed soul, into thine eternal rest with God, forever and ever. Amen." As he finished speaking, he traced the sign of the cross on her forehead, and she opened her eyes once more and silently mouthed, *"Amen."*

Several minutes more and the pastor shook Grandfather Christian's hand, softly telling him, "God be with you, dear brother, through this time of trial."

When he left, the family crowded around the bed once more, the women dabbing tears, men somber and still, the smaller grandchildren looking from face to face to get some measure of what was going on. The children found themselves moving slower than they ever remembered moving, shouldering in to peek between the adults to get a look at Grandma with her mouth wide open, making strange sounds.

Somewhere during the endless hours of night, the other three daughters and their families arrived to join the long vigil of death. All through the night, family members drifted in to stand in silence by the bed for a while, many softly stroking Grandmother's cheeks or gently rubbing her arms.

During the long hours, the women rustled up sandwiches, and neighbors started bringing in sausages and breads and dishes of food.

Katherina saw the haggard look of utter exhaustion on her father's face and finally said, "Papa, why don't you lie down awhile. If anything changes, we'll wake you right away."

At first he didn't want to leave his beloved's side, but when he could hold himself together no longer, he finally went into another bedroom and lay down, squeezing between several sleeping grandchildren.

All through the long night, Karolina struggled to die, and death would not come. Her breathing grew shallower by the hour, and more labored, until each breath was followed by an agonizing pause. The family began praying for the end to come, but life would not leave her.

Suddenly her eyes snapped open wide, and she whispered, so softly that only those next to the bed heard, "*Herr, nimm mich Heim*, Lord, take me home." And just as suddenly, her eyes closed, her hands flinched ever so slightly, and she seemed to shrink smaller in the rumpled bed.

Then as the first faint glimmer of light crept into the eastern sky, her breathing turned into a rattling sound, the "death rattle" the adults knew only too well. When it became more pronounced, Katherina told Gottfried, "Go wake up Papa. He wants to be with her at the end." As the neighborhood roosters competed to call forth a new day, gentle death hushed Karolina's rattles and softly snuffed the wick on her dimly burning candle.

She had seen much and lived well, and now she belonged to the angels. Gottfried led the entire family once more in the Lord's Prayer, Katherina reached down to close Mamma's eyes for the final time, and it was over.

After the funeral, all the families returned home, and life went on, now without the glue that held the family tightly together, but it went on.

It would be by far the hardest for Grandfather Christian. For the time being, he would stay in his lonesome little pioneer house and keep puttering in his leather shop. And with all the families now owning cars, they could hopefully look in on him regularly, maybe bring him out for occasional visits in their homes and keep him going.

****

Before long, it was GP's turn to be confirmed, and he also memorized all of Martin Luther's Small Catechism, a dozen hymns, forty Bible verses meant to hang on to and live by, and portions of a book of all the great Bible history stories. Many a night at home by the kerosene lamp, Father and Mother drilled him over and over on all his memory work. Two months before confirmation, Ricka ordered his first store-bought suit with long pants from Montgomery Wards, and now he was ready.

Sunday morning, the church was absolutely packed with nervous parents, adoring grandparents, and a few jealous adults who were secretly hoping that some of their snooty neighbor kids would embarrass themselves.

All the confirmands, in their finery best, were lined up in front of the altar rail, facing the congregation, and the stern pastor sat on a chair in the aisle facing them. Calling name after name, he grilled them about everything they had learned. The pain was excruciating. To miss an answer was bad. To miss two brought tears of shame to parents' eyes. Hardly ever had so few sweated so much over so little.

After church, a huge dinner was laid out by each thankful mother who had also enlisted a number of aunts to stay at the house and get the spread all put together.

Before dinner, the families called their confirmands to the overflowing table and presented them with either their own Bible or a hymnal with their name inscribed in silver on the front cover. The confirmand, boy or girl, was then given the seat of honor to eat with all the grown men who always ate first. Then the women and children ate, over much laughter and joyous celebration. This pattern was time-honored from the old country, and these pioneers would under no condition depart from it in the New World!

Shortly thereafter, Father and GP both decided that seventh grade was enough book learning for GP too; and when the Jake Eisenbeisses just up the Valley asked for GP to come live with them in their childless house and help them run the farm, it didn't take long to reach neighborly agreement. They would give GP room and board and pay him five dollars a month. That he was still in his teens did not matter. He was judged old enough and strong enough to do a man's work, and Father John had more sons coming up, so everyone was happy.

Several years seemed to fly by, with GP doing the full round of Eisenbeiss farmwork: milking, manuring barns, birthing, castrating, feeding animals, running the horses for plowing, seeding, and harvesting. In short, everything needed to make a well-rounded farmer in his own right. As time went by, he often did the work alone, with Eisenbeiss staying home to work around the yard or sitting on his porch looking out over the Valley. Saturday nights, Eisenbeiss smiled at GP and nodded him down the road.

"A young man's got fancies he has to satisfy," Jake loved to say with a smile and a wink, as Mrs. Eisenbeiss joined in smiling.

Sunday mornings, after chores were done, he was also free to go to church with his family and spend the day at home, returning in time for evening chores. Winter evenings he often cranked the ice-cream freezer after Mrs. Eisenbeiss put together a mouth-watering batch of her rich chocolate-walnut mix, and the three enjoyed their delightful dessert over a few hands of cards. Other nights they sat by the fire while Jake regaled them with stories about life in the old country. He could expand events just enough to make them hilariously memorable, and at his feet on those cold winter nights, GP learned the fine art of storytelling that would later make him a wanted companion and friend.

Then one day, word reached the farm that the newly formed Knife River Coal Mine just outside of Beulah was hiring mule skinners to haul coal out of the underground mine. GP didn't much fancy himself as either a mule driver or an underground coal miner, but the idea stuck in his brain and wouldn't let go.

On a lark, he asked Eisenbeiss's permission to ride in and talk to the mine's "Muley Foreman," as he was unofficially known. Eisenbeiss was not at all thrilled at the thought of losing his good farmhand but reluctantly agreed.

GP had no "mule experience" and seemed a little young, yet the foreman sensed something positive in him and gave him the job. Now, as a mule driver, he was officially known as a "skinner."

GP knew horses, but mules were a breed apart. The second day at work, though he had been duly instructed, he couldn't get a stubborn mule to pull, so he stepped close and slapped its back rump. The mule, Spider, took high offense, bucked with both hind legs, and kicked him with such force that he was thrown against the rough wall of coal. Luckily the shod hoof just grazed his thigh.

"One inch further over," he hissed at Spider, "and you bloody bugger woulda busted my leg to bits." He wanted to scream at the cantankerous critter and whup him good, but that would have attracted attention, which at that moment he didn't want at all.

Life in the bowels of the earth, he quickly discovered, was a mule of a different color. While the temperature was constant and comfortable underground where they worked, it was always musty smelling, always dusty, always total dark just beyond the light on his cap. The air in the tunnels was charged with tiny particles of coal dust that hung like an endless fog. After several hours on the job, he coughed black phlegm and blew black mucous from his nose. No one thought of masks.

One day GP mused to another miner, "I suppose our lungs are full of that crap too, just like the air we're breathing."

"You want the money," replied the other, "don't complain."

The money indeed was better than any job around, so complaints were few.

The mine was dug into a sidehill and gradually angled down, following a fifteen-foot coal vein that ran from thirty to sixty feet underground. As the tunnels went further in, narrow gauge rails were laid, and on these rails the loosened coal was hauled out in four-wheeled one-ton cars. The cars were latched together into a mini train, and the mule skinner's job was to harness one mule to the train and pull it out to be unloaded in the tipple at the mine entrance.

The skinners soon discovered that the mules had some gray matter between those big ears and could do very precise math. The men could gang together nine cars. But try ten and the mules balked.

One day, one of the skinners was driving old Snus and hooked up ten cars. Snus leaned into the harness, felt the extra weight, and backed off. The skinner yelled at him. Nothing. Cussed fiery words. Snus stood block still. Finally the skinner swore loud and swung his short whip. Snus bucked and brayed and locked down. The skinner swung his whip again, with everything he had, but before he finished his swing, Snus lashed out with a hind leg and caught his irritating skinner, shattered his knee, and promptly ended his mining career.

The foreman ordered work halted and packed the screaming skinner out for medical care. When they started back to work, GP was stunned to hear the foreman utter, "The dumb sombitch shoulda knowed better."

For GP, this underground world was new in a number of ways. He had to get used to coming out of the mine every day with face and skin and clothes totally grimy black that never completely washed out—the only thing left white in this world were eyeballs, and even they were often tinged an irritated red. He also had to learn to adapt to totally different temperatures in the world above when he came out, both summer and winter.

Another new page in his world was the nationality thing. His had been a German world, and growing up in the Valley, he really knew no other. Now he was tossed in with Norwegians and Swedes, Scotts and English, Irish, Finns, and French among others, along, of course, with a heavy majority of Germans.

"I didn't know there were that many different kindsa people in the world," he told the family at home, "or all the tongues they talk."

"They sure sound weird too," he added, and when he imitated a few, the younger children roared with laughter at the strange sounds.

The aspect of his job, however, that deeply distressed Ricka was the rough language he was picking up. Many words she didn't understand when he occasionally slipped them in around the younger children, but from the very tone she knew they were not good words, no matter the language.

Their German culture was nuanced with very earthy language already, with bodily functions bluntly named, but these new swear words seemed vulgar and ungodly.

"Gottfried Peter," Ricka went into Mother Voice on overhearing him, "I don't want to hear that kinda of talk around here anymore. You hear?"

"Oh, Mamma, don't worry, it's not that bad."

For GP, the thing that wore on his mind was the situation of the mules. The mine had gradually discovered that moving the mules from light to dark and back every day was resulting in a number of the animals going blind. So the decision was made to build a full stable inside the mine and keep the mules permanently below ground. That meant that when the forty mules on the regular work herd went into the mine, they would never again see the light of day, except for several weeks once each summer, until they were led out to have their life ended in the glue factory.

GP, like the other skinners, learned that each mule indeed had a very distinct personality, and they grew to appreciate each of them much like a person, even as the mules did the skinners. To see Maud and Cheesy, Big Red and old Mike treated like so many mindless machines gradually made him more and more uncomfortable.

Something needed to change, but what could he do?

Chapter 10

TR Rides Again

Several years in the mines taught GP that money isn't everything. Thus, when he heard that Theodore Roosevelt's old Elkhorn Ranch near Medora was looking for cowhands, he jumped at the chance for a change.

Ever since sixth-grade American history class, when the teacher painted a glowing portrait of Teddy Roosevelt and his close connection to their North Dakota home, GP felt a personal bond with this twenty-second American president. It grew stronger yet when he read the stirring article about TR in their school's new set of *Funk and Wagnalls Standard Encyclopedias.* Later, he remembered stories Father told about TR's presidency and days in the White House. Now the news of a job on the old TR ranch rekindled all those romanticized childhood images, and his heart said, *"Get out there!"*

At the first opportunity, he begged a day off from the mine and rode the Northern Pacific rails to Medora. There he rented a horse at the livery and threw in with several cowboys riding north who said they'd show him to the Elkhorn.

The ranch foreman wanted to know about his horsemanship skills, and though his roping abilities were lacking, his farming and mule-skinning experience, along with his openness, appealed to that honcho.

"Well, I'll take a chance on you," he told GP.

"Sounds good."

"When can you start?"

"How about if I come back Sunday night and start early Monday."

"Good. But get some clothes before you come!" were the foreman's parting words as he walked away.

GP looked around at some of the other hands on the ranch and realized that his clothes required a major makeover. He needed to convert from farmer to rancher.

To start with, his cap would have to go, and he'd need a wide-brimmed hat to protect him from the elements. He'd need waist-high jeans, no more overalls. The lace-up work boots had to be replaced with stirrup-hugging, high-heeled cowboy boots—tall, since this was big-time rattlesnake country. Four-buckle overshoes would be stored away in favor of tall, boot-fitting rubberwear. And to keep reasonably dry in freezing spring and late fall rains, a long, black oilskin raincoat, high-collared, lined, and split high up the back for marathon hours in the saddle.

On the way home, he stopped at the Ferris store at Medora and stocked up on ranching gear. The storeowner was glad for the business but chuckled to see another greenhorn coming through, so eager to become a bona fide cowboy: *"Blessed TR, here comes another one!"*

Walking down to the railway depot on Main Street with his precious bundle to catch the train home, GP passed the large, gnarled oak tree about which the coal miners had told him. It was known around the state simply as the Hanging Tree, where one of the miners had witnessed Old West justice meted out and now loved describing it in graphic detail. In the several short decades since Medora was established, the tree had seen ample use, and GP shuddered as he pictured men gasping and swinging at the end of the dreaded rope from these very branches.

On Sunday, at home after church, when John drove away in the car to take GP to the train, Ricka clutched her chest. A tiny spark flamed out inside her as she waved them good-bye. *"My little boy is gone,"* she whispered to the wind, *"he's mine no more."* She lifted her apron and wiped a tear as she walked back to a full house that suddenly breathed a strange emptiness.

When GP arrived at the ranch, the foreman took him to the bunkhouse and introduced him to the Elkhorn cowboys. He shook hands all around, and then his eye caught a rumpled pile of old clothes in the dim far corner. It was topped with a sweat-stained Stetson, and GP's first thought was *"Looks like a broken dummy from the Ferris store."*

"That there's ol' Whiskey Jack," the foreman shouted toward the still figure to make him hear.

"Took a likin' to th' jug," chuckled one of the men under his breath.

Finally the Stetson tilted up, revealing a weary, leathery face and a pair of heavy, hooded, rheumy eyes. The straggly, salt-and-pepper beard below them parted, showing several brown stubs in a mouth that had lost its struggle to hold teeth.

"Yo, Sonny," came a weak, raspy voice as old Whiskey Jack raised a bony, withered hand tipped with brown-stained fingernails.

Years ago, Jack rode the badlands for Roosevelt and other spreads longer than anyone could remember; and recently, with no kin and no home, the Elkhorn had taken him in for his final ride. He spent long years in the saddle, pulled long draughts from the jug, and splurged on some unfortunate liaisons with infected pleasures in the upper rooms of the Mad Bull Saloon. Now this triangle, combined with brawls and a spittoon full of years, left him feebly addled, content just to sit quietly in his corner and smoke his hand-rolled Bull Durham.

The foreman coughed softly to get GP's attention back. "Listen, I'm going to pair you up with Swede here and Spotty."

Swede, grizzled veteran of the range, bowlegged, wrinkles as deep as badland ravines, hands gnarled and scarred, quick looked him up and down, saw GP's light facial hair, and promptly labeled him "The Kid."

Spotty was an ornery gelding, so named by an earlier hand for his Appaloosa coat. This horse not only bucked with no provocation but also loved to turn his head and bite the horseman in the butt while he was putting on the saddle.

"Turn your back on him when you bend over to grab the cinch, and you'll have teeth marks in places you only let your girlfriend touch," one of the hands told GP as the whole bunkhouse roared.

The next morning, the cook, whom with great imagination they named "Cookie," was up at the breath of dawn and woke the roosters as he rattled around and fired up the cookhouse stove. In a matter of minutes he rang the bell for breakfast. The bunkhouse crew quickly devoured their eggs with potatoes and slices of ham, washed it all down with stand-up black coffee, and clapped their Stetsons on for another day on the ranch.

GP took the cowboy's advice about Spotty, and after breakfast he asked Cookie for a few carrots. He held them up and let Spotty nibble them as he gently rubbed his nose. And before saddling up, he held Spotty's head, looked him steady in the eye, and quietly talked to him. It seemed to pay dividends. Spotty carried his new rider with feisty pride.

When their horses were saddled, Swede reached into his back pocket and pulled out his little round can of Copenhagen. After the ritual triple-tap on the cover with his middle finger, he reached in with his index finger and thumb, squeezed a pinch of the rich-smelling, dark-brown fibrous compound, tucked it between his lower lip and teeth, and he was good to ride.

The foreman told them to ride south to check on the cattle in the breaks along the Little Missouri River, and they hadn't gone more than a mile when GP reined in his horse and stopped. Ever since they left the corral, he was struck by the clear sky and the beautiful-smelling air, which carried the soft scent of cedar and ripening leaves. *"This sure ain't the coal mine,"* he thought to himself.

"Kid, what'r ya doin'?" asked Swede, turning around and stopping his horse as well.

"Just listen how quiet it is," replied GP softly, turning in his saddle and tipping back his gray felt Stetson.

"So?"

"So there is absolutely no sound out here. Nothin'."

"Oh, crap," Swede muttered. "Jeez," and spat a brown stream downwind as he kicked his horse into a trot, irritated at this senseless stop. While Swede silently wondered about his new partner, GP rode on in awe. After several years of breathing thick air cloudy with coal dust and the constant noise of drills and iron wheels grinding on iron rails in the mine, this open country with no farms for miles around seemed like the center of paradise to him. He felt the delight of a young colt fresh out of the barn after a long winter and kicked his spurs into Spotty's flanks, galloping to catch Swede.

The rugged buttes surrounding him were painted in soft rose reds and yellows and chalky whites, pale lavenders and blues, beiges and grays, with streaks of soft black lignite coal that lightning sometimes set on fire. GP was struck with all this beauty and its constantly changing shades of color and told Spotty, "Hey, this is just like riding into the picture in Funk and Wagnalls back in school." Swede just rolled his eyes and kept riding.

Each of the hands was issued a long-barreled Colt double-action .38 six-shooter and a .30-30 Winchester lever-action rifle, along with boxes of shells. And each was told to practice so they could stop varmints of the rangeland, snakes, and miscreant cattle rustlers. For rustlers, range justice sometimes simply meant leaving their bones on the prairies with no questions asked. GP practiced until he could pop a tin can off a fence post eight out of ten times, and Swede grudgingly told him, "You'll be aw'right, kid. Keep at it."

The gnarled cedar trees and tall timber in the long ravines were a constant source of joy for GP, especially since they hosted birds of a thousand voices. After a time, he recognized their songs but remained largely a stranger to the singers. This Juilliard Saddle School of Avian Song taught him compositions but not composers.

Fall brought another new encounter. GP rode through a long ravine and listened to the magpies scolding him for invading their domain when suddenly he became intrigued by the rhythmic, rustling sound of Spotty's hooves brushing through the deep layer of leaves. "Whoa, Spotty," he whispered and slid off into the inviting, ankle-deep, crunchy blanket. Bending down and scraping a small pile together, he picked up all that his arms could encircle and tossed them high into the air, something—since their farm had no trees—he had never experienced in his whole short life. With a high-pitched laugh he shouted, "Hey, Spotty, ain't this some fun?" The horse was busy nibbling grass and, at the mention of his name, turned and juked his head up and down and snorted, as if saying, "Man, you're some kinda weird, dude."

GP grabbed the saddle horn and vaulted up, touching his spurs to Spotty's side, and burst into singing at the top of his lungs. With Spotty trotting through more leaves, his rider serenaded the buttes, first with raucous, bawdy folk songs, then segued into the great songs of faith he remembered from confirmation: "*Jesu geh Voran,* Jesus Still Lead On," and others. Spotty trotted on, surprised by the sudden exuberance of his rider. When they reached the top of the ridge, GP stroked the horse's mane, rubbed his neck, and shouted, "Ah, old Spot, I bet these buttes haven't ever heard good German singing for as long as they've stood here." His face relaxed into a satisfied smile. A soughing wind turned the brittle cottonwood leaves into a million Lilliputian drums that gave him a new longing. "Wish I had my accordion here," he sighed with a sad smile. Spotty flicked his ears and trotted on.

Before long, one of the other hands came galloping up, shouting, "Hey, what the devil's goin' on? You aw'right, kid? Somethin' wrong?"

"Naw, just a little singin'," GP shouted back, "just a little happy singin'." And Spotty trotted on.

With the colors of the buttes all around him changing from sunrise to noon to sunset, and all of nature joining in, GP stood up in the saddle and whispered, "How blessed I am, Spotty."

Too soon the stands of whispering cottonwoods and rustling ash, the scattered oaks and maples laid down their brilliant coats of many colors and stood naked against the biting winter winds. They signaled the crew of cowhands that it was time to buckle on their leather chaps and ride the miles of the Elkhorn's brush and grasslands; time to mount every hilltop, scour each ravine to drive the herds into the Little Missouri bottomlands closer to the ranch; time to settle down for the snows and harsh, bitter cold that was beginning to breathe stronger out of the north with every passing night.

The chuck wagon went out with them and served as their central camp for several days in each location. Two days of biting wind and bitter freezing rain chilled GP to the bone. He tried to keep from bouncing too much in the saddle and hunkered down low into his oil-skin, thankful for the wide-brimmed Stetson that kept at least a little of the stinging sleet out of his eyes. The cattle were just as miserable, humping their backs and turning away from the sleet, refusing to budge when the cowhands tried to move them.

GP and the other hands finally untied their twelve-foot, braided, leather bull snake whips and twirled and cracked them over the heads of the anxious cows. When the sharp cracking sounds still didn't move them, the men snapped the whips sharply into their hides until the stinging pain got them going.

When the crew finally got the woeful critters shouted and whipped into a ravine near the chuck wagon, they huddled under the cook's spreading canvas and wrapped their fingers around steaming, hot tin cups of black coffee. After their teeth stopped chattering, Cookie had thick T-bone steaks with fried potatoes, cooked cabbage, and warm bread waiting for them. Their tin plates and crooked forks had never borne a feast as welcome nor as tasty as this.

Cookie had girdled the chuck wagon with canvas, and the grass under the wagon box became their hotel for the long uncomfortable night. They took their boots and socks off and hung them on sticks by the roaring fire, watching them steam while they warmed their tingling feet as close to the fire as they could stand it. As soon as their socks and boots were partially dry, they slipped them back on. Then with all the rest of their clothes still on, they wrapped themselves in the extra blankets Cookie brought along and crawled under the wagon, huddling close to capture a little warmth from each other's bodies. After a while they shivered less, but warmth was no closer than Kansas.

"Hope we make it through the night," muttered one of the greenhorns.

"Keep your mouth shut, you idiot," Swede snapped, "if you don't wanna let all the warm air out."

GP couldn't remember a time when he had ever been colder, or slept less, but somehow they survived to ride another day.

As the blowing snows piled deeper across their bleak badlands country, the world became ever smaller. Life now was mostly hitching up the sleds and, after hard snowfalls, hauling hay out to the cattle in the trees close to the ranch and keeping the bunkhouse fire going in the black potbellied heating stove. Sometimes they rode out into the herd and practiced calf roping, although GP could never quite master the art of roping both hind legs of a wild, running calf.

On occasion, the foreman's wife would invite them all up to the main house for supper, and every so often they saddled up and went out hunting whitetail deer or shooting coyotes.

During one particularly bitter night, the fire in the black heating stove went out. In the morning, the windows were frozen over in amazing artistic designs, and the roof nails coming through the ceiling boards were all tipped in frost. Cookie shivered awake, restarted the fire in the stove, and boiled coffee for the frozen crew. Pulling their boots on was like sticking their feet into a hole in the frozen Little Missouri, but they shivered and got up. Cookie took a tin cup of coffee over to Whiskey Jack and shook him, but his whole body moved like one big log. His face was turned to the wall, and when Cookie bent down to look closer, he saw Jack's eyes glazed over and his mouth open wide. Cookie was no stranger to death, nor were his potatoes knocked out of the frying pan now.

With his hand still on Jack's cold shoulder, he turned to the table and announced, overloudly, "Hey, boys, old Jack's gone."

The cowhands were still too cold to react strongly to anything, but losing their quaint old companion without the opportunity to say "Farewell, happy riding," left them uneasy.

They set breakfast aside to join Cookie in pulling Jack's boots on, flattened his hat on his chest—the sum of his goods from a cowboy lifetime—crossed his arms over his hat, and double-wrapped his worn-out body in the sheets. When they were finished, one of the men said, "So now what?"

"What do you mean?"

"Well, in this frozen tundra we sure can't plant him now."

"Guess we gotta store 'im in the granary," Swede put in. That was not what anyone had in mind, but what else could they do?

While Cookie ordered a hand, "Get up to the big house and call the boss," the rest put on heavy gear to carry Jack's body to the granary, where they laid him in a bin of oats. When the boss arrived, he looked things over and said, "Too bad. We'll miss the old guy. But hey, this ain't gonna do it. The critters'll get in here and chew on him." He told the men to get some ropes from the barn, and they fashioned a sling around the body and hung him from the rafters to keep him safe until spring.

The long nights of winter continued and gave them opportunity to do more talking. Some of it was getting acquainted, much of it was lying. Some nights they gambled, played poker, and drank whiskey. On others, Spud got out his accordion and taught GP some basic chords.

GP found the other five cowboys to be a tough bunch: hard riding, heavy eating, immensely rich in earthy swear words, enough to stretch clean across the river at flood stage. Mostly Irish, they took insults from no one and came out swinging over almost anything.

Much of their sparring was good-natured, like wolf cubs biting each other's tails, and they worked on teaching GP some head-and-body-saving basics for barroom battles.

Several times, however, as winter closed in deeper, tempers flared for real, chairs and tables were trashed, bodies flew, and Cookie had to bandage wounds, applying whiskey inside and out for pain.

"Say, you guys ever Indian wrastled?" asked one of the hands on another cold night.

"How you do that?"

"Well, you lay down on your back, next to each other, facing opposite ways." With a lot of gestures, he continued, "Then you hook arms, and you raise your inside leg straight up."

When GP and another hand did so, they laughed. "Doesn't feel much like wrastlin' to me."

"Well, just wait," replied the new coach. "Now you hook each other's leg and jerk down hard to roll the other guy over in a somersault."

Soon all but Swede and Shorty were taking turns and rolling each other over with bruising somersaults. After several nights, GP discovered that he had a talent for this new sport and earned the bunkhouse title of "Wrastlin' King."

None of the men were married, though they still felt the need of a woman's companionship every so often and oft made big talk about little conquests.

Shaving stopped when winter started. So did bathing. *"Long johns are meant to ripen on the body"* was the unspoken rule of the day.

When summer came, GP was given a week off to go home and stand up for brother Phillip's wedding. When he came back, he brought along several small bags of sunflower seeds and tried to convert a few of his bunkmates from spitting snus to the more refined "Russian peanuts." It didn't work. Not even on lazy nights after work when they took down the long bamboo poles hanging on the outside of the bunkhouse and walked down to the river. Holding them out over the muddy water of the Little Missouri and watching their cork bobbers, GP got out his sunflower seeds and put a handful in his mouth. "Try some," he cajoled the rest.

It was too complicated. They couldn't angle for the whiskered catfish and chew seeds at the same time. "You gotta work them seeds around with your tongue," GP coached, but it was all for naught. To the rest, snus was a whole lot more relaxing than "those dag-nabbed Roosian nuts."

But what GP enjoyed most was to get Swede and Shorty talking about Teddy Roosevelt.

Shorty, from his name up, was small statured. In his younger days, stretched out full he stood the wall at five-foot-two. Over the years the saddle shook him down some. "But his heart come up to six," the men said. Now his fence-post legs were bowed from years in the saddle, face weather-leathered from hard days out where the deer and the antelope roamed. Wrinkles deeper than wind tunnels on the Little Missouri bluffs carved his visage. Missing his left incisor, he sported a straggly, dapple-gray beard and owl tufts of ear hair, but he was tougher than a starving coyote. While his arms were short, his right hand was a sledgehammer.

Outside of Whiskey Jack, he and Swede were the two oldest hands in the bunkhouse, and both of them worked for Roosevelt when he still owned both the Maltese and Elkhorn ranches back in the eighties and nineties.

"What was Roosevelt like?" GP asked.

"He was differen', that one," Swede replied.

"Yeah," Shorty continued, "'member when he first step off'n the train in Medora with his fancy al'gator boots an' silver spurs?"

"Jes' wanted to be one o' the boys," Swede laughed.

"An' his buckskin shirt with the swingin' strings, an' tanned leather ridin' pants?"

"Don't forget tha' pearl-handled Colt pistol."

"An' that fancy hand-'graved Winchester .45 rifle musta' set him back a bunch."

"Did he learn to ride good?" one of the young hands wanted to know.

"Sure did. Sat a horse good as any man, an' he spent more hours on't than any cow-punch in the spread," Shorty replied, "hot 'r cold, he loved ever' bit of it."

"Summer 'n' winter, didn' matter. Tough nut, he was."

Their enthusiasm for the remembered Eastern cowboy was infectious, and they couldn't stop describing him in every detail.

"An' he was dead on wi' that Winchester. He could plug a coyote at a hunert yards, jes' like he done buffalo 'fore he got here," Swede added.

"Yeah, an' we got ta callin' him 'Old Four Eyes' behin' his back, what wi' them thick glasses he wore."

"Didn't they call 'em Pink Noses?" someone asked.

"No, dummy, pince nez," replied one of the more bookish young hands, recalling a thing he had read about the old days, "'cause they pinched 'em on their noses."

The rest rolled their eyes and let it drop.

"Turned out tough," mused Swede, "but he was kind of a twit when he got here. 'Member how he tried to get the cows movin' more quicker one day, and yelled to O'Malley, 'Hasten forward quicker there'?"

"Tried to sound tough," laughed Shorty, "but that high-pitched, squeaky voice made it hard to take him fer a tough guy."

"But after a coupla summers," added Swede, "he learnt to castrate an' stick the brandin' iron with the besta' the boys, an' he didn' hang back none."

"An' he never become Teddy or Theodore out here. It was *Mr.* Roosevelt. Period."

Before they knew it, the seasons cycled, and they were at the shortest day of the year, December 21, which also happened to be GP's nineteenth birthday. One of the hands had wheedled that fact out of him, and Cookie baked a special three-layered chocolate cake with creamy double chocolate frosting to celebrate. But before they cut it, the rest of the hands wrestled GP to the floor and carried him out to the eight-foot stock watering tank beside the windmill and heaved him in. The water was covered with a thin layer of ice, but he broke through and went to the bottom, almost taking his breath away.

In one motion, he shot to his feet, leaped out of the icy water, and raced to catch those wretches on the way to the bunkhouse, screaming every word of profanity he had learned in the coal mine and ranch, adding some special German ones as well. He roared into the bunkhouse, ready to kill, but they grabbed him once more; and after they stripped off the icy clothes, they peeled off his long johns that stuck to him like glued wallpaper and stood him stark naked by the stove, to thaw out before he caught pneumonia. "Wouldn't this ha' made ol' Whiskey Jack cackle?" someone cracked.

While the rest roared and slapped their knees in glee at finally being able to properly initiate young GP into the bunkhouse, Cookie cut the cake and passed it around. Someone else got a towel for GP, along with an extra-large piece of his birthday cake, and Cookie dosed him up with a cupful of Jack Daniel's. "To keep the pneumonee down," he said.

"Ranching," GP thought later in his bunk, *"is not for sissies."*

One winter weekend, the hands braved the cold and rode to Medora for some much-needed break time. After Dame Whiskey sated their cells in the Mad Bull Saloon, they got into a terrible brawl with cowpokes from several different spreads.

GP tried his bunkhouse moves but quickly found his novice skills no match for the veteran brawlers around him. He ducked several vicious blows and thrilled at the resounding "thwack" of landing his own but missed seeing one coming and heard his nose crack, followed by several more quick blows to his cheeks that sent stars spitting around his head. An instant later he was swallowing bitter blood, with more gushing down his face.

He backed against the wall and slid to the floor, touching his nose that was already swelling big enough that he could see it with both eyes. Chairs and bodies were flying in all directions as he got out his red handkerchief and held it over his nose, crazily convinced he'd bleed to death before the sun came up.

When the uproar finally ended, the bartender walked into the middle of the wreckage and shouted, "That'll be ten bucks from eacha' ya stupid bastards, or I'll have your sorry ass throwed in the slammer."

The pain in their wallets stung almost as badly as their bruises.

The other Elkhorn hands, with cuts and scrapes of their own, finally got GP up and on his horse for the long and painful ride home through the dark of freezing night. It took weeks to heal their bruises. For a long time, the silence of the bunkhouse made it feel like a morgue.

Letters rarely came for the men. Nor were they letter writers themselves. Occasionally Ricka wrote to GP, keeping him informed about things at home, but only seldom did he answer. Writing too often would have branded him. One day a letter told him that Grandpa Christian had died in Krem. He dearly missed being with his family for the funeral, but by the time the letter reached the ranch, it was long over. His heart was heavy for days. He never told the men why he didn't talk for a while. And no one asked.

The next spring during roundup, when GP and Swede rode through the many-colored buttes north of the ranch, they came on a sight GP had never seen. The grass on a long, sloping hillside was stripped down to bare dirt, with foot-high mounds for half a mile around. And popping up out of the mounds were short-tailed little gray critters barking high-pitched, screechy yelps that could be heard a mile away.

"What are those things?" asked GP. "Sure ain't gophers, and they got a yippie little bark."

"Prairie dogs," Swede answered, "an' they're a bloody nuisance."

With that, Swede pulled his Winchester from its scabbard and popped one of the little beasts, which shot a foot into the air and came down dead. Before the echo of the shot died down, every one of the stubby-tailed little critters had vanished down its hole.

"Shoot all th' little buggers ya can," Swede shouted, "'cause they strip a lotta pasture away from the cows."

GP watched them darting around like little kittens, calling back and forth like so many kids in school, and he found himself strangely drawn to them, but his reverie didn't last long.

"Ranchers hate them li'l crappers like alkali water," Swede groused as he spurred his horse and kept riding. In seconds, the prairie dogs popped out of their holes again and scolded them away.

Glancing up, GP spotted a ferruginous hawk, wings out wide, drifting lazily on updrafts, keeping a sharp lookout for careless prairie dogs or rattlesnakes sunning beside a rock. The prairie dog guards barked a shrill warning that kept the great hawk aloft as hundreds of the tiny-eared little critters yipped and darted back into their maze of underground burrows.

Through all these times, GP's heart was drawn back to TR. To GP, this early hero of the open range seemed as much at home in these rugged buttes as in the smooth halls of power in Washington. *"Maybe,"* he thought, *"these rugged buttes and tough weather were what made him strong enough to face the battles he had to face in politics. Makes you wonder . . ."*

Out here in these majestic Badlands, he felt a kinship to Roosevelt, riding with him across the wide-open spaces, lying under the vast canopy of stars at night, the Big Dipper and North Star always in their places. Seeing the great hawks circling, and smelling spring flowers, all of nature rolled on in balanced harmony. He fell in love with this place, just like TR had, and though there was no church out here, he spent many a time in the saddle quietly engaged in prayer. "God seems so close I can almost reach out and touch him," he whispered to the wind.

Toward evening, when he rode in from the range, a dulcet breeze with an iron grip wrapped its fingers around the strong southern winds of spring, throttling them down to pulsing whispers and coaxing the cottonwoods leaves into a beautiful chorus. As the melodious sound struck his ear, GP smiled, *"Sounds like a thousand angels whispering prayers to God."*

In this magnificent land of ever-changing hues, GP sometimes felt enveloped by another dimension. In those mystic moments, it seemed as if some sort of strange gossamer cathedral arched over him, occupied by a Presence that he could only describe as a shimmering column of moving Light. Here he became Michelangelo's Adam, from that mysterious colored picture in the family Bible, reaching up to touch the hand of God.

"I don't know if Roosevelt felt that when he came out here after his wife died, and his heart was crushed," he thought one day, sitting in the saddle. *"I don't know, but something out here must have healed his heart."*

In the long dark of another winter's night, when the smoky kerosene lamp threw ghostly shadows against the wall, the men pulled chairs up to the rough bunkhouse table to play cards.

GP was still hungry to learn more about TR.

"Why did Roosevelt come out here in the first place?" he piped up before the cards were dealt. "Seems like a rich guy from the East had about everything he wanted back there."

Swede and Shorty were quick to pick up on his question, because this was, after all, not cold history. This was their life.

"Well, first of it," Shorty pitched in, "Roosevelt really liked outdoors."

"He like' nature no end, fer sure," Swede continued.

"Knew all that stuff, an' he could talk on it for hours."

"An' then, he really like' ta hunt—"

"Jus' 'bout anything that moved," Shorty cut in.

"Y'know, thirty-five years back, we still had herdsa' buffalo 'n elk runnin' round here," Swede quipped.

"An' lotsa' ugly gray wolves."

"Boy, that's hard to believe now," GP mused, shaking his head.

"Well, th' man was really good wi' tha' fancy Winchester."

"Some of the papers made fun of him, because he couldn't see worth a Roosian peanut without those thick glasses," added a young hand. "Fact, one of the old papers said he was nothing but teeth and eyeglasses."

Swede and Shorty both clinched their fists and nearly came off their chairs but caught themselves while the rest just rolled their eyes and kept quiet.

"Anyways, like I said, that Winchester was his baby, an' it never lef' his side."

"When he point that rifle at somethin' it was dead, no quesshun aksed."

"Was he any good on the ranch?" GP wanted to know.

"Never learn' ta rope worth a crap," Swede went on, "but he sure done everythin' else needed doin' round here."

"So," GP's curiosity wouldn't let up, "how did he get hold of two ranches?"

"Well, in eighty-three he come out here ta hunt," Swede chimed in.

"That's when th' NP railroad come through."

"An' he was alla' twenty-four years old," Swede added with a smile.

"'Fore he went back east, enda' summer, he give Sylvan Ferris $1,200 an' tol' him ta buy the ol' Chimney Butte Ranch six miles southa M'dora, an' maybe four hundred or so heada cows," replied Shorty.

"Called 'er 'Maltese Cross Ranch,' 'cause that's the shape a' the brand he drew out fer his stock, a square cross wi' little square ends on it."

"Next spring, his wife an' mother died, both th' same day, back in New York," Shorty added, "jus' a few hours 'part."

"Near done 'im in."

"An' he come back here, to put hisself back tagether, much as anythin'."

"Didn' hunt much tha' summer," Swede reflected, "jes' got on 'is horse an' rode off by hisself, sometime days at a time. Musta' been tough."

"But he got better," Shorty put in, "'cause 'fore he went back East, he scout' out this place here, both sides a' the Li'l Missura."

"An' give Ferris 'nother $50,000, an' tol' him to buy this place too, and 'nother twenty-five hunert heada cows."

"But this is thirty-five miles north of Medora, and the Maltese is six miles south," GP questioned, "that's a long ways apart to run a ranch."

"Well, he really like' this spot tucked 'way down in th' Li'l Missura valley, wi' th' Badlands 'n all, so he put up th' big house an' th' main buildin's here."

"Ev'nins he liked nothin' better'n to sit 'n his rocker on the big porch, readin' a book, or jus' lookin' out over the river and lis'nen to the night hawks dive."

"An' once a while, we'd walk up there an' he'd tell us stories, till the moon was up there," Swede chimed in, pointing up to the southern sky.

"So," GP wouldn't let go, "how much land did he have here?"

"Kid, ya sure a curious pup, aint'cha," Shorty smiled.

"He run over five-thousan' acres, both sides a' the river, 'n more outn' the hills," Swede replied.

"'Course he didn' really own all that. Some of it was jus' open range the fedrals ownt, and a buncha ranches all run cows on't," Shorty added.

"And what happened to all of it?" GP had to know.

"All went good 'til the winter of eighty-six and eighty-seven," answered Swede, his voice suddenly turning wistful and softer. "Worst a body ever saw."

"Awful," Shorty remembered, looking down at his gnarled hands, "jus' plain awful."

"Started with a terr'bl blizzard, first weekend 'n November. Over two foota snow. We couldn' see t'other buildin's fer three days."

"Few days later we get 'nother big snow, then rain, turns to sleet, and leaves a sheeta solid ice."

"Tell ya, it was like hell froze over. We couldn' move. We couldn' get hay t' the cows. Range stock couldn' dig through to find grass."

"She was so cold you couldn' breathe, hit forty below, bunch'a times."

"One time she blowed fer over a week straight, total white-out so you couldn' see yer hand if ya stretched it out in frona' ya."

"An' we was socked in here, drifts higher'n th' windows, door drift shut, couldn' budge 'er."

"Nothin' left ta eat, whiskey drained dry."

"They come down from the big house 'n dug a tunnel to get us out. Otherwise we'da end' up like them dead cows out there."

"Them damn blizzar's come nearly every week, all winter through, reg'lar as kids to an Irish coal miner's wife."

"Yeah, 'n when she was done, there was four foot of snow on the level, and drifts to fifty-foot deep in places."

Gottfried and the younger hands felt chills up their spines and a new appreciation for these grizzled partners who had lived through all this and survived.

Both Shorty and Swede were talking slower and softer, unnerved even now by bringing up those times more painful than they wanted to remember.

Slowly Swede picked it up again. He had to finish, to get it out of his soul.

"When we rode outn' the spring, there was piles of rottin' carcasses the size'a houses. Cattle run wi' the wind an' piled up like carloads of gunned-down buffalo. Bottom ones choked, an' more jes' kep' pilin' on top of 'em. You can't imagine."

"Some coulees was packed fulla' decayin' carcasses."

"I seen rottin' carcasses hangin' high up in trees where they walked up on hard snow banks to eat tree twigs an' broke through, endin' up dead in twenty-foot-high cottonwood trees."

"Stink was so rotten," Shorty grimaced, "I puked fer two days."

"Even coyotes and vultures was sittin' around sick."

"Yeah, an' then some."

"Womenfolk on differen' ranches got cabin fever so bad they end up takin' their own life."

"An' in the white-outs, men got lost 'tween the house 'n barn, 'n froze to death. Did'n nobody find 'em till spring, curled up in a ball."

"One day in the spring, when it melt' an' the river was floodin' wide, I look down an' the water was nothin' but dead cows floatin' wi' all four in the air, an' here 'n there a' antelope or deer all bloated, goin' down the river."

"Almost more'n you co' take."

"Body couldn' never know what she was like if they wasn't there."

"The cows that was still alive was jus' walkin' skelt'ons, an' most of 'em never had calves that spring."

"It was like they los' their minds."

For a long time no one said anything. The lamp burned low, but no one noticed. The young hands couldn't begin to imagine living through such terror day after day. For the two old timers, it was like yesterday, the hurt still fresh enough to pump bile into their stomachs.

"That was about the enda' things 'round here," Swede whispered, the pain locking his mouth in a deep grimace, his cheek muscles rippled with the distant agony.

"Roosevelt lost three quarters a'all his cows tha' winter."

"Like all the ranchers 'round here."

"What did he do?" one of the hands asked.

"They said over winter he'd gone someplace in the Old Country, but he busted 'is tail gettin' back here in spring. First day we rides out t'the breaks and he sees all the decay an' rot, I thought he was gonna not make it. His face turn' to ash an' he jus' sat fer a lo-ong time, hands on the saddle horn, an' shakn' his head. Couldn' say a thing."

"I think it was jus' 'bout as bad fer him as losin' his wife."

"Not long after, he sold out to Ferris fer the price of a coupla blind horses."

"Couldn' do'er no more."

"Lost hi' shirt out here."

"Oh"—Swede suddenly brightened up—"didja know he had a' armchair made here, all outta big steer horns?"

"An' a lamp, outta elk horns," Shorty quickly added.

"An' when he come back here in ninety-two, he tol' us he had 'em in his office up in the White House?"

The memories lit up Shorty's tired face. "An' he sure did make a great pres'dent."

"I think livin' here helped him in lotta ways."

"Too bad he had ta die so young."

"Sure wish we coulda gone t'the fun'ral," Swede added wistfully as he pulled his boots off. After a long minute of silence, Shorty sighed, "I'm tired out. Enuf," leaned over, and blew out the lamp.

When the sun again rode higher in the sky and the snow was down to a few finger banks on the north side of building and bush, the men scouted out a beautiful little knoll with a small grove of cottonwood trees on the banks of the Little Missouri. All agreed that, looking into the setting sun, it would be right proper ground for old Whiskey Jack's private boot hill.

Spreading out, they found some brush and tree limbs which they dragged to the spot and burned to soften the ground. With equal parts of pick, spade, and swearing, they were able to dress a shallow grave for the burial.

"Tonight, sunset," Swede ordered.

As they were taking Jack's body down from the rafters, a young hand chuckled, "Well, spring, and time to plant old cowboys."

Swede nearly came off the ground and cut him off, "Listen, you dumb bull-shipper, yours is coming!"

None of the hands, nor the foreman, was big on religion; and since they had seen GP reading his Bible on a number of occasions, they assigned him the task of "preacher." His Bible was German, and he knew that wouldn't do, so he asked the foreman for the Bible he had seen on the mantel of the great stone fireplace in the big house. He found the twenty-third Psalm and the Lord's Prayer and he was ready. After short eulogies from Swede and the foreman, GP read the psalm, the Lord's Prayer, made the sign of the cross as he saw pastors do, and with a final "amen," the sojourn of John "Jack" O'Reilly on this harsh frontier was done.

During these times, the government was allotting more of this area to homesteaders while the Northern Pacific was also selling off some of its land-grant properties. At the same time there was talk of reserving this whole badlands country as some sort of park for all people. The cowpokes on the little piece of the Elhorn that remained were still burning the two-pronged Elkhorn brand into the rump of little Texas long horns and Herefords, but they knew their days, too, were numbered.

With so much changing, GP decided that his cowboy days were finished as well, and told the foreman he was leaving.

One last time he rode up on the high bluffs. On the way, going up the side of a long draw, Spotty was following a weaving deer path when suddenly he put down all four and stopped dead. GP clicked his spurs, but Spotty only twitched his ears and snorted, horse talk saying, "Trouble, boss." When GP bent in the saddle and looked a few steps up the trail, he saw a thick rattlesnake, coiled and rattling. GP pulled his pistol to nail the slithery snake when a strange biblical word snapped into his mind, *"Righteousness and peace have kissed each other."*

"Ah, Spotty, King David's word just hit me too strong. I can't kill the little bugger, let's go around her," he whispered to his mount and quietly rode a wide circle around the fretting heir of Eden's fateful tree. "Let 'er hiss, and kiss in peace," he told Spotty, leaning back for one last look and chuckling at his inspired addition to David's psalmodic poetry.

Up on the high ridge, he sat looking over the lush river valley and the special buttes that reached out to him in a host of colors. Up here in the quiet he could almost feel again the crushing ache of death, the pain of anguished loss that Roosevelt must have felt. After a while he dismounted Spotty and, sitting on the virgin grass, soaked in this vibrant painting stretched out before him. Slowly, another feeling sifted in.

The wings of the wind carried a profound peace, a subtle solitude that filtered deep within, and made him breathe full and slow. *"Yes,"* he mused, *"here in this place righteousness and peace really have kissed each other."*

In the stillness, he reflected for a moment on how in this majestic country he had experienced strange new mysteries: fire-red scoria rock, fossilized fish skeletons, and little pockets of seashells a thousand miles from the ocean. He had picked up pieces of petrified wood turned to stone, millions of years old, inhaled the sickening sulfur of burning underground coal veins, and handled huge bones which Swede said that Mr. Roosevelt had called "dinosaurs." What it all meant, his mind couldn't quite put together.

Out here, he remembered, he also heard his first mourning doves, with their long, haunted cooing. At home, with no trees, there were no mourning doves.

Just then he heard a pair calling back and forth from the trees in the coulee below, and the mournful sound seemed to him like the sound of angels whisking to heaven the souls of those who perished in the blizzards of '86.

Off in a far ravine, a cow switched to Mother Voice and told her careless calf, "Pick up your ears, we're moving." Closer in, two magpies on the wing were sharing sweet secrets. GP's heart sang at the beauty of it all.

"All this," he reflected, *"and these rugged buttes that have stood up even against the mighty glaciers, and they're still standing now, strong as ever."*

As the Native Americans experienced long before him, there was healing here, and his heart felt lighter. He thanked God and rode away. All this, and the stories of a hero's heartbreak and healing, would color the rest of GP's days.

"I wonder," he said to the wind, "what's gonna' happen now?"

Chapter 11

Sack Full of Money

The first thing GP wanted to do when he returned home was to visit the graves of Grandpa Christian and Grandma Karolina in Krem. When he walked into St. John's Cemetery, a half mile south of Krem, he was pleasantly surprised. All their children had gotten together and sent pictures of Christian and Karolina to a company that baked them into ceramic tiles and set them permanently into the tombstones. Those clear pictures would endow both stranger and kin to look into their sober faces for generations to come.

Now, as GP knelt in front of the stones, remembering so many times spent with his precious grandparents, he was bathed once more in the distinct aroma of Grandpa's hammered leather and the mouth-watering taste of Grandma's choke-cherry jam on a slice of fresh-baked bread, dipped into a bowl of fresh cream.

"Good-bye Grandma, good-bye Grandpa. God watch over you," he whispered softly, rested his hand for a moment on the tombstones, and got back in the car. The trip home was full of happy conversations with both of them, especially about life in the old country.

Returning to the farm, GP walked into a different world. Older brother, Phillip, was married and gone. Siblings, Emilia, Robert, and Fred were sometimes home, sometimes hired out to the neighbors, while the younger girls were now teens with some grown-up ideas.

GP was a welcome member of the family again, but everyone was on a much different level with each other. He was a mature adult now and related to John and Ricka as fellow adult, though at times they would sooner have had him back as little boy. The younger kids especially loved to get him started telling stories about his life during the past few years, and many a night they came near laughing themselves sick as he brought to life the characters that colored his days. Mother and Father took it with a grain of salt but still enjoyed this "new" son of theirs with fresh appreciation.

With the little sack full of money he had earned, GP bought his own Model T coupe to get where he wanted to go. And a better accordion. He and Brother Freddie spent evenings taking music lessons from some neighbors, and before long he was playing both the accordion and the fiddle, while Freddie became proficient on guitar and banjo. They never got far into reading notes, but after learning key structures, they both played all their music by ear. Soon they were playing for family occasions, then small gatherings, and before long, wedding dances.

They didn't do the fancy new stuff. Waltzes and polkas, two-steps and schottisches were their forte, and usually they ended a night's stand with a number of the beloved old German folk songs that every respectable kuchen eater joined with lusty singing.

The two Oster Brothers, along with Brother Robert at times, slowly gained a reputation as good musicians. But it was GP's mellow baritone voice that got the young women excited. Soon more and more came out to hear them, with girls skipping a turn on the dance floor just to edge close to that voice that seemed to reach out and caress them. GP didn't mind the attention and enjoyed returning all the adoring smiles.

One of the girls worked in the State Capitol and fancied herself quite a band connoisseur.

"That voice is chocolate for my ears," she told her boyfriend.

"I guess it's all right," the boyfriend replied and muscled her back out on the floor.

****

To bring GP up to speed on the farm, John took him out to the fields to see a new invader. Drought had brought some devastating failures to their fields and pastures during these years, along with grasshopper invasions almost as bad. But now a new weed had sneaked into every piece of plow land, and word was that it had traveled all the way out to the West Coast.

"I want you to see this stuff," John said as he bent down and circled his hand over a round globe of a plant. "They're *hexa*. The English call them 'Tumble Weeds.' Them suckers got more prickly spines than ten mamma porcupines."

"Ja, I saw them in fields when I rode the train home from Medora," GP responded. "Where'd they come from?"

"Well, the paper's sayin' they first came in with some flax seed somebody shipped in from the Ukraine or maybe Russia."

"That's why they call 'em 'Russian Thistles' then, I guess. We heard about 'em out in the ranch country."

"Same thing," John answered.

"Where'd they start?"

"They tracked it to Bon Homme County, close to Yankton in southern South Dakota, in the 1870s, the papers say."

"And they spread all the way up here that quick?"

"They claim that every single plant makes from a quarter million to a full million seeds."

"I can't even think numbers that big," GP responded, "but I guess when they start rolling in the fall, one of those buggers can spread a long row of seeds."

"All they need's a little wind."

"Plenty of that around here!"

"Ja, we ate the salt of Mother Russia," John said slowly, surveying the fields, "but now she sends us bitter gall."

Looking across the fields, GP could see these two-foot round green balls—with some up to four feet across—dotting the whole area. "Somebody's gotta figure out a way to lick those suckers," he said.

But before that would likely happen, GP knew some other things needed attention. Spending time at home, he noticed that Mother and Father were both getting older and slowing down, Mother getting Grandma-rounder as well, her ankles grown thick to calf size. They got up slower from their chairs. They sighed and groaned more, grew tired and out of breath quicker.

The same was happening to Uncle Gottfried and Aunt Mina. And GP realized that with Grandma and Grandpa both gone, these four dear hearts were now the older generation, and he and the brothers and sisters and all the cousins would need to step in and do more of the work than before. Father couldn't spend twelve hours on the plow anymore. Mother couldn't do all the family's laundry by herself on the washboard as she once did.

Earlier, Father had been family dentist, tying string around teeth and giving a quick pull. But now when two of Mother's teeth went bad, they drove over to Gottlieb Keller's to get them pulled. They loaded Mother down with three stiff drinks of whiskey and waited while Keller finished boiling his narrow-nosed pliers. Then, when her eyes started to drift and come unfocused, he stood in front of her, gently lifted up her head, and asked, "Ready?" She grimaced, wrinkled her face in fear, and nodded. "Open wide," he said and, with his narrow-nosed pliers in his right hand, took a tight grip on the tooth.

For a moment he wiggled the tooth front and back, then with one motion, he brought his left hand up hard in a jab against the right and snapped the bloody ivory out of her jawbone. Though she tried hard not to scream, she couldn't help it. Once more for the second tooth, and after another hard scream, it was all over. She sat with a cold, wet dishrag clamped between her teeth for a long while, leaning on the table until the bleeding slowed down.

"Here, take some of this," Keller said, handing her a bottle.

"What is it?" she asked.

"Laudanum. They say it's got some stuff called opium in it. Good for pain."

GP now realized he needed to pick up more of the load around home. At the same time, it dawned on him that he couldn't live at home forever. He needed to think about a place of his own. And more and more often the thought crept across his mind, *"One of these days I gotta find me a wife."*

Girlfriends were plentiful, hints abounded from many quarters, and dances brought some delightful romancing, but so far it was all short-lived, appealing though some of these lithesome, sweet-smelling fair maidens were.

****

At the same time there was sadness for the family, since there had not been any letters from sister-in-law, Natasha, in Russia, for quite some time. They had no idea of what might have become of her and the boys. The last packages and money they sent were never returned, but they could only guess that someone else purloined them, so they stopped sending the help she perhaps desperately needed.

For Ricka, it was a particularly difficult time. For over a year, her sister, Mina, complained about not feeling well. She had no appetite, her stomach hurt, and headaches plagued her days. Ricka had the boys drive her to Mina's place several times a week, and often she massaged Mina's stomach and abdomen and rubbed her down with Watkins Liniment or Witch Hazel. It seemed to help for a while, but by the next day the pains returned. Lately nothing seemed to interest Mina, and now she took to sitting for hours in her rocker, doing no knitting, no crocheting, not reading her Bible as she loved to do in earlier times. Then her stomach began to swell, food wouldn't stay down, and she vomited for no apparent reason.

"I'm so terribly tired, I just can't do anything," she said when the family tried to interest her in doing something or going places. Then she took to her bed and only got up to nibble a bite or limp to the outhouse.

Ricka now had the boys drive her every day to spend time with Mina. Although Mina didn't have the energy even to sit up in bed, they had long conversations about their family's futures, about life in old country, and how much they missed their sainted parents. They remembered those frantic first days in this wild new land and how blessed they both were in so many ways. Mina became especially energized when they talked about what heaven might be like and the wonderful hope that God would have a beautiful place waiting for them.

"We have here no lasting city," Mina reflected one day, going back to that wonderful Bible verse, "but we seek a city which is to come, which the Lord has waiting for us."

"That's such a precious hope," Ricka quietly answered, "how true."

That night Ricka had just blown out the lamp and crawled under the covers with John when they heard a car speeding toward their house. John jumped out of bed in his long johns and cracked the door open enough to look out. It was one of Mina's boys, and the car hadn't even come to a stop when he shouted, "Come, quick. It's Mother." Before they could ask any questions, he turned the car around and roared back down the trail.

John and Ricka quickly slipped on some clothes and raced their car to Gottfried's place. They ran into the house where the lamps were on, and the family gathered around Mina's bed. The girls were crying, the boys grim-faced, Gottfried sitting beside the bed and holding Mina's limp hand. Her eyes were wide and unfocused, staring at the ceiling, mouth open wide, chest rattling with every shallow breath she took. Suddenly she stopped breathing, lay still for half a minute, took another shallow breath, stopped again. Death gripped her shoulders, drew back, and squeezed again as anguished suffering hung in the crowded little room.

Ricka held her sister's other hand and finally said softly, "My precious sister, it's all right. You can let go this life. God will take care of you, and he'll take care of your Gottfried and of us too. Good-bye." Then she added, "Tell our parents in heaven, 'Hello.' *Der Herr behuete dich*, the Lord keep you safe." One more long, agonized stillness, then the smallest of gasps. Just then the mantle clock tolled midnight, and Mina's soul took flight.

For Ricka it was a crushing blow. She had lost not only her only nearby sister but also her closest confidant and friend, as well as the only tie to her parents and family at home. All that was gone now. She felt terribly, terribly alone. Tears poured out of her soul like she hadn't cried in years. In the kitchen, dishwater was suddenly mixed with salty tears. Darning socks by the lamplight, she couldn't see the needle through a flood of tears. For many nights she couldn't stop herself from crying quietly in bed. "Ricka, what's the matter?" John asked. No answer. "Ricka, are you sick?" No answer. Finally he stopped asking.

Life had been so good, but now it would never again be quite the same. Her soul was anchored in the bright hope of resurrection, but a wispy cloud girdled her heart for a long season of sorrow.

Despite her grief, life swirled on around her. The county was building a brand-new, fully graded road from Beulah up through the Valley. They straightened and relocated it along section lines and made it state of the art, graveled, and with ditches to drain the water off the roadway. No longer were they driving in dirt ruts. Now they could load trucks and haul wheat on this early superhighway at twenty-five miles an hour! They could make several trips in half a day. And young hotbloods could wind their special four-wheeled beauties up to a blinding fifty and a cloud of dust.

To be sure, in numerous places the roads wore into hard, corduroy washboards that rattled many a lose screw in the dashboards. And in the spring, soft spongy spots still mutated into axle-deep ruts of pure gumbo that could sling a vehicle like a new-feathered arrow straight for the ditch if the driver didn't steer just right—as many a new driver learned after he slogged through the mud and asked a neighbor to hitch up the team of horses and pull him out.

Life seemed to speed up in the Valley as travel now took considerably less time and became more dependable during inclement weather. But to many, the best gift this new road brought to the Valley was regular visits by the Watkins Man. When his black panel truck, with "Watkins Company" emblazoned in bright letters, arrived on the farm, the whole family dropped everything they were doing and turned out to meet him, eagerly waiting for him to swing the magical back doors open.

"Oh, John, doesn't this remind you," Ricka said with an excited smile, "of old Avram back in Klostitz before we came, with that rattly wagon and his little song, 'Garn und Knoepfe'?"

"I was just thinking the same thing."

"Except here his name is Olson."

The Watkins Man soon became a regular and welcome figure on these remote farms. As soon as the younger children came near his truck, Olson shouted, "Here, sporty, have a stick of gum." Or he'd toss them a piece of peppermint candy or a licorice stick. For the adults he had an endless supply of stories that relaxed them for spending their hard-earned money on his bountiful "this'll help you with that" stock of products.

His treasured stock held a cornucopia of things helpful for daily living. He brought veterinary medicines for chicken lice and cattle grubs and horse worms, home remedies for catarrh and bowel problems and stomach cramps, exotic tongue-tingling spices from places far across the seas, along with the best pepper and cinnamon and vanilla extract. And chief of all his items was his most famous product, liniment, soothing balm for the aches of man and beast alike. Made from a secret blend of Asian camphor and red pepper extract, it became the standard salve for nearly everything that hurt.

One day when he noticed a burn on Ricka's hand, he brought out a tin and said, "Here, rub some of this on it."

"What is it?"

"It's called Pain-Oleum, and it'll heal that burn in no time."

Sure enough, it did.

When he looked across the yard and saw a horse that had cut itself on a barbed-wire fence, he told John, "Rub some of this Petro-Carbon Salve on it, and it'll be healed in a hurry."

It was.

Another favorite part of his calls was giving Ricka and the girls samples from a whole chest full of creams and powders and other beauty aids and hints on how to use them. Ricka, of course, felt she was too old to indulge in such youthful extravagance; but when Olson slyly winked at her and gave the girls some samples, telling them, "You'll be the prettiest girls in church and at the barn dances up and down the Valley," she felt a little surge within and couldn't help but picture the princesses they might just become.

Within a short time, Olson would become almost a member of the family, often invited in for quick coffee and lunch. Usually on the last visit of the year, he also brought along a much-anticipated "Watkins Almanac" for the coming year. This paperback gem was a combination weather forecaster/home doctor/cookbook with helpful hints for just about anything prairie folk needed to know, from animal doctoring to "rheumatiz cures" to making root beer for summer picnics. Ricka saved hers every year for handy reference anytime.

****

With time, GP became settled in at home again and realized just what a serene cocoon he was nestled into. He missed the Elkhorn with Swede and Shorty and the vari-hued Badlands buttes, but he discovered that the sunflower seeds and sauerkraut, the kuchen and strudel and Sunday church were a bigger part of his soul than he had known. And all the beautiful girls in his life each weekend made him say to himself one day out in the field, *"Ah-h, this is home, and this is really who I am. Sure feels good."*

Saturday evening they stopped work early, and as soon as the milking was done, Ricka had hot water boiling on the cookstove. The men peeled off their shirts and undershirts and took two washbasins outside, setting them on a board laid over the wheelbarrow. Adding a little cold to make the water from the boiling kettle bearable, they flicked open their straight-edge razors and each took a turn honing his razor to scalpel-edge on Father's boar-skin strop. Ricka earlier moved three little hanging mirrors to hooks on the wall outside, and now each man performed a rare study of his face in the mirror. Next, each stirred up a batch of shaving lather in his heavy mug and, with his soft-bristled badger-hair shaving brush, slathered the hot mix over every inch of his face, leaving only eyes and nose unlathered.

Then, with much scrunching and stretching, each painstakingly swung into the practiced celial surgery that in the day's judgment would make him more attractive to his fellow beings, especially the more delicate among them: carefully slide the razor for several inches at a quarter angle to the face, dip and swish in the steaming water to clean the blade, repeat. And repeat again until face is clean of all unwanted hair; lift nose, stretch mouth, tighten skin on cheek, slide razor again, oh so carefully, gently, gently—a process slowly but forever embedded in each man's brain. No surgeon hath skill more refined, the ads proclaimed, than the straight-edge man tonsured by his own hand.

GP, like the others, nicked himself several times and asked Father to pass the styptic pencil around. He dabbed each of the bleeding nicks and with each dab winced in pain.

"These things sure work," he said, "but the darn pain is worse than the cut in the first place."

"You can say that twice an' mean it," replied Fred.

Supper, a quick bath in the tin tub, and they were ready for another exciting Saturday night. This particular Saturday night, GP and Fred, "The Oster Brothers," were engaged to play for a barn dance south of Krem.

On the way, Fred reflected, "You know, old Krem sure ain't what it used to be."

"What do you mean?"

"Well, with the railroad not coming through up here, and the steamboats not running on the river anymore, things have really gone downhill."

"I bet a lot of businesses are in trouble too."

"Some closed, some moved to Hazen to get on the rail line."

"What about the church?"

"Aunt Katherine says they're hanging on, but lot of people have moved out of town, so that's tough too."

"But this is such good land around here," commented GP, wondering out loud.

"Some of the best in the country, I guess, and the farmers up here are doing real good right now."

"Should make for a good dance tonight."

"I think real good," Fred replied with a big smile.

At the dance, GP especially noticed two particular young women. One had been fed too much homemade Red Eye hootch by some young studs with designs for things later in the evening. "Man, she's *verschnutzed*, half drunk," he whispered to Fred. She was getting noisy and sloppy on the dance floor, hanging on to her partners to stay upright. Whenever they danced past the musicians, she made eyes at GP and blew kisses at him. After a while it grew irritating and he stopped meeting her gaze, though the kisses kept on coming.

"What a *gatch*, weird duck," GP said softly across his accordion to Fred as she passed.

"*Ja, wahrlich*, for sure," Fred answered, amused by big brother's annoyance but not missing a note.

The second young woman was a dark-haired, attractive type who seemed to be enjoying herself every minute. She smiled easily at grandparents and romping kids alike and looked like she was having fun with every dance partner who took her out on the floor. There was something beguiling about her, something in the way she floated when she moved that seemed to draw GP's eyes to her every time she danced by. She must have felt him staring, because on the next pass around the floor, she smiled a little more broadly at him; and when her partner swung her in a waltzing circle, her eyes came back to GP again, this time, it seemed, with a little extra sparkle. Another turn and they were gone in the crowd.

After the dance, GP described her to one of his friends and asked if he knew who she was.

"Sure, that's Bertha, Joseph Wulff's daughter."

"She from here?" GP continued.

"Ja, but she's working in Bismarck right now, for some rich family down there."

GP and Fred casually walked through the partying crowd, then around the parked cars trying to spot this daughter of the Wulffs, but his new heartthrob had vanished.

Several weeks later, quite by accident, GP was introduced to her older brother at another dance and jumped at the chance to ask if his sister was spoken for.

"No," the brother laughed. "Why, you interested?"

"Well, I saw her at a dance a while back, and I'd just like to meet her, that's all," GP replied, trying to sound nonchalant but still appropriately interested.

When the brother thought a moment, he remembered that she was going to be home several weekends from now and most likely going to another dance. They quickly settled all the details to work an introduction and agreed to meet at the dance. Then, shaking hands, they both walked away, curious, excited, and with a stack of questions rolling through their minds, more in GP's than in her brother's.

GP was enthused by this turn of events but a little hesitant. Word was going around that one of the Wulffs' neighbor wives was into witchcraft. Stories circulated that in the old country her family owned a "black Bible," which many called "The Sixth Book of Moses." It was considered a textbook of witchcraft, with instructions in the black arts. Word was that she knew them well and would not hesitate to use them.

Neighbors were careful not to offend her and wary of close contact with her. The situation grew yet more skittish during a neighborhood gathering when all the adults threw their coats on a bed, as was the custom, and during the evening someone walked in and discovered her picking hair off a man's coat.

"Magdalena, what are you doing?" he asked.

"Oh, there was some fuzz on this coat here and I cleaned it off," she replied. And with her best smile added, "Wasn't that nice of me?"

"Um, ja, I guess so," was all he could answer. And with that, she walked back to join the rest in the living room.

Nothing more was said until several weeks later when the coat's owner got his fingers stuck in some machinery and lost his hand.

The neighbor who saw Magdalena pick hair off the man's coat remembered that moment and connected it with the accident. Soon word spread throughout the neighborhood, and outrage against Magdalena went over the fence.

Stories grew about more strange accidents, about dogs mysteriously dying without being sick, about black cats that appeared out of nowhere, hissed, scratched people, and vanished.

What was true and what was made up was debatable, but it was a moot point. The rumors had a life of their own.

It left GP with some qualms about driving into that neighborhood, but finally his attraction to this winsome Wulff woman did battle with his fears, and attraction carried the day.

"Besides," he said to himself, *"I'm not gonna let the devil run my life."*

****

Passing days brought more flying changes. Older brother, Phillip, and his wife brought the first grandchild to an overjoyed John and Ricka. Sister Emilia got married. John bought a new Model T Ford truck to haul grain and cattle. And after talking with Ricka and then with GP and Fred, he decided to expand his farm and buy more land. When neighbor Jake Eisenbeiss agreed to lend him the money, he took the plunge and bought another quarter of land to raise more cattle and grain.

"My wife and I still remember your GP and how good he was to us when he worked for me," Eisenbeiss told him. "Maybe, John, you can help him out with this land someday."

"Maybe," John replied and left it at that.

Owing that much money left John terribly unnerved. He felt he had to do it to keep up with the times, but it scared him to the bottom of his soles. After signing the Eisenbeiss note, he tossed all night in bed, his mind in anxious turmoil. Strangely, some Russian proverbs from the old country kept running through his head.

"Debts are not rabbits—they don't hop away," rattled around for a while. How true. He knew this debt would hang over his life a long while. Then, when he thought maybe he shouldn't have bought the land, came *"One who sits between two chairs will be on the floor."* "If you can't make up your mind," he silently whispered, "you'll lose everything."

Then into the jumble came yet another: *"As you cooked the porridge, so you must eat it."* "Yes," his mind went on, and he blew a big sigh of relief as resolution seemed to scroll across the dark bedroom ceiling, "I have to answer for what I do. Whatever happens, I have to pay the fiddler, and I can't blame anybody else."

Another word flew through the darkness, this time one the pastor had read in church last Sunday, "Let not your hearts be troubled; neither let them be afraid." Finally, he could only pray and put it all into the Lord's hands, trusting that, in this as in all things, God would somehow see him through.

During fitful hours of sleep he found himself running and marching in the Russian army with officers screaming and lightning flashing. Suddenly fellow soldiers were being kicked to death, and he tried to escape, in terror of being discovered. Each time he woke, soldiers with heads of dogs were just a step from catching him.

When daylight finally cracked the dark of the East, he wasn't sure if he had slept or not during the turmoil of the night and felt as if a herd of wild things had run him over. But just waking up and having work to do was a giant relief.

Still feeling frazzled, later that afternoon he told Ricka, "Let's drive over and visit Gottfried tonight."

While they were visiting at the kitchen table, Gottfried looked at the floor and remarked, "Ei, without my wife this place is so lonesome now I can't stand it." Neither John nor Ricka quite knew how to reply, and finally Gottfried packed his pipe, then reached over to his little three-legged tobacco table and picked up the last *Staats-Anzeiger*. With the heavy silence hanging like the smoke from his pipe, Gottfried changed the subject: "Did you read there was a big money crash all over the country?"

"Ja, didn't they call it Black Friday?"

"Says a whole bunch of banks went belly up too."

"Lotsa people lost everything."

"They say some men jumped out of high buildings, took their own life."

"Don't know how anybody could do that," John replied.

"Just glad I keep my money at home, not in them banks."

"Ja, me too."

John wanted to tell his brother how nervous he was over being in such a hole of debt, but somehow Gottfried seemed all wrapped up in his loneliness, and the moment wasn't right. John glanced at

Ricka and couldn't bring himself to open his heart, brother or not, and in this moment could not respond to his brother's broken heart.

****

While John stewed for days over being in debt, GP was not bothered. Work around the farm was prelude for dances to come—some to play for, one to meet a special young beauty that had his mind spinning.

On the prearranged Saturday night, he took special care shaving and bathing and putting on good-smelling aftershave lotion. Before they left, he stuck a packet of Sen-Sen in his pocket to make sure he'd have clean breath.

He and Freddie drove to the dance, and it wasn't long before Bertha and her brother rolled in as well. GP walked over and shook the hand of Brother Otto, who smiled and with a mischievous wink introduced his sister to GP and Freddie. Otto and Freddie both knew the score and immediately excused themselves.

"How about a dance?" GP asked, coughing as the words stuck in his throat.

"I'd like that," she replied, her easy smile making him feel better already.

Bertha, too, had been cued by Otto about a special young man who seemed clearly interested in her; and she also took particular care to get ready, making sure hair was done, rouge just right, seams straight, and the right amount of cologne applied in just the right places. They danced five dances, each enjoying the rhythm the other displayed, the easy conversation about a lot of nothing over the noisy dancers all around, the relaxed feeling they got from each other after the initial nervousness.

Through the evening, a number of young men in turn cut in and asked for Bertha's hand to dance. So did several of her married relatives, as partners changed freely all night long. When the last dance was announced, partners all scurried to find each other, and GP nervously looked around for Bertha, hoping no one would nab her for the slow, romantic finale. She had also managed to keep moving, staying close to several girlfriends in case GP might come looking for her. He did, and they thoroughly enjoyed the close, easy last dance of the night, feeling wonderfully comfortable without any hasty artificial intimacy.

After the music was over, GP asked, "Can I give you a ride home tonight?"

"I'll have to ask my brother," she replied, but all that was already worked out between Fred and Otto, who would ride together in Otto's car so the two new warm-bloods could get better acquainted.

On the way home from the Wulffs, after dropping Bertha off, GP blew out a big breath and exclaimed, "Man, she sure turns my crank!"

Freddie just laughed. "Looks to me like that crank'll get a lotta turning. But will it start the engine?" That thought struck him as hilarious, and he continued laughing. GP didn't think it all that funny.

Chapter 12

One Special Woman

Wonderful girls walked through GP's life—women, to be sure, but to him, girls—and Ricka hinted broadly that some of them came from just the right families. In fact, she invited several families, including their eligible daughters, to Sunday dinners after church. The visits went well, the young people were sociable and seemed to enjoy the day, but, alas, no fires were kindled, not even sparks.

After one such lavish dinner, when the "kids" just waved casual good-byes to each other and their families, Ricka announced to John in a too-loud voice, "Well, that was sure a waste of good sausage." GP just shook his head, "Ach, *Mutter*, Mamma."

Now with the new Wulff girl attracting such strong attention, Ricka casually said to GP one Saturday night when the men were shaving, "This Wulff girl, you know she comes from a way different *dorf* than ours. She sounds nice, but, you know, sometimes people from other places have different ideas about things."

"Mamma," GP shot back, "I'm not a little boy. Let me decide."

That exchange triggered in Fred's mind a proverb the old folks sometimes tossed around, *"You live with wolves, you howl like a wolf."* Just saying the words in this moment struck him as uproariously funny and made him and Dad double over with laughter. GP failed to see the humor in it and scowled through his shaving lather. Perhaps a pause might have been a good idea, because he nicked himself half a dozen times before he was done.

For GP, life seemed to revolve more and more around this one special woman. It seemed as though in everything he did, his mind somehow came back to Bertha. Bertha, always Bertha.

The favorite times of his heart were when she had time off from her housekeeping job in Bismarck and he drove to her farm to see her. Just sitting on the porch together in the evening, listening to the nighthawks swooping in their whistling, popping dive, and hearing it together with one he loved was pure music to his soul. No accordion had such celestial power in its keys, nor any fiddle in its strings.

"You know," he whispered to her one warm summer's night, "my mother and father talk about sitting on my grandfather's porch, just like this, back in Russia."

"Really?"

"And they say they still remember seeing the Big Bear in the north."

"Oh," Bertha replied excitedly, "we can do the same thing." She grabbed GP's hand, and together they ran around to the side of the house and looked into the majestic night sky where the Big Bear stood in silent glory, surrounded by a million other stars twinkling to get their attention.

"Same bear, new crew," mused GP as they returned to their swing.

Several weeks later, as GP was driving to get Bertha for another dance, he had a terrible encounter. Driving along the section line trails, where grass grew running board high on either side of the worn trail, he suddenly saw something flash into the trail just ahead of the car, a fuzzy black-and-white something. Before he could react, he ran over it, and in an instant the entire car stunk with such an obnoxious stench that it took his breath away. He got the skunk. But the skunk got him first. He braked to a stop, threw the door open and ran off to the side, but it was all too late. "I knew it," he spit out, "I just know it's the witch out to get me."

He drove the rest of the way to the Wulffs with all the windows rolled down, trying to air out the car, but it didn't help. When he drove into the Wulff yard, the two dogs that usually ran up to greet him lowered their heads and skittered away sideways with troubled yips, tucking their tails between their legs as if they'd been yelled at for lapping up the cats' milk. They knew bad news when they smelled it.

Even the chickens stopped their noisy clucking and cocked their heads sideways in wonderment as the pungent odor from this rotten machine began to permeate their yard. GP's entire proud Model T had been turned into a motorized waste pit that reeked of the awful stink that could only come from one source.

When Bertha came out of the house, she got only halfway to the car until she clasped her hands to her mouth and gasped, "Phew, where'd you hit a skunk?" It was awful. Even his clothes had absorbed the smell by now, and when he got out of the car and walked toward her, she backpedaled as fast as she could move.

"Yech, I'm not going anywhere with you tonight," she exclaimed, and he had to agree. There would be no carefree dancing this night, much less kissing.

All he could do was sadly drive home and park the car for a week at the edge of the yard with all the windows open, hoping nature, which provided the nauseating smell, would also find a way to evaporate it.

This was the season when the Sears and Wards catalogues were nearly used up in the outhouse, and the whole family was secretly getting nervous waiting for new ones to arrive in the mail, hoping they'd come before they would have to use corn cobs for personal hygiene. There were no peach wrappers in this season, so things were getting dicey. The men tried to help by doing their bathroom duty in the barn where they could twist handfuls of straw to clean themselves.

It was also the season when the men were out manuring the barns. Their three-man team worked just perfect, with Fred cleaning stalls in the far end of the barn and pitching the manure to the middle of the barn, John pitching it from the middle to the front door, and GP pitching it up on the sled to haul it out to the fields. On the way to the snow-covered field, they had time to talk, and talk turned to the farm and their futures.

With GP and Fred both starting to think about marriage and having a place of their own, Father had been turning some things over in his mind.

"What would you think, Gottfried, if I sold you the quarter of land I just bought, and then, Fred, I'd sell the homestead to you?"

The brothers looked at each other in shock for a moment at this turn of events.

"Well, I suppose . . .," Fred stammered.

"I guess we could all work something out," GP added.

"But we don't have that kind of money," Fred quickly piped up.

"I'd sell it cheap so you could afford it," John replied.

When they arrived in the field, Father climbed off the sled while GP and Fred pitched the manure out over the field as far as they could fork it. On the way back, John picked up the conversation again.

"Gottfried, how would a dollar sound for that land?"

"You mean a dollar an acre?"

"No, a dollar for the whole thing, including the eighty-acre pastureland to the north."

"Well . . .," GP started to say.

"Not much money, but remember," Father continued, "you still have to put up a house and barns and dig a well, and get some machinery and horses."

"I guess. But what about you? What would you and Mother do?"

"I thought Fred would get the place here, and the machinery. But he'd have to take care of Mother and me. We'd stay here and live with him."

A free farm sounded good to Fred. But what would a new wife think of this arrangement? Would it be more costly than any of them knew? He looked at GP and shrugged his shoulders.

"Let's think about all this," was all Fred could say for the moment, and there it was left to simmer until another day

Not long after this, Bertha came home for the weekend; and since the brothers were to play at a dance, GP picked her up to go along. While the brothers played, Bertha enjoyed dancing with a number of young men, with several grandmothers whose husbands didn't like to dance, then with a man who sported a silent-movie pencil mustache and who threw a big shadow, carelessly swinging hands that were big as T-bone steaks nailed to cedar corner posts.

He was none other than the spitting Emil Wiedeman, with whom GP had a history, and now to see his girl dancing with that lowlife riled GP so badly that he missed several notes of the song he was playing.

"That filthy skunk," he mumbled after he got his fingers back on the right keys.

Wiedeman had developed a reputation for being a skirt-chaser. And more. When the number was over, he hung around Bertha, smiling, talking, gesturing. The next several dances he had her out on the floor again, laughing, bending his head down to fill her ears with chatter.

"He's kinda fun to dance with," Bertha told her friend between numbers, "'cause he's a four-buckle overshoe bigger than any guy I ever danced with."

The girlfriend giggled as she pictured the four-bucklers walking.

"And that big barrel voice makes his laugh rumble like a Rumley engine."

More giggles.

"When he wraps those big arms around me, I feel like I'm floating in the air."

"Ooh," the girlfriend responded, ready to fold into his arms if he'd just ask her.

When they were driving home, GP grew angrier by the minute.

"That Wiedeman's quite a dancer," he said, trying his best to sound calm.

"Nothing special," Bertha shrugged, quickly sensing from his short breaths that there was a whole lot more to his comment than Wiedeman's dancing skills.

"Surprised he didn't ask to take you home."

"I didn't give him any reason to," she answered quietly.

When she reached over and put her hand on his throttle leg, he thought better of taking the conversation any further and didn't want to tell her of his history with Wiedeman. She noticed GP was quiet for the rest of the drive home but didn't quite feel free to pry into his thoughts.

At the next dance, the same thing happened. Wiedeman was there again, and he seemed attracted to her like a honeybee to sweet clover. Soon he was hanging all over Bertha, dancing with her entirely too many times, holding her much closer than GP could stand. He also noticed that as the night went on, Emil "Valentino" was doing a considerable amount of drinking.

GP went into a slow burn, growing angrier by the minute. Although "Valentino" was scary big, GP had to settle this thing; and when the dance was over, he followed him outside.

"You lay off my girl, you got that?" GP shouted.

"Hey, Ostie, you don't want me to plow with your heifer?" Wiedeman laughed, nose up but unsteady on his feet.

The slur enraged GP to instant fury.

"You stinkin' ox," he shouted and swung his fist with everything he had into Wiedeman's stomach. Wiedeman gasped and returned an arching haymaker, but he was unsteady enough that hand didn't follow brain and struck nothing but air.

Just then, friends of both men stepped in and pulled them apart.

On the way home, neither GP nor Bertha said anything for a long time. Finally Bertha broke the ice, "I didn't think there was anything wrong in dancing with different guys while you're playing. You can't dance with me anyway."

"It's not different guys. It's that stupid Wiedeman," replied GP.

"He doesn't mean anything."

"Maybe not, but he's a *schleiger,* a crooked sneak, and I don't trust him."

"Well, I won't dance with him anymore, all right?"

GP shrugged but said nothing. *"Someday I'll tell her about him,"* he thought to himself, *"but not tonight."*

He thought the better part of wisdom here might be silence. Now both felt awkward, and in that awkward silence they finished the ride home. A quick kiss at the front door of Bertha's house and the evening was done.

Still another dilemma, however, faced GP. While he felt this antagonism toward Emil, Wiedeman's father had learned to play the balalaika in the old country, and he teamed up with an accordion player to form a dance ensemble that played wonderful old-time music. GP thoroughly enjoyed the father, but the son sure gave him fits.

Several weeks later, GP picked Bertha up on a Saturday night to attend a dance in the big Dreamland Pavilion in Beulah. Locals knew it as "the Sheep Shed." This night, a traveling band from Strasburg, in German country across the Missouri River, close to the South Dakota line, was playing. Their lead man was a sharp young accordion player named Lawrence Welk. GP was fascinated by his outstanding fingering skills, and during a break he talked with Welk and picked up some hints on accordion technique.

On the way home, GP was still picturing Welk's playing in his mind and asked Bertha, "Wasn't that accordion player, that Welk, something else?"

"Ja, I got a notion he'll be around a while," she replied. "Their music is smooth as chokecherry wine, and so easy to dance to."

"I think he might have a future in music, if he sticks with it a while."

After GP dropped Bertha off at her house, he was driving home when suddenly he broke out laughing. During another break at the dance, GP was relaxing with a group of energetic young swains gathered outside, most of them rolling Bull Durham or packing snus along with passing around a few paper sacks with beers made illegal by Prohibition. After some moments, the talk turned to a right heavy young woman who came with her brother from south of the nearby town of Zap.

"She sure has some layers of *schpeck, fat,* on that chassis," snorted one of the smokers.

"But hey, can she lay a jingle to that *schpeck* on the dance floor," laughed another with a wink as the group guffawed, wondering secret wonderings on their next Bull Durham drag. Soon the music started back up, and they stashed the paper bags under their car seats and went back inside.

Occasionally, GP and Bertha attended a movie at the Roxie Theater in Beulah and were totally enthralled when they experienced their first movie with full sound. Heady stuff, making movies a whole new experience.

During the next months, their relationship blossomed and grew, and finally he asked her to marry him. She had been hoping he would and accepted with no hesitation. When GP asked Father Wulff for her hand, he gave his blessing, and both parents were excited to help plan their only daughter's wedding.

"Is the wedding gonna be pretty soon?" Mother asked.

"I'm afraid it can't be for a little while," GP said, "'cause right now we'd have no place to live."

"You can live with us for a time," her father replied.

"Oh, but . . .," Bertha started to say.

"That's nice," GP cut in, "but I'll be putting up a house and buildings on the farm my father's selling me. He offered me a good deal."

"Good. I'll get our boys to help," Father added quickly.

"Hey, is he just a little too eager, or what?" GP wondered.

Chapter 13

Wedding Bells

With the help of GP and Bertha's brothers and several cousins, house building wouldn't take long. The little house would make a good home. Bertha's brother, Emil, was a strong worker and would keep the rookie builders on target, while the women would keep their stomachs satisfied with a steady diet of scrumptious soul food.

For his new farmstead, GP had selected a small plateau of high ground, rising up from the valley floor, with a long high hill just behind it to the east. The spot looked out over broad, two-mile-wide Antelope Valley to the south and west and into another range of tall hills on the far side of the valley. "This place," he told Bertha, "is halfway between my folks and Uncle Gottfried's, a half mile from each."

The house would sit on the plateau, sharing the high ground with the pig and chicken sheds. An earth barn for cattle and horses would be dug into the sidehill of the ravine below the house.

But before the final spot for the house was determined, they had to locate a well for water. GP drove over to get their old "water-divining" neighbor further east, and he brought his forked willow stick to douse for water. To their surprise, his rod showed a little underground stream about twenty feet from where GP wanted to build the house.

"Should be water right here, maybe six, eight feet down," said the neighbor. They drove a stake on the spot, and after a promise of dinner in the new house, GP drove the neighbor home.

The next week they began digging a dirt cellar for the house. Using Father's two-horse scraper, they quickly had the cellar hole a foot deep. Then they hit a glaciated layer of blue clay that was hard as any cement. Only sharp pickaxes could break it, and each miserable swing made only a little hole in the clay. After five long backbreaking hours, it seemed like they were making no progress at all.

"Maybe we should get John Bauer with a couple sticks of dynamite," said one of the cousins.

"Sure would be easier, but maybe kinda messy," GP replied as they took turns swinging the picks. After two days their shoulders and arms ached so badly they could hardly unbutton their pants, and they decided to switch to another job. They split into two teams, with a wagon each, and drove across the surrounding prairie hills gathering cap-sized rocks to cement into the rubble-stone foundation for the house. After a long day of walking and picking stones, their backs ached, but their shoulders were rested enough to challenge the blue clay and finish the cellar.

When the rubble-stone foundation was cemented and level, they were ready to begin building the house. But first they would dig two more holes—one for the well, another for the outhouse—on the opposite side of the dwelling, away from the well.

The second hole, for the outhouse, would be easy.

The first hole, five by five feet square, with straight sides, would have to keep going down until they hopefully hit water. They all groaned when they thought of the miserable work that lay ahead, swinging the pickaxe again in tight quarters, one man in the hole at a time, picking for a while, then shoveling the lose clay and dirt out of the hole.

They battled down eight feet and needed a ladder to get down and back up out of the hole. Still there was nothing but backbreaking blue clay, bone dry and rock hard.

The temperature hit a scorching one hundred degrees, and in the hole it was considerably higher.

"Man, you could *verschmacht,* suffocate, down there," said one exhausted digger climbing out of the hole, sweat running down his whole body, every bit of clothing soaked.

"I hate to say it, guys," GP said with a big question mark in his voice, "but let's go down another foot or two, and if we don't hit water, we'll give it up."

Bertha's brother was in the hole, the rest all on their knees around the top of the hole peering down through the dust and taking turns pulling up the rope with a bucket of dirt every time the digger filled it at the bottom. Suddenly there was a loud whoop from the deep, "Hey, I hit soft sand!"

The next digger leveled off the bottom of the hole down to the sand, and several inches more, and within minutes water began seeping into the bottom of the hole. GP quickly climbed down and started lining the walls with flat sandstones they had hauled in from outcroppings on the high hill behind the new place. Now they'd have fresh water, and house construction could begin.

Before long, their little prairie bungalow of two rooms and low roof was hammered together. The one entry door, facing east, opened into the kitchen, with windows only on the south and east to protect against the bitter winter winds sweeping down through the Valley from the frozen Arctic. There was no insulation to defend against biting cold, only a clapboard-covered outer wall and a plastered inner wall, with two-by-four studs in between. A quick coat of robin-egg blue paint on the clapboard outside and soft yellow on the inside walls, with Ricka and Bertha laying out a steady supply of sandwiches and coffee, and they were soon finished.

Now bride and groom were ready to finalize wedding plans. They set it for early November, with the wedding at Bertha's church, north of Hazen, and a wedding dance at her parents' house.

There was, however, a great shadow hanging over their hope-filled plans. The previous two years had been terribly dry, with scarcely any crops at all. Now hay was in short supply. Animals were growing thin and bony, some starving and dying in the pastures. There had recently been a stock market crash that crippled the finances of the whole country. Banks failed, and broken men took their own lives. In the face of all this, some people questioned GP and Bertha's wisdom in even thinking about marriage in such an anxious, volatile time.

"Remember June in '29," one well-meaning friend told GP. "That was the driest month ever on record in North Dakota, and we aren't out of the woods yet, by the looks of it."

"You got no crops on your land this year, and hardly any hay. How can you even think of getting married right now?" another counseled.

But love is not susceptible to weather. Nor was theirs.

Bertha's wedding dress, purchased with the money she earned in Bismarck, reflected the new age ushered in by the recent World War. She dressed at home and now walked down the church aisle in a V-necked, white satin sheath dress, knee length and adorned with a beaded, floral headband. Flowing down from the headband, a white, full-length, wrap-around, sheer organza veil. At her neck a beaded broach, and on her feet, flat leather shoes, since she stood five-feet-five, an inch taller than GP, and didn't want to appear awkwardly taller than her beloved. In her hands, a white embroidered handkerchief lay atop a white leather-covered German Bible.

Before they left for church, her mother got out her own wedding picture from twenty-nine years earlier. It showed her looking stern in a white veil and sash over a solid black dress—black because they could only afford one good dress, and after the wedding she could remove the veil and sash and wear the dress for funerals and holidays.

"How different weddings are today," she commented to Bertha before they got in the car.

The little country church was completely packed, and when the pastor pronounced them "man and wife" and spoke the final benediction, both the bride and groom had a terrible urge to shout "yea" and run headlong down the center aisle of the church. All the families and friends would have been aghast, and all proper Lutheran decorum broken, so of course they did neither and instead walked solemnly down the aisle with sober faces and out to Fred's waiting car to be driven to the Wulff home for a festive wedding meal. There were no rings, but the knot was tied.

As soon as supper was finished, all the young men helped rearrange the living-dining-room furniture and the celebratory wedding dance began. When the music started, the guests soon discovered that dancing in those close quarters was a challenge indeed but not nearly as challenging as trying to avoid stepping on the eager little children that darted between the tall timber of constantly moving adult legs.

Halfway through the evening of dance and revelry, they stopped the music and two young men came up behind Bertha and hoisted her into the air while a third removed her shoes. The best man held one shoe up high and shouted, "Now we're gonna auction off the bride's shoe." He walked through the crowd of guests and nudged each man until he coughed up some paper money to put in the shoe. When some were slow to produce, he poked them in the chest and loudly yelled "hey, hey, hey" into their face until everyone looked and they were embarrassed enough to produce. As was the custom of that era, this was the bride and groom's "start-up fund" for their new home.

The other shoe, meanwhile, was poured full of Red Eye home brew and passed around for all to take a nip. It was refilled a good many times and increased the generosity level to green up the first shoe as well. That the shoe was a little sweaty caused a lot of good-natured joking but no loss of thirst. And that it was squishy for the rest of the night when it was given back to the bride was of precious little concern as well. These were times for full-throttled celebration with loved ones, not for standing on formality, *"and prohibition and the drought be hanged,"* someone shouted.

When the eastern sky started to hint light, the music ended, and the women brought out sandwiches and cakes, kuchen and pickles, along with stout, black Russian coffee. The wedding couple greeted their guests one last time, and GP drove his bride to her new home.

For them, there was no lavish wedding trip as the storied well-to-do were wont to enjoy. He parked his Model T in front of the little blue house and carried her inside. They did no work on the farm that day.

After the sun had set, Fred and Selma, his new bride of two months, walked over from their place to visit; but when they approached the house, there was no light, no sound, no sign of life.

"Let's let the newlyweds be," Fred said after a moment of standing silently outside the front door.

"Yeah. I wish we'd have had time to ourselves like that," she said.

Fred knew what she meant, moving in with his parents right after their wedding. But what could he do now? "I know. I wish so too."

The second day, the bride and groom awoke thirsty and starved. Bertha thoughtfully brought a small bag of sandwiches, some chocolate cake, and a jar of cider from the wedding.

"And that," GP joked later, "was the first meal my wife cooked for me."

Now they could leisurely relax in their new home and get settled in. One room was the kitchen, with a small table and chairs for eating, and a cupboard for pots and dishes. In the corner stood a homemade washstand and basin, above it two twelve-penny nails on the wall at eye level to hold a small mirror and hang a towel. The command center of the kitchen was a new black Majestic cookstove that John and Ricka gave them for a wedding present. On the wall beside the entry door, GP mounted a horizontal two-by-four, into which he pounded half a dozen twelve-penny nails to hang jackets and coats, bonnets and caps.

The second room held a double bed and wardrobe, presents from Bertha's parents, Joseph and Salomina. Across from the bed, a potbellied coal-burning heating stove, a rocking chair, and two straight-backed chairs with woven cane seats for company. Bertha also hung up an eighteen-inch, colored, hard-paper picture of a sober Jesus above the bed. Between the bed and the potbellied stove, she put down a woven, six-foot oval scatter rug to keep their feet from freezing on cold winter mornings.

The little house was not exactly what Bertha was accustomed to, especially in the upscale Bismarck doctor's house where she worked as nanny and hired girl. Instead of going to the bathroom and pulling the chain, now she had to endure a trip outside in the harshest of elements. Instead of pushing a button to turn lights on, now she had to lift the kerosene lamp's smoky glass chimney, strike a farmer's stick on the bottom of the table, and light the soaked-up dimly burning wick. But she was an exuberant twenty-two-year-old, her man was twenty-seven, and it was all their own. They had each other, and now they were off on a grand lifetime adventure.

In the middle of their second wedded afternoon—a sullen, stormy November day—they decided they'd better drive to Beulah to lay in some food and supplies to begin housekeeping. While Bertha got the necessary groceries, GP stopped at the station of the new Flying Red Horse, where the attendant washed his windshield, checked his oil and tire pressure, and filled his gas tank for ten cents a gallon.

Driving back in the gathering dusk, they were busily talking as they drove past Wittenberg School a mile from home. Suddenly a dozen frightful figures appeared out of nowhere and jumped in front of their car. GP slammed on the brakes and sprayed gravel as the monsters banged on their windows, screaming unearthly cries and stunning them with a terrifying cacophony of clanging metallic thunder.

In a moment they regained their wits, and the ghastlies slipped their handkerchiefs off their faces, letting GP and Bertha see that it was their loving neighbors treating them to a splendid shivaree, a noisy "welcome to the newlyweds" in which they all hid in the tall ditch grass and jumped out, screaming and banging pots and pans, making a horrible noise. After a few minutes of hilarious joking and backslapping, they all got their cars from behind the school and accompanied the newlyweds to their house, where the women got out baskets of food they had prepared and cheered the joy of a brand-new couple in the neighborhood, celebrating long into another Valley night.

The next morning their world was dusted with wintery white. Outside there was precious little life in this frozen world, except a flock of tiny, bouncing, black-and-white snow buntings that flew into their hard-packed yard to pick up period-sized gravel pebbles. Other days, a handful of hearty, winter-proofed sparrows in speckled-brown jackets bounded around and sang cheery sparrow songs to them. GP had run some wheat through the fanning mill and now scattered handfuls of broken wheat kernels and weed seeds out in front of their door, and it soon became a picnic ground for the little feathered ones.

Winter wore long and harsh. The snow was deep, cold, and intense. Getting to the earth barn and the outhouse both became a challenge. They tried to keep a small fire burning all night in the potbellied heating stove in the bedroom, but by morning the water in the reserve pail on the kitchen stove, along with that in the wash basin, were frozen solid. When they woke up, the yellow inside walls of their little house were glistening white with frost.

GP spent long days shoveling snow to keep the pig barn, chicken shed, earth barn and stock tank all open and accessible, while Bertha kept him supplied with strong coffee and tackled the challenge of preparing meals and baking new cakes and canned-fruit kuchen in her wood-fired Majestic oven.

Nights, after chores and supper, they played a few hands of cards until GP gave a weak yawn. "Must be about time for bed." He cupped his hand over the lamp chimney and blew it out.

"Gonna be a cold one tonight again," Bertha mentioned as she undressed.

"Pile on more blankets and cuddle tight."

"Won't be hard," she smiled, jumping into the cold bed and curling full against GP. For newlyweds, hard winter was private and pure delight.

"*Holy cats*, your feet are cold," GP shivered with this new experience. Bertha giggled, and life was good.

Chapter 14

Depressing Depression

Spring was exciting for Bertha, because she could now put in her own garden for the very first time. Down the ravine several hundred yards from the house, and around a low curving hill, an artesian spring ran out of the hillside. Beside it lay a small, flat piece of ground which would make a perfect garden. After GP plowed it up, she dug a small canal from the spring to her new garden. As soon as the ground was warm enough, she planted rows of peas and potatoes, cucumbers, carrots and cabbage, and sweet corn and carrots. She put in beets and beans, hills of pumpkin and muskmelon, lettuce and dill, and onions and garlic. And at the end, she spotted two full rows of sunflower seeds.

When her back grew sore from bending over, she stood up, and the sound struck her. She couldn't help being cheered on by a score of red-winged blackbirds perched on nearby podiums of buckbrush and water reeds. Their brilliant song surrounded her with symphonic trills of encouragement: labor now, savor later. "Thank you, little friends," she chanted back to them, and suddenly the weariness was lifted. Whatever else might happen, she would feed her man well this summer and winter.

GP had his own excitement with new life. Father gave him two sows, and now each bore piglets—one six, the other ten. He enjoyed nothing more, when work was done at night, than to light his kerosene lantern and settle into the straw in a corner of the new pig shed, letting the pink-skinned, soft and clean little grunters look with ever curious eyes into his while they oinked and snuffled his fingers with moist little noses and jumped all over his lap without a care in the world.

Over the past several years, John also gave GP several heifers of his own. In addition to these, last fall GP purchased three milk cows and five bred range cows; and now, one by one, they were all throwing calves.

The first chore each morning for the new couple was milking the cows and feeding calves, sticking their hands into the steaming milk pails and letting the calves suck their fingers as if they were feeding on mamma's four faucets. "Those little gums can sure squeeze your fingers," Bertha laughed.

After milking was finished, GP drove out to the plow land where, with five horses on the two-bottom plow, he turned over two furrows with each pass up and down the half-mile fields.

The previous fall, he and Fred broke up twenty more acres of sod on his new farm, and now he disked it several times to break the clods of earth into smooth soil. After all that slow, grinding work, seeding with the big drill was a cinch, and hopefully by fall this year they might again have a crop of grain along with calves and pigs to sell.

Late every Saturday afternoon, their routine began with early milking and chores, a bath in the round tin bathtub, and clean clothes for a trip to town. Anticipating visits with neighbors and friends, their hearts were light as they climbed into the Model-A, and GP maneuvered the half mile of a two-track trail around the prairie hills from the farm out to the gravel road. Then thirteen miles to Beulah. After they dropped off the five-gallon can of cream at the Beulah Creamery and Bertha's crate of nine dozen eggs at the RCU Grocery, GP's usual word was, "You get groceries here, and I'll stop in the Mirror Bar to see who's around." With Prohibition in effect, the Mirror served some non-alcoholic drinks, and with care, for a few trusted customers, upstairs in a little back room, stronger stuff.

"All right," and Bertha was off to the store.

"Meet you in the Sweet Shop around eight thirty." There they'd meet friends and catch up on the latest news over coffee before picking up their sacks of groceries out of the pile waiting to be picked up at RCU and heading home to sleep and be ready for church on Sunday.

But with the passing days, '33 was also turning sour on them. Spring rains were sparse, and the haying grass grew stunted. As spring turned to summer, both the pastures and fields slowly turned brown and dried up. Day after day, temperatures soared and scorching heat bore down on the earth. Clouds blew up dark and threatening, but the much-needed rains would not fall.

Anxious farmers helplessly watched prices go into free fall. Wheat sank from $1 a bushel to 35 cents, a 64 percent drop. Cattle selling for $100 a head were now under $30, more than a two-thirds drop, leaving no profit. Corn, hogs, milk, all sank to the lowest prices in memory.

GP hauled a hundred bushels of wheat into the Peavey Elevator, and the manager cut him a check for thirty-five dollars. "Hey, you gypped me here," GP told the manager.

"Sorry, GP. Little while ago you'da got a hundred dollars for that load, but everything's down the dirt now."

"Doesn't even pay to haul the stuff to town!"

Those who borrowed money to buy land or machinery were losing everything. Many a confident soul felt hope slip away and fingers of desperation set in.

If all this misery wasn't enough, Mother Ricka began complaining about stomach pains that wouldn't go away. Both Selma and Bertha gathered small chamomile buds, with their unique five petals and bright yellow buds bearing a distinctive faint odor of apple, and made medicinal camellia tea, but it didn't help. Finally, GP and Fred were able to convince John to take her to the doctor in Beulah. The diagnosis was grim.

When they returned home, Selma saw Ricka's eyes red from crying. "What is it?" she asked.

"*Es ist krebs*, it's cancer," Ricka replied.

"Can't they do something?" Fred wanted to know.

"They said not."

"It is serious?"

"They said I only got a few months to live."

There were a lot of tears and hugs. But what else was there to say? Hardly had that news been digested when John's sister, Katherina, in Krem, who had also been ill for a time, suddenly died in her sleep. Now the Krem connection, where Ricka had memories of so many precious shopping trips and visits in those early days with her husband's parents and with his Baisch sister, was all gone. "Lord, where are you?" she cried on her pillow at night. "This just isn't fair."

For Ricka, the cancer and losing her sister, Mina, then her sister-in-law, both close to her own age, along with still painful memories of three infants she bore and nursed and laid into the buffalo grass, was more than she could bear. After Katherina's funeral, Ricka's health spiraled downward at an alarming rate. Within two months she lost her appetite and could not eat. Soon she was too weak to get up.

Two weeks more she suffered and prayed, prayed and hurt. John sat with her. The children came and were a big comfort, but they could not lift the pain. Then in the dark stillness of a night in the third week, a strange mysterious thing happened. There at the foot of her bed stood a tall figure wearing a long robe that seemed more shimmering light than cloth. He said nothing, but his eyes shone out a peace that eased her breathing. In a moment he raised his hand with his palm toward her, and from it streamed a beautiful ribbon of light in which her past flowed like a river.

There she was, feeling again the profound joy of holding her beloved Johnny in her arms after being so afraid the Russian army would claim his life. She held children she brought into this world and nursed at her breast, and those she washed and cried into the prairie sod, tasting again the salt of bitter tears running into the corners of her lips. She found herself smiling as she sat with the Charging Bears after being so afraid of their different skin and tongue.

In a sudden flash of light, the memoried stream vanished and was transformed into a mystical sight that left her gasping. Never had she seen anything so breathtaking, so totally beautiful. She was walking in a large field of flowers with colors glowing in a luminescence that could only be angel powered. In the far distance rose a vast city gleaming like dazzling gems of rainbow colors. It was bathed in a brilliant golden aura that moved and shimmered like northern lights but had no source. And coming out of the city was a large group of people in sparkling robes but still too far away to see their faces. They were singing a song so melodic, so full of rich harmony that only heaven could bring forth.

Then, as she waited for the throng to come near, another light flashed and it was all gone. Disappointed, she took a deep breath, now robed in a golden treasure of both memory and surprise that colored her heart.

Once more there was a soft glow in the room, and when she opened her eyes, there stood the tall, silent man in a column of light that continued to send out waves of the most beautiful music. In his right hand he held an open book, his left hand resting on a page.

"Ricka," he said with a deep voice so inviting that she held out her arms, "Ricka, your name is right here, when you are ready." And just as she began sitting up, he was gone, leaving behind a joy, a peace, a blessedness more powerful than she had ever known. She lay back and took another deep breath, and it felt like she was back in the tub at the Salem Hotel. Suddenly, breathing seemed so easy, her heart totally at rest, her soul bursting with a deep inner light.

"I'm ready," she whispered and fell asleep.

The next morning when John sat on her bed with a small bowl of porridge for her, she took his hand and whispered, "Something I have to tell you." Her eyes glistened as she relayed the wondrous visit she had during the night.

"Ja," John replied, "for sure the Lord is here." He was amazed but not really surprised that the Lord had visited his faithful mate in this way.

"John, I'm ready," she whispered once more and closed her eyes.

Despite her peace and the deep faith of her loved ones, the scepter of healing stayed in heaven. She endured a few more days and grew weaker still.

When her breathing became labored, Fred and GP sent word to the uncles and aunts, and soon all were gathered at the homestead. The angel of death called with merciful swiftness, and soon Ricka's trials were over. Fifty-nine summers of grace, and now with a stomach full of cancer and a heart full of peace, her walk among the rolling tumbleweeds was finished.

Walking away from the grave after the sad funeral, with the girls holding his arms, John couldn't hold back the tears. "She never got her 'threescore years and ten' that the Bible holds out," was all John could say.

He was devastated to lose his beloved. "I don't know what I'm living for," he said at supper. Living with Fred and Selma helped, but he still felt all alone. "The young people have different ideas," he told his brother, Gottfried. Ricka was his heart, and now that heart pumped gall into his soul.

Along with John, her death was hard for Fred and GP who had spent so much precious time with her; and though they were both now married, Ricka was still Mamma in their hearts. Grief walked with them like a shadow for many a day. With Grandmother Karolina,

Katherina, and Mina all gone, Ricka was the glue that held the family together. Now even that glue was gone.

During the funeral, the black-robed pastor focused on the long-term blessedness of eternal life. For the family, short-term anguish ruled the day as another death had come too soon, and the dutiful McShane bell of Peace Lutheran tolled another grave into the front row of the rain-starved cemetery.

Hardly had the families put away their black mourning clothes when Uncle Gottfried's second wife died. He had remarried after his precious Mina died, and now he laid a second wife into the bone-dry earth. For him, homestead became dungeon, and he had to move away.

"How much death can we handle?" the family began asking each other. But there was nothing they could do to change it. Between death and drought, the depressing days rolled on like summer thunder that knew no end.

Uncle Gottfried gave his homestead to his son, Adam, and moved to a little shack on the outskirts of Beulah. He let his square, mottled gray beard grow unruly, and soon he took on the look of a homeless indigent, shuffling around lonesome and rumpled and unwashed.

When John stopped by to visit, Gottfried groaned, "I get so awful lonesome . . . I can't eat . . . I need a wife." John didn't need to be told—the condition of the house told the story.

"Ja, I know how it is," John slowly responded. How well he knew!

"The days drag by like a bull snake in long grass."

"Ja, we both walk around like blind horses trying to find the barn door."

Through all these sad days, the blistering sun continued to burn everything that grew. And what the sun didn't burn, the scorching east winds crumpled over, as if some angry Homeric deity was blowing his searing breath across a mythic primordial Sahara.

Believers prayed earnestly for rain. "Open thy heavens, O Lord," prayed the pastor, "and mercifully let thy gentle rains water the parched earth, that thy people and thy creatures may not perish." And several Sundays later, "As thou didst answer the earnest plea of thy servant Elijah and send forth rain upon the earth in that day, so do thou again in our day." But high heaven seemed as closed as the low heavens, and there was no rain. Dark clouds were impregnated by mighty thunderbolts but gave birth to bags of wind.

GP managed to get hay only from several slough bottoms and long ravines. Some of it was needle grass, loaded with barbed hay needles that stuck in his clothes and dug into his skin. Worse yet, the needles got into cattle's eyes and noses and into the lining of their mouths, causing severe infections. It was not the grass he hoped to put up for hay.

Then, while he was mowing that miserable grass and bemoaning his fate, a flutter of translucent blue dragonflies went flitting through the milkweeds dotting the grass. Their diaphanous double wings fanned in a hummingbird blur. "Whoa," he called to the team and pulled them to a stop. For long minutes he watched the dragonflies enjoying God's bounty, and suddenly his heart beat with a new rhythm.

"Those little things are so amazing," he told Bertha at home. "They can fly in any direction, change speed, stop on a pin."

"I like how your voice gets different when you talk about 'em," Bertha smiled.

"They're like Ezekiel's wheels in the Bible," GP remembered, "going every which way without ever slowing down."

"Nice, huh?" she chuckled, seeing how excited he was about these little creatures.

"Couple of 'em flew up on the horses an' sat on the hame balls and never moved for a whole round, like they were paying good money for the ride."

****

The next day, when he walked into the fields, he noticed that only the grain in the low spots was filling out. The plants on the high ground were so shriveled they weren't even worth cutting for hay. Moving on to the lower ground, he was astonished to see that the gumbo flats had turned rock hard and split open into jagged pieces, with cracks big enough to stick his hand in.

"But what's growing?" he asked Bertha. "The blessed tumbleweeds!" When nothing else could survive, they thrived in the dry weather and grew in every field, some to enormous sizes.

"If only we could harvest them suckers," said one of the neighbors, "we could maybe sell thistle seeds and make a fortune."

"And our cattle would sure have plenty to eat," replied another.

Fortunately, through the entire drought, GP's artesian spring kept pouring out water from deep inside the hill. Day or night, neither cow nor horse ever lacked for water.

Bertha dug a channel from its run-off water to her garden and had an automatic irrigation system. Her garden knew thirst only at high noon. In the cool of the evening she opened the little water channel for an hour and slacked the thirst of every plant until it stood tall and thriving.

Crickets and grasshoppers, mosquitoes and horseflies all thrived as well. Wherever beast or man trod, it seemed that one or more of this quartet of misery chirped in an ear, jumped on a body, sampled blood, or snatched a mouthful of flesh. "If we all die off," GP said one evening, coming in from the field, "I got a pretty good idea who's gonna make it."

Bertha could handle all of this, but she shuddered each time she opened the trapdoor in the kitchen floor and descended the wooden steps into the dirt cellar to get canned vegetables or cool cream. Shining her flashlight down, little pairs of reflectors stared back at her. When she swung the light on them, it was *grattler,* crawly, eight-inch, spotted salamanders. They sported round toothless jaws, shiny bodies, and long, sweeping alligator tails. They burrowed little holes in the dirt walls of the cellar, backed in, and stared at Bertha's light.

"Those ugly things make me shiver something awful," she told GP.

"I know, but they won't hurt you."

Finally, she carried a spade, chopped their toothless heads off, and scooped them outside.

"Yech," she shuddered again, "even after I chop their head off, their ugly tail keeps swishing back and forth."

"But they can't chase you anymore."

"Ja, but one of those headless little devils moved his tail till the sun went down."

****

During these difficult times, people still sought at least momentary relief, and dances were one way of finding it. GP and Fred continued to get dance dates, and though their playing did not earn big money, it certainly helped. By cramming themselves, two wives, cased accordion, fiddle, banjo, and guitar all into one car, they saved a little more and made the small earnings go further.

In the midst of hardship all around, Bertha woke up one morning feeling awful. As soon as she got out of bed, a wave of nausea flooded over her, and she ran outside vomiting.

When she got to the barn, she was nervous and not sure exactly how to break the news to GP, or whether to tell him at all right now. "I don't know," she finally blurted out, "but I kinda think maybe we're going to have a baby."

He got up from under the cow he was milking and took her in his arms.

"Hey, that's great," he said. "I'm so happy." After holding her a moment, he stepped back and held her at arm's length. "But it kinda scares me too."

"I know. Me too." They weren't sure if this was the best of times to have a baby, but it was too late to ask the question.

This would be the first grandchild for Bertha's parents, and she couldn't wait to tell them the news.

"I'm so glad," her mother replied. "But now you better get rid of your cat."

"Why?"

"Because cats lie down on the baby and suck the air out of them."

"Oh, Mother, you don't really believe that."

"I sure do. In the old country, there were two families that came in and their babies were dead, with the cat lying on top of them. I know."

Several days later, Bertha mentioned the conversation to Selma.

"Ach, that's old wives' tales," Selma replied, "but get rid of it if you want."

Still, Bertha took her cat along to church the next Sunday and gave it to another family.

Before long, Selma found she was also expecting, and the two of them enjoyed commiserating over nausea and wild cravings and driving their husbands to distraction.

GP was secretly hoping for a boy. He looked forward to having a son whom he could guide in the secrets of shepherding the earth as John taught him, as generations of fathers in their family had faithfully done before that. A little hunting partner would be fun too.

When Bertha went into labor, GP drove to tell Selma and Fred, and then on to get the midwife. While Selma helped with the birth, Fred was busy trying to keep GP from panicking as they impatiently sat on the ground outside, waiting for midwife's call or infant's wail. A strapping baby boy it was, and they settled on Clinton Leroy for a name.

The new mother spent long hours cuddling the precious babe, nursing, changing, talking to him, and singing childhood rhymes. Occasionally, as she sat on her rocking chair nursing him, he would shiver a little. She mentioned it to GP, but it never happened when he was around, so they dismissed it. John loved holding his little Clinton and just looking into his eyes.

When they drove to town for groceries, GP filled the car with gasoline. At ten cents a gallon, it cost him a dollar and forty-three cents. "Ei, there goes four bushels of wheat I don't have," he told the attendant.

The spring rains, meanwhile, were sparse at best. The ground was still dry, but GP, hopeful like the neighbors, planted a full crop and trusted for a good harvest.

Summer came on drier and hotter than last year, everything wilting by the day, plants dying a leaf at a time. Dogs panted at noonday, tongues lolling out the sides of their mouths. Chickens fluffed in the dirt on the north side of the shed, seeking cool shade, and sat with beaks open.

GP's entire farm had not one tree on it, nor did Fred's homestead place, so cows had no place to find shade except to gather in tight clumps on high ground to draw shade from each other, or else lie flat and let the sweltering sun roast their fur coats. But then pesky flies crawled into their noses and ears or burrowed into their eyes until they bawled for relief.

Grasshoppers and tumbleweeds loved the drought and continued to flourish. Nature seemed to be in rebellion against man's efforts to tame her, while some questioned God. One of the neighbors, whose piety was questioned by some, finally said it out loud, "If there is a God, why doesn't he step in and do something here."

"You'd better be careful," replied a friend, "or he might start with you."

In midsummer, rumors circulated about a terrible grasshopper infestation coming from the south. But so far they hadn't come. Then one day GP came racing into the house with a crazed look in his eyes, pointing south and shouting, "They're coming! They're coming!"

When Bertha joined him at the door, they saw a single dark cloud low in the southern sky, rising and falling, getting darker, then spreading out. An instant later they heard a high-pitched humming roar as millions upon millions of hungry green hoppers settled into the field to their south.

As the roaring hordes descended into a field, they landed, often several to a single stalk of grain or blade of grass, and nibbled it down to bare ground. When those in the rear of the thrusting mass finished their voracious gorging, they flew up and landed in front to gorge some more. They formed a roiling river of endless motion, like the great Missouri in flood stage, and as wide and devastating. In a matter of minutes they would annihilate an entire field of grain. Now they were scorching the earth in a swath three miles wide. Other swarms devastated areas to the east and west of them.

John had come over, and as they stood looking at this living disaster, he softly said, "Reminds me of the rolling ocean waves on the *Armenia* when we came over."

"I can believe that," Bertha said. "And listen, you can actually hear them chewing."

Their new dog, Schatzie, heard it before they did and cringed behind them, hugging close to Bertha's legs, frightened by the terrible, spectral sound.

GP was reminded of the song the English were singing and put in, "If ever God *has loosed his fateful lightning with a terrible swift sword*, we're seeing it right now."

"Or maybe it's the antichrist coming to take us down," replied John.

Several neighbors came driving up with gasoline cans and yelled, "Let's set fire just ahead of 'em and burn 'em out."

They quickly fanned out and lit the fires. Mounds of hoppers were burned, but many more just flew over the flames and moved on. Fire would not stop them.

The mass followed the Valley, and only some thousands came over the farm, but they were soon on everything, in everything, crawling, jumping, chirping, clicking hind legs together, as if saying, *"Take that, you puny intruders!"*

After they passed through, the ground was covered with stinking, dead grasshopper corpses, perishing from who knew what—maybe overeating—but still dead. All the mushy hopper carcasses turned the roads slick for driving.

The chickens were delighted at the cheap banquet. But soon they had the *eggles,* the yucks, on this overfeast and sat down with their eyes closed, wanting no more.

The next day when GP drove to town and walked into the café, all the talk was about the great hopper invasion.

"Yup," a grizzled retired farmer spoke up, with his hands hooked into his bib overalls, "they're even worse than they were back in aught-nine."

"Let me tell you," GP told the group, "I was out mowing hay, and when I stopped for dinner, I left the team out in the field. When I came back, the horses were gone."

"No," gasped an out-of-state traveler who had been listening, "what happened?"

"Gosh, you won't believe it, but the grasshoppers had eaten the horses."

"Oh no-o," groaned the shocked traveler.

"And there were the grasshoppers," GP whispered secretively, looking around the room, "split into groups and pitching the horseshoes to see who'd get to eat the harnesses."

The visitor gave a shallow laugh and walked out mumbling.

When GP returned from town, Bertha was nursing the baby and called out, "He shivered again, a couple times. It's so strange."

"I don't know. Maybe next week we'll have to take him to the doctor."

The next day GP hitched up the grass mower and went to mow the old slough bottom to the east that the hoppers had somehow missed. The good grasses had mostly dried up, but wild, weedy foxtails were growing tall. They had four, some up to five-inch heads with long, soft, prickly white "hair" that were good cattle fodder if they were cut green. But when they ripened and grew stiff, the hair turned into reverse barbs that burrowed into cattle's eyes and noses, leading to major infection. GP thought he could get them cut down in time to get at least a little hay for winter.

From the slough bottom, he moved to road ditches and mowed the thin stand of fuzzy pigeon grass and rich-smelling sweet clover, and that was the hay for next winter.

Sitting on the mower, he looked up toward the farm and suddenly saw Bertha frantically jumping up and down and waving a white dishtowel. Quickly unhitching and throwing the harness off, he jumped bareback on one horse and galloped home.

Before he reached the house, he could hear Bertha screaming, terrified. As he bolted through the door, she shrieked, "He's dead! Oh, dear God, my baby's dead!"

GP knelt beside her and felt for signs of life. When there were none, he snatched the infant and shook him, then laid him on the table, pumping his stomach, trying to push some air back into the lifeless lungs. The little one's eyes were rolled back, already turning darkish, mouth agape.

"What happened?" GP cried.

"I was holding him and he just went into *gichter,* convulsions, and wouldn't stop."

"Did you do anything?"

"What could I do? Before I could get out of the chair, he went all limp and stopped breathing, just like that."

All GP could think of doing was to drive to his father's, to get him and Fred and Selma to come over. For several hours all they could do was hug and shed tears and join in asking, "Why? Why?" Selma made coffee on the stove, and finally they decided to take the body to the undertaker in Beulah and begin preparations for a funeral.

After they got home, Selma told her husband, "At least I'm glad I told Bertha to get rid of her cat, so we don't have that to deal with."

They dressed little Clinton in the white baptismal gown that Mother Ricka had sewn on her Singer before she died and that he had so recently worn. They arrived early at church for the funeral, and Bertha got out the new Kodak box camera she received as a wedding gift and snapped several pictures of her precious firstborn in his tiny, cloth-covered white casket. Her grieving heart needed something to remember him by.

With one toll of the church bell, they laid their son-of-promise into the pitiful little row of baby graves opposite of Mother Ricka and Sister Mina. Mothers, especially, stood circled in that wind-swept cemetery filled with weeping that would spider into every mother's bed and haunt the dark with unwelcome questions.

"The pastor said God is merciful," Bertha sobbed that night in bed, "but I think he's not a good God. He's cruel."

"Sh-h, *liebchen*, my dearest, I know how much it hurts. But try not to feel that way."

"I can't help it. It hurts too much, and it's all God's fault," she shouted into the dark.

"Sh-h, don't make the Lord angry on top of it," GP softly whispered, taking her into his arms and holding her tight. "Somehow we'll make it through. Even with all this, try to remember, God's mercy is everlasting."

That note struck a bitter chord in her heart, and she shot back angrily, "Well, I wish he'd take his mercy someplace else and just leave us alone for a while."

GP stroked her hair and said no more until she cried herself to sleep.

The next days they both walked around in a fog. Everywhere they went, everything they did, brought their white-haired little cherub back to their minds. Bertha, especially, felt his little hands caressing her face, heard his cry. Her breasts were hurting to be nursed and needed relief, and the pain echoed in her soul.

She had a little sister who was hydrocephalic and died at twelve. But that death was somehow more relief than anguish. This was a hole so raw inside her, so visceral that it made her shiver, almost like her baby.

"Dear God," she finally prayed weeks later with tears streaming down her face and more down her heart, "my heart's completely broken. I don't know how to go on. Help me. Please, God, help me."

GP found solace by walking up to Raven Feather's high grave, which was part of his farm now. Sitting on the cairn of stones, he imagined all the darker-skinned fathers of long ago who also lost sons, some of whom were now resting under these very prairies, and felt a bond of peace. *"In death, all our skin is the same color,"* he thought to himself as he eyes swept the great Valley and returned to the silent stones on which he rested.

Later in the week they had visitors who brought them deep comfort. Two Indian couples drove in, separately, and wanted to talk. The Broken Arrows had lost two little ones, one stillborn, another dying at several months old. The Charging Bears were now getting on in years but had watched GP from a distance all these years and still thought of him as family, even though their hoped-for adoption had not happened. GP and Bertha could feel the hurting hearts in these brothers and sisters from the long, tight hugs they gave and from the tears that flowed.

The Broken Arrows brought them a venison roast; the Charging Bears brought a pair of deerskin mittens they had made for Bertha. Those heart-touching visits started a long road to healing. *"Was it all coincidence?"* GP thought.

It wasn't long before Selma's days were upon her, and they had a beautiful blond-haired baby girl. Grandfather John held her in his arms and rocked her, his heart full of joy.

"She reminds me of Ricka," he said, though he wasn't quite sure why.

Selma felt happier than she had ever felt in her whole life. "How blessed I am," she whispered as she held the precious bundle to her breast. Then it happened. Two days of life the little one was given and she died.

Selma and Fred were devastated. "What is God trying to tell us in this family?" Selma cried.

GP and Bertha drove to Fred's, and Selma ran into Bertha's arms. Bertha held her tight and rocked her back and forth. "I don't want to stay here anymore," Selma sobbed. "I hate this place."

"I know, dear sister. I know," was all Bertha could say.

And, with one more toll of the bell, another little grave was added to the tragic baby row beside the church, with a little carved lamb atop the little tombstone.

Selma and Bertha, such joyous young mothers, and now no more, spent long afternoons sharing every smallest detail of their darling babies, flesh of their flesh so cruelly snatched from their breasts.

Sometimes they talked. Sometimes they cried. Sometimes they sat in silence, feeling their little ones stirring inside them.

As despondent as Fred and GP were over the deaths, they were still deeply thankful that their wives had survived the births. They knew only too well how many area graves were filled with young mothers who died in childbirth. The price of populating those prairies was much higher than anyone really wanted to talk about.

Within another month, Uncle Heinrich died as well. Unfortunately, in his whole life they had never gotten a photograph of him, so they decided this was the last chance. After the funeral they propped Uncle Heinrich's casket up against a cemetery fence post as straight as they could without sliding him out, opened the cover, gathered the family tightly around him, and took their family picture. On the prints they noticed that the pastor wore a dreadful scowl, but they still made enough reprints so all in the family could have a photo of Uncle Heinrich.

When the reprints were sent out, one of the nieces was heard to say, "Wow, Uncle Heinrich sure looks dead." Her prescriptive remark lived long in family lore.

As summer bent into fall, the days got hotter still. It didn't seem possible, but the soaring temperatures climbed higher and scorched everything. Wells went dry. There was no grass left, and cattle ate more dirt than vegetation as they gnawed at the dried-up roots. They were nothing but skin on bones, with every rib showing through.

Then another dust storm hit. Was it the tenth, eleventh by now in these bitter years? Nobody quite remembered. The arid, scalding winds ripped across the dry grasslands and over the barren grain fields and hoisted the powdery soil high into the air. These winds had gathered from the far corners and flexed their maws seeking a new menu, and they found it in the floured earth of the great Midwest. Picking up scoopfuls of choice Canadian topsoil, they roared on, lifting huge truckloads of Dakota-lite ground and mixing it into a dirt salad for the puzzled residents of Chicago.

GP was working outside when he saw the dark wall coming atop the high hills across the Valley. It rose hundreds of feet into the air and came rolling in like the angry waves of the Atlantic that had scared the wits out of his shipboard parents.

"Hurry, close everything tight," he yelled to Bertha, "and cover all the stuff in the kitchen."

When they had finished, they walked out to the west side of the house and watched it come. Field after field disappeared as it came on with the speed of a galloping horse. Soon the wind blew harder where they were standing, and everything turned dark. They barely got into the house and closed the door when everything went dark. They lit the kerosene lamp and noticed a fine powdered dust filling the air around them, forming an indoor fog. Soon they began to cough and covered their mouths with handkerchiefs, but the dust was so fine it went right through the cotton cloth.

"Here," Bertha said, walking to the washbasin, "soak your hanky in the water, maybe that'll help."

The washbasin was already covered with a thin film of scum.

With short, quick steps, GP walked to the window to look outside and pulled back the white lace curtain. A puff of fine dust drifted down. He could not see the buildings yards away. On the other side of the glass everything was totally black.

"Looks like a cloudy midnight in November out there," he blurted out.

Six terrible hours the thick wind howled around the eaves. Outside the animals hunkered down and closed their eyes with their noses against the ground, trying to find a place where they could breathe without choking. Finally, after what seemed like days, the wind died down.

When GP walked into the yard, the cows had dirt rings around their noses, with black pus draining from their eyes. Chickens flew off their roosts and fluffed their feathers, spraying mushrooms of dust into the air. The pigs were in hog heaven with mounds of fresh dirt to wallow in.

Bertha began the long job of dusting. "I wish the wind would have blown a little in here," she said out loud, "to clean off this blasted dirt." Her dishtowels needed to be washed; the clothes in the wardrobe shook out and brushed off. Underwear and socks in the drawers were pickled in black powder. Windows were grimy, sills layered with dirt. Cold pork on a cloth-covered plate in the cupboard had to be thrown out. The butter under glass next to it wore a thin film of dust and had to be scraped off. She lifted the glass dome, scraped it off with a knife, and sat down and cried. She couldn't even think about the bed and the floors. Her brain reeled. It was too much.

Tumbleweeds by the thousands blew against the fences and became windbreaks for the blowing dirt which piled up on both sides, causing drifts as high as the fences and forming bridges hard enough for the cattle to walk over. Ditches were level full of black grit, with drifts reaching across the roads like fingers of snow in the winter. Even a covered can of cream hung down in the well to cool had a film of dirt on top of the cream.

The next evening, after they finished milking, Bertha and GP walked over to Fred's. John had just purchased a new floor-model RCA radio that could be run off a six-volt battery. When they found Bismarck on the dial, the newsman said the storm was the worst one during the years of drought, sweeping across five states and carrying topsoil from the plains all the way to Cincinnati and some as far as Nashville.

Early winter brought little snow, but for days on end the mercury hung way south of zero. Then Dakota December hit. The strong-willed arctic winds that knew no weakness shot sleet BBs with such force that it brought worry to rocks. No living creature wanted to stay outside for long. The range Herefords that had no choice huddled together on the lee side of the hills, heads down, eyes closed, seemingly praying cow prayers for relief.

When Bertha sat down on the frozen board seat of the outhouse, it sent shivers up her spine. Even the Sears Roebuck catalogue pages were iced and stiff. Her stay was short. GP made use of the straw pile in a corner of the big barn. Winter on the prairies was not for the meek of heart.

In church, before services, Sunday after Sunday brought the question, "Is this weather never gonna get any better again?" Others reflected more somberly, "Have we done some terrible sin that God is angry with us?"

More than one was heard to mutter, "I'm about ready to give up on this miserable land and move out west."

"Ja, at least they don't freeze to death out there."

"Or choke to death from dirt."

Chapter 15

The Rope

Recent winters outside were harsh. But for John, the winter in his heart was much more severe.

Several times he asked Fred to drop him off to visit brother Gottfried in Beulah, but in their loneliness they found little to talk about and mostly just sat quietly together until Fred came to pick him up. Usually Gottfried, with brown-stained shaking fingers and nails uncut, rolled his Bull Durham and lit it up until his long tangled beard momentarily vanished in a cloud of smoke. John mostly drummed his fingers on the hand-crafted pine kitchen table that bore scars of both love and anger from Gottfried and three wives and a wagon-load of prairie children. The silence between the two old pioneers was heavy with memories. On the drive home, John couldn't help but think, *"My dear brother was such a good man, so full of life."* He thought back to their journey on the *Armenia*, the painful days of breaking sod, *"He stood by me through thick and thin, always ready to help, and now he's nothing but a broken shell. Ach, it hurts."*

With Ricka gone, John realized more than ever before that she was the anchor for his life. Now, with his anchor pulled up, he felt adrift. Fred ran the farm, GP ran his, and that left John being a spare wheel for a wagon that was not broken.

Living with his son and daughter-in-law, John spent more and more time just sitting in his little bedroom in the cardboard-lined attic of the house. It was not that he didn't like Selma, but since she rearranged the whole place, it just didn't feel like home anymore.

"Oh, Ricka, why did you have to go?" he said silently, over and over. The words, "I love you," were not words that ever crossed John's lips, nor Ricka's, in all their life together. But one measure of the depth of his love for her was the depth of the hurt in his broken heart now.

For long days he sat silently, hours at a time, on the edge of his rumpled bed in the cold attic, head down, mind reeling, thoughts tumbling in agonized confusion. *"Es ist alles ganz eitel,* vanity of vanities" came back to him from the book of Ecclesiastes, "all is vanity," useless, chasing after the wind.

How terribly he missed his dear old wife. Memoried tears streamed down his leathered cheeks as he saw her again walking by on stiff ankles, padding around on the cold dirt floor in the soddy, starting a fire to make his morning coffee. He watches as she barks a creaky cancer cough and runs arthritic fingers through her thinning hair. Slowly she reaches into her apron pocket to pull out a white handkerchief turned gray with age and blows her nose. Stiff fingers run over her hips, trying to smoothen her frayed apron. Now he finally realizes how her whole body is weathered with furrowed wrinkles, like a freshly plowed wheat field, but her voice is full of summer as she shifts about, softly singing "Jesus Still Lead On" while she rinses dirty dishes. As she brushes by him, her passing walk trails the strange smell of old age, but to John it is the elixir of life.

"Dear God, how I miss that old woman. She fed my heart, raised my children, kept my dreams alive all these years. Oh, God, why did she have to go? It hurts so much."

A flick of the brain and his heart is in the motherland, in a streaming vision of an alluring Russian *Maria*, wiggling her bewitching hips down the dusty street of Frumuschika. He's in the saddle, his whole body hungering for her; he wants to scoop her up into the saddle behind him, like a Cossack of old, but he's riding by faster than he wants to, heart pounding out of his chest, and *Maria* is left behind. The memory brings a smile: *"Ah, what a princess that one was."*

Another flick and he's sitting with his beautiful young Ricka in the double swing of her father's porch in Russia. How good her hair smells as it flows over his shoulder, how warm her sensuous body nestled so trustingly, peacefully against his, turning all his senses into pudding with mad, overpowering longing for her. And he tastes again the sweet, sweet fruit of the Garden of Eden in the New Salem Hotel like it was last night. "Oh, my sweet Ricka," he laughs, and weeps.

"We were twenty-three and no wrinkles," he chuckled to himself before the pain returned. "Precious daughter of Eve, you have been my heart, and now I have no heart." The awful ache rolled across his soul like the tumbleweeds of November. *"Dear God, why did she have to go?"*

"Tomorrow morning," his shadow says. *"Tomorrow morning."*

Across his mind scrolled the deep, life-giving memory of sitting on cane chairs close together here in front of their new wooden house in recent years, Ricka with her frail arm on his shoulder spending long delicious minutes ever so gently combing her fingers through the back of his thinning hair. He inhales again her earthy smell that carries a hint of musk, feels her deep faith rolling out with every note as she quietly hums, "Oh, take my hand, dear Father, *and lead thou me."*

Her exquisite womanly gentleness provides a peace so strong that it lifts him out of this world for a moment and bonds their minds into a knowing that goes beyond all description, forging their hearts into a pulsing, life-giving engine with a life all its own. *"She has the power to spin gold out of our Dakota straw, does that woman."*

Now it's all over. When he wakes in the middle of the night and reaches over for her, the bed is empty and cold. Joy is gone like the songbirds of summer. His soul is scorched, his heart as cold as the frozen stones on Raven Feather's grave. *"Oh God, the pain, the awful, never-ending, soul-destroying pain."* It chews off a little more of his heart with every passing day.

"Tomorrow morning," he says once more to himself. *"Tomorrow morning."*

Early in the morning, before any of the family is awake, he gets out of bed and slowly shuffles to the barn. The cows hear him opening the door, and as he walks in, one of them gently lows. He knows her voice.

"Ja, Molly, *gute kuh,* good cow," he calls to her.

Here, in and out of this warm barn, where so much of his life played out, giving meaning and richness to his days, raising his sons, fathering precious daughters, shepherding the gentle animals, each of whom he knows by name, here he now sees empty nothingness. All that exists now is the consuming pain that bites into his fingers and gnaws up his arms until it pulls all of him into its monstrous jaws like a giant serpent whose bent-in fangs will only pull in and never release.

Slowly, with trembling fingers, he winds the knot that will end the pain and throws the rope up over the beam. With the rope now adjusted firmly around his neck, he slowly steps up on the milk stool, which he has carefully set in place.

"Good-bye, dear Ricka, good-bye. I'll see you soon," he calls out loud.

****

In the house, as soon as the family was awake and breakfast ready, Fred called upstairs for Father to come and eat. When there was no answer, Fred's heart sank and he ran up the stairs. Seeing the old bed empty, he felt relieved and walked back down to call outside. When another louder call still brought no answer, he pulled on cap and coat and walked down to the barn, now dreading what he might find on the barn floor. "Father?" he called once more into the dark, "Father, time for breakfast!"

Pushing the door open, he looked into the darkness and at first saw nothing. Then a dark shape caught his eye, and he let out a scream, "No, Father, no!"

He raced back to the house, and as he rushed through the door, Selma knew at once from his guttural rasping that it meant death. She knew not how. With tears streaming down his face, Fred looked at her with terror in his eyes and pointed, "Dear God, he's hanging out there in the barn!"

She wanted to see, but he pushed her down on a chair and raced to the door. Without stopping, he ran the half mile to GP's place, shouting before he got to the house, "It's Father. Quick, you gotta' come."

GP jerked his cap and coat off the hook and met him outside.

"Is it bad?"

"Gottfried, he hung himself!" Fred rasped, choking on the hellish words.

GP's knees almost buckled, like a pig shot between the eyes, sinking down.

They raced to his car and sped over to Fred's, skidding to a stop in front of the open barn door. They both ran in and still could not believe the unholy sight that met their eyes. For a moment they were afraid to touch him.

"What should we do?" asked Fred.

"I don't know."

Finally they decided to drive to Beulah to get the undertaker.

"But I can't stand to let him hang like that for so long," uttered Fred, suddenly breaking into huge sobs.

"You're right," GP blurted through his own tears.

They loosened the rope and slowly lowered their father to the dirt floor. GP was mortified when he touched the body, for now in the freezing cold of early March it had turned clammy and stiff, like a ham with the skin left on hanging in the smoke house.

Averting each other's eyes, they carried the body and laid it on the hay in a stall, both still in tears, and left to get the undertaker.

The next day, neighbor men gathered at the church cemetery. Their hearts were heavy even before they got there, because they all knew that since suicide was viewed by the church as an unforgivable sin, John could not be buried in the church cemetery.

They had to dig a grave outside the cemetery, at the edge of the adjoining field. There they built a large fire to thaw the frozen ground, and after an hour they started swinging their heavy picks. They wrestled the earth for several hours, inch by tortured inch, until the icy sod finally gave up space enough for the tear-filled grave.

They dreaded the funeral at church, and their fears were not misplaced. The pastor's words offered more fire and brimstone than comfort. Making it even more abhorrent, when the funeral service was finished in church, they had to carry the casket out, plod past the barren rows of granite markers all the way through the snow-packed cemetery, lift it over the fence, and bear it to the lonely black hole outside the cemetery.

The six silent pallbearers carefully inched their way around either side of the grave and slowly let the cold canvas straps slide through their hands, lowering the casket into the ground.

As Fred stared into the frozen maw of earth coldly waiting its fill, he turned and through clinched teeth whispered to Selma, "I should be down there."

"Sh-h," she whispered back, shaking his coat sleeve.

"Go ahead," rasped an ugly, dark voice in his ear, *"one step and you'll be where you belong."*

Selma's sudden iron grip shaking his arm brought him back to the moment, but he heard nothing of the pastor's final words.

Frozen clods thudded heavy, echoing around the wooden box as the men shoveled dirt into the grave, joining to bury their friend of so much blessed memory, their loved one for whom no love could buy another day. The women watered the frozen earth with silent tears.

Every heart there was bleeding, especially those of the family who were left not knowing if their loved one's life of faith might have led him to God's glory or if his final act condemned him to the fiery realm of the devil.

Family members were not bashful about pointing fingers and laying blame, while Fred and Selma felt almost overwhelming guilt, wondering what they might have done differently, or not have done, to prevent this dastardly deed. But it was over, and nothing could be done to change it now.

Cars driving home from the funeral were filled with silence as people in speechless shell shock tried to process the twists the last several days had taken.

Only Fred would understand the tear stains in his brother's dusty red handkerchief weeks later as GP got off the plow and walked behind it in the long silent furrows, letting the horses turn the wakening soil at their own pace.

Father's tortured death snuffed the song from GP's accordion for a long and pain-filled season of weeping. GP, in his own wilderness, joined that anxious chorus of those left behind with freezing soul in the noontide heat and cried numb into the north wind, "What made him walk into that devil hole? Why, God, why! Answer me!" And there was only silence.

****

Still, spring came and greened the earth. Purple crocuses stood tall in the grass, cheery meadowlarks warbled courage to GP and Fred, and new hope into the hearts of weary Valley folk. Surely in '35 things would turn around, and it would be a better year. The drought could not last forever!

GP had just enough wheat from last fall's failure to put in a new crop and continued to spend long days on the plow to get the land ready. The horses had only poor hay and little grass to eat and hardly had the energy to pull the plow, even though the ground was powdery.

Pasture grass came back thin, but wild onions grew in riotous profusion. The cows loved them and ate every one they could find. The result was distressing, to say the least. It produced flatulence in the cows that made the milkers cringe and, worse, loosened the cows' bowels.

"Ach, desch eklich, eklich, oh that's so disgusting!" Bertha exclaimed.

The milk became richly onion flavored, and the creameries would not buy it.

But before the crocuses were done blooming, the scant moisture again retreated into the earth, and soon the land was brown. Once more everything seemed to be turning against them. These were people of deep faith, but now more than a few were asking, "Is God turning against us? What sin have we done that has made God so angry?"

"Repent," the pastors proclaimed from the pulpits, "and turn from your sinful ways. Seek God and his righteousness." Prayers rose on every side, but the endless drought would not break.

One Sunday after Easter, Bertha suddenly turned pale and excused herself in church, hurrying to the spider webbed outhouse. The women looked at each other and nodded their heads. Several minutes of the pastor's long, learned sermon were lost while they did mental calculations. *"Have the baptismal water ready this fall,"* thought the deacon's wife, with a knowing nod to her neighbor.

During the next hymn, Selma leaned over and whispered, "We've been trying too, but nothing's happening." The men glanced over, hoping Bertha's stomach flu would not spread.

****

Roosevelt's government agents now went around buying cattle to save the dry pastures. They were roundly hated, especially in the hill country, because people still remembered them snooping around all over during Prohibition looking for moonshine stills. They were even more hated wherever stills had been found.

Going from farm to farm, the "Revenuers" were buying cattle for almost nothing. If the farmer didn't sell, they confiscated what they wanted.

A team of agents stopped at GP's, picked him up, and drove out to the pasture to see his cattle. "We're authorized to buy five head. You pick 'em out, and we'll send a truck next week."

"What will I get?" GP asked.

"Fifteen bucks a head."

"That's robbery. I can't sell 'em for that."

"If you don't, they'll haul you in and you get a big fine or jail. You pick."

There was no choice. Some farmers hauled their cattle away to be slaughtered for fertilizer. The weakest ones they took into the pastures and shot.

****

After supper one hot evening, GP opened the paper and suddenly shouted, "Ei, yei, yei!"

"What?" Bertha shot back, nearly dropping her dishes.

"It says, 'Man Eaten.'"

"What do you mean?"

"Says a man was eaten up by his pigs."

"They're joking, right?"

"Says there were two Johnson brothers, over across the river, living alone on their farm. Philip they called 'Farm Brother,' 'cause he ran the farm, and Oluf they called 'House Brother,' 'cause he kept the house. The House Brother ran into town to get groceries and spent some time talking to a friend in the garage. Later, when he came home, Philip wasn't around. When he still didn't show up for supper, Oluf went outside, and when he looked in the pig pen, he finally found a couple torn chunks of his brother's pants and a piece of his skull that the pigs were nuzzling around."

Bertha's shoulders shook, and her whole body shivered at the horror of it. For days, nearly every conversation, far and wide, opened with that gruesome occurrence. Some were stunned by its animal grisliness. Others opined that the biblical pigs of the Gerasenes, which were demon-driven into the sea, were here seeking long-overdue revenge.

For weeks, whenever men walked out to the pigpen, wives stood by the kitchen window and watched, wringing their hands in silent worry.

****

In these years, horses were among the most important elements of any farm. They and the soil were the lifeblood of the farm. Now things were so desperate that several of the neighbors had to shoot some of their starving horses. These men were not given to idle sentimentality, but they cried bitter, anguished tears inside when they had to shoot the beloved creatures that were almost family, as much pet as laborer, each with a name, each a special personality. They wanted to take them out into the prairie to do the ghastly deed, but things had gotten so extreme that they led the starving horses into the pigpen, shot them once in the head, and slit them open for the pigs to eat. At least the pigs wouldn't starve as well, and they would make food in turn. After such a deed, the men were never quite the same. Some went into depression so deep that the neighbors feared for their life. Others took to the bottle and never recovered.

With this kind of strain, some families unraveled. Women became so despondent that they couldn't keep up the house. Men took to beating their wives in frustration over their own failures. Children beat the dogs and told lies, got into fights in school, earned failing grades, and had horrific nightmares. There were no counselors, no programs to turn for help. Only the faithful neighbors and pastors who were untrained for counseling but saw their neighbors dying by inches quietly stood by them with prayer and a soothing arm around the shoulders to keep them going. Other times, a hot meal and long visits far into the dark nights of the soul saw many of them through to wholeness on the other end of this anguish beyond all imagination. There were enough tears to water the wheat, could they have been saved. This people knew the meaning of "neighbor." And they would never forget.

Many wondered whether a brighter day would ever come to this benighted land, many a heart silently thought of giving it all up, and more than a few did.

Chapter 16

Knee Deep in Tears

Saturday night, April 13, Fred and Selma came over to GP's place, and from the looks on their faces, they were not bringing good news.

"The radio just said there was a bad dust storm coming again, maybe yet tonight, maybe tomorrow morning," Fred said when they sat down.

"They said it's already blowing dirt something awful northwest of here."

Blow it did. The howling winds began during the night, and all the next day the whole country lay shrouded in total darkness. It brought soil from who-knows-where and carried it on to who-knows-where as well. The screaming wind sounded like nothing less than angry demons from the netherworld itself.

As the storm continued, Mr. Weather on KFYR, Bismarck, had his own dramatic version of this event as he put on ghosty music and continued, at six in the morning, "We are privileged to have in our studios this morning Dr. Stavros Pappas, a weather expert from Athens to give us his analysis of what is currently transpiring in our area. Good morning, Dr. Pappas."

Then shifting into a silky, dark voice with a soft Greek accent, he continued, "Thank you, Mr. Weather, for having me. Ladies and gentlemen, it has been reported in some circles that the ancient mythological god, Zeus, great king of all the natural world's forces, long thought by civilized cultures to be only a figment of prehistoric imagination, has actually materialized and swept down from the upper heavens. Taking gigantic breaths, he is blowing them out with savage, extraterrestrial strength over the Northern Hemisphere. The strongest blasts seem directed right over your great American Midwest.

"Other reports suggest that he has enlisted the aid of devouring Boreas, the ruler of the North wind, and Zephyrus, ruler of the West wind, both of them chill winds that rend men's hearts. They are each said to be holding the end of an immense diamond-studded dragnet, and starting in the vast spaces of Canadian Alberta, they have dragged it across the plains, and with roaring, otherworldly shouts they are mingling unimaginable volumes of earth and sky, forming a blinding, herculean wall ten thousand feet high. Such events, dear listeners, have not been seen since our Greek poets described them three thousand years ago."

Finally, shifting back to his own voice, Mr. Weather continued, "Thank you, Dr. Pappas. Yes, dear listeners, we ask you to stay tuned for any forthcoming developments, which KFYR will bring you immediately as they unfold."

The brief minute-and-a-half segment caused a stir from Winnipeg to Yankton, putting not a few people into mindless panic and jamming telephone lines. Other calmer people just laughed and said, "I think God is angry, *gel*, right?"

The storm, driving fine grains of dirt, sandblasted everything both living and dead; and by evening, GP knew he still needed to make his way to the barn to milk the cows. But two steps away from the house, he could no longer see it. In panic he spun around and thanked God for being able to get back inside before he became a statistic. His brief excursion out the door and back in filled the kitchen with a cloud of choking dust.

"Look at your clothes," Bertha said, "it looks like you got shot through with a shotgun fulla' dirt."

Bertha put down her cleaning rag, wiped her hands on her apron, and placed both hands on her abdomen, thankful that her baby was not yet born, afraid that with all this choking dirt its life might be snuffed out. She couldn't handle losing another baby. Quietly she went in and sat on the bed, alone in deepest prayer, as a wave of nausea swept over her and awful fear rocked her heart. "Dear Father, please, oh, please take care of my baby," she pleaded.

If last year's storm filled everything with dirt, this year it was twice as bad. Many ditches were level full of dirt. Tumbleweeds had a foot-high finger of soil nestled against their lee side. Ravines had four-foot drifts of someone's land. Hilly fields were stripped of topsoil down to the subsoil clay.

When the wind finally died down, the air gradually cleared, but everything smelled of dirt.

"You should see the haymow in my barn," Fred exclaimed. "The hay is covered with two inches of dirt, and it's worthless. Cattle can't even eat it."

When GP read the *Beulah Independent,* he remarked, "They're saying now it was the worst dust storm that's ever been. They're calling it 'Black Sunday.'"

"I can believe it," Bertha answered, "just from the dirt in my house. Half an inch of somebody's farm on my windowsills. I need a shovel to clean it all out."

She spent two days cleaning every inch of the house. Even the walls were draped with a layer of gray grime. When she finished, she sat down and wept.

Before she could dry her tears, GP came back in. "Bertha, what's the matter?"

"It feels like I'm knee deep in tears in this place."

Soon the scorching sun returned, and it needed but a fleeting season to burn everything to a dried-up crust. Grasshoppers flourished once again, since last year's millions dutifully left ample eggs behind. Horseflies seemed to grow bigger and bite harder than ever. Tumbleweeds were in love with this new desert and planned great fall rallies with fencerows full of progeny. At least so it seemed in this awful scheme of things.

Finally, late one hot afternoon, fecund rain clouds blew up dark and heavy, filled with heaven's dew to water all things with leaf and every anxious throat. Unbelievable bolts of ozone-laden lightning sizzled the skies, and ear-splitting cracks of thunder shook the foundations of the earth. Surely this time they would break the chains of the great wellsprings of the deep and send forth watery streams of life. Every living thing with nerves was on edge, witnessing nature ready to explode.

GP and Bertha retreated to the safety of the sod-roofed earth barn and stood in the doorway, astounded at this frightful and beautiful display of nature's fury, expectantly awaiting the promising downpour.

"Have you ever in your life seen anything like it?" Bertha asked.

"Not even out in the dry badlands."

But before long the great spectacle once again passed over. The rain was stillborn. Only scattered drops watered the desperate earth.

One by one the chickens and geese stepped out of their sheds, warily cocking their heads and wondering just what was going on. "No?" they seemed to be asking, "Again?"

Valley dwellers, along with the whole wide area, were totally distraught.

The unrelenting drought was exacting a heavy price in every arena of life. Animals, both tame and wild, were suffering, people discouraged, plant life shriveled up. Only Bertha's irrigated garden, recovering from the storm, stood strong and green, filling their plates with the choicest of vegetables.

Church continued to be full on Sundays, hymns rang out, but voices were muted and enthusiasm gone. Prayers were prayed, but deep down many a believer began to wonder if prayer was doing any good at all.

In June, Fred said, "Why don't you come over next Wednesday night for the boxing match. Max Schmeling is fighting Joe Louis."

Fred dialed the program on the scratchy radio, and they were on edge as the boxers danced in the ring, trading jabs and blows round after punishing round.

"Our German boy, Schmeling, was the World Heavyweight Champion for a few years, you know," Fred remarked between rounds.

"But *der Schwartze,* that black boy, is supposed to be real tough too," answered GP.

In the twelfth round, when Schmeling knocked Louis out, everyone cheered. "That's our man," GP sang out. At least for a moment they could forget the drought.

Summer saw *dreeb,* overcast, days and one rain shower, but it wasn't enough even to settle the choking dust. The artesian spring, together with a long and deep ravine that bubbled water coming down from below the Indian grave, produced just enough grass to keep the cattle and horses from starving. But beyond that, the pastures yielded only ground cactus, coiling cedar, and buck-brush. Hardy sage bushes also thrived, but cattle couldn't stomach the sour taste and left them alone.

During these wretched times, public dances decreased as well. People had no money and even less energy. Though they loved to dance, it wasn't a necessity, and they stopped going.

"You know, a lot of people are selling out and leaving," GP mentioned to Fred, "and there are only a few auctioneers around here, so what do you think about me and you taking up auctioneering?"

"Funny thing, I just noticed an ad in *Successful Farming*," Fred replied.

"What's it about?"

"Well, it's called 'Joe Reisch's American School of Auctioneering,' and it's in Minnesota, a town called Austin."

They looked it up, wrote in, and both were accepted into the month-long August session. After a long train ride to Austin, they paid their sixty-dollar registration fee, and were soon in daily classes with twenty-six other men from around the country.

Mornings they attended lectures, afternoons they were divided into groups to practice the auctioneering lingo, and evenings they were assigned stacks of reading—in business practices, appraisal, product identification, and math skills. Some of the men were not the brightest candles on the Christmas tree and had only limited education, so reading was a slow go for them. But they were willing students and determined to beat the bitter Depression misery.

One afternoon the men were taken on a tour of the Hormel hog-butchering plant in town and, among other things, introduced to a new canned meat which Hormel was introducing. It was to be called "Spam," shortened from "shoulder of pork and ham," the name for which a company officer's brother was given $100 in a naming contest.

"What did you think of that new canned meat?" Fred asked when they got back to their rented room.

"Well, not bad," GP reflected, "not too bad."

"Wonder if it'll ever sell?"

The brothers found their dance-band experience stood them in good stead, with their sense of rhythm enhanced by the music and their cadence sharpened by singing a host of different songs. They were naturals at the auctioneering patter.

"I'mbidadollarandaquarterwho'llgiveadollarandahalf . . . doIhearahalfanybodybidahalf" seemed to roll off their tongues like songs off a meadowlark's beak.

When they put on suit and tie and lined up in carefully staged rows for their graduation picture with Mr. Reisch himself, there was not a hint of a smile, but they felt as bright as any class of Princeton's finest. And they were entitled to use the honorific title of "colonel." They were now "Col. GP Oster" and "Col. Fred Oster."

Returning home, they put an ad in the *Beulah Independent*; and since many people already knew them from their musical ventures, within two weeks they already had their first auction engagement. Their partnership allowed them to rotate—with one crying the auction, the other spotting bids—changing off every half hour to protect their voices and stay fresh. The faster they could chatter the auctioneering patter, the better they were judged to be. But they also had to keep putting out full volume from the bottom of their diaphragm, so they could be heard at the far edges of the crowd.

Looking for a distinctive introduction to begin sales, they turned to the state flower and often began with a loud, "All right, all you healthy rose buds, thank you for coming, and we are ready to start the sale." On occasion GP added, "We are the Colonels Oster, headquarters for Mercer County auctioneering." Fred quickly cut in with, "Hey, GP, don't let it go to your head. Remember there's only two letters difference between 'headquarters' and 'hindquarters.'"

Their apt sense of humor, honed from playing dances for diverse, sometimes bleary-eyed crowds, proved a godsend as well and often helped relax bidders when things got tense during a sale.

"Hey, Conrad," GP would yell to an acquaintance out at the edge of the crowd, "get in here and spend some of that moldy money!"

"Yeah," Fred picked up on it, "you can't keep it buried in that old tobacco can forever." That always brought a horselaugh from the crowd and on occasion a deep crimson color to the face of the man singled out for a bit of fun.

They quickly mastered the fine art of judging just when to back off and tell a story, when to push hard on a bid or pull back and joke with a bidder, and how to spot those subtle bids when neighbor did not want to be seen bidding against neighbor.

Since money was scarce in that shrunken economy, auctions were not high-volume affairs. And their 2 percent fee of the gross did not amount to big dollars earned, but every penny helped protect their farms and their families.

Unfortunately, all too many auctions were sad affairs, because they meant the end of a dream for the owners. The terrible Depression was exacting an awful toll, and the auction was the final price. To make matters worse, few neighbors had any money either, so many items sold for almost nothing and didn't help the owners out of the deep lake of debt in which they found themselves.

Sometimes, seeing the wrenching pain on the faces of both those selling out and those buying, left both brothers in their own depression. Bertha and Selma both had to learn to lift them up and work hard to find cheerful things to talk about when they got home.

GP also discovered that it buoyed his spirits to stay in touch by mail with some of his Reisch classmates.

"How is the auction business in your area?" one from Montana wrote back. "Around here the only thing that's bringing any money is horses. Sold a young team of black Belgians for three hundred dollars the other day. The auction business helps, but I sure work for every dollar I make."

How well GP and Fred knew that feeling.

****

During these dry years, there was an explosion of jackrabbits. There were many, and they grew large, measuring up to two feet tall when they sat up erect. On occasion, a number of men got together to have some fun hunting the jacks. They surrounded a quarter of prairie land, a half mile on every side, and started working toward the middle, using only shotguns so the shot wouldn't travel too far and wound another hunter. Often they were hardly out of their cars before shots rang out and boys began running to pick up the dead rabbits. They could sell the jacks for a few cents each to the Unruh Cream Station in Beulah that was buying and shipping them out, some to make rabbit-fur trim for women's clothes, some to grind up for dog food.

On one hunt they were tightening the square, with hunters drawing close from every side. The hunter to GP's right got excited when a rabbit ran between them and took a wild shot. The BBs spread out, and one lodged in the lobe of GP's ear. It bled for a while, but they couldn't get the BB out.

Finally GP said, "Leave it. We gotta finish the hunt, and I gotta' get home. My wife is having a baby anytime now."

By now Bertha knew the signals, and several nights later, in the middle of November, she woke her husband, "It's time."

He quickly dressed and drove to get the neighborhood midwife. That woman had also grown older, and her "hurry up" was not as fast as before. GP was afraid they might not get back in time, but everything worked out well. The hours of labor were excruciating for the unnumbed mother as well as the frightened father-to-be. But before long the lamp-lit silence was rent by a squeaky cry and they had another baby boy. They chose Cousin Christian and his wife, another Bertha, who lived just across the valley, as godparents and baptized him "Edward John." "Eddie" he would be.

Their lonesome little prairie home, from which not another house could be seen in any direction, was almost impossible to keep warm enough for the baby. They piled every blanket they owned and several borrowed from Grandma Wulff on the little crib to keep him warm. Every time the little one cried for feeding, Bertha nursed the baby and GP nursed the potbellied stove to keep up the heat. They were almost paranoid with fear, watching the baby for any signs of shivering. Every time he stretched and shivered just the slightest, they panicked. But there were no convulsions.

For Christmas, GP pulled out a chunk of his auctioneering money and bought Bertha a new Maytag washing machine with a pedal-start gasoline motor to turn the agitator and a metal flex hose to run the exhaust fumes out the window. Now she could just rinse the dirty cloth diapers in a pail and then drop them into the machine tub. He still had to carry buckets of water in from the pump, and she still had to heat the water on the cook stove and carry out the tub of dirty water from the machine. But it surely beat bending over to hand scrub the diapers—and everything else—on the tin washboard. The new machine even had a hand-cranked wringer to squeeze most of the moisture out of the clothes, so they'd dry faster on the string he nailed up across the crowded living room/bedroom.

The winter was as bitter as ever, and more. In January, the temperature fell to forty-eight degrees below zero on GP's thermometer.

"It was even worse in Parshall," Fred reported the next day when he walked over to check on them, "the radio said it was sixty below there last night."

"Where's Parshall?" Bertha asked.

"About fifty miles north of here, across the river."

"This is getting too cold even for Eskimo dogs," GP put in, tired of it all.

The jackrabbit population, meanwhile, turned some bright mind to creative imagination, and word spread that there were jackalopes on the loose out there. They were super-jackrabbits, as much as five feet tall with racked horns like deer stags, and they ran like the wind, twenty feet at a bound. Locals loved to sidle up next to outstate travelers in the cafés and furtively warn them, "When you're driving, watch out for jackalopes around here. They're vicious, especially in breeding season."

"Ja, last week one attacked a man, and it took three shots to bring the sucker down," added his friend.

"If you see one, don't stop, and don't get out of your car. Gun it, 'cause with those sharp horns they can roll your car over like nothin'."

Several visitors left wide eyed and more than a little nervous to be on the highway.

People had high hopes that '36 would be the turn-around year. Again, it greened up well in the spring, with winter's snow bringing a burst of new life. But it was soon over. Before the grasses could grow to mowing height, they slowly turned brown and finally wilted.

When the grass and weeds dried out, somehow a prairie fire started to the northwest of them. The strong spring winds soon turned it into a fiery inferno racing across the high hills on the eastern edge of the Valley, sending flames and a wall of gray smoke high into the air. In a short time, men and their sons gathered from miles around to fight the fiery monster. Neighbors came with plows and broke up rows of sod to create a firebreak. Others raced up with wagons carrying barrels of water and shovels and gunnysacks to beat the flames. Several farmers quickly shot cows and slit them open. Then, tying long ropes around the critter's hind legs, they teamed up, with one riding in the burnt area, the other in front of the fire dragging the carcass between them directly on the flames.

GP joined a group of men, beating at the flames with his sand shovel. Suddenly his boot brushed against a smoldering little pile of something mushy hard. Glancing down, he noticed that it wasn't the cow pie that he half expected. Looking closer he saw it was the charred body of a mamma skunk with four furry little kittens that had succumbed to the flames. The mother's body was tightly curled around the little ones, her legs encircling them to shield them from a terrible death. Sadly, her motherly bravery was all in vain. They had probably run as far and as fast as they could, but the relentless fire-breathing dragon was faster still and overwhelmed them. When she saw that the little ones could make it no farther, she quickly gathered all four into a little knot, curled herself around them, and waited for the flames.

Her scorched jaws were frozen open in a last silent, pain-filled scream that no one heard. GP was not a particular friend of skunks, but this sad sight gave him a start and brought a lump to his throat. As tragedies go, the death of these little creatures was perhaps rather small, but for that one tiny family it meant extermination from off the face of the earth. There was no skunk stink, only the faint sickly scent of singed hair and burnt flesh. "Ugly, blasted fire," he muttered to himself and kept beating the moving flames that seemed to have a life of their own and fed by taking away other life wherever they could.

When GP got home, he was a sooty, disheveled mess. The bottoms of his denim overall legs were frayed and burned, his hands blistered from swinging the shovel. While he went to the well outside and pumped water to wash off, Bertha set out slices of fresh bread she just took out of the oven. They dipped the bread in cream, and with slices of farmer sausage they had a fast picnic.

GP told her about the skunk family, and she too felt the pain of that little animal-cousin mother. For a moment, she caught herself trying to shake her precious little Clinton back to life but quickly pushed the stinging image away. Turning away for an instant, she replied, "At least we can be thankful the fire didn't come this far."

"Ja, the Lord was good to us," GP answered. Then holding a slice of bread still warm from the oven, he inhaled the delicious aroma. "Reminds me," he continued, "of the old folks' saying, '*Ein Mahl ohne Brot ist garnichts werdt,* a meal without bread isn't worth having.'"

****

In the high country, not far from them, GP's younger brother also had a farm, and he had borrowed money to buy more land. When he couldn't make payments, the farm went into foreclosure, with a date set for a sheriff's sale of everything he owned. The night before the sale, brothers and cousins got together and loaded everything they could pile into an old truck with an extra high rack on it, and the brother and his family left in the darkness for Montana. The sheriff and the banker were terribly perturbed, but in these bitter times, people did what they had to do.

Several weeks later, the Valley was on edge as word spread that a company of dark-skinned, strange-speaking gypsies was making their way up through the area. They had a dozen covered wagons, with a lot of ragged, unwashed children, and several cows and goats in tow. They told people they were looking for work erecting windmills and camped where they pleased along the road, driving up to farms asking for water. Wherever they camped, a cow or a pig or several chickens seemed to disappear from nearby farms. This time they camped in the alkali flats a mile from the Osters and not far from an artesian spring, making the whole Valley nervous.

GP owned a Winchester .22 Special rifle, and now he slipped ten bullets into the loading tube and propped it beside the door, along with the 12-gauge shotgun and a belt full of shells that John had given him. All the neighbors armed as well.

Wherever the gypsies camped, neighbors came from farther out and helped the closest farmers stand guard during the night. Brother-in-law, Adam Baisch in Krem, heard about the gypsy foray and brought a friend to help. GP hauled straw into a corner of the chicken coop, and Adam slept there overnight, shotgun loaded and ready to ward off any night visitors looking for free chicken. His friend did the same at Fred's.

Finally the sheriff and a car full of deputies came from Stanton, and although they could not hang any crimes on the band, they ordered them to clear out of the area. GP and a number of neighbors also drove to the camp and stood at a distance, careful not to get involved. Several of the gypsies grew belligerent and made ready to fight, but when the deputies cocked their guns, the band thought better of it and hitched up, trekking farther west out of the Valley. Rumors about things disappearing continued to swirl for several weeks, but then the band vanished into thin air.

All through the terrible summer, there was no relief from the drought. The dry winds continued to blow. Dark clouds gathered and blew over, but the hoped-for rains did not fall. More dust storms devastated the land. Grasshoppers and crickets chirped and chewed whatever grew. Horseflies and mosquitoes thrived, as did buckbrush and tumbleweeds. The government shot more pigs, and farmers gathered in town and poured cream cans of milk on the streets to protest the miserable starvation prices.

By early June, in the height of the green season, the prairies were burned September-brown.

One evening, after chores and supper, GP hitched up the team and drove the family out to the wheat fields. "Ei, yei, yei, look at that," he said, "the wheat stalks are just little brown sticks with no heads."

He and Bertha climbed off the wagon, and he lifted Eddie down. Then GP knelt and touched the ground. "This is awful," he whispered, "I can put three fingers into these deep cracks in the ground, they're so big."

All around them, the fertile plowland had broken into thousands of jagged jigsaw pieces. "Looks kinda like black dragon dandruff," Bertha said. They laughed at the humor of it, but both knew it wasn't at all funny.

Gumbo ground turned to rock-hard cement, and the alkali flats on the valley floor became choking powder that blew like smelly snowflakes in the hot wind.

Sunday, when they drove by the alkali flats on the way to church, Bertha held her nose. "Ach, smells like manna from hell," she said.

While prices went down, the temperature went up still more. For weeks the mercury hung in the high nineties, and in July when GP came into the house, his eyes were big as saucers. "The thermometer," he shouted at Bertha, "says it's a hundred and nine degrees out there."

"Gotta be wrong," Bertha replied. "Did you give it a tap?"

Later in the evening, when they walked to Fred and Selma's, Fred was all excited. "The weatherman from Bismarck reported 120-degree readings in Steele, over east of Bismarck," he said.

"Can't hardly believe it."

"Said it was the hottest temperature ever recorded in North Dakota."

The chickens walked around with beaks open, Schatzie dug a hole on the north side of the house to cool off, cows and horses stood like silent statues, too hot to move even for a drink of cooling water at the artesian spring.

Through the heat, as more people gave up and moved out, the Oster brothers were busy with auctions. The auctions and a few dances were their only sources of income. But they didn't drink or smoke or chew, and they bought no new clothes, no items for the house except coal from Bauer, so expenses were few and they survived.

Bertha got some baby clothes from relatives and neighbors, and they exchanged no presents on special days, except what Bertha could make from thread or GP could make from wood. They butchered their own beef, pork, chicken, and goose and had meat every which way: fresh, canned, dried, salted, and stuffed into sausage. Bertha made bars of soap, mixing lye with rendered pig lard and pouring it into pans to harden and dry. It didn't smell good, but it got dirty stuff clean. They produced their own eggs, milk and cheeses, raised their own vegetables, which further held down expenses. When Bertha hung her lye-cleaned clothes on the line outside to dry, they danced in the wind. "Look like children learning to polka," she laughed.

Unlike their city cousins, they had no electric bill, no telephone, no running water, no mortgage payment, so they could stretch their meager income a long way. Flour, sugar, some spices from the Watkins man, gas for the car and an occasional tire, along with a few veterinary medicines and, of course, taxes, and they were nearly finished spending. They were dirt poor, but they had their health, good neighbors, food to eat and a house to live in, and felt blessed of God.

"I guess, toward a lot of other people," GP told Bertha, "maybe we're not so bad off after all."

****

Indian families still found their way to GP's as well. Some with cars occasionally needed a can of gasoline, those who still drove wagons to town stopped in on hot days for a drink of cool water for themselves and the horses. In return, they wanted to show GP and

Bertha that they appreciated having a welcome place of respite and often brought along a chunk of fresh venison.

"If you're interested," one of the men told GP, "you can come to my land by the river and cut diamond willow saplings for fence posts."

"That'd be great," GP replied. "We don't have any around here, and I really need some for fencing."

"Wait till it freezes so you can drive down on the low ground, then come."

With all the dust storms, since '35 the county agents encouraged farmers to rotate crops and do more strip-farming—planting crops in narrower strips rather than in half-mile fields which were easier for the wind to attack. They also encouraged summer fallowing: letting a portion of land lay idle each year both to preserve moisture and to control weeds. But Valley farmers were not quick to jump on changes.

"I don't know," the county agent told GP one day, "but I sure can't get the men around here to sign on."

"Well, remember, our families have lived off the land for a pot fulla' generations," GP replied, "and by now the men think they know how to handle stuff without the government telling them how to do it."

Later, when GP visited with one of the neighbors, the man furrowed his brow and said, "I don't know, but I sure don't like the idea of planting all them small fields. Lotta extra work doin' that."

"Ja, sure is," GP replied, "but I know one thing: I sure don't ever want to live through another dust bowl if I can help it."

Area farmers watched and talked on it, and every year a few more adopted the new ways. They wanted their land to last and their children's future blessed.

In the bitter winter, when the snow became too deep to drive the twisting half-mile pasture trail from their house to the Valley road, GP parked the car on their approach at the side of the Valley road and left it there. Now they could slog the half mile through the drifts, sometimes thigh deep, and still get to town. GP didn't want to risk losing the keys, so he left them in the car's ignition. "It'll be all right," he told Bertha, "honest folks around here." The car was never disturbed.

'37 brought no relief. The unrelenting drought would not break. Dry as previous years and drier. But the abundant tumbleweeds led one of the neighbors to a special brainstorm. "Why not cut those miserable tumbleweeds while they're green and the spines are still soft," he said. "Then we rake 'em up and stack 'em in piles and pack 'em down for hay." Didn't sound good at all to the men until yet another neighbor said, "Hey, maybe we could pour half a dozen five-gallon cans of molasses over the stack."

"You mean like a molasses sundae?"

They tried it, and the cattle went wild over the stuff. The tightly entwined stacks of mowed tumbleweeds nearly broke the backs of the men who had to fork them onto hay racks, but it was hay. It was cheap, it was weed control, and it was a treat that almost made the hungry cows smile. The nutritional value was almost nil, but it filled empty stomachs.

The miserable tumbleweeds were an endless topic of conversation, and when the men gathered before church one Sunday, one of them jokingly asked, "You think there are more grasshoppers or more tumbleweeds around here?"

"Maybe more grasshoppers," came the reply, "but at least hoppers don't stack up against the wire and take the fences down when the wind blows 'em full of dirt."

The year again brought yet another total crop failure. But by late in the summer, Bertha noticed something most interesting. They had planted watermelon on low ground at the edge of a field where the spring runoff thoroughly soaked it, and all summer the melons grew and grew and grew. By late fall, they were record-sized and made for watermelon parties across the entire Valley as neighbors all around experienced the same wonder.

"Best melons I ever saw, big, sweet, tasty," was the word from nearly everyone.

Bertha sat Eddie in his little red Radio Flyer wagon, propped up one of the big melons beside him, and took a picture. It showed a melon almost as big as her nearly-two-year-old son. Later neighbors laughed when they discovered that the rest had all taken watermelon pictures as well. To Bertha and the neighbors, it was *"Das grosse Arbussa Jahr*, the Great Watermelon Year" that yielded a season of sweetness amid the years of drought.

The dry summer's unwanted crop of rolling weeds led to another job that Valley men did not relish. "About as much fun as pickin' rocks," GP said when he started. In the fall when the round balls broke loose and rolled in waves against the fences, he had to walk the line and fork them away from the barbed wire. Then when the wind died down, most often in the evening around dusk, he set fire to the rows and burned them. He wasn't alone. Standing beside the burning rows, he looked around and the whole valley was pocked with bonfires of tumbleweeds burning as neighbor after neighbor did battle with the vicious weed and labored to save his fences.

In early winter, after the ground was frozen, GP hitched up the team and drove to the Reservation to cut fence posts. The Indian friend showed him the patches of diamond willow saplings in the Missouri River lowlands, and GP spent three days cutting, trimming two hundred saplings into fence post length, and loading them on the wagon.

The bitter drought when the heavens were sealed still did not break during the next year. It was the same as '31 and '32. Same as '33, '34, '35. On into '36 and '37.

At the beginning of '38, the pastor ordered daily devotional calendars for every family in church and encouraged the fathers to tear off the little page each day and read the Bible verse, short devotional message, and brief prayer with the family at supper.

As GP was reading the devotional in the drought-stricken middle of summer—again hot, dry, and windy—he commented, "You know, the terrible biblical drought in Egypt lasted seven years, when Pharaoh had a dream and told Joseph to hand out grain to the starving people. This makes eight years for us. It just has to break this year."

"Are we worse sinners than those pagan Egyptians?" Bertha wondered.

About the only thing that could turn talk away from the drought was a Joe Louis fight, and another one was scheduled for June 22. It was a return match with the great Max Schmeling who had beaten him in '35. But since that time Louis defeated everyone who went into the ring with him, and now he was the clear Oster favorite as well.

A radical upstart leader named Adolf Hitler was making war noises in Germany and bragging up Aryan superiority in all things and now touted Schmeling as the true champion of the world. The fight had become more than a boxing match.

GP made sure Monday chores were done early, and the families were settled in front of the RCA radio at Fred and Selma's place well before fight time. They could hardly hear the scratchy voice of the announcer over all the audience hoopla, but soon the fight began. Louis had prepared well, and this time the fight was only in the second round when he knocked Schmeling out. In less than six minutes, the "Fight of the Decade" was all over. While all the Oster adults shouted and cheered, even little Eddie woke up and joined the happy clapping. Big, tough "Fightin' Joe" was their man. "Wonder what Hitler thinks now?" Fred laughed.

During these times, GP and Fred continued to be sought out as auctioneers. Sometimes it was for area families that were struck with illness and had to give up farming. Sometimes it was for a widow who lost a mate and couldn't keep up the farm or the household. All too many times it was for families who were caught in the jaws of both unyielding drought and unforgiving debt. They had no other way out but to sell everything and move away, usually somewhere out West, to start over.

For their work, as the auction bills advertised, "Starting at 10:00 a.m. sharp! With free lunch served on the grounds," the Oster Brothers together received a 2 percent commission on the total money brought in from the sale. Usually that amounted to somewhere between five and ten dollars to each man for a day's work. One day, GP came home and laid his entire day's earnings on the table. Two dollars and seventy-eight cents. As he sat down, Bertha noticed a tear running down his cheek and held him as they both silently lamented what they had to go through to survive.

Then, in the midst of these harsh times, events in the area took a horrendous, grizzly turn that shook even the strongest to the core.

Chapter 17

Murder in the Manse

In a nearby Lutheran church, the pastor's wife left for a brief vacation back to her hometown. While she was gone, the parsonage went up in flames. The neighbors arrived to fight the fire, but the flames were too high for their buckets of water to do any good. As the fire died down, Reverend Reinhertz came driving up and asked about Melita, their maid. When no one could account for her, Reverend Reinhertz went into a panic, crying, "Dear Lord, she was in the house when I left. Didn't she get out?"

When the embers cooled, they found the maid's horribly burned body curled against the foot of the sofa, and Undertaker Chilson took the remains to Beulah to prepare for a sad burial. As he worked on the charred body, he made a stunning discovery. Her stomach contained traces of strychnine. The poison raised flags for Chilson, and he moved on to carefully examine the girl's seared womb. His knees went weak when he discovered the remains of a tiny fetus.

He didn't want to face this situation alone and immediately called Dr. Rasmussen. He rushed over and also examined the body. After a long silence, he shook his head, "Looks like a bad deal all right." Then, with hearts pounding, thinking of the enormity of what they were facing, they drove to Stanton and summoned the sheriff. When they had all reviewed the findings, they decided to have a talk with Reverend Reinhertz. Even though it was now late at night, they found him staying at a church member's house and asked him to come out to the car with them.

When they laid out the details, the pastor was totally aghast and wondered how such a loathsome thing could have taken place. But the more they pressed him, the more nervous and convoluted his talking became. Several minutes more and the sheriff told him, "Reverend, I'm taking you in and booking you for murder."

When the news got out, GP and Bertha were in shock, as was their pastor and everyone in the state after the *Bismarck Tribune* picked it up. This news of a shepherd of God feasting on the flock was enough to sear the soul of many a true believer. Death was served on the plates of these pioneers as regular diet, but death at the hands of another was rare and despised. Sadly, there was worse to come.

The trial established the setting in which the pastor had gotten the maid in trouble and convinced her that *her* bad sin needed to be forgiven, so he gave her Holy Communion, lacing the wine with strychnine. She naively drank the sacramental wine and died an agonizing, tortured death. When she was dead, the pastor set the house on fire and drove away to make a spiritual visit to a family of the church.

As the ugly, unbelievable details began to unfold in trial, Melita's family found the pain too heavy and, with hearts torn by picturing their loved one's agony, broke into quiet, bitter sobs. Throughout the stifling little courtroom, women pulled their hats down low and dabbed their eyes to staunch painful tears they could not stop.

The pastor, in freshly pressed black wool suit and starched white shirt, spent much time during the proceedings with head down, eyes closed, hands folded in prayer, attempting to portray the wounded servant of God, and roundly declared his innocence, claiming he was set up by his enemies.

"That must be somebody else's baby. I never touched her," Reinhertz testified under oath, "and maybe that man started the fire, because Melita was fine when I left the house."

His defense attorney brought a parade of character witnesses to testify that this righteous man of God could not possibly commit so heinous a crime. The jury was not persuaded. They found him guilty, and the judge sentenced him to life imprisonment in the state penitentiary in Bismarck.

"What happens," GP wondered, "that a man of God can sink that low?"

"What he did with her is bad enough," Bertha answered, "but to poison the Communion wine, and give her that to drink just about makes me vomit."

That night in their devotions after supper, GP was at a loss over what to pray. He could only manage to get out, "Oh God, have mercy on dear Melita's family, and on us all. Amen."

People were angrier over this than over anything they could remember. There was talk of breaking the preacher out of jail, before they took him off to the state penitentiary, and hanging him. Others still believed the pastor to be innocent and gathered in prayer meetings asking God to find a way to overturn this whole tragic affair and send an angel to set the suffering pastor free from prison, like St. Peter of old.

No matter how bad the drought, this sordid event with the preacher was "badder" still and weighed heavier on their souls than any demonic thing they could imagine. For weeks, nearly every conversation in the county centered on "that monster," or "poor Melita," or what her family must be going through.

Their hearts were bruised by the tragic death of the Ballhagen children some years earlier. But that fire was from nature. This one was different.

"First off," said one neighbor, "Reinhertz couldn't keep his pants on around the maid."

"And behind his wife's back yet," another continued.

"Then his teeth are dripping with the poor girl's blood."

"And he tries to cloak it all with the blood of Christ."

"Just that blasphemy should be enough to hang him."

"Anybody thinks there's no devil is short a wheel on his wagon."

As the talk continued about Reinhertz, someone thought of the meaning of that name: "clean heart." "Some people grow into their name," he said, "but that piece of dirt wouldn't recognize a 'clean heart' if you gave him a trunk fulla' silver dollars."

The next Sunday in Peace Church, not many miles away, their pastor really did not want to get into this sordid business. But he knew it was at the top of every member's thoughts, and clearly he had to address it. Slowly he climbed the steps of the high pulpit.

"When evil breaks into the heart of a man," he began his sermon, "things happen that are so ugly you can't begin to describe them." With one sentence, he had the whole congregation's immediate attention.

"Yes, yes," heads silently nodded, eyes wide and waiting.

He was speaking both to himself and to every person there. "And only God can break that iron band of original sin, which has a grip on us stronger than the bone-crushing bite of a mighty lion."

"Where's he going here?" they wondered.

"Sin climbed to the mountaintop so recently in our area, sin so monstrous it marches under a black satanic flag—"

Yes, his listeners nodded.

"And it dare not be excused—"

No, no, they shook their heads.

"And must be justly punished—"

Yes, yes.

"And grieves the very heart of God—"

Surely!

"But which of us here this morning, which of us here today, can stand up and say . . . *I* have not sinned . . . *My* heart is clean . . . *I* am innocent . . ."

After each quiet phrase, he paused and looked from face to face.

Then he dropped Jesus's words on the stunned listeners: "Let any man among you who is without sin, cast the first stone."

One by one the faces before him turned down, studying their hands, looking at the floor.

"Now are you beginning to understand why God had to plant a bitter cross on Golgotha's hill? Why he had to give his son to die? Why he raised him back to life in a mighty resurrection?"

"Remember," he dropped his voice to a whisper, "there is a balm in Gilead that makes the wounded whole."

After a long pause in the absolute silence where all breathing had suddenly ceased, he ended in slow phrases, so quietly they leaned ahead on their chairs to hear, "There is a balm in Gilead that heals the sin-sick soul. That makes . . . the wounded . . . whole. Amen."

"Remove the scales from our eyes, O Lord," he bowed his head and prayed, "and let us see the threatening peril of our own sin, that we might be led to repentance unto eternal life. Amen." And sat down.

After worship was finished, GP walked over to one of the deacons in the parking lot. "Did we just get good news or was it bad news?" he asked.

"I don't know. Kinda like eating stale bread," the deacon replied. And both left it at that.

In the car on the way home, GP's mind was turning in circles, "Ja, I remember the Psalmist said, 'Thou hast made man only a little lower than the angels,' but that twisted Preacher Reinhertz must have crawled out of hell."

"You think," Bertha reflected, "that monster will ever be able to cleanse his soul of this ugly sin?" For a time, both their faith in God and their faith in humanity were shaken.

Besides the Missouri, a second river ran through their country. It was called the Knife, and now the Knife River was seen by some as more metaphor than river. "The guy that named our little river must have been a prophet," Fred said to a group of men the next Sunday at church, "to see a knife run through us."

Chapter 18

World Turned Green

In '39 the rains finally returned. The thirsty earth sucked up raindrops like a thirsty camel ten days in the desert. One day GP walked into the house and brightly announced, "I don't remember our world ever being this green. Sure feels good."

"Like the Garden of Eden," Bertha replied with a smile.

Another event that some took as a sign of the drought breaking was the '38 election of John Moses as governor of North Dakota. The word going around the area was "If Moses could lead the people of Israel to water in the wilderness back then, maybe Moses can lead North Dakota out of the drought now." When GP heard it, he told Bertha, "Well, you gotta keep hoping, you know."

But while they were not naive enough to think that one season of rain meant the drought was over, the change in attitudes was amazing. Neighbors who hadn't smiled in months went about wearing smiles again. Hymn singing in church had new zest. The chickens laid more eggs. Horses whinnied and bucked with pleasure in the pastures.

Bertha put on her bonnet and took little Eddie's hand to walk to the garden. On the way, they walked alongside the small earthen dam that GP had put up to hold water from the artesian spring. In front of them, several skinny-legged, black-and-white killdeer birds skittered along the muddy edge of the dam, bobbing their heads and singing their distinctive "kill-DEER, kill-DEER." Eddie was fascinated and sang out a cheery "kill-deer" in return, but they couldn't seem to understand his people talk. Suddenly one of the birds flew up and landed just a few yards in front of them, dragging its wing and limping.

"Look, Mamma, the bird is hurt," Eddie shouted.

"No, she must have a nest close by, and she's doing that to get you away and make you think you can catch her," Bertha replied.

"Bet I can," he cried out and ran to catch her. One flap of her wings and she skittered away, dragging her wing again to pull him farther from her nest. Several more failed attempts and he finally shouted back, "Guess you're right, Mamma."

Eddie's biggest fascination during this time was the horses, and he wanted to be with Dad whenever the harnesses went on. He loved to have Dad lift him up on the horse's wide back at the end of the day. His little legs had to do the splits, but he hung on to the hame knobs and rode home while Dad drove. And Dad was thrilled to have a little son who enjoyed the labors of the earth as much as he did. Sometimes Eddie came into the house as caked in dust and grime as his father, saying, "Mamma, we had to work real hard out there today." She smiled, wondering who was more proud, she or Dad.

That fall they finally got a full harvest. GP found huge joy in getting up each morning and looking out over the fields of grain rippling in the wind like waves of a great rolling ocean.

"Oh, this does my heart good," he thought to himself as he walked into the field when it had turned to brilliant gold. He picked several heads and with his right thumb crushed them in the palm of his left hand, freeing the kernels from their form-fitting jackets. *"Thank you, dear Lord. Tomorrow I put in the binder."*

Across the whole area, teams of horses were soon straining into the harness for long hours, pulling the binders up the rolling fields and down to harvest the first good crop in eight years. And on each farm, whole families worked dawn to dusk shocking the wheat bundles with the heads up, eight bundles against each other in teepee fashion, to keep the heads of grain dry and ready for threshing.

When the grain was all cut, neighbors gathered in teams, and the ponderous threshing machines began to chew bundles and blow straw into the clear North Dakota air. That led the harvest sun to collect the dust and do a celebration of its own. It set the Dakota heavens on fire with such brilliant sunsets that neighbors paused from their labors and spent long reflective moments soaking in the splendor of it all. Flaming reds and burning yellows and fiery golds were mixed into the endless horizon of clouds and air-brushed into great expanses of overpowering lavender that surged into the brain and stilled the soul like the healing amethysts of ancient lore.

"I'm so glad we're living in this good land," GP told Bertha on one such evening as he carried Eddie piggyback and delighted in the vast heavenly wonder that arced high across the miles of western sky, stretching as far north to south as eye could see.

"Maybe God's giving us this beauty to lift us up after all the bad years," Bertha answered, knowing only too well how transient all this goodness could be.

Some weeks later, GP drove the family for a Sunday visit with Grandpa and Grandma Wulff. No sooner were they seated in the house than Grandma Salomina said, "You remember Magdalena, our neighbor that some said was a witch?"

"Sure do," Bertha replied while GP felt the hair on his arms stand up.

"Well, it got so people wouldn't talk to her anymore, and when she brought food to any potluck dinner, nobody would eat it."

"Sounds bad."

"Well, I talked to her some, but people started giving me the evil eye too."

"Then what?"

"You won't believe it, but a week ago she walked into the creek and drowned herself."

"Oh no," was all Bertha could say, and stealing a glance at GP, she saw it was nothing but relief to him. "Poor thing," she added, "that's a shame."

"At the funeral they wouldn't let her casket in the church," Grandma replied, "and she was buried outside the cemetery fence."

Strong feelings bounced around the room, but nobody wanted to start an argument. An uncomfortable silence followed, until finally Grandpa lit his pipe and began talking about the weather.

With all the adults in the house, Eddie had no one to play with except Grandpa's dog. While they were cavorting noisily in the yard, Grandpa's two frisky black-and-white goats also caught the excitement, and soon all four were a blur of constant motion. On a whim, Eddie ran several times around Grandpa's brand-new, black Model T car with its soft canvas roof, which was parked just outside the house.

The two little goats took a short cut, and with one light, bounding leap, both landed on the hood of the car. A second stiff-legged leap put them on top of the canvas roof. Their tiny, sharp hooves sliced the canvas like jackknives, and both crashed into the car, trashing and flailing until Eddie could jerk the car door open and let them out—only after one had urinated in the car and left a stench second only to the smell of a skunk. In a flash, boy, dog, and goats disappeared down behind the barn, three wanting to run some more, Eddie desperate to find a big hole.

Several moments later, Grandpa led all the adults out to show them his exciting new automobile. It didn't take long to figure out what must have happened during all that barking and yelling and bleating they heard a few minutes earlier. He took one look at the trashed car and bellowed like a bull in a barn full of heifers in heat, "*Donner wetter*, balls of fire, if I catch that kid I'll skin him alive!"

Grandpa Wulff was normally a man of few words. In these few minutes, he spoke many. And these were the kindest by far.

When they finally found Eddie, Dad put him over his knee in front of everyone and spanked his bottom until his hand was sore.

"What can we do about the car?" Dad asked Grandpa after setting a crying Eddie down on the hard ground, where he collapsed out of both shame and fright.

"Well, I got a big field with a lot of rocks. Next week I'm gonna drive the team, and he's gonna pick every gosh-darn rock he can lift on that field," Grandpa replied, still furious about how much repair the car would need.

On the way home, Bertha and GP spent a long time in conversation over Magdalena.

"Some will say that proves she was a witch," GP insisted.

"But think a minute," Bertha replied, "if she really was, such talk going around would just have made her laugh. Maybe she really wasn't a witch, and people finally hurt her so much she just couldn't take it anymore."

"Sure glad we're not part of her family now."

"Must be just awful for all of them."

"Pity the poor preacher that had to bury her."

"I even feel awful."

"Yeah, suppose so," GP finally replied, but he couldn't agree, and they drove in uncomfortable silence the rest of the way home. Eddie wanted to speak, but he thought better of it and kept his questions to himself.

Some weeks after Eddie's painful goat ordeal, another school year opened and he was back in school with his friends. But that summer Eddie had received an education in the school of life that no book would ever teach him.

That winter, GP and his family spent a lot of nights visiting back and forth with the nearby families of brother Fred and cousins Adam and Christ and other neighbors. Many a card game of whist went down, sometimes over heated exchanges about "dumb" or brilliant bidding. They cranked up gallons of rich homemade ice cream in all sorts of experimental flavors. And the little cousins spent hours on the hills, sledding every slope and stuffing snowballs down each other's necks. Life was good again, and hymns of praise ended many an evening's gathering of neighbors during those evenings on the quiet prairies.

As winter began to break, they entered the weeks of Lent, which meant special worship services remembering Jesus's great sacrifice. On Thursday noon of Holy Week, Bertha hauled water and set it to heating on the cookstove. It was Maundy Thursday, with Communion, and that meant everyone taking a bath before church. This was special, because it was one of the few times during the year when they would take two baths in one week. After they finished, GP threw the bath water outside. Bertha wiped up the water that had been splashed out of the tub, then got out the box of Arm & Hammer Baking Soda and all three brushed their teeth. Finished, GP led them in family devotions, and it was time to drive to church.

After hymns and a forty-five-minute sermon, the pastor uncovered the Communion elements and invited the congregation to the altar. The young boys sitting on backless benches on the front right side, and girls on the left, watched as row by row of men solemnly filed out and walked up to the circular white altar rail to receive the bread and wine. When it was time for the women on the left side of the church to take their turn, a number of them had babes in arms that they passed to the men who were now seated again, only to have a handful of the infants burst into cantankerous squalling. Most of them had been sound asleep, and suddenly being shifted to a few nervous fathers brought them to instant irascibility. When one infant began howling, the rest soon followed. The youngsters up front snickered and whispered at the irreverent scene, while the men were totally chagrined and the poor mothers completely lost their concentration on the holiness of the Last Supper.

The pastor was clearly irritated and unconsciously began shouting the words of Communion into the ears of the women kneeling in front of him, rattling them even more. When the pastor finished serving the women and they returned to pick up their precious bundles, the raucous crying soon stopped and quiet returned. But there was little spirit behind the singing of the final hymn, and both pastor and people left with the suffering in the Garden of Gethsemane sadly tangled with echoes of bellicose bawling.

The next day was Good Friday, and all work across the Valley stopped as they gathered in church to worship at the foot of the Cross. Fred was the church organist, and he brought his family to church early to begin playing prelude hymns on the pedal organ as families silently filed into the church. The pastor's deliberate tone in Bible readings and sermon, together with the slow, dirgeful hymns, heightened the air of remorsefulness as they remembered again the painful price God was willing to pay to secure a place for them in heaven, there where the pastor said, "Death and depression and drought will finally be no more."

When they got home from church and finished their meatless Good Friday dinner, GP took Eddie's hand and said, "Come, I want to show you something."

Together they walked through the ravine behind the barn and up on the high ridge that ended in a large sandstone outcropping. When GP earlier walked out to get the cows for milking, he ran across a nest which a mallard hen had dug into a small depression hidden by the prairie grass.

Eddie loved walking up here, since the sandstone formations reminded him of King David's fortress in Jerusalem that Dad told about in family devotions. It was a magic place. Suddenly Dad said, "*Dort*, there," and pointed to a spot in the grass. In an instant there was an explosion as the mottled brown mallard hen, fearing for her life at the sight of these advancing giants, erupted out of the nest with furious fluttering and angry quacks. She flew a short distance away and landed in the grass, squawking her irritation at having her ordered life so rudely disrupted and threat brought to her unhatched children.

Eddie bent over to touch the eggs, but Dad quickly said, "No, no, don't touch them, or she won't come back." Eddie squatted down and studied the marvelous sight of this clutch of nine pale-green eggs nestled together in a warm featherbed of softest down that the hen had plucked from her breast and carefully packed down to make a protective cocoon for her little hatchlings. When they got back home, Eddie ran ahead and skipped into the house. "Mamma, mamma," he shouted, "me 'n Dad found something really nice!" Over the next ten minutes Mother learned every little detail of their wonderful discovery.

Worship on Easter Sunday for the first time in years felt like true celebration, as did worship on Easter Monday as well. Hymns seemed to have a life all their own as the glad "alleluias" bounced off the high wooden ceiling. They knew all along that the Resurrection was real and God indeed cared for them, but somehow rains and wheat in the granary made it much more real and close at hand.

For several weeks Dad and Eddie walked up the ridge to check on the nest, and there was no change. Then one day they noticed one of the eggs give just the slightest quiver. In a moment, it clicked against the other eggs, and then the shell cracked. A tiny yellow nib of a beak poked through the membrane inside the egg, and in a twinkling, a whole beak and a little wet head wobbled out, eyes glued shut and fuzzy down all slicked back. For long seconds it just lay there, looking more dead than alive from its hatching struggle. Then it jerked erect as the shell broke apart and a whole sticky-wet body emerged, only to fall once more, exhausted by its hard struggle to enter an uncertain world. "Yuck," Eddie said drawing back, "I sure don't wanna touch that thing."

Mamma mallard sensed the hatching and flew up from her nearby grassy lair, dive bombing the intruders and nearly strafing their caps as she loudly scolded these pesky meddlers with highly annoyed duck talk.

"Come on, Son, let's leave," said GP, "because Mamma's getting mad at us for hanging around her new baby."

That night, when Dad knelt at his bed and led him in singing his "*Muede bin ich, geh zu Ruh*" prayer, Eddie was still bubbling with descriptions, over and over, of the little miracle on the prairie.

Several days later, after chores and supper in the evening, Dad and Eddie again walked up to the nest. Now all the eggs were hatched, and Mamma had cleaned out the nest. But only six tiny yellow fluff balls remained in the crowded downy living room. Eddie squatted beside the nest, dying to pick up the tantalizing, soft ducklings that pulled on his heartstrings. "Look," he whispered, "there's three duckies missing."

"Ja, sometimes they die, just like people." GP got a catch in his throat and coughed as a vision of his little Clinton in the casket suddenly rolled across his mind.

"Please, Papa, can't I hold just one of them for a little bit?" Eddie begged.

"You better not, or she'll kick it out of the nest and it'll die."

The next week, when they checked on their duck neighbors once more, the nest was empty and the ducks all gone. There was no trace to show if coyotes had gotten them or if Mamma had marched them all away to safe haven.

When summer turned hot, Eddie loved to take his shoes off and play barefoot outside. He was captivated by the red-winged blackbirds that sat on the nearby buckbrush, fluffing their red wing epaulets and trilling their long, rolling warbles back and forth. But a bigger source of fun was to team up with Schatzie and run around the shores of the stock dam below the artesian spring to catch the croaking green frogs that had moved in. Problem was, the ground at water's edge was soft, and one day he sank to his knees in the waterlogged mud. Struggling to get his legs out of the muck, he fell, and his overalls were mud up to his chest. To his mind, the problem was simple: take the muddy clothes off.

The bottomless freedom felt so good he took his shirt off too, and seeing GP coming home with the horses for dinner, he ran buck naked and laughing to meet Dad. GP met him and took his hand as they walked the horses to drink at the watering tank below the spring. On the way, they passed the dam, with Eddie's muddy clothes lying in a heap. Dad let the horses walk on by themselves and, taking Eddie's hand, walked him to the edge of the dam.

"Wow," Eddie thought, *"Dad's going to catch frogs with me."*

Instead GP gently sat his son down and, without a word, scooped up handfuls of mud and slathered Eddie in thick goo until only his eyeballs were showing white. Leaving him sitting there like a stunned tar baby, Dad walked to the tank to finish watering the horses.

Eddie cried his heart out, and after trying to wash off some of the sticky mud, he ran screaming to Mother, "Mamma, I fell in." She took him to the well and pumped cold water to rinse him off. When GP came into the house, he looked at her and winked, and that was the end of that adventure.

Eddie never again repeated that episode. Instead he and Schatzie made a game of running around the edge of the dam to catch frogs, and when he yelled "Siccum," Schatzie would do a flying leap into the water, trying to snatch one of the enticing green leapers.

Often the frogs would lie submerged, with only eyes and nostrils above water, and it took a sharp eye to spot them. When he did, he aimed a rock to smush them. Luckily for them, his aim was poor and few were struck.

Finally Eddie learned to draw more enjoyment from sitting on the rocks and quietly listening as the frogs sang majestic a cappella "Black-Spotted, Green Frog Concerti" in multi-voiced harmony that Beethoven surely would have incorporated into his grand *Pastorale Symphony* had he been privileged enough to hear it. Occasionally black-and-yellow-striped garter snakes would slither through the water, and Eddie raced to catch them on the opposite shore, but somehow they were always faster than he was, and all he could do was throw more rocks at the weaving creatures.

One of the next Sundays in church, Eddie was sitting beside one of his friends on a backless bench in the little boys' section, on the right-hand side in front of the men. Suddenly, during the middle of the sermon, he remembered the snakes, and he simply had to tell his friend about trying to catch them. They whispered ever so quietly for the briefest of moments. But it was a thing simply not done nor tolerated in church. While the pastor continued his sermon from the high pulpit, GP got up from his chair toward the back of the church, silently walked down the boards of the center aisle, leaned in behind Eddie, and smacked him over the head with his little black hymnal. The blow knocked Eddie backward, clean off the bench, and he crumpled down between the legs of the man behind him. Hitting the floor, he was showered with a hundred German songs as the hymnal exploded and rained down pages all around him.

Terrified, Eddie sprang up, half surprised, half stunned, and jumped back into his spot on the bench. GP walked back to his seat, the pastor never missed a beat in his sermon, no one said a word, and Eddie never talked in church again. After that incident, if any little one whispered a word or two in church, on the way home all the parents had to say was "Remember Eddie?" It was a powerful lesson that never needed to be repeated.

****

"Isn't it strange," GP said at supper one night, "the roads are all full of cars and trucks now, but all the farming is still done with horses."

"Well, with the terrible dry years," Bertha replied, "I guess nobody has money to buy all that machinery."

"Long as you got hay, horses are still the way to go."

"Guess you better feed ours pretty good then."

Fall rains soaked the ground, and abundant snowfalls helped even more. Then days of slow spring rains topped it off to set the stage for renewed life not only in the Valley but across the entire Midwest.

When Uncle Gottfried, now advanced in years, decided to sell a quarter out of the land he still owned, GP jumped at the opportunity. The hundred sixty acres were half pasture, half plow land, and Uncle wanted a thousand dollars. GP's old boss, Jake Eisenbeiss, was willing to loan him the money, so for $6.25 an acre, he nearly doubled the size of his farm.

Some neighbors were skeptical. "What if the drought comes back? You'll lose everything." It was unnerving, but with Bertha's approval, GP went ahead.

The rains held, crops were bountiful, and when another eighty acres across the road opened up for sale, GP bought that as well.

In short order, he increased his herd of beef cattle, built a large barn with high haymow and a lean-to on each side, and purchased a tractor to farm all the new land.

It was a heady time, although GP woke up a number of nights with his heart pounding from recurring dreams of running endlessly in bitter dust storms, of walking parched fields where nothing grew, of the well running dry and the pump spouting sand into the water bucket he kept trying to fill.

His sense of trepidation was not lessened by the news swirling around the Valley and indeed around the world. Germany had once again embroiled most of Europe in another war, with Hitler proclaiming a "thousand-year Reich," while Japan was attacking her neighbors on the other side of the world.

The war fever led President Roosevelt to declare a national draft, ordering all men between the ages of twenty-one and thirty-six to register and be ready to serve in the Armed Forces should America be drawn into the conflict.

GP and Fred drove to Beulah and nervously walked down the steps to the basement below the post office to register at the new Mercer County Selective Service Office. At age thirty-four, GP was on the cusp, but both of them were worried.

"I'm sure afraid of this whole thing," GP whispered as they started down.

"Boy, I hope I don't have to leave Selma and the kids," Fred answered.

"And who would run the farms if we were gone?"

Fortunately, before long they received notice that because they were family men and engaged in farming, their service was considered "essential to the war effort" and they were classified 4-F, meaning they were permanently deferred from the draft. That night they got together to play a few hands of whist and enjoyed a Pabst Blue Ribbon brew that Fred had picked up earlier. But their celebration was tempered by knowing that a number of young single men in the Valley would surely have to serve.

In early September, Eddie disappeared. Around midmorning Bertha called him to come in for lunch and was not concerned when there was no immediate answer. He often got so involved in play somewhere around the yard that he didn't hear her. Several minutes later she called again, and when there was still no answer, she turned up the volume, this time shouting "Edward John" at full mad-mother level. After checking in the barn and the dam, with more shouting and finding nothing, she walked over the Fred's, only to learn he wasn't there either. Now she panicked and ran out to the field to get GP.

When he saw her frenzied running, arms unhinged, hair disheveled, her eyes glazed and frantic, he knew there was big trouble. Immediately, he shut down the tractor and ran to meet her.

"Eddie, he's gone," she shrieked between puffing breaths, "and I can't find him anywhere." GP caught her as she broke into a flood of tears, in her mind's eye seeing again, only too clearly, her dear baby Clinton in his terrible little white box of death.

Since the steel-wheeled tractor had no road gear, GP took her hand and began jogging for home, half dragging her, moving as quickly as Bertha's exhausted legs would carry her.

"I have an idea," he said, panting between breaths, "let's drive down to the school."

GP put the gas pedal down on the Model A, bouncing over prairie ruts and rocks as fast as he could keep control while Bertha stared ahead unseeing, wringing her hands and mumbling, "I'm going to die if anything happened to him . . . I'm gonna die . . . I'm gonna die."

"*Nu, sei Ruhig*, be quiet." GP responded sternly, "Nothing happened to him. You'll see."

But she wasn't convinced. Wringing her hands until they were white, she couldn't stop, "I'm gonna die . . . I can't take it."

When they arrived at the school, Schatzie came bounding off the front steps, happily barking, jumping up on the running board, giving their pounding hearts a burst of hope. The teacher, Miss Hafner saw them driving up and met them at the door. "Are you looking for someone?" she asked, knowing why they were there and seeing the fright on their faces.

"Is our Eddie here?"

When they walked in, Eddie was sitting at a desk with the first graders, busy coloring a picture Miss Hafner had given him.

"He came about an hour ago, and I told him he'd have to go home again, but he asked if he could just color a while, so I let him do that."

Eddie was lucky at that. When he came to school he knew no English, since they spoke only German at home. Fortunately, Miss Hafner also came from a German home; and when he walked in the door, she called him to her desk, whispering to him because she didn't want to break her rule: "No talking German in school."

"He sure had us worried," Bertha responded.

"I have to ask you," Miss Hafner said, "how old is he?"

"Well, he's five. He won't turn six until the middle of November."

"Yes, the district rules say anybody with a birthday after the first of October has to wait until the next year to start."

Bertha motioned for Eddie to come, and they drove home. GP was irritated by having to miss two hours' work and said, "You do that again and you're going to get the strap on your back end. Understand?"

"Yes, Dad."

The next week, Eddie went missing again. This time Bertha walked the mile and a half to school and unceremoniously hauled him out of the desk to head home. Half the way home she lectured and cajoled and filled his ears about the dire consequences that would shortly befall him.

Toward evening when GP returned home, Bertha told him the story, and he called Eddie into the house. He took down his shaving strop and told Eddie to bend over a chair. GP had to keep his word, even though his heart was not in this spanking. *"How do you spank a kid who wants so bad to learn things?"* he thought to himself. Two smacks of the leather strop and the job was done. It smarted enough to make little Eddie burst into tears and run to the barn, silently vowing to run far, far away and never come home. Supper that night was a silent affair, and GP's family devotions felt more like a funeral.

It wasn't a week until Eddie ran away for the third time.

This time, when GP and Bertha drove to the school, Miss Hafner came to the door and met their angry looks with a smile.

"I've decided," she told them, "that anyone who runs away from home three times to go to school is maybe ready to start, no matter what the rulebook says."

"Really?" GP asked, totally surprised. "You mean that?"

"Yes, I've assigned him a desk, and tonight he'll bring home a reading book so you can help get him caught up. Oh, and here's a list of things you should pick up for him to get started."

The shocked parents drove right to Beulah to pick up the needed school supplies, and that afternoon when Eddie came home, he talked their ears off for an hour about how wonderful school was and how he was already learning so many things. He even tried out some new English on them, some of which they had to correct to get his German tongue making the right new sounds.

Soon he was busy learning not only the basic things that he and his two first-grade classmates would digest but also listening to each of the higher grades reciting their knowledge and gleaning bits and pieces from their scholarship as well.

****

Threshing season that fall was a glorious time. The harvest was plentiful, bins were filled with grain, the men worked well together, and the women outdid each other with feasts that could have led to gastronomic overdose had they not been forced to work so long and so hard day after day.

During the next weeks, GP made arrangements for the Valley farmers to sell their cattle in St. Paul, and soon the men were busy rounding up their stock and forming a large herd of several hundred, which they drove down the road ditches thirteen miles to Beulah. A dozen men on saddle horses kept the herd together, and GP's ranch days came in good stead when the men chose him to be drive-foreman in charge of the two-day drive.

"Ei, does this bring back memories," he thought to himself a hundred times as he sat in the saddle, his mind flashing scene after scene of Elkhorn past.

GP rode point on the herd, careful to gauge the ebb and flow of the herd's movement, with time for hard walking, time for quick grazing, and time for watering in little Antelope Creek along the way. He knew only too well that these cattle were nearly all strangers to each other and could easily be spooked, since they had never before been away from the safety of their own familiar pastures.

After they got the cattle loaded into boxcars, GP and neighbor, Herman Waltz, rode along in the train caboose to oversee the unloading and final sale in the stockyards at St. Paul.

Another reason GP wanted to go along with the livestock was to make sure they were fed and watered along the way and also after they reached the stockyards in St. Paul. Much to his dismay, the train personnel told him that they had strict instructions not to feed or water the cattle. The same rules held in the slaughterhouse stockyards, where GP was mortified by the constant din of loud, bawling animals so desperate for feed and water. *"Sounds like a thousand growling tractors pulling plows through heavy gumbo,"* GP thought. Their desperate misery crushed his heart.

When GP and Waltz approached the yard foreman about at least getting some water to the desperate animals, he curtly told them, "Makes the butchering easier, less waste that way."

Walking away from that depressing conversation, GP was struck with a choking cough and noticed a cloud of dust that hung over the yards. It came as thousands of empty stomachs cried out and set milling hooves to stomping on the powdered dirt in overcrowded pens before the final hammer.

The next day, on the caboose ride home, GP couldn't get the misery of the animals out of his mind. "I just got a lump in my guts over how they treated our cattle," he told Waltz.

"Ja," Waltz replied, "worse than dirt." They rode on in silence, depressed and wondering. When GP took the substantial check out of his pocket and looked at it, he shook his head, "Money'll do such good stuff for the folks at home, but it just feels dirty."

"Like sin money," Waltz nodded.

Before church the next Sunday, when the men were gathered between cars, GP handed out the money and then described the events in St. Paul.

"You know," he said looking down at the ground, "I think the hellish sound of those bawling cattle begging for water and a mouthfulla hay will haunt me the rest of my life."

It took a long while until he could once more feel that his Dakota prairies were a good life.

But the good life of their little world was soon to change.

Chapter 19

Whole World at War

A few weeks later, on Sunday, December 7, 1941, GP and the family had just returned from church and changed clothes when Fred came roaring over, with his tires churning dirt on the prairie trail.

"The Japs," he shouted, wide-eyed, before he was even out of the car. "The Japs just attacked us this morning in a place called 'Pearl Harbor' in Hawaii."

"Was it bad?" GP asked.

"The radio says the Japs killed thousands of our people and sank a bunch of our big ships."

"*Jammer elend,* Oh my gosh, what's gonna happen now?" was all GP could get out. GP quickly got Bertha and Eddie into the car, and they spent the rest of the day at Fred's, anxiously glued to the scratchy radio news reports coming across KFYR in Bismarck.

Monday morning they quickly did chores and drove back to Fred's. At 10:30, President Roosevelt came on the air describing those events as "a date which will live in infamy" and in six short minutes set the course for war. A half hour later, Congress responded with a declaration of war on Imperial Japan.

Tuesday morning a hush lay over the school, and Miss Hafner—a Lutheran, as were most of her students—asked them to stand at their desks and bow their heads while she led them in prayer for their land and for all going off to war. After the "amen," she led into the Pledge of Allegiance, and those words stirred each young heart like a continuing prayer as well. Each of the little patriots suddenly felt an urge to rise up and march off to fight their evil enemies to the death.

Miss Hafner then asked all the students to come to the front while she pulled down the wall map of the Pacific Ocean and the Far East. She handed the pointer to one of the seventh graders and asked him to find Japan and point out Tokyo. Another was to find Hawaii and point out Honolulu on Oahu Island. Then she pulled down the map of Europe and asked the sixth graders to find Germany and Great Britain and Russia.

"Will our enemies attack us here?" one of the youngsters wanted to know.

"Well, they're a long ways away, so I don't think they'll get this far."

"How far away are they?" asked another.

Then she gathered them around the globe on her desk and had the eighth graders again find Japan. When they located it, she had them find the mileage scale and gave them a string to measure a line from Tokyo to Bismarck.

"Looks like maybe a little over five thousand miles," slowly came the calculated answer.

"And how far to Germany?" she asked.

Another eighth grader took the string and measured to the other side of the globe. "Maybe around five thousand miles too, looks just about the same."

"So I think we'll be safe here in Antelope Valley," Miss Hafner assured them. They all returned to their desks feeling a little safer. Still, to these little scholars, five thousand miles meant very little, except to know that the adults around them were anxious and disturbed, and it must be bad.

Eddie's world, however, became much smaller for a moment when they were all gathered around the teacher's desk. When the students crowded in close, Eddie ended up being pushed against Miss Hafner's chair; and as she was talking, she happened to put her arm around him and held him tightly against herself. In that magic moment, fireworks exploded in Eddie's brain. The curves of her attractive body pressed into him with a warmth he had never known before, the luscious perfume that softly drifted from her sweater reminded him of a fairy princess, and it almost overwhelmed his senses. Her soft tone became the voice of the princess, speaking only to him. In that enchanted moment, fire and glory flooded his brain.

As Miss Hafner looked at the worried faces around her, and glanced down into Eddie's upturned eyes, his face suddenly burned hot and he quickly looked away. He had never experienced such feelings before, and when he returned to his seat, he found himself thinking, *I like Miss Hafner, and I wanna marry her when I get big. I really do.* He knew he would love her forever.

At the end of the school day, Eddie was walking home with his cousins. All the talk was back to war, and love was soon forgotten. At least for that afternoon.

When Eddie came home, he burst into the house shouting, "Mamma, Mamma, I know where Japan is, and Germany too." Since they had no maps in the house, Eddie sat down and drew two maps so Mom and Dad would know too. "I think we should drive over there," he blurted out, "and Papa should shoot that Hirohito for bombing our ships."

That night in bed he closed his eyes and saw the Lone Ranger and Tonto riding in, six-guns blazing, and they did just that. He clenched his fists under the covers and, with a silent *yes,* said a prayer and went to sleep wrapped in the heavenly perfumed arms of Miss Hafner holding him tightly against herself.

Two days later, Germany and Italy declared war on the United States. Having already invaded Russia, and forcing America to fight two wars at the same time, it now seemed like they had suddenly drawn the whole world into this war.

A month later, GP took the family into town to see a Gene Autry movie, and the previews included an RKO News Brief with martial music and clipped commentary on the war, showing several scenes from the bombing of Pearl Harbor. The crowd in the theater sat in stunned silence as they watched the billowing black smoke of huge ships exploding and burning, with deadly shrapnel flying, men screaming in horrendous agony, and grotesque bodies floating open mouthed and lifeless in the oily water. It suddenly brought the war home to people who heard daily radio reports and felt anxious but still rather undisturbed as they went about their normal lives on the prairie. Suddenly, with these images, the war became terribly, disturbingly real.

After the movie, GP pulled into the gas station. "Fill 'er up," he sang out to the attendant.

Then he noticed the price on the pump: twelve cents a gallon.

"She's sure shootin' up. Last fill it was only a dime."

"Yup," the attendant replied, "war, y'know."

****

One evening after supper, when Eddie had gone outside to play, GP sat at the table with Bertha and reflected on their son sleeping in the same room with them, just a few feet from their bed, and how it was affecting their intimacy.

"You know," he said, "our boy is getting old enough to where he knows about things."

"For sure. But what can we do about it?" she replied.

"Well, maybe we ought to think about getting another house."

"I think I'd like that."

Several weeks later GP heard about a house for sale in Beulah, and they stopped in to look at it. It had two small bedrooms, a kitchen/ eating room, and a small living room. After some intense negotiation, they agreed on two hundred fifty dollars and closed the deal.

As soon as the frost went out, they dug a basement close to the old house, poured cement for the walls, hired a house mover to move the "new" house slowly the thirteen miles from town, and set it on the foundation. Now they had a new coal-burning furnace with central heat, a basement coal bin, and a cool room to store vegetables and canned goods. The unfinished attic also made a new indoor play area for Eddie, even if it was unheated in winter's cold. Unfortunately, there was still no running water and no bathroom, so the "two-holer" outside stayed in daily use.

Soon word got out that their ten-year-old, little blue starter house might be for sale, and August Little Soldier purchased it and moved it to the Ft. Berthold Reservation.

Bertha's favorite part of the new house was the cement basement, which meant she didn't have to face the ugly, steely-eyed salamanders every time she went downstairs. *"Oh, is this nice,"* she whispered to herself for several weeks as she went down the steps.

In the spring, one afternoon when Eddie got home from school, he walked out to the stock dam. On approaching it, he noticed a mallard hen on the water, with eight little brown ducklings all in a line busily paddling behind her. Every time one darted out to catch a water bug, the duck mother quickly quacked it back into line. She brooked no disobedience during this day's lessons. *"I wonder,"* Eddie thought, hearing frogs busily croaking at the same time, *"do frogs eat duck?"*

He ran to the house and asked, "Mamma, do frogs eat duck?"

"I don't know, why?"

"Because some baby ducks were swimming on the dam and the frogs were sure croaking about something. I think they were getting ready to hunt the ducks."

He had barely gone outside when he came running back in.

"Mamma, Mamma, a bunch of really big birds just flew over. They're kinda brown, and their necks are this long," he shouted, stretching his arms as wide as he could reach. "They sang a real different song. What are they?"

"I don't know. Maybe storks or whooping cranes."

Only half listening to the answer, Eddie was already back on his way outside. The cranes had disappeared, but Eddie charged up the hill behind the dam and collected a handful of crocuses. "Here, Mamma, gotcha' some flowers."

"Thank you. They're beautiful," Mother replied, appreciating his thoughtfulness.

For Eddie, this was a busy time of learning, and school was only a part of the education that was awaiting him. Nature had wonders that were unfolding their beauty to him every day, and he couldn't soak it up fast enough. Every night he seemed to have some new mystery for which to thank God.

One piece of learning that Eddie did not relish was fixing fence. On Saturday, GP hitched up the team, loaded the wagon, and they drove along two miles of pasture fence, up steep hills and down. Every fence post that broke off during the winter had to be replaced: pull the staples out of the old post with a fencing pliers, position a new post, pound it into the ground, and hammer in new staples to attach the four strands of barbed wire to the post. Eddie's job was to carry the diamond-willow fence posts and hold them in place while Dad pounded them into the ground.

"Dad, this is kinda scary," Eddie said as he held one of the posts, "I sure hope you never miss with that heavy maul, or my hand'll be slivers."

"I don't miss very often," GP chuckled.

His humor did not help Eddie's confidence in holding the next few posts.

When they returned home, the fencers were totally exhausted. They put the team in the barn and slowly walked up to the house. "Hey, what do I smell?" GP shouted as he opened the door.

Bertha decided to surprise her workers and was ready with a big supper of sauerkraut and sausage, mashed potatoes and gravy, canned peas and fresh bread. When they finished their plates, Bertha got up and put a plate of German chocolate cake topped with a double dollop of whipped cream on the table. She would have had cloth napkins and her best china out—if she had any, but she didn't. Her best china was four plates that had no chips on them.

"Ei, best meal I ever had," GP said, laying down his fork and patting his stomach.

"Me too," Eddie added copying Dad's stomach rub.

"Well, I thought as hard as you two had to work, we could make this into a Fencer's Holiday," Bertha chuckled.

"Maybe we could do that every year, huh Mom?" Eddie quickly chimed in.

Later, between haying and harvest, GP took Eddie's hand and they walked a half mile across the prairie hills to Dad's favorite haven, the Indian grave atop their highest hill. As they sat on the large stone cairn and looked across the vast expanse of land, unbroken miles in every direction, GP told Eddie about the Indian grandmother who used to circle these stones many years ago. Then taking Eddie's hand, they circled the large cairn, just as she had done, and followed the stone path to the smaller cairn on a lower point, still tracing her footsteps. Eddie tried to listen, but his mind was busy imagining buffalo hunting and tepees on the hills with boys his age darting in and out chasing their dogs.

Dad pointed north to the Missouri River, stretching as from the west to the east as eye could see, and Eddie could smell its silt-laden waters wafting on the breeze. Now enjoying this special moment to the full, Dad turned south and said, "See that highest hill way, way off in the distance where everything's kinda hazy blue? That's Medicine Butte, and it's thirty miles away. That hill was a holy place, too, for the Indians a long time ago."

Now Eddie's mind was filled with wonder at what he was experiencing in this moment. "Kinda like church, huh?" he asked.

"Ja, kinda like church."

This bit of ground indeed felt sacred to GP, the hallowed ground of a private cemetery where lay an ancient brother, Raven Feather, kin to the red-skinned, little grandmother whom he so clearly remembered walking here in the days of his youth.

When GP began talking again, his voice had a strange otherworldly sound to it, his eyes looking somewhere beyond the horizon. "I wonder," he said softly, "who his wife was, how many children did they have . . . how many buffalo that his arrows brought down did she skin and tan the hide?" GP fell silent while Eddie's mind churned with stampeding buffalo. Then, "How many times did she wake up on cold nights and pull the heavy buffalo robes up over his sleeping shoulders to keep him warm? How many times did she see him paint up and ride off to battle and wonder if the Great Spirit—"

"You mean like God?" Eddie cut in.

"Yes, that's the name they called God . . . and she'd wonder if the Great Spirit would bring him back from battle to warm her tepee again?"

GP's mind wouldn't stop now, and he wanted Eddie to know the story. "The lady I saw walking around up here when I was young was Raven Feather's granddaughter. Little Soldier told me that. And he said she was his grandmother."

"Wow," Eddie exclaimed.

"Raven Feather must have done some brave stuff to become a chief, and be buried here on the highest ground."

This spot of earth towered above all the rest in the area, and here the grass stretched closer to the sun than any other for miles around. The sun kissed this spot first in the morning, and this hand-laid tomb was the last to bid the sun good night. GP felt all this again and wondered.

"What I wouldn't give to know," he added as the strange sacredness of the place silently enveloped him again and left him feeling mystically, totally at home.

"Dad, your voice sounds kinda funny," Eddie said, glancing sideways at his father, now almost a little afraid to look right at him.

GP looked north, down into the wooded Missouri lowland area that was part of the Reservation, and silently wondered about Raven Feather's kin living there today, amid so much hardship. *"They're living in lousy shacks,"* he thought to himself, *"getting miserable government checks that keep them on the edge of starving. They're driving rattletrap cars that pull into our yard for quick repairs, or gas, or fixing a tire. They're serving our country across the oceans in the army now, but they can't get hospital care here at home."* He shook his head at the irony of it, with Eddie wondering what was going on with Dad. *"They're driven out of their old hunting grounds, hooked on the white man's firewater, and our 'good white folk' make fun of 'em . . . what can be done? What hope is there for my red-skinned brothers?"*

With his mind still reeling, he took Eddie's hand again and, as they walked the high ground just below the stone cairn, showed him a dozen tepee rings in the grass, scattered across the high ridge.

"Here they had their tepees, and from here they could see the buffalo herds from miles away."

"Boy, wish I coulda gone hunting with them."

"Wouldn't thata been great?" Dad replied, his mind still spinning.

Then it was back to the fields. His new red Farmall-H tractor only pulled a two-bottom plow, like his five-horse team did, but it moved three times faster, so he could accomplish a lot more. The tractor had steel wheels with six-inch steel lugs and was a bumpy ride on hard ground, but it had good traction in the heavy gumbo soil on parts of the farm where the horses struggled with everything they had to keep the plow moving.

And even though there was no room for a passenger, GP could hold Eddie on his lap and let him enjoy steering the tractor. Little Eddie was far from able to steer the straight line that GP insisted on for all his furrows, but with Dad's hand lightly on the wheel, the furrows were still laid at least reasonably straight.

Before doing any seeding, GP pulled Eddie out of school for two days, and the two of them and Bertha took the wagon out to the fields to pick rocks. Walking over every yard of all the hills and high ground and bending over to pick up every rock bigger than a grapefruit was about the most miserable work any of them could imagine. And every year they had to do it all over again.

"I'd swear them darn rocks hatch little ones every spring," GP called out as he bent over to pick up a heavy rock and carry it to the wagon.

"Ja, they hatch better than my turkeys do," Bertha answered.

Eddie picked up a rock and couldn't help but wonder.

After spring planting, GP also bought a two-row cultivator that he could hook onto the Farmall, as well as a long-toothed buck rake to stack hay. Then he converted the seeding drill, the harrow, disc, and binder, all to be pulled by the tractor instead of horses. With grandnephew, Gilbert, hired to drive the tractor, and GP on the binder, they could harvest three times as much cropland as before. Farming was taking on a whole new cast.

Meanwhile, in the papers and in movie "shorts," they were learning names they had never heard before: Midway and Corregidor, Tobruk and Anzio, and a host of other horrific battles where friends and relatives were fighting and dying, some coming home horribly wounded and disfigured for life.

On the home front, every citizen was asked to use less and give more. The government issued Ration Books with red stamps for meat, fish, butter, and dairy products; blue stamps for flour, sugar, coffee, and other processed foods, with a "spare" stamp for miscellaneous goods.

"You can only buy what you got stamps for," the grocery man said, "and no more."

All these rationed items were in short supply, partly because the government ordered a lot of production shifted from consumer goods to war supplies, and partly to supply the millions of troops fighting in Europe and in the Pacific, along with war aid being sent by shiploads to Great Britain and Russia.

Shoes, lard, cheese, and canned fruits were all rationed. At the gas station, the pump jockey told every customer, "I can only fill you three gallons a week, with your ration stamp, and no more, that's it." When that was gone, they had to walk.

A special certificate was required to buy rubber overshoes. Rubber tires were pulled from the market and could not be bought or sold, with severe penalties for those caught in any such transaction. The Office of Price Administration, OPA, became policemen of the cash register.

GP and other farmers were given exemptions and could buy more gasoline and tires and rubber overshoes if they could prove the need; and even though some things could be obtained on the black market, pity the poor lout that got caught!

Posters and ads went up urging every loyal citizen to "Defeat the Nazis," and "Wipe Out the Japs," with grotesque caricatures of Hitler and Tojo featured in gaudy, eye-catching colors and dripping blood. One sure way to do so was to buy War Bonds. For just $18.75, all loyal Americans could help win the war, and in ten years, their patriotism would be rewarded by getting back $25 for helping to make the world safe for democracy.

Students, from first grade on, were urged to share in the war effort as well. The county superintendent issued Miss Hafner and all teachers an express kit containing a supply of U.S. Treasury folders and books of ten-cent war stamps.

"Uncle Sam wants you to help win the war," Miss Hafner told the students, "so try to bring some nickels or dimes to school every Friday and you can buy these special stamps."

When Eddie had accumulated 188 stamps and pasted them into his U.S. Treasury folder, Miss Hafner gave it to him and told him to have his parents take it to the post office in town and exchange it for a War Bond in his name. When he received the bond with his name on it, he felt as proud as General Patton winning a big tank battle.

One evening, when Fred and Selma and the children came over, Fred told about the president's recent fireside chat in which FDR described the serious shortage of rubber for army jeep and four-by-four truck tires and urged all citizens to help the troops by bringing any kind of rubber to collection points in town. Fred tried to remember just how FDR put it on the air, "I think he said something like, 'Look around your place for anything made of rubber that you don't absolutely need, from old tires to overshoes, worn out raincoats to bathing caps, leaky garden hose to broken rubber toys, and give them to win this terrible war,' something like that."

"I've got several old inner tubes," said GP, mentally doing farm inventory.

"And I have a broken rubber horse," added Eddie.

"And we can give those old rubber crib toys that are cracking, and my rubber bathing caps I got from working at the doctor's place in Bismarck," Bertha commented as Fred and Selma and daughter Lorraine added to the list.

The next Sunday in church, the members voted to dismantle the chain-link fence around the cemetery and donate it for scrap iron. The following Monday, as they gathered to tear it down, many brought along worn-out plow shares, disc blades, and other metal and loaded them on GP's truck to haul into town. He also took all the family rubber donations and threw them on the large mound of rubber contributions behind the Unruh creamery in town.

The Ration Board in town, meanwhile, was working overtime, getting ration books out to every man, woman, and child in the county. While it meant shortages of many items for city dwellers, for Valley farmers the hardship was lessened, since they raised all their own meat, dairy products, eggs, vegetables, and had their "Victory Gardens" long before the government asked all citizens to grow home produce behind their houses.

And while car tires could not be purchased by ordinary folk, and gasoline was limited to a few gallons per week, the Valley farmers could buy gasoline and tires for trucks and tractors, so rationing did not limit their daily life as sharply as it did their city cousins. Sugar was in short supply, coffee very limited, and some got terribly frazzled over tobacco shortages. Others lightened the pain by brewing their own beer and wine at home, while a few quietly made stronger stuff for battling all the bad news from every side.

Before church began one Sunday, Bertha and the women were visiting on the left side of the sanctuary when one of the younger women softly remarked, "I sure don't feel right coming to church without stockings, do you, girls?"

"Doesn't it make you feel almost naked?" Bertha added as a number of the women giggled.

"I miss my silk stockings almost as much as anything," added another.

"I just got runs in my last pair."

"We haven't really had nylons all that long, have we?" flew the comments.

"But we've sure gotten used to them in a hurry."

"And they make you feel so dressed up."

The conversation abruptly ended when the pastor walked in.

Several of the women were wearing their "old" brown cotton stockings and blushed, hoping none of the other women would comment on it. They all felt frumpy, but not being able to buy sheer stockings was one more price of war. Before the war, they could buy a pair of nylons for the price of a bushel of wheat. Now they were just glad to have their husbands declared 4-F and spared from the draft.

The men felt another pinch when orders came down from Washington to impose a national speed limit of thirty-five miles an hour on all driving. Every driver was to follow the newly proclaimed "Victory Speed" to conserve gasoline and tires—and thus help crush their evil enemies.

****

When GP came into the house one day, he commented to Bertha, "Boy, my throat is really sore. I can hardly swallow, it hurts so bad." Within a few weeks, it had grown increasingly worse; and when he went to Dr. Vinje in Beulah, the doctor recommended an immediate tonsillectomy. After nearly a week in the Hazen hospital, GP returned home, but still terribly ill and in immense pain, and had the neighbors worried.

Bertha pushed small spoonfuls of warm chicken soup down him as gently as she could, hoping its magic would work. The pain of swallowing was excruciating, and he was trying to take some crushed aspirin when Eddie came running into the house, "Mamma, there's a big black car coming."

In just moments, county coroner Harry Chilson and his assistant, each in black suit and tie, knocked on the door; and when Bertha answered, he said in his most solicitous undertaker's voice, "I'm so sorry to hear about your husband."

"Thank you," Bertha replied, "ja, he's been really sick."

"I just heard in town this morning that he died, and if it's all right, I came to pick up the body now," he continued.

From his bed of pain, GP faintly heard the conversation, and in shocked distress, hoarsely yelled out, "Hey, I'm not dead! At least wait a while!"

The horrified undertaker spent five minutes apologizing to Bertha, using every word, every gesture he could to amend the ghastly *faux pas* that he had in all innocence just committed.

"Without a phone . . . I heard . . . I really didn't know . . . I'm just so terribly sorry . . ." His voice finally trailed off, and he walked back to his hearse, shoulders slumped, a proud man defeated.

At the moment, GP failed to see any humor in this sad mistake, but the entire Valley soon learned of it and thought it was the funniest thing they had ever heard. The story was told over and over and grew as it went.

When they cried their next auction, before GP called for the first bid, someone shouted, "Hey, there's the dead man walking!"

"Ja, that was enough to make you wish you had a telephone," GP fired back, and the crowd roared. Never had he faced a gathering of more enthusiastic bidders.

At his retirement party years later, "the Chilson," as he was known, would recall that incident as the single most embarrassing moment of his entire life.

Chapter 20

Pow-Wow

Several weeks later, August Little Soldier drove into the yard and invited GP and his family to stop in and see their old house, which he had moved and fixed up on the Reservation. "We sure like it," he said with a soft smile. Then he added, "Me and my wife wonder if you'd like to come over and see it early next Saturday night, then we'll all go to the Pow-Wow."

When they got to the Reservation and walked into the main hall at Ree for the Pow-Wow, Bertha looked around and whispered to GP, "Did you notice, we're the only white people here?"

"Ja, but that's OK," he replied, surprised by how many faces in the room he knew, many from having stopped at Father John's in years gone by, and others more recently at their place.

Within minutes they were absorbed by the pounding rhythm of the big drums. Seven men sat around each of two drums at opposite ends of the room and alternated drumming. Each group of drummers was also called a drum, and swung their leather-knotted, two-foot drum sticks in high arcs, pounding the four-foot buffalo-leather drum tops in perfect precision and singing centuries' old tribal songs of lament and grief, of hunt and hope and thanksgiving.

Soon the floor was awash in whirling bodies, many clad in softest hand-stitched deerskin pants and shirts, skirts and tops, handsomely embroidered in stunningly intricate designs of beads in a rainbow of colors. Some wore huge feathered headdresses of many colors, round and wider than their shoulders, that stretched from crown of head to heel, and were passed down in their families for generations. Others wore simple headpieces with spiked hair or fur or tails from happy hunts. Their feet were shod with silent, deerskin moccasins, colorfully beaded in elaborate patterns as well.

The dancers were adorned with shiny beads in the rich bird colors of red and orange, of yellow and white, with sky blues and grass greens, along with earth browns and blacks. Reddish-tan faces shone with an exuberance that knew delight in life, even in dire circumstances. Tiny tinkling harness bells on straps around their ankles added to the driving enthusiasm that recalled centuries of living free.

There were dances for hunt and dances for war, dances for rain and dances for peace. The Osters couldn't understand the words, but from the cadence of the drums—now a steady throbbing, now a syncopated beat, sometimes soft and slow, then frenzied and ferocious—they still felt themselves becoming part of the spirituality deep within.

The drumbeat was matched by the expressions on the dancers' faces, sometimes pleasant, dreamy, relaxed, other times fierce and wild as they stabbed the air with slender wooden spears. They danced Creation and they danced Wounded Knee. They danced the circle of Mother Earth and Sister Sun, of Brother Buffalo, and of the People coming up out of the center of the earth. And they danced the loss of all in this Reservation not of their own choosing, where they had to beg for handouts from a Great White Father they neither knew nor wanted, who turned them into benighted orphans in a land that was theirs no more.

The young dipped and whirled in their double-stepped patterns, with every part of their body moving to the throbbing rhythm of the drums and the wailing vocal choruses. Ancient words poured through stamping feet and lively arms as bodies spoke in volumes. Old warriors, some cradling long clay pipestone pipes, danced their dreams again, just as determined as in days of old but with feet that now stayed closer to the earth. Silver-haired grandmothers with braids down to their hips, many with grandpapoose in arms, glided along like sinuous sturgeons in Missouri waters.

Beaming maidens, with long, shiny, undulating braids and darting jet-black eyes betraying hope and shy *I'm-here-see-me* smiles, danced with just enough flair to make their bodices bounce and young men notice. Fertile young mothers, with the fruit of their womb now covered in layers of beads, gently danced hand in hand. Sacred stories were rolled out here in unbroken procession, the memories of the old translated by the feet of the young. As the celebration went on, Bertha found herself mesmerized by the native liturgies unfolding in praise and intercession.

Seeing that unbroken chain of moving feet, GP's mind turned back to a verse they had recently read in family devotions: "How beautiful upon the mountains are the feet of the messenger who announces peace." *"May it be so,"* he thought, *"yes, may it be so."*

Somewhere toward midnight, the drummers laid their drumsticks across the taut drumheads, and suddenly it was over.

While the dancers headed for the doors to cool off, a team of young men came in, hoisting the ends of two copper boilers—one filled with meat, the other with fresh, hot Indian fry bread—and set them down in front of the Osters.

Little Soldier came along and, stepping in front of them, pointed into the first copper boiler and announced, "This is as fresh as it gets. The left half is venison, the right's beef."

"Sounds good," GP replied with a smile.

At that, Little Soldier cupped his hand over his mouth and bent close to GP's ear. In a low, guttural voice imitating the cowboy-Indian movies he rasped, "White man beef, heap good. M-m-m."

Both men guffawed while the people around them wondered what could possibly be that funny about a kettle of meat.

Then, with a mischievous smile, Little Soldier turned to Eddie and added, "There was some fresh roasted puppy too, but it might be all gone."

"That's all right," GP quickly shot back.

Bertha glanced down and noticed Eddie's face turned ashen, eyebrows raised high, and lower lip trembling. She reached down and took his hand. "Sh-h," she whispered, "sh-h-h."

GP leaned ahead on his log bench, suddenly taken aback when he saw that all the meat was raw. The powerful aroma of fresh-butchered beef, and venison even more pungent with a unique smell all its own, wafted up and drenched their senses. Like fresh blood sausage, once smelled it would never be forgotten.

Bloody, raw meat was not on the top of GP's list for evening food choices, but to refuse this generosity would be a high insult to their hosts; and since they were served first, all eyes were on them.

GP cleared his throat, put his hand in, and picked up a piece of blood-dripping beef. He softly nudged Bertha, and she followed suit.

When it came little Eddie's turn, he slowly slid off the bench and peered into the kettle. One look at the dripping raw meat and he knew this was a far distance from grandmother's fried chicken.

The parents soon realized, to their chagrin, that this was one treat he just couldn't handle. Bertha nodded to him and whispered, "Just take a piece and I'll eat it." But the tears welling up in his fear-struck eyes and his lower lip trembling even more told her he simply couldn't do it.

"Quick, take some fry bread," she whispered, and as the wonderful fried-dough smell coming out of the second copper boiler struck his nostrils, he smiled a tight smile, took a large slab of fry bread in both hands, and the day was saved.

Several weeks later, Bertha baked a batch of homemade bread with a yeasty, baked smell so rich that neither man nor dog could resist. For supper that night, she cut some slices and all three dipped them in fresh cream mixed with a dollop of chokecherry jam. A ring of fried sausage and several scoops of cottage cheese and GP commented, "This is about as good as it gets, don't you think, Eddie?"

Eddie suddenly remembered the pow-wow and grimaced but kept eating.

For Bertha, however, there was another problem. The second loaf she cut into had a large air space in the center of it. As soon as she saw the hole, fear stabbed like a knife into her heart. The old Tantas had a long-held tradition that now almost overwhelmed her. *"This means that someone close to us will soon die,"* her mind shouted. Without thinking, she tore the loaf into little pieces and ran outside, wildly scattering them for the chickens to eat. As disturbing as this awful incident was, she couldn't bring herself to share it with GP and spent the next days worrying over him and Eddie every minute they were out of the house. Nights only heightened the stress, and every time sleep fled she pleaded, "Oh, God in heaven, if it be thy will, have mercy on our family, and hold death away from us. Amen, amen."

She found herself hovering over Eddie, rubbing his back, mussing his hair until he began looking at her with quizzical eyes, wondering about all this sudden feeling-touching attention.

In bed at night, she curled up into GP just to feel the security of his body safely beside her. He took her cuddling to be an invitation and began slowly caressing her curves. When she drew away—wanting only security, not marital bliss—he was left adrift on a wedded sea, and in disappointment turned his back to her, leaving them both isolated and alone until they finally fell asleep.

Several days later, after morning chores, she walked over to Selma's and shared her story.

"You know, same thing happened to me a while back," Selma replied. "Scared the sauerkraut out of me, but nobody died."

With that assurance, Bertha felt the gnawing fear begin to melt away and, with one final prayer, left it in God's hands.

Not long after, Eddie asked, "Mamma, when you gonna make some good fry bread again?"

"When you learn to eat it with good raw meat," she chuckled, surprised at the ease of her laughter.

"Yuck, don't think so."

Finally the warm pow-wow with its fry bread memories had overcome the dreadful bread-hole memories and left her at peace once more.

Chapter 21

Incense of the Valley

For most of a year, news sources were reporting that the war was not going nearly as well as FDR and the military brass had hoped. MacArthur and the Allied Forces were driven out of the Philippines with many thousands of troops captured and forced on a horrendous Death March. Nazi forces swept over much of Europe and North Africa as well. German U-Boats were sinking American ships just off the Eastern coastlines, and there were fears that Japanese submarines would surface and attack the big cities along the West Coast. Blackouts were ordered on all windows facing the ocean on both coasts.

While Midwesterners were somewhat isolated from the immediate effects of the war, they soon experienced the wider impact. Before long, residents of Mercer County were joining a growing stream of thousands moving to the West Coast to work in huge new shipbuilding yards and factories of every sort. Women were putting on pants and working alongside the men in every kind of work. No longer were they mostly teachers and nurses and secretaries. Now they were pilots and riveters, truck drivers and welders.

When Selma and the family were visiting at Bertha's, Selma mentioned, "On the radio they're calling those women 'Rosie the Riveter.'"

"Well, then I guess maybe we are Rosie the Farmer," Bertha replied, holding up a piece of kuchen, "'cause they all gotta eat, you know."

"That'll be the day," Fred answered, "when they honor farmers for anything."

As the war intensified, concerns mounted in the Valley as well. At threshing time, when Keller shut down the threshing machine for morning lunch, the men gathered in the shade of a loaded rack; and as the women passed around kuchen and coffee, one of the men commented, "You know, the way the war is going, I'm getting a little worried."

"Ja, you think they'll take away our 4-F?" added another.

"You think they might draft us anyway?"

"Sure don't know."

"Could happen. Big shots in Washington can do what they want, you know."

"And not much we can do about it," GP said after a long silence.

Nothing more was said, but the topic weighed heavier on the men than a scoop shovel full of fresh manure.

Despite his calm at the threshing machine, GP was haunted all night by the thought of going off to war and his little son possibly growing up fatherless. He knew the American military was not the same as the cruel experience his father had endured in the Russian army, but it still caused a knot in his stomach. Just before morning light was fresh-born in the east, he got up quietly and walked outside. God's haunting question to a troubled Job suddenly whirled in his mind: *"Where were you when I laid the foundations of the earth . . . when the morning stars sang together, and all the sons of God shouted for joy?"*

Looking up to the great starry heavens, he saw the myriad morning stars with a new eye and felt God's quiet reassurance. With Schatzie leaning against his leg, looking quizzically up at him, ears cocked for any possible command to action, GP suddenly felt a strange surge of joy that made him want to shout. But he knew a shout in the morning mist would cause mayhem in house and yard alike.

As he continued looking up, the fading stars twinkling the last watch of the night sang a soft song of peace to his soul, and the whispering North Wind bathed his heart in a gentle bliss. It rolled through every fiber of his body, like the mighty Missouri calmly streaming along in the dog days of August.

"Thank you, Father. 'Great is Thy faithfulness, Thy mercy without end.' Thank you," he whispered, and Schatzie nuzzled his hand as if to add, *"Me too."* He smiled at Schatzie and, patting his head, told him, *"Guter Hund,* good dog," and wandered back into the house for another quick hour of sleep.

When GP went outside in the morning, he walked into a beautiful sight: a thousand diamonds gleaming from the tops of the needle stems of grass. The wet years brought morning dew back again, and it lifted his heart. When he went back into the house, he mentioned it to Bertha.

"That sight's more beautiful than the czarina's diadem that the folks talked about in the old country," he said.

"And sure a lot cheaper," she replied as they both chuckled at the strange silliness of the truth she had just spoken.

Several days later, when GP took a load of grain to the elevator, he ran into a man who had a '35 Chevy sedan for sale. The man was moving away and needed to get rid of the car by the next day. It looked in good shape, the price he asked was low, and GP bought it on the spot. On the way home in the truck, he began to worry, afraid Bertha would be upset and think he was getting *hochmutig,* uppity. But when they drove back to town and she saw the clean "new" green car, she loved it and felt they had finally moved into the modern age.

GP paid cash for the car, as he did for everything. Most all the neighbors operated the same way. The Great Depression left tentacles stretching into every nook of their brains, and their motto for the rest of their lives would be, "If you can't pay cash, don't buy it." The dry years would color their whole generation to their death. The only thing for which they would borrow money would be land and possibly a house. Nothing else.

The fall rains sprouted thousands of vigorous tumbleweeds in the stubble of the harvested fields as well as in the summer fallow. Since the disk left many tumbleweeds standing, GP hooked up the harrow to rake them out of the ground. Then he hitched up the hay rake and dragged them into piles to burn. The miserable, thousand-armed weeds caught in both the harrow's teeth and the rake's tines, clogging them something awful. Every few hundred feet he had to stop the tractor, lift up a section of the harrow, and use a pitchfork to wrestle the stubborn knots of weed out of the machinery. Same thing happened when he tried the rake. As he tugged and pried and yanked, he shouted an extended list of first-hand German and second-hand Russian words of malevolent disgust. They didn't reduce the trouble, but they made him feel better.

When he had the weeds raked into large piles, he climbed up on the tractor with a big sigh and drove home to do chores. After supper, as early dusk began to settle in and the afternoon winds died down, he tore off a fistful of outhouse Sears & Roebuck pages and, taking

Eddie's hand, walked out to the piles of weed balls. Late harvest dust had turned the setting sun blood red, painting the scattered clouds across the western horizon into an unforgettable explosion of color. It was so breathtaking that their feet stopped moving to let their souls bathe in the wondrous beauty.

After the colors faded, Eddie whispered, "Gee, Dad, that was really something."

"Aren't we lucky that God would bless us like this!"

"Yeah."

Then, kneeling with his hands cupped close to the ground, GP struck a wooden "farmer's stick" on his pants leg and lit a catalogue page to set the first pile of weeds on fire. The tumbleweeds exploded into crackling flames, shooting sparks high into the air, and produced such a satisfying aroma that it seemed to release a tight knot in GP's stomach. *"Ei, this feels better than a drink of homemade chokecherry wine . . . on a cold winter's night . . . after a long ride in the sleigh,"* GP's mind stretched on in pictures as he continued working.

Father and son stuck their pitchforks into the burning pile, and lifting out a flaming forkful, they raced on to the next piles and set them on fire. Looking across the Valley, they noticed more flames shooting into the air as several neighbors joined in battle against the dreaded, tumbling, Russian thistle. Each little bonfire quickly erupted into a hot blaze, then burned out quickly as well in a brilliant explosion, shooting up a shower of orange sparks and yellow-red flames.

As Eddie watched the fiery bursts up and down the Valley, his imagination shot into high gear, and he suddenly shouted, "Dad, it looks like Tonto's sending signals to the Lone Ranger!"

"Bet the Lone Ranger and Silver are on the way to help," Dad shouted back with a smile.

By the time they finished burning the last of the big tumbleweed piles, darkness crept across the Valley and they started for home, their way lit by the fall full moon. It beamed full orbed and pumpkin orange over the eastern hills, like another tumbleweed fire, then grew whiter and bigger until it seemed to be standing right over the nearby ridge of hills.

"Hey, Dad," Eddie whooped in amazement, "it looks like the moon is floating right down to us."

"Looks like the man in the moon is smiling at us, *gel?*" Dad replied.

Eddie reached up for Dad's hand, and they walked in silence, awed by the brilliant, friendly moon, their nostrils filled with the pungent, ambrosial smell all around them.

As the last fires died, a low cloud hung over the valley. To GP it grew into something strangely magnificent. "Smells like incense," he chuckled, "like a kind of earth perfume." Bertha, who had joined them, laughed, "Don't bother to buy that for me."

GP couldn't get the smell out of his brain. The intoxicating aroma gripped his mind, and when he got home, he got out his accordion. His fingers rolled over the keys, and slowly words of a two-stanza song began to gather.

There's a sweet-smelling incense in the valley.
There's a sweet-smelling incense of earth.
It's a strange plant th'world rolled upon us,
It's a thistle that feels like a curse.

But light it on fire, it's an offering,
And the sweet-smelling incense of earth.
It lights up the hearts of believers
And bids them lift a song of new birth.

At the next dance they played, GP paused for a moment and announced, "Last week a lot of us burned tumbleweeds, and a funny thing happened. A song rose up from the flames." Fred played an introduction, and they swung into the new song. The crowd paused to listen, and when the song was finished, there was stone-cold silence. For a long minute no one moved, and GP's heart sank at the awful thing he had so happily created.

Then a man called out, "Hey, do that one more time."

"Yeah, try it again," two more shouted. GP gave Fred a long questioning look, and they did it again. When they finished, a woman sang out, "One more time so we can all do it with you." This time the whole crowd joined in lustily belting it out together.

"What'r you gonna call it?" someone shouted.

"Don't know. How about 'Incense of the Valley'?" GP replied.

Every fall thereafter, that was to be their new theme song.

****

After school one day, Eddie and Schatzie discovered new fun by climbing over the gate and into the pigpen. Eddie found a stick and began chasing pigs, beating them as they ran. Schatzie thought the sport exciting and soon joined the chase, nipping at back legs, catching tails. Both of them were totally delighted at all the different squeals that came out of the distressed pigs.

When Mother heard the noisy commotion outside, she had visions of a pack of coyotes attacking, grabbed the broom, and raced to the pigpen. Shocked at the sight, she screamed at Eddie, "You dumb little poop, get out of there, right now!"

As Eddie climbed out, with Schatzie following through the boards, head and tail down, Bertha swatted Eddie's bottom with the broom, yelling in anger, "You do that again and we'll send you to reform school in Mandan!"

Eddie didn't know all the particulars about the reform school, but he knew that's where bad boys were sent for stiff punishment, and the tone in Mother's voice made the threat even more foreboding.

"I won't do it again, Mamma, promise."

Eddie would do anything he could for her, especially now. She was in the middle of having all her teeth pulled and dentures put in, and all the pain and stress were making her sorely irritable. GP and Eddie tried to be understanding, but her short fuse was making it difficult for all of them.

Several weeks later, Eddie and Schatzie were busy attacking the evil forces of Hitler's Nazis in the barnyard. Racing around, Eddie swung his swordstick and clipped a turkey's tail feathers. The shocked turkey gobbled wildly and flew off. Schatzie picked up the cue, and soon the two were bravely attacking these Nazi turkeys to win the war for America.

With wild war whoops, dog barking, and turkeys in fluttering panic, it didn't take Bertha long to figure out the scene in the barnyard.

Running out of the house, she screamed, "Stop that right now, you little dummy! Once more like that and you *will* be going to the reform school!" Eddie and Schatzie spent the rest of the afternoon dejected and sitting on the rocks at the stock pond, waiting for Dad to come home.

At the supper table, Bertha, still upset, launched into a review of the afternoon, clenching her case with, "And I told that kid if he does that one more time, we'll send him sure to the reform school."

Looking at Eddie for emphasis, she added, "Isn't that so?"

GP was surprised at his wife's anger but said nothing; he simply laid down his fork, raised one eyebrow, and silently shook his finger at his son.

"But, Dad," Eddie whimpered, "we were just trying to kill Hitler and stop the war. Don't you see?"

With that he burst into sobs, ran into his room, and threw himself on the bed, crying salty tears into his pillow until he fell asleep. For the first time in his life, he felt totally unloved and unwanted in this house. The night was long and hard as dark, scary monsters clawed at him and terrorized his soul through the endless witching hours.

The next morning both parents seemed cheerful, with the evening before long forgotten. But in Eddie's heart there was a yawning sadness he had never known before.

Hardly had he begun to recover from this frightful angst when late one afternoon a shiny new car drove into the yard. Two tall, well-dressed men in dark suits and Stetsons got out of the car and walked up to the house.

Eddie was playing in the barn with Schatzie when he looked out and saw the two strangers knocking on the door. Immediately, he just knew they were there to pick him up and haul him away to reform school. As fast as his young legs would carry him, he raced out the back door of the barn, Schatzie running beside him, sensing the terror in his master's eyes.

In short minutes they covered the distance around the hills and across the prairie to Uncle Fred's farm, shouting out of breath to his surprised cousins, "Me 'n Schatzie are killing Nazis! We need help!" He hoped the cousins would believe his story and not notice the terror gripping his insides.

He felt better when Aunt Selma called them all inside for a glass of orange nectar, and he tried to appear nonchalant as he announced, "Mamma's not feeling good, with her teeth, and said I don't have to come home for supper if I don't want to."

Selma wasn't so sure about all that but set an extra place for him, with the cousins glad for company.

After supper, Eddie piped, "Thanks, Aunt Selma," and slowly started for home, leaving Uncle Fred and Aunt Selma hoping everything was all right with Bertha. As soon as he was out of their yard and over the first hill, Eddie turned north and made a mile detour around his home, circling behind the hills to stay out of view until he reached the high bluff behind the house to see if the dreaded car was gone or if they might still be waiting for him.

Crawling on hands and knees through the sparse grass atop the hill, and keeping puzzled Schatzie down, he crept ahead until he could see the yard and the house. The hateful car was gone. Noiselessly he backed up until he was out of sight of the farm and retraced the mile-long circle back around to come home on the trail from Uncle Fred's. By now it was black outside.

"*Jung*, child, where have you been?" an anxious Bertha asked him, now more concerned and worried than he had seen her for a long time and ready to start searching for him.

"Oh, Aunt Selma made *fleisch kuechla* and asked me if I wanted to stay for supper."

The two strangers were never mentioned again, but they left an indelible print on Eddie's heart.

That Saturday, GP took Eddie along out to the field and let him ride the harness, hanging on to the hames. The easy motion of the strong, gentle horse and Dad's reassuring arms as he lifted Eddie off the horse spoke of love once more as a young boy's fractured heart began to mend.

****

After Christmas, the family was going to spend an evening at Uncle Adam's place to do haircuts and homemade ice cream. Eddie had received a pair of skis for Christmas and left early to ski the three quarters of a mile to Uncle Adam's while GP and Bertha would follow later with horses and sled.

Eddie thoroughly enjoyed going across the snow-covered prairies, taking the skis off and climbing up the hills through deep snow, then putting them back on to zoom down the other side. His balance was not yet good, and lots of wipeouts marked his path, but he finally maneuvered through the strands of two barbed-wire fences that stood between their farms and made it to his cousins' place. His two boy cousins also received skiis, and they were all enjoying short, easy runs down the hill behind their house when Ronald, several years older and wiser than the younger two, suddenly had another idea.

"Last week I licked the pump handle," he taunted smugly, "and I didn't stick at all. Bet you can't do that." That was a challenge the younger two couldn't pass up, and all three unstrapped their skis and raced for the water pump not far from the house.

When they reached the pump, Eddie grabbed the handle and stretched out his tongue to lick the frozen iron.

In the next instant, all they heard was a horrible muffled "aaarrrrggghh" as his tongue stuck tight and he couldn't pull it away. The other two grabbed his shoulders and tried to pull him away, but he only screamed louder, trying to hold his head close to the handle to avoid tearing his tongue out by the roots.

In the house, Adam was busy squeezing the handles on the hand clipper, cutting GP's hair, and almost dropped the clipper when they heard the blood-curdling scream outside.

"Uh-oh, there's big trouble," GP exclaimed as all four parents jumped up and bolted for the door.

They just opened the door when Ronald burst in, "Quick, come out, Eddie's tongue is stuck on the pump handle!"

Aunt Emma grabbed the big blue coffee pot on back of the cookstove and poured some into a bowl, handing it to Adam as they raced out to the pump.

"Hold still," GP told Eddie, "and bend you head sideways as much as you can."

Adam held Eddie's shoulders and added, "Don't move, and we'll pour some coffee on the handle to heat it up so it'll let go of your tongue."

As the hot liquid ran across his face and all over his coat, Eddie screamed like a wildcat, partly out of pain and partly out of fear that his tongue might end up torn to pieces.

When the pump handle finally let go of his tongue, they walked Eddie to the house, sat him at the edge of the table, and gave him several aspirin, the only thing they had for pain. A little older and a good snort of whiskey might have been used, but not for little Eddie.

While the rest cranked the freezer to make canned bing-cherry ice cream, Eddie sat at the end of the table, whimpering in pain as his blistering tongue seemed to swell into a hunk bigger than his mouth could hold.

When school started again after Christmas vacation, Eddie's tongue was still sore enough to keep him from talking, until the teacher finally remarked, "Eddie, you sure are quiet."

He mumbled, "Ah'm oshay," and the other students snickered, but for all of them it was a sobering lesson that none of them felt a need to repeat.

****

Before long it was spring, when another season of wild onions swooshed through the milk cows and meadowlarks trilled their sparkling songs atop the fence posts. Bertha wanted to get out, so GP took the family to see a Western movie. Before it began, Uncle Sam, in well-coiffed goatee and patriotic red, white, and blue ensemble, came on the screen and, pointing out at each member of the audience, again implored every loyal citizen who loved America to buy War Bonds, bring in all the scrap iron and rubber they could find, plant Victory Gardens, and save wherever they could. That announcement was followed by a universal news brief bringing a terse update on the raging war. The audience was encouraged by seeing the Allies driving the Axis forces out of the sands of North Africa and invading Italy; and they saw American GIs crawling across black volcanic rocks on the way to winning a costly victory on a tiny Pacific Island called Guadalcanal, which few German tongues could pronounce.

"Six thousand casualties they said," GP whispered to Bertha. "That's nearly half the population of Bismarck, we paid for one lousy island."

"But remember, they said we stuck the Japs with twenty-four thousand casualties."

"Well, I suppose that's a pretty good trade-off," GP grumped. He couldn't help but think of all the heartbroken mothers and fathers who experienced a knock on the door and a telegram delivered beginning with the terrifying "We regret to inform you . . ." Luckily, so far there were none in the Valley.

The entire audience erupted in cheers a moment later when footage of the brutal naval battle of the Bismarck Sea was played. It showed American and Australian dive bombers threading bombs down the stack of the Japanese ship *Kimbu Maru* and blowing up its load of aviation fuel and ammunition in a horrific exploding fireball. The cheering continued as the war correspondent brusquely intoned over martial music and the roar of explosions, "With the loss of only five planes and no ships, our brave Allied air and naval forces routed the Imperial Japanese naval force steaming for New Guinea and sank eleven enemy ships, inflicting thousands of casualties on the Japs. Our brave men showed them what America is made of." The fortunes of war seemed to be turning.

The theater crowd was relieved when Gene Autry and his horse, Champion, finally galloped across the screen, displaying their heroics in the new movie, *Tumbling Tumbleweeds.*

The movie's theme music was the lilting song of the same name, and GP couldn't get it out of his head. When he got home, he picked up his accordion and practiced until he could play it. When he wrote to KFYR in Bismarck and got a copy of the words, he and Fred soon turned it into their own theme song to open their gigs at dances and parties, alongside their own "Incense of the Valley." Every person who ever heard them play it could relate to the dreaded weed with the glamorized song:

Cares of the past are behind,
Nowhere to go but I'll find
Just where the trail will wind,
Drifting along with the tumbling
tumbleweeds.

I'll keep rolling along,
Deep in my heart is a song.
Here on the range I belong,
Drifting along with the tumbling
tumbleweeds.

It seemed like whatever event they played for, someone was also sure to ask for some of the old-world folk songs that were crowd pleasers, and everyone sang along. One that always brought smiles to the partyers was "The Bachelor's Lament" in their Schwabian dialect:

Heirata tu ich net, o net,	*-Marriage—I will never do;*
Heirata tu ich net.	*-Marriage not for me.*
Aber wenn a Schoene kommt	*-But if a real Beauty comes along*
Heirata tu ich doch.	*-Marriage it'll be.*

This year at Christmastime, there was another favorite everyone wanted to hear. Bing Crosby had sung "I'm Dreaming of a White Christmas" in the movie *Holiday Inn*, and it struck a deep emotional chord in the heart of all who knew a man or woman in the military, which was almost everyone.

"Do 'White Christmas,'" someone would yell out, and an immediate hush fell over the crowd as soon as the first chords sounded, many quietly singing along, others dabbing their eyes in quiet, heartfelt loneliness and prayerful concern.

After Christmas, at the end of a night's playing, when GP put the accordion down and set his wailing fiddle to crying the sweet melodies of the homeland, it flooded the heart of the old with profound memories that brought tears to many and a bittersweet end to the evening. They were so glad to be living where they were, but the good old days of life in the old country—when life was slower, simpler—also had a sweet taste that would forever flavor the tongues of these first-generation pioneers.

Chapter 22

Tired of Rationing

The war, it seemed, would never end. And it was bringing unimaginable suffering to people in lands where the fighting raged on a scale and in ways more terrible than any people had ever endured.

Rumors circulated about the Nazis having some kind of horrible prison/labor camps where unspeakable atrocities were being carried out.

"But," one neighbor argued, "our German people would never let that happen, even if Hitler and his crazies wanted to do it."

City cousins across America complained about their life being shrunk down in countless ways, but when the movie RKO News Brief showed them the devastation happening in Europe and in the Far East, they soon realized that their grumbling had much more to do with inconvenience than with suffering. With gas tightly rationed, people had to either walk wherever they wanted to go or stay home. "But that's a small price to pay," the pastor said in a sermon after he heard a number of people complaining over coffee downtown.

In the Valley, however, the war still seemed far away. So far, no Valley men were killed in battle, and the biggest shortages were sugar and rubber tires. Some car inner tubes had blown out so often and were taken off the rim and patched so many times they looked more patch than rubber. And sugar for canning peaches and pears and bread-and-butter pickles and for baking the always necessary kuchen was strictly rationed and ever in short supply.

"If you want kuchen," Bertha told GP, "you better cut out sugar in your coffee."

And for Eddie, her word was "If you want canned peaches next winter, you better start eating your puffed wheat with no sugar on it."

Neither liked it, but changes had to be made.

In church, the pastor led them in fervent prayer for an end to the awful war. And at home during family devotions, GP led the family as well in nightly prayers for peace and an end to the killing that was making the whole nation weary and depressed. The future appeared terribly uncertain. "Just seems like you can't plan anything past a week or two," Bertha told GP over the *fleisch kuechle* she made for supper.

Despite all the grim news, the spring and summer rains were plentiful, and the harvests filled the bins with grain for several years running.

GP and Bertha decided that since their son was doing rather well in school, this might be a good time to get him a pony. When they mentioned it, he was so excited that he streaked out into the yard, running and shouting until he set Schatzie into frenzied barking that in turn set the chickens squawking all across the yard. Even the pigs caught the fever and began squealing and running in their pen. "Ja, I think he'd like a pony," GP laughed.

At one of their auctions, GP had heard about an Oelke family in nearby Hazen having a pony for sale, so they drove to look it over. When they got there, the owner had two ponies, one a filly and her brother a perky gelding. They were half Shetlands, both jet black, the gelding with a white star on his forehead.

When Mr. Oelke took them into the fenced-in pasture area, both ponies eagerly came toward them, sniffing for a snack. Eddie petted each of them and instantly fell in love with both.

"Which one do you think you'd like?" GP asked.

"I like 'em both," Eddie replied, looking hopefully at Dad with an ear-wide smile.

Suddenly the little gelding nuzzled Eddie's arm and rubbed his head on Eddie's shoulder, and that decided it.

"What's his name?" Eddie asked Oelke.

"Barnie."

"Well, I suppose we'll take him then," GP said slowly and half grudgingly, trying not to sound too eager so the price wouldn't shoot up before they were done.

They shook hands, and GP said they'd be back the next day to pick up Barnie.

On the way home, they stopped at Christ's and asked if Cousin Gilbert, five years older than Eddie, could go along tomorrow and ride Barnie home. He would have an eighteen-mile ride across country, and riding bareback meant a long, rump-wearying, bouncy ride.

The next day, when dusk fell and Gilbert still had not arrived at GP's place, they grew worried and drove over to Christ's to see if he stopped there instead. When he wasn't there either, the men got on GP's Chevrolet and started to drive the back section-line prairie roads toward Hazen. When they got several miles out, they spotted a rider silhouetted against the night sky as he came over a high ridge and knew immediately who it was.

Christ breathed a big sigh of relief and chuckled, "The old folks used to say *'At night all cats are black,'* but we'd know that cat anywhere, *gel?*"

When Gilbert rode up to them, he explained, "I'da been here earlier, but I kinda got lost back there someplace and had to ride in to a couple of farms to find where I was."

The next few days, Eddie practically lived on Barnie's comfortable, warm back, galloping him out to the pasture, then back into the yard. There, with legs dangling, he lay on the pony's back and watched the lazy clouds drift by as Barnie noisily munched mouthfuls of grass.

GP and Bertha had never seen their son happier. Every time Eddie raced into the house and picked up the dipper for a drink of water, he beamed and said over and over, "Thanks, Mom. I sure like Barnie." And for several days when GP was still at a distance, coming in from the field Eddie shouted, "Barnie's so much fun, he's my favorite. Thanks, Dad."

In these times, even puffed wheat without sugar wasn't so bad, and Father drank his coffee black without complaint.

Chapter 23

Barnie's Chain

Since Barnie was new to the farm, GP didn't want to turn him into the pasture with the other horses; so after several weeks, he borrowed a twenty-five-foot, light-link chain from Cousin Adam and staked Barnie out to graze at the edge of the yard. With the war on, metal chains were impossible to buy, so the borrowed chain was some valuable equipment.

Watching Barnie slowly move around on his light chain gave Eddie a brilliant idea: *"I could take the chain off the stake and clip it on my Red Flyer wagon and let Barnie pull me around the yard while he's grazing."*

It was so wonderfully relaxing that Eddie lay back in the wagon with eyes soon restfully drowsy. Then it happened.

A monster horsefly bit Barnie in the neck, and he snapped his head to shake it off. The chain clattered and rattled the rickety old Red Flyer whose wheels were already worn wobbly, and totally scared the wits out of Barnie.

The frightened pony did the only thing he knew how to do—get out of there—and bolted like a streak of lightning. In two jumps he was thundering out of the yard and headed north, across the prairie, into the hills. Eddie's frantic yelling only frightened him more.

Several yards of super-speed travel and Eddie was separated from the Red Flyer, with grass stains on his face. The wagon was bouncing high in the air, with Barnie's arched neck just as high, tail arched even higher, sharp hooves churning up buffalo grass.

Picking himself up, Eddie screamed and tore after pony and wagon, which suddenly lived out its Red Flyer name and was already growing small in the distance. Soon Eddie, with tears running faster than feet, started coming across scattered Red Flyer pieces and knew immediately that big trouble lay waiting at home.

When he finally found Barnie, in the farthest corner of the pasture over a mile away, the pony was still snorting, wide-eyed and terrified, and refused to let Eddie approach him. After half an hour of slowly circling each other, with Eddie doing a lot of tear-filled talking, Barnie finally stood still long enough for Eddie to catch him. But Eddie's heart sank into his leather high-tops when he saw that the precious metal chain was gone.

For several hours, Eddie rode across the rolling prairie hills, following the path he thought Barnie had run, but the chain was nowhere to be found.

As dusk descended, he rode home and put Barnie in the barn. Mom and Dad had finished milking and chores and were sitting at the supper table.

"Where in the world have you been?" Mother asked.

"I had to get Barnie."

"What happened?"

"Well," he stammered, "I was sitting watching Barnie graze, and a horsefly must have bit him, and he snapped his chain and took off running."

"This long?"

"Well, I couldn't catch him. He was really scared."

"You got the chain?" Dad asked sternly, suddenly seeing a deeper story here.

"I guess, I guess maybe it got lost."

"What do you mean, 'I guess'?"

"Well, it musta' come off when he ran."

With the Red Flyer missing and Eddie coming home this late, it didn't take an Eisenhower to figure out what had happened.

"Tomorrow you're gonna find that chain," Dad scolded, leaving no doubt, "or you're gonna get the strap! *Verstehscht du,* you understand?"

That night Eddie prayed more fervently than he had for a long time.

When the rising sun hit his window, Eddie lit out of bed, soon with overalls up and high-tops laced. Breakfast was a silent affair, quickly over, and he clapped his cap on to start his desperate mission.

During that whole long day, he covered every square foot of that pasture, followed every rutted cow trail, looked into every buffalo wallow, searched around every single fence post and every large rock and boulder across the hills. The chain had simply vanished.

Several times he barely missed stepping on clumps of prickly pear cactus that lay half hidden in the buffalo grass on the high ground. Their nasty two-inch-long, needle-sharp spines could puncture a worn leather sole, and he silently cursed both cactus and bad luck with some of Dad's favorite grown-up words of fire.

As he half walked, half ran over the whole prairie area, erect purple cone flowers and black-eyed Susans with blazing yellow petals stood lonely sentinel among the grasses, waving to get his attention, but his eyes were blind to everything but that dastardly metal chain.

That night when he slumped into his bed, dog tired and afraid, he turned again to prayer: *"Dear God, I'm in big trouble, and I really, really need your help. If I don't find that chain, Dad'll strap me good. Please, God, please help me."*

With his stomach churning and mind reeling in review of every detail in that large search area, sleep came in spurts most of the night. But somewhere close to cock crow, he had an amazing dream. He saw a large, four-foot-high granite boulder which was a favorite of his out in the high pasture, and curled up in the grass beside it rested Barnie's chain. *"Thank you, God,"* he silently prayed and slept until Mother woke him.

He gulped a quick breakfast, telling Bertha, "I think I know where the chain is," and left the house running. It didn't take him and Schatzie long to reach the boulder, and he raced toward it, already feeling the cool chain in his hand. To his shock, he found . . . *hootzla,* nothing. Several times he circled the huge stone, but there was nothing. His heart sank, his trusting faith crushed, and through bitter tears he screamed, "God, why did you do this to me?"

At dusk Bertha saw him coming and knew from the slump of his shoulders what the story was and wanted to hug him but thought better of it. Supper that night was another silent affair. Both parents noticed several tears rolling down Eddie's cheeks but said nothing. Another day of fruitless, dusty walking in the hot wind, and Eddie felt more forsaken than ever. On the fourth day he climbed up on another large boulder to look over the area while Schatzie ran around the back of it. Suddenly Schatzie came around the side, snarling and growling and twisting every which way. As he turned, Eddie saw why: he had hold of a huge diamondback rattlesnake and was snapping it from side to side with every ounce of his strength. The frenzied snake repeatedly tried to strike Schatzie, and once he yelped, but finally he shook his head so fiercely and bit so hard that he killed the snake. While its tail was still wriggling, Eddie jumped off the other side of the rock and stroked Schatzie's head, "Good dog. What a fighter you are!" Schatzie wagged his tail, seemingly appreciating the compliment.

When they got home that night, Eddie described what happened, and Dad went out to check and see if Schatzie was all right. He was wagging his tail and seemed fine, eating his pork chop bones from the table with his usual delight.

By now GP's threatened use of the strap on Eddie had cooled down, but he said, "Tomorrow we're going to drive over to Adam's, and you're going to tell him what happened to his chain."

When he was told, Uncle Adam replied, "Well, you know I paid a hundred dollars for that chain, and with the war on, it's worth a lot more right now."

Eddie's heart sank, afraid of what was coming next.

"So I was thinking," Uncle Adam went on, with a wink to GP, "maybe I'd have your Dad sell it at an auction and make some money on that thing, but I guess that's all gone now."

"You think that chain really cost a hundred dollars?" asked Eddie on the way home.

"I don't know," GP replied. "Maybe not quite."

Eddie felt sick, still wondering what consequences were yet to come over that whole thing.

When they got home they noticed that Schatzie didn't come out to meet the car, as he always did.

GP grew concerned and went out to the barn, where he found Schatzie lying on the straw in one of the horse stalls. When he called his name, Schatzie finally got up but seemed to have no energy. Dad noticed a swollen area below the dog's right eye.

"I don't think Schatzie's feeling very good," Dad told Eddie and asked him to take some food to the dog. He ate a few bites, licked his lips and stopped, resting his head back on the ground.

The next day Schatzie didn't get up at all, and when Eddie sat down beside him, he raised his eyes but didn't lift his head from between his outstretched paws.

"What's the matter, Schatzie?" Eddie asked as he curled up beside his pet and softly stroked his head. The dog slowly turned his head and looked at Eddie with eyes that broke his master's heart. Never, neither on man nor beast, had Eddie seen eyes that were so crushingly forlorn and sad. Eddie thought he saw a tear standing in the corner of those heavy-laden eyes and started to cry.

When he held a little bowl of water for Schatzie to take a drink, the dog took several laps and, whimpering ever so quietly, slowly turned his head and began licking the back of Eddie's hand. For long, long seconds he just softly, slowly licked and licked, then laid his head back down between his paws and closed his eyes.

A few moments later he was terribly still, and Eddie noticed that he wasn't breathing anymore.

When he shook him, he realized his beloved pet was gone, and he lay down beside him and wailed great heart-wrenching sobs until his whole body shook.

Just then GP walked into the barn and put his hands on Eddie's shoulders. "Dad, he's gone," Eddie cried out. "I think he knew he was going to die, and he licked my hand to say good-bye."

Then he laid his face on Schatzie's neck and wept bitter, salty tears until tears would come no more.

When Dad finally reached down and stood Eddie up, he held him tight for a few moments, then quietly whispered, "You know, that rattler got him in the cheek, and that's what made him die. Schatzie saved your life out there."

Slowly they made their way to the house, and Eddie lay on his bed and wept until he fell asleep. *"Come back, Schatzie,"* swirled through his frazzled mind over and again, *"come back, Schatzie, I need you."*

He wanted to pray, but try as he might, words simply would not hang together.

Chapter 24

Black Cow Down

The weather turned cloudy in late afternoon. With supper finished, GP walked outside and noticed the barn swallows all a-twitter, swooping around the yard. Usually that behavior signaled a storm coming.

Sure enough, angry black clouds were soon churning in the western sky, lightning rent the heavens, and thunder rumbled through the ether. Since the cattle were grazing in the pasture toward that direction, he grabbed his denim jacket and raced out to drive them home.

"*Donner Wetter*, thunderation, *this is a big one coming*," GP muttered to himself as he ran.

When several sizzling lightning bolts shot straight down into the tall, blue-clay buttes on the western slopes of the Valley two miles away, it looked like the Archangel Michael slinging javelins at the firmament, and GP felt a touch of panic.

By the time GP had the cattle rounded up and nearing the yard, driving rain was slashing sideways, and he held his jacket over his head, shouting to hurry the nervous cows. Just then, as Bertha and Eddie were watching from the house, a horrific bolt of lightning struck straight down into the middle of the little herd, and in the same instant thunder crashed with such a deafening explosion that it nearly knocked them to the floor.

"Oh, dear Lord, no!" shrieked Bertha, afraid that the deadly firebolt struck GP and scorched him to an instant death.

In one burst, the mass of flying hooves shot ahead, and through the pouring rain Bertha caught a flash of GP's jacket, still running with the cows. Without stopping or slowing down, he left the cows milling around the barn and sprinted to the house with a speed his legs had never reached before, eyes big as coffee cups, ears blown shut.

"Are you all right?" Bertha cried.

He couldn't hear her but shouted, "I—I can't hear, but I'm OK."

A while later, when the rain lifted, GP looked out the window and noticed that their black cow, Nellie, lay dead where the lightning struck, hooves burned black, legs in the air.

"*Lieber Gott.* Oh, dear God," GP shouted through trembling lips, "Nellie was running right beside me when the lightning hit, and she's down."

That evening, when GP read the usual chapter in the Bible for family devotions, Bertha could not keep her mind on it. And though she seldom prayed out loud during these times, after GP finished his prayer she couldn't keep still.

"Oh God, dear Father, I can't thank you enough for saving my dear Gottfried tonight. You are so good to us." GP didn't hear it, but when he saw her lips stop moving, he added, "Amen."

Later in bed, he continued silently, *"Lord, my hearing is gone, and it's so scary right now. Please, if it be thy will, let my hearing come back again. Amen."*

The next morning, he was startled when the crowing roosters woke him up. He bolted upright in bed and nearly scared the wits out of Bertha yelling, "I can hear!" Quietly he added, "Thank you, my Lord, so much."

****

Soon the Valley turned a brilliant gold, the season when the wheat fields ripened into golden waves rippling in the wind like the waters of the swift Missouri, the season when the grasses lay down for shivering rest, and tall cottonwoods began whispering winter to each other in the Missouri bottomlands.

One evening when chores were done and the fiery late-summer sun was nearing the western horizon, GP said, "Let's climb up the hill behind the house and look over the valley."

When they reached the top and sat down on the outcropping of large shale boulders, the scene was breathtaking. The sun was blood red, huge, standing just atop the closest hills. Miles of gilded wheat fields stretched up and down the valley in every direction.

"Looks just like the ocean waves that Grandpa Oster talked about coming over on the *Armenia,*" GP mused.

"Seems like all of a sudden the whole world is turned to gold," Bertha observed, thrilling at the majestic sight in front of them.

In the distance, a meadowlark trilled the closing song of day.

"Look at those two hawks circling up there," Eddie said, pointing up, "they're so high you can just barely see 'em."

"You know, I'm so glad our parents took a chance and came over here from the old country," GP mused. "Living in this beautiful place is the best life I could ever think of."

Bertha nodded in agreement, "God has been so good to us, hasn't he."

Eddie was glad to see his parents so happy. "But I sure wish Schatzie was here with us," he whispered forlornly, "I still miss him."

"He was such a good dog," Mother added, hugging him. She took his hand, and they started back down the steep slope, just as the sun slid behind the western hills.

Above them, two sleek, brown-and-white, speckled nighthawks were hunting insects and doing their whistling dive over the stock dam, ushering the family into the house with contented smiles on their faces.

The next week GP strapped in the canvases that were driven by the heavy bull wheel of the binder and put the binder into wheat. As the machine whirled and clattered through the wheat stalks, he kept a sharp eye on all the moving parts; and every fifteen yards he pushed the bundle carrier pedal, dropping piles of bundles in straight rows across the half mile width of the field.

When Bertha was done with house chores, she slipped a pair of denim pants under her cotton work dress and set out on the long walk to the fields. She would rather have skipped the dress, but she didn't. *"Men wear pants. Women are meant to wear dresses."* That was the dictum of the day, and Bertha followed it.

In the mighty war production plants out on the coasts, women were now wearing pants, and in one of the Universal News Briefs in the Roxy Theater, a clip showed women with kerchiefs on their heads, wearing pants as they worked on the line, some even smoking. One of the women in the audience was heard to say, a little overloudly, "Nu, are those hussies, or is this what the world is coming to?" No one answered, but many wondered.

Still, in this mini breadbasket of the world, the old ways held sway. Here pants could be worn but only under a dress, even in the relative privacy of a large Dakota wheat field.

Now, with pants under her dress and wide-brimmed straw hat tied under her chin, Bertha hooked two fingers in the handle of the clay water jug and headed out to the field. The gallon jug, wrapped in old cut-up denim pants, had been soaked in water to keep it cool and now felt comfortable when she brushed it against her leg as she walked. In her other hand she carried a three-tined pitchfork, and soon she was setting the long rows of piled-up bundles into shocks, with Eddie helping as he could.

When the men finished bindering the field, they shut the machinery down and joined Bertha in shocking the bundles. Half a mile on a single row, eight bundles to a shock, and on to the next row. All that work, in the scorching hot south winds of August, and it seemed like they got nowhere but thirsty. Never was there a drink more refreshing than walking back and getting the clay jug out from the shade of a shock back in the first row. Never mind that the water was lukewarm by now. It was wet.

As they continued shocking in the heat, all motion became mechanical and talking ceased. The scorching wind sucked all the moisture out of their skin without them feeling it drain away. They were relieved when GP said, "Let's stop a minute and make some gum."

Each of them took a handful of the heads of wheat and ground them in the palm of their hands until the kernels were separated out. Blowing away the chaff, all popped a handful of kernels in their mouths, ground them up, and had a delicious mouthful of gum to chew.

"Good stuff," Bertha commented with a smile.

"Helps keep my mouth from drying out too," Eddie added.

GP wielded his fork in steady rhythm, but his mind turned to the changes that were sweeping the land, and he was glad for tractors to spare the horses from the misery of long, waterless hours on the binder as they had for a number of years. But his heart grew heavy as he reflected on how the tractors also caused a lot of horses to become useless in a short time as farmers downsized from six and seven horses to just two or three. Cattle buyers now became horse buyers and bought them from farmers by twos and threes and fours until stockyards were filled with thousands.

For GP, like so many, selling several of his beloved horses seemed like betrayal as he thought back, *"These weren't just some 'dumb animals,' they were like my family. Each one had a name, a personality, a history. Some worked better in the furrow, some in the lead. Others on the left of the hitch, still others on the right. Ja,"* his thoughts jumbled on, *"and a few were lazy and needed a touch of the whip once in a while to get them to lean into the collar and pull."*

He thought of old "Bill," and a tear welled up as he remembered, *"He used to nuzzle my hand and nod his head when I slipped the bridle over his head to tell me he was ready to go to work. And now he's gone."*

The men of the plains became deeply attached to these workmates, and selling them left many a man with guilt and sharp pain. They hurt with crippling grief over the loss of these soul mates who had labored so long and hard, who knew the men's moods by the inflections in their voice, and shared so many exhausting days together on plow and disk, drill and binder, mower and hayrack, manure spreader and heavy sled. For the men to know that their faithful companions would see green pastures no more, and that they were now headed instead for slaughter in some distant glue factory, brought nightmares to many a man of the soil, even as it did to GP.

Meanwhile the grain shockers were nearly finished with one of those endless rows, and GP's mind returned to the work at hand. Just then an explosion shook the stubbles.

A covey of speckled brown partridges erupted from the wheat stubble just ahead of them and shot into the air, wings whirling in furious motion and chattering loudly in disgust at being disturbed.

"Boy, a scare like that," Bertha quipped, "and you could end up with wet pants."

"Ja," GP shouted back, "they could blow the rivets off your overalls!"

The rest agreed and laughed at being that startled by such innocent little creatures.

One more large field to shock, then four smaller ones, and GP's crops were in. As soon as all the neighbors were done as well, the threshing machine would roll in and harvest would be finished for another year.

It was a good year not only for crops but, as they discovered, also a great hatch for crows. They descended on the ripening cornfields by the thousands, and tens of thousands, darkening the sky when the great flocks flew in and descended on an area.

Their shrill, raspy cawing could be heard a mile away. Each, it almost seemed, had matriculated with honors from some Northern States Crow College, and all had majored in voice projection. Sadly, their magnificent voices proved all the more irritating to human ears, right up there with fingernails on blackboards.

Farmers up and down the Valley got out their shotguns and blasted away at the winged corn huskers, but their feeble efforts were of little avail. GP with his 12-guage and Eddie with his BB gun joined the hunt as well. They got to the cornfield early, and as the black cloud of scavengers descended around them, GP shouted to Eddie, "Them suckers sound like a thousand auctioneers gone crazy on moonshine!"

Father and son both shot at the same time, and several crows went down. "Dad, I got one," shouted Eddie.

"You sure did, Son. Good shot."

GP shot a dozen more of the sharp-beaked scavengers, but the flocks just moved to the other end of the field, landed on the stalks, and kept pecking the ears of corn until the cobs were stripped nearly clean. The flocks were almost frighteningly organized, with guards around the edge of the feast, hopping along the ground in their unique two-footed hop, constantly sending reports of any danger to the noisy eaters. For days on end, sunup to sundown, they plagued the fields, retiring at night and roosting in the trees of ravines several miles away. Early the next morning they were back.

When cold weather and sleet finally moved them south, the corn harvest, much to the irritation of the Valley farmers, was reduced in some fields by almost half.

****

Soon the weather turned colder and it was hog butchering time, and that meant neighbors getting together to do the job. When GP and Bertha decided on a day, Christ and his wife came over to help. As soon as all the sausage was ground and mixed and stuffed, the men finished trimming some meat cuts while the women lit a fire under the big cast-iron rendering cauldron to heat all the excess chunks of fat that had been trimmed from the meat. As it melted into liquid, they skimmed off the impurities and ladled it into used tin syrup buckets to cool into pure white lard for baking and cooking.

Bertha set two buckets of lard aside, and on their next trip to Beulah, they took it to Unruh's Cream Station where it would be scraped into large barrels and donated to the War Victory Drive. President Roosevelt asked all Americans to help win the war, and this was one of rural America's donations that would be turned into glycerin, which in turn was used to make bullets and explosives, to help the men on the front lines defeat their implacable foes.

"Doesn't it make you feel good," Bertha said, "to know that we are really helping the boys win this terrible war?"

"Seems like such a little thing," GP replied, "but it sure adds up when everybody pitches in together."

While they were in town, Bertha stopped at the Five and Dime to pick up some bobby pins and rubber bands for her hair.

"Sorry, but we haven't had either one for a long time," said the storeowner. "The war, you know."

When she asked for work socks, for GP's Christmas present, she got the same answer. She'd have to darn the holes in the heels and make the best of it.

As they were driving down the street on the way home, Eddie noticed a curious little flag in a house window. "What's that little white flag with a gold star and a red border back there in the window?" he asked.

"That's a gold star flag," Mother replied. "It means they had a man killed in the war."

"Hope we never get one of those," Eddie spoke up, deep in thought.

When they got home, Bertha unpacked the groceries, and she poured out a little pile of strange things that looked like dried bananas.

"What's that?" Eddie wanted to know.

"St. John's Bread," Bertha replied. "My mother told me about it, from the old country."

"How you supposed to eat it?"

Bertha held one up, and it looked like a brown, wrinkled banana. She tapped it on the table and said, "It's kinda hard, but you can chew it. But be careful—it's got some real hard little seeds inside that can crack your teeth if you bite down on 'em."

Eddie took one and carefully bit into it.

"Tastes kinda funny."

"It grows on trees and comes from the Holy Land and countries around there. They call it locust, and that's the stuff John the Baptist ate in the Bible story."

"Wow, I'm eating Bible stuff." Eddie laughed.

"And those hard little seeds are carob, and that's what they made chocolate out of."

"Wish we could grow some of that here, and we could give some to Jesus if he comes by."

GP drove the car into the garage, and when he came to the house he called out, "We have a little time before chores. Eddie, let's walk up to the Indian grave."

"Oh, yeah, let's go."

GP took Eddie's hand, and they walked in contented silence, each wrapped in their own thoughts. Twenty minutes hard walking and they reached the top of the high hill. Sitting on the stone cairn, both enjoyed surveying the wide horizons stretching in every direction, now turning a soft, shrouded blue in the far reaches.

Turning northeast and looking over the Missouri, GP pointed and asked, "See that point where the river turns south and the land sticks out like a little thumb?"

"Think so."

"You remember, in school, learning about Lewis and Clark?"

"Yeah."

"Well, a little over a hundred years ago they explored this country for the first time, and August Little Soldier one day told me that his great-grandfather was there when Lewis and Clark made camp on that point, on their way out West."

Eddie's eyes grew wide. "Wow!"

"The grandfather said they came in the biggest canoes he'd ever seen, and those were the first white men he ever saw too."

"Must'a seemed weird, huh."

"Ja," GP chuckled. "August said his father told him, 'My grandpa always said those white men with hair all over their faces looked like the Great Spirit only got them half baked in his fire.' Then grandpa'd look at his hands and add, kinda quiet, 'But their blood was red and warm, just like ours.'"

On the walk home, Eddie kept seeing Mom pulling loaves of bread out of the oven, looking all lumpy white and doughy.

"Yeach," Eddie finally mumbled.

"What?"

"Half baked!" Eddie looked up at Dad's face and laughed.

Cold weather also meant getting all the hay hauled in from the hayfields and stacking it close to the big barns. But first they had to clean up the leftover hay from one of last year's stacks. As GP and Eddie were pitching the musty old hay on the rack, several mice ran out from the pile. The three yard cats anticipated just that happening and were on the spot, catching the mice before they could escape and eating them whole.

"Look at them cats go." Eddie laughed.

"Hey, count how many they get," GP replied.

"Must be half a dozen already."

When they were done, the three cats had captured forty-three mice. "Boy, they look sick," Eddie said.

"They won't need supper tonight, that's for sure."

Later, when they were milking, only one cat showed up for the nightly ritual of getting a squirt of milk from GP.

****

The holidays were soon upon them, and for Christmas Eve worship services the Oster brothers, with wives and children, formed a choir of seven. They sang *"Stille Nacht,* Silent Night," and Martin Luther's beautiful *"Vom Himmel Hoch,* From Heaven Above to Earth I Come," the moving hymn which all the adults knew by heart and silently hummed along. More than a few wiped tears, remembering grandparents and Christmases past and babies laid into the cold ground just beyond the windows outside.

A skinny, seven-foot-tall, short-needled Christmas tree stood in the corner beside the high pulpit, bravely trying to add cheer to the evening with a scattering of multicolored balls, foil icicles, and five-inch white candles in holders clipped to the branches. It was carefully guarded by deacons sitting next to the flickering flames and armed with buckets of sand in case of any errant flare-up.

All the children were dressed in their best Christmas prairie finery, *strublich,* tangled, hair slicked down by Mother with a quick lick of her fingers and a few swipes across the hair. Each had a special verse of Scripture or a Christmas rhyme they had to stand up and recite in front of the congregation. Most of them, with great fear and trembling, got through it. Their reward was a little brown sack filled with hard Christmas candy, a handful of peanuts, and a big shiny apple.

When they got home from church, it was time to open presents. Bertha and GP exchanged gifts they had made for each other. Eddie received a pair of magic Scottie-dog magnets—one black, the other white—and an eight-inch, rubber-tired, iron Farmall-H tractor that had somehow made it through a toy factory without being seized by either the rubber or iron police of the war effort. As much as he loved the Farmall, he loved the Scottie dogs more for all the tricks they could perform.

After church on the second Christmas Day, GP and Eddie were munching nuts when GP split a peanut open and held it up to Eddie.

"Look close at this tiny little chunk at the top," he said. "See, it's got a pointy hat, eyes, nose, and a double-wedge beard. That's Santa Claus, and he's in the middle of every peanut." Eddie never ceased being amazed at the Christmas mystery of peanuts.

Chapter 25

"I Will Fight No More Forever"

The *Beulah Independent* carried an article quoting Chief Joseph, chief of the Nez Perce Indian tribe. Just a few years after Custer was killed in the Battle of the Little Big Horn, Joseph's people were chased in bitter pursuit across three northwestern states to corral them into a reservation and were finally brought to terrible devastation. When Chief Joseph and his people at last gave up to the American armies, he laid down his rifle and ended his memorable words of surrender with, "From where the sun now stands, I will fight no more forever."

"Sure wish Hitler and Tojo would say that," GP commented as he read the paper.

"Guess we haven't got them cornered yet," Bertha replied.

Still, by '44, the fortunes of war were definitely turning in favor of the Allies. When GP took the family to the Roxy Theater in Beulah, the Movietone News Reel showed the bloody, thundering battles of Saipan and Guam as the Allies bombarded those islands. With aerial attacks and with the mighty sixteen-inch guns of several heavy battleships hurling frightful, explosive shells, they finally captured the islands and moved across the Pacific, ever closer to Japan.

Then the news reel, with Lowell Thomas's succinct commentary, switched to Japan itself and showed high-altitude pictures of Tokyo in flames as great B-29 Super Fortresses, new off the production lines, dropped tons of bombs on that city. Finally, the reel switched to the European Theater. Thousands of ships were trailing wakes and belching smoke, and the sky was dark with wave after wave of droning planes. Suddenly the big screen was filled with beaches awash in bodies and blood, shells exploding all around in terrifying confusion, the air thick with smoke. Wounded men screamed in agony, and the dead floated by in silence. The theater goers watched in shock as body parts bobbed on the waves. The sand was washed in blood, the heavens angry with death. In seconds, the faraway war came home and tore through the Roxy hearts. The horror of war became only too real. That night in the theater they were witness to the costly invasion of France on D-Day, drawing the noose ever tighter around Hitler. Even after the feature movie ended, the crowd walked out in total silence with dark shadows dogging their steps.

"Holy cows," Eddie piped up from the backseat of the car on the way home after the movie, "did you see all them airplanes flying?"

"Almost as thick as the grasshoppers a few years ago," GP replied.

"Reminded me of Armageddon in the Bible," Bertha responded.

GP was glad Eddie hadn't focused on the lifeless bodies bobbing up and down in the raging water. He couldn't help but think, *"Like our poor old horses, they'll see green grass no more."*

In school, Eddie had his own little war to fight. Miss Hafner was gone, and their new teacher was a rigid young man who was a part-time preacher and a conscientious objector to the war. Instead of going into the military draft, he took the government option of serving his country by teaching in the rural school system. He was part of a small Christian denomination with whose worship practices the Wittenberg families strongly disagreed and warned their students to be careful.

One of the mothers said, "Remember the saying in the old country, *'There'll be trouble if the cobbler starts making pies'?*" The saying meant that people should stay in their own field of expertise and not mess around in stuff they don't know about. "Ja, ja," came the reply.

All Eddie knew was that this new teacher was a gruff sort, and he didn't like him at all; and besides, he didn't smell good like Miss Hafner.

One day Eddie had just brought his money up to the teacher for his War Bond purchase, and while the older students were bringing theirs, he got his little Scottie magnets out of his overalls pocket and ran them around on the top of his desk. When another student snickered at the neat tricks of the magnetic Scotties, the teacher looked up and saw them. For some unknown reason, it infuriated him; and with several giant steps and a scowl, he stomped across the room and slammed his map pointer so hard across Eddie's desk that the pointer shattered into splinters.

"Don't you *ever* bring those things to school again!" he shouted at Eddie, the veins bulging in his flushed face.

The whole school was frightened by the sudden outburst, and Eddie's dislike was stronger than ever. "Oughta call him Teacher Grump," Eddie whispered to himself.

Earlier, through the teacher's position on war, they had learned the meaning of the difficult word "pacifist," but out of the corner of his mouth Eddie quietly sneered, "Doesn't seem like much of a pacifist to me!"

Just before the school day ended, there was a stir of excitement as the students looked out the windows and saw Duke calmly walking up the road and into the schoolyard. Duke was Albert Keller's big, spotted St. Bernard, and he was hitched to his two-wheeled cart come to pick up the Keller girls, Elsie and Irma, from school.

Every morning they got on the cart at home, a mile away, and drove Duke to school, then turned him loose and he walked home alone. In the afternoon, Mr. Keller harnessed him up at home, told him "Go get the girls," and off he went with a glance at his master and a wag of his tail.

During all the time that faithful Duke did this important family job, no neighborhood drivers ever met him on the wrong side of the road, nor did he ever run off after a rabbit or skunk or baying coyote on a nearby hill.

As soon as Teacher Grump rang the closing bell, Eddie and the rest all ran outside to pet Duke, who happily wagged his tail and knew every one of the students, if not by name at least by smell.

****

When GP was reading *The Dakota Farmer,* he ran across an article about registered Hereford cattle, describing them as rather docile animals, good beef producers, and well suited to survive outside during the harsh Midwest winters. As he read the article a second time, the idea of raising his own herd began to intrigue him. Several days later, he talked with Fred, and they both thought it worth a try.

The article mentioned the Albers Hereford Ranch near Hannover, and the next Sunday, after church, GP put the family in his car and drove to see the Albers.

Driving down the road with the car windows open, they were bathed in the distinctive smell of sweet clover that once inhaled is forever branded on the brain. The road ditches were full of the yellow-flowered clover, moving GP to remark, "Kind of smells like heaven, doesn't it?"

While the women visited in the big ranch house, Ted and Martin Albers took GP and Eddie on the pickup and they drove through miles of the Albers' verdant, rolling pasturelands inspecting the herd.

"I'd like to get three cows," GP said after several hours of looking, "with another three for my brother, Fred, and a young bull that we'll share, at least for a while."

"I could make you a good deal on young, bred heifers that'll have calves next spring," Martin replied, and soon they had six and a young bull picked out, all in the Domino line.

"They're all registered," Martin pointed out, and all had the perfect Hereford markings—reddish-brown body with white face and brisket, white underbelly and "socks," white "scarf" along the top of the neck, and white tip on the tail.

By the end of the week, the cows were in their new pastures, and the Oster Brothers were launched into the Registered Hereford business.

****

One night during the middle of winter, the snow was deep and an Alberta Clipper was gripping the Valley with blistering cold and BBs of sleet and icy snow. The family were all deep in the middle of dreams when Bertha woke up to voices outside.

She poked GP, "There's somebody outside."

He got up, grabbed a flashlight, and opened the front door, which was always left unlocked. The dim light illuminated two unfamiliar Indian men and a woman standing on the porch, all dressed in light jackets, no overshoes, and nearly frozen, eyes pleading for help and begging for warmth.

One of the men seemed wobbly, hanging onto the woman's arm. As soon as they were inside, they explained that their car had quit running some distance down on the gravel road.

"We didn't know what to do," said the shorter man. "There was nobody coming along, and if we stay on the car we freeze to death. So we had to try and walk."

"You did the right thing," GP replied. "I'm glad you made it here."

"We didn't know what to do, but we were hoping maybe you could help us."

After GP got them up the steps and into the kitchen, he offered them chairs and went to get Bertha up. In a few minutes she had wood in the cookstove and a fire going to make coffee and some sausage sandwiches. With the leftover heated water, she filled the rubber hot-water bottle and laid it on the cold floor for the woman to put her feet on.

"Oh, I don't remember when I ever felt anything as good as this," the woman said, wiggling her stiff, numb toes.

"By the way," the short man spoke up, "I'm Andrew Crowfoot, and that's Frank Running Wolf and his wife, Anna."

"Hello," GP replied.

"Maybe you noticed that Frank can't see. He was blinded in the war."

"What happened?" GP asked.

"A shell exploded too close, and it got my eyes and my face. Kinda rough," Frank replied.

"Sorry you had to go through that," GP replied, feeling bad for the man across the table who looked right at him but saw nothing. "That war's been bad for way too many people."

"Yeah."

"Well, let's wait till morning, and we'll take a look at your car," GP continued.

"Trouble is," Bertha put in, "we don't have any beds for you to sleep on."

"We don't want to be any trouble," Anna piped up, waving her arms in the air.

"Best I can do is put some blankets and quilts on the floor," Bertha replied.

"That'll sure beat freezing in the car all night," said Andrew, nodding his head and shivering at the thought of what might have been.

In the morning, after milking and finishing chores, Bertha cooked up steaming bowls of cream of wheat with fresh milk to fill the six empty stomachs. After they finished eating, GP harnessed the team to the sled and he, Andrew, and Eddie drove down to see what they could do with the stalled car.

By now the sleet had stopped, and GP's first thought was to check the gas, but the gauge showed half full. Against all odds, the battery had endured the cold and still cranked the engine, but it would not fire. After checking a number of things, GP unclipped the distributor cap and found moisture, now turned into ice crystals, in the distributor.

"Wish I had a blow torch," he said. After thinking a moment, he got a farmer's stick match out from the dozen he usually carried in his side pocket and struck it on the engine block. When the flame flickered, he cupped his hand around the distributor and held the match close to the metal wall until it burned out.

"Not much happening," he said, but after five more matches, the ice crystals had turned to tiny droplets of water, and he wiped them out with his handy red handkerchief and replaced the distributor cap.

"OK, Andy, hit the starter, and choke 'er a few times," GP instructed.

Several cranks and several sputters and the engine caught and began running.

"Man, you ought to go into car repair," said Andrew, thankful and impressed by GP's automotive diagnostic skills.

After they had run the car long enough to get it thoroughly warmed up, GP said, "Let's shut 'er off. The snow's too deep to drive the car to the house, so let's drive the sled home, and I'll bring you all back in the sled too."

When they got home, Bertha fixed a quick early dinner of fried eggs and potatoes, a panful of bacon, and homemade bread with chokecherry jam. As an afterthought, and without thinking of Frank's situation, she warmed up a small bowl of canned peas she had left over from supper the night before.

Eddie was all eyes, since he had never seen a blind person up close before, much less a blind man eating. He tried not to stare, but he was awed by how gently Anna took Frank's hand and softly touched it to the different food items on his plate, after which he took the knife and fork and comfortably fed himself until his plate was clean.

After a big round of thank-yous, the visitors climbed into the sled, wrapped in blankets Bertha sent along, and GP and Eddie hauled them back out to the car. When they were safely on the road, GP took Eddie to school and explained to Mr. Grump why they were late.

At recess, Eddie couldn't stop talking about what had happened at his house, and especially about the neat blind soldier who was an instant hero to Eddie.

He was still bubbling when he got home from school. No sooner had he raced into the house than he shouted, "Mom, Mom, did you see Mr. Frank? He never even dropped a single pea when he was eating!"

"Don't you wish you could do that?" Bertha replied. "And you can see!"

"I sure am glad, Mom!"

That night, and for a number of nights to come, Eddie's prayers included heartfelt thanksgiving to God for the wonderful gift of sight and to watch over the blind man.

****

For a number of years, GP plowed across a knobby hill south of the farm, and each year it produced nothing but rocks.

"You know," he told Bertha, "I wonder if there could be gravel in that hill. A lot of real fine sand, and little stones turn up every year when I plow it."

The next day he drove over to Bauer's coal mine and borrowed a core drill. He drilled down some ten feet, pulled it out, and checked the drillings. Just as he suspected, and deeply hoped, he found soft sand and the smallest pebbles of gravel, the best cement-sand you could find anywhere.

Within the hour he had the front-end loader hooked to the Farmall and started pushing the very thin layer of topsoil off the little hill. Then he moved to the base of the hill and put the loader in, dumping a pile off to the side. When he got off the tractor, he picked up several handfuls of sand, ran them through his fingers, and let out a full-bellied "whoop" so loud that Bertha heard it in the house a quarter of a mile away. It wasn't long before word got out that some of the best gravel to be found was at the Oster place, and GP was busy loading it out at four bits [50 cents] a yard at the pit.

"What's a yard?" some asked. "And why don't you sell it by the ton?"

"Well, first of all, I don't have a scale to weigh it out," GP answered patiently time after time, "and second, gravel is sold by volume, not by weight. So a yard comes out to two thousand seven hundred pounds instead of two thousand in a ton, and you get more for your money. Fair enough?"

The further he got into the deposit of gravel, the better it got, just the perfect consistency of sand and fine stones for making cement. GP liked to stop the loader and walk around in the pit, picking up handfuls of the fine mineral and letting it run through his fingers. "Dear God, what a treasure you gave me here," he sang out time after time.

Before long, several trucks a week came for gravel, and some weeks several dozen. Other people wanted gravel hauled to their site, so GP invested in a two-ton Ford truck with hydraulic dump box, and soon he had a fairly profitable side business going, gravel at a dollar and a half a yard.

****

On one of their gravel-delivery hauls, GP and Eddie drove into a yard where several children were playing with a litter of winsome, half-grown puppies.

While GP dumped the gravel, Eddie ran over to see the puppies.

"What kind are they?" he asked.

"They're mutts," came the reply.

"Why, would you like one?" asked another child.

Just then, one of the little pups jumped up and licked his face. "What's his name?" Eddie asked.

"We call him 'Cuddy,'" the youngsters chorused.

In just a few minutes, with Dad's OK, Eddie had another dog of his own, to replace Schatzie.

When they got home, Eddie ran into the house carrying Cuddy and shouted, "Mom, Mom, look what I got!"

"Oh, I think he'll be nice," Bertha replied, taking the bright-eyed little tail-wagger in her arms, as he wriggled to lick her face. "I like him already."

That night, Eddie patted down a soft bed of straw in the barn for Cuddy, gently laid him in it, and brushing his head once more, bade him, "Good night, Cuddy. We're going to be good friends."

But no sooner had he slid the barn door shut than Cuddy began crying and scratching on the inside of the door.

"Mom, I just can't let him cry all night. He's really lonesome, and he'll get too scared," Eddie begged. "Can't I stay in the barn with him tonight? Please?"

What could Bertha do but get out several blankets for GP to take to the barn, where he made a little straw bed in an empty stall, ready for Eddie to curl up with his new puppy. GP hung the kerosene lantern on a peg and turned the wick down low, letting it guard against the shadowy specters of the dark. For two nights, Eddie and Cuddy shared their barn bed, bathed in the rich barn smell and the soft grinding of cows chewing their cud, with sparrows fluttering in sporadic flight among the timbered joists. After that, Cuddy had to settle for Barnie and the cows to keep him company during the long, dark nights. Soon the animals all seemed a well-adjusted four-footed company, ready every morning to join their people in the tasks of the day.

Chapter 26

"V" Days

Selma was busy doing dishes, with the radio tuned to KFYR, Bismarck, when the program suddenly stuttered. "We interrupt this program to bring you this important announcement: The President of the United States, Harry S. Truman, has just announced that Germany has surrendered to the Allied Forces, and the war on the European front is over. I repeat, the war in Europe is over!"

Selma almost dropped the plate she was washing but managed to land it in the rinse water, and grabbing a dishtowel she raced out to the field where Fred was working. Running, jumping, crying, wildly waving her dishtowel, her incoherent screams scared the wits out of Fred, whose mind flashed a thousand terrible things that could have happened at home to make her this hysterical.

Fred shut the tractor down and heard her screaming, "It's over! It's over!"

"What? What's over?" he shouted back.

"The war. Germany just gave up, it's over."

Fred gave a big yell, unhooked the tractor, and with Selma standing on the hitch behind his steel seat, he pulled the throttle all the way over and lumbered home as fast as the steel-wheeled tractor could travel—which now seemed unbearably slow. "Gosh," he shouted back at Selma, "fast gear on this thing is slower than molasses in January!"

When they got home, they jumped in the car and raced across the prairie trail to GP and Bertha's. At the gate, Selma had her hand on the door handle and bounced out before Fred got the car stopped. She sprang out like a cowboy leaping off his horse roping a calf and in one motion lifted the wire loop to release the gatepost and flopped the wire gate down to the ground. Fred gunned the engine to drive through, and the tailpipe barely cleared the wires when she had the gate lifted back up and flipped the loop to close it.

Honking the horn to alert a now frightened Bertha, they both shouted, "Hurry up. Get in the car," and as soon as she was in, they both bubbled out the wild news and raced out across the summer-fallowed field to pick up GP.

"Quick, get in," Fred shouted as he drove up to GP's tractor.

GP's heart sank, wondering what awful death he was about to have to deal with.

"Did someone in the family die," raced through his mind, *"or another big shot like Roosevelt or Hitler or like Mussolini hanged upside down?"*

As he got into the car, the other three were shouting, arms waving, the wives crying, and the words "war, over" reverberating off the windows. When he slid into the backseat, Bertha, wild-eyed, jumped on his lap. *"Ei, yei, yei, like a heifer in heat,"* crazily boomed through GP's mind in that frantic twinkling until sanity returned and the big picture of a suddenly changed world came into focus.

"Ach, lieber Gott, danke schoen. Oh, dear God, thank you, thank you," was all he could get out, choking up on the words after three and a half years of anguished prayer for the terrible war to be over.

After several more minutes of hugging, with all talking at the same time, the full enormity of the moment began to strike home and they slowly became still.

"Let's drive down to the school," Bertha suggested, "because a lot of the families don't have radio at home and haven't heard the news yet."

Fred put the foot feed to the floor, yelling, "The hell with the Victory Speed. Let's kick the lead out and get there, now!"

When he turned off the gravel Valley road and started up the hill into the schoolyard, he leaned on the horn button and didn't let up until he braked to a skidding stop in front of the flagpole.

The blaring car horn had all the students thinking terrible emergency, and they erupted out of the school door, followed by their frowning, scowling teacher.

Selma and Bertha charged out of their passenger doors, shouting, "The war is over! Germany just surrendered! The war's over!"

The students went wild, cheering, jumping, yelling at the top of their lungs. One of Eddie's classmates ran back inside, grabbed the teacher's hand bell, and raced around the schoolyard, ringing it so furiously that the clapper got warm from being slapped against the bell.

The commotion got so loud that several nearby neighbors heard it on that warm and still May day and came speeding up to help deal with whatever had gone wrong, and soon they too were part of the exuberant, dancing prairie celebration. Their shouting hushed the meadowlarks into silence for half a mile around.

When things finally settled down somewhat, Selma held up her hands and declared, "The president said tomorrow the whole country should celebrate V-E Day."

"What's V-E?" asked one of the little ones.

"Victory in Europe," she replied. "It means we won the war, and that ugly Hitler's finally dead."

Cheers went up again until the teacher finally announced, "Let's all come here and join in thanking God for this victory." He led them in a stretched-out, adult kind of prayer and after the amen told them, "All right, we've had enough for today. I want you all to go home now and tell your parents the good news."

The next day, officially declared by President Truman as V-E Day, was mostly another day of work in the Valley. At noon, GP and Bertha had a quick lunch of fry bread with strawberry jam and knoepfla soup, and Bertha looked deep into GP's eyes and whispered, "You know, I think I'll remember this special Tuesday, the eighth of May in '45, for the rest of my life."

"Well, the war in Japan sure isn't over yet," GP softly replied, "but this day is just about as big as the day we got married, isn't it."

They both smiled in deep gratitude, as she was now at the stove heating a small kettle of lard to make *fleischkuechle*. GP walked up behind her and put his arms around her. Surprised, she moved the kettle off the burner and turned around, kissing him with a long, heavy kiss. Their hearts flowed together and they celebrated this joyous moment with a freedom they had not felt in years.

"You know," GP whispered, "through all these terrible years of the drought and then the war, I didn't realize how tired out I was getting."

"Ja, seems like I'm ten years younger all of a sudden," Bertha whispered in return.

Then it was back to work . . . with a smile.

"Happy V-B Day," GP tossed over his shoulder as he walked out the door whistling "The Bachelor's Lament."

That week's *Beulah Independent* bannered the historic moment with two simple, four-inch, heavy-print black letters—*V-E*—and followed the headline with several columns summarizing the end of the war in the European Theater.

Church on Sunday gave the whole Valley a chance to celebrate and give thanks. The celebration, however, had a bittersweet taste to it. While they were thankful for victory and part of the war being over, how could they be thankful that a people who shared their own mother tongue, many of them Lutheran believers as well, were now ravished and destroyed, left homeless and starving?

For worship, Pastor Gunter Grossmann had chosen "*Nun danket alle Gott*, Now thank we all our God, with hearts and hands and voices" as the opening hymn, and never was it sung with more fervor or deeper emotion. The pastor spoke movingly about the meaning of the victory that had been achieved by the Allied forces in Germany. "But remember," he continued, "God won a far greater victory for us on a cross in a lonely place called Golgotha, and three days later beamed hope all the way to eternity with a mighty Resurrection."

But during the prayer at the end of worship, the congregation was stunned when the pastor's voice trembled and abruptly stopped, his shoulders shaking, as he dug into his gown pocket for a handkerchief to stem the flowing tears that suddenly overwhelmed him.

After he regained his composure and ended the service, people were buzzing in the parking lot wondering what happened to him. Many thought it was a profound sense of gratitude for the war being over. GP, who was on the church board, was also concerned and, after quickly checking with Bertha, invited the pastor and his wife home to dinner.

During a moment of small talk, when dinner was finished, GP got up his courage and asked, "Pastor, we couldn't help but notice your tears today. Is everything all right?"

"Well," Pastor Grossmann replied, after picking up his fork and studying it for long seconds, "as you know, I grew up in Germany and did all my pastoral training there. They sent me as a missionary to the German immigrants in America, and I ended up here among our Germans from Russia."

After a long pause, he continued, "I've never mentioned that I grew up in Dresden, one of the most beautiful cities in the world. My family's still there."

"Please don't tell anybody," he went on, "I hope I can trust you and Frau Oster that this doesn't go any further, but I have a short-wave radio, and I've been listening to broadcasts from Germany. You know I love America, and support her in every way as a loyal citizen, but I'm terribly concerned about my family back there. Do you understand?"

"Of course," GP and Bertha replied as one.

"Well, our news here hasn't said much about it, but the Allies sent a thousand bombers over Dresden in February, on the night before Ash Wednesday as a matter of fact, and firebombed the whole city. Out of six hundred thousand people in the city, they said as many as one hundred thousand might have been killed. A report from England said the second wave of bombers could see the glow of the fires going up from a great many miles away."

His lips began to tremble, and after a long pause he slowly continued, so softly they had to strain to hear. "The broadcasts said 90 percent of the city was wiped out, and I haven't heard from any of my family since that time. I don't know if they're alive or all dead. My heart is so heavy."

When tears began to stream down his face, Mrs. Grossmann broke down sobbing and, picking her lace handkerchief out of her sleeve, buried her face in her hands.

Bertha got up and leaned over the back of Mrs. Grossmann's chair, holding her and gently rocking her back and forth.

No one quite knew what to say after that, and they sat for a long time in silence. Finally GP asked the pastor if he would lead them in prayer. After his heartfelt imploration, they all got up, and the Grossmanns took their leave.

Neither guests nor hosts were huggers, but in this moment they all hugged as the Grossmanns expressed effusive thanks for this kindness from these dedicated sheep of his flock. "And please, dear Herr und Frau Oster," Grossmann said as they stepped into their car, "please keep this in confidence, won't you?"

"Of course we will," GP replied. "Is it all right if we just tell people you still have family back there, and you're worried about them, and hope we'll all pray for them?"

"That would be kind of everyone, yes."

With that brief explanation, the curiosity among the congregation was quickly turned to deeper caring, and many a prayer was sent heavenward for their hurting shepherd and his family.

****

Over the next few months, GP and the family found the movie newsreels to be more gripping than the movies as they showed footage of the horrendous Pacific battles of Okinawa and Iwo Jima. The reels captured the unbelievable bombing and ear-shattering explosions, the sixteen-inch guns of navy battleships hurling tons of munitions, flamethrowers shooting burning streams of napalm into caves, and enemy soldiers bursting out, on fire and screaming in agony. It culminated with Gabriel Heatter detailing the marines raising the Stars and Stripes on the rocky top of Iwo Jima's Mount Suribachi. To nine-year-old Eddie, it all seemed somehow terribly exciting, and he told his cousins, "Wow, I sure want to be a soldier when I get big!"

But for all three of the family, the most brutal newsreel of all was Edward R. Murrow's soul-wrenching commentary as cameras recorded the atrocities during his harrowing coverage of the newly liberated Nazi concentration camps at Buchenwald and Dachau. They saw thousands of people with huge eyes staring out over sunken cheeks, ribs showing through, arms and legs starved down to thin sticks of skin-covered bone. Mouths with teeth missing were hanging open in mute agony beyond all feeling. The starved people were more skeleton than alive, hardly able to move, and the sight left everyone in the theater sick to their stomachs. When the cameras panned to mounds of contorted dead bodies piled up like great jumbled stacks of chopped wood, then focused on a huge wire bin full of human hair that was to be used to stuff mattresses, many in the theater were too shocked to watch and too stunned to turn away.

The brief reel concluded with requiem music and the haunting comment, "Every one of these unfortunate souls was so recently an energetic, vibrant human being, with fond hopes and talents and dreams, and now the vacant stare on their gaunt faces looks through you like a wounded animal begging to be put out of its misery."

After those horrific scenes, very few in the audience remembered the movie that followed.

During the ride home in the car, Bertha, GP, and Eddie each silently replayed the awful scenes they had witnessed, and for a long time no one said a word.

"How in the world," Bertha finally said, "could anybody do something like that, much less people that speak our own mother tongue?"

"If somebody doesn't believe there's a devil," GP replied softly, "he should be made to see those pictures. We just saw the devil at work."

Back home, they walked into the darkened house. GP struck a farmer's stick on his pants leg and lit the kerosene lamp on the kitchen table. "Let's sit down," he said, "we need to pray." When all hands were folded, he bowed his head: "Holy Father, with the world aflame on both sides of the globe, we humbly pray forgive your people their sin and bring an end to this awful suffering." After a long pause, he slowly continued, "And thank you that in your mercy you have spared us in this land from such terrible pain and death. Amen." To see that horror and be sitting in the warm comfort of their humble home left both GP and Bertha feeling guilty for days on end.

****

GP was working on the binder, getting ready for harvest, when he remembered something Fred brought up back in March and how disturbed Fred was about it. "The radio said that yesterday the Allies sent hundreds of those big B-29 bombers over Tokyo," Fred had told him, "and it said they killed more than one hundred thousand people by dropping over a million firebombs."

"I can't imagine a million anything."

"They said it made a firestorm so hot all over Tokyo that it melted bricks and turned asphalt into running globs."

It had sounded like Dresden all over again, and now a terrifying thought flashed through GP's mind, *"Will this slaughter never end . . . or are we standing at the door of Armageddon?"*

Then after supper, Fred knocked on the door and invited them over to listen to radio broadcasts coming in about a new bomb so frightening that the newscasters could hardly find terms to describe it. "They're calling it an 'atomic bomb,'" Fred said.

As they gathered around the radio, the stentorian voice of Lowell Thomas came on to describe it once more. "This Monday past, August 6, at eight fifteen in the morning, Japanese time, a lone American B-29 aircraft has changed history. The plane carried just one bomb, a terrible new weapon just developed for our American military forces. When this one single atomic bomb was dropped, it exploded with the brilliance of a star coming in and blowing up a few thousand feet above the ground. In just seconds, the blinding light of its enormous explosion and resulting blast forces leveled much of the city of Hiroshima, Japan, melting everything for several miles in every direction."

As the devastating words continued to pour out of the radio, they stared dumbfounded into each other's faces and one after another muttered, "Ei, yei, yei."

Lowell Thomas went on, "The explosion of the bomb, which with no little irony was dubbed 'Little Boy,' sent a glowing orange fireball cloud mushrooming some sixty-thousand feet into the Japanese sky. Follow-up air surveillance, several hours later, showed only the stillness of smoke and dust where just a short time before there had been a thriving city of some three hundred fifty thousand people. Military analysts have estimated that as many as one hundred fifty thousand people may have been killed in this one flash of blinding light, with a stunning power never before seen in all of human history."

As the report ended, GP spoke what he had thought earlier, "Is this God's way of starting Armageddon?"

"I don't know," Fred responded, "but it sure could be."

"But remember," Bertha put in, "the Bible says there'll be angels flying and signs in the sky."

"Yeah, I guess we haven't seen anything like that," GP replied, shaking his head, his stomach in knots over the meaning of what they had just heard and the possible import of it for the days ahead and for their children's days to come.

Two days later Fred came walking over again and told them, "The radio just said that we dropped another atomic bomb on another Jap city. They said it was made of different stuff and was even stronger than the first one. They said the explosion might have gotten seven thousand degrees hot, and the blast made winds of six hundred miles an hour. Not much left of that place either."

"That's more than my little brain can put together," GP surmised.

"Dear God, what's happening to our world?" Bertha added, shaking her head.

Such figures were way beyond anything Eddie could grasp, but from the adults' reactions, he knew it was bad, really bad.

GP and Eddie spent the next days bindering, and all three joined in shocking the wheat. Several evenings when they stopped and then finished the chores at home, Bertha sliced some cold cuts of *schwarta maga* and with fried eggs, bread, and strong coffee made a quick supper. And each night they walked the half mile to Fred and Selma's to listen to more broadcasts about the war.

On Sunday, without anyone discussing it, nearly all the families arrived for church an hour early, and animated talk centered on "the bomb" and the war.

The men, gathered around Renner's car, kept repeating, "I just can't imagine anything with that kinda power." It was as if each one was saying it for the first time.

Reports had described the bombs as having the force of twenty-thousand tons of TNT exploding in one horrendous blast.

"Just think what a coupla sticks of Bauer's dynamite can do to a rock," said another. "Now multiply that times a million or something and see what happens."

"You could fill every house in Beulah with all that dynamite and still have a pile left over."

"Blow that up all at once and see what a hole that'd make!"

"And that's still nothing compared to what they dropped on Japan."

The women, gathered in a back corner of the church, talked a different direction, going to concerns of the heart.

"I can't help but think of all the children that are horribly burned."

"And don't have any parents left. What are they going to do?"

"They don't have a home left to go back to."

"Or food to eat, or water."

"Or medicine for pain."

"So many people are just terribly burned, they keep saying."

"And there aren't even bandages to wrap them up."

"And most of the hospitals are gone."

"Doctors and nurses gone too."

"And stores and schools and everything."

"And what about all the Tantas and crippled old people who somehow made it through alive and now can't take care of themselves?"

These dear believers quickly saw a side of war that no one really wanted to talk about, especially the slightly voyeuristic news reporters, and least of all the ardent military whose priorities were body counts and turf control, with human suffering left out of all the careful calculation.

Back home, each night Bertha made sandwiches or fresh kuchen to take to Selma's for lunch, while Selma put another fresh egg into the big coffee pot on the back of the kitchen stove and added more strawberry nectar to the Redwing cooler. Lunch lifted worried spirits, but the radio broadcasts became more gruesome with every passing day.

Now the descriptions turned from "thousands killed" and "square miles devastated" to the suffering and the slow, tortured death of those not instantly obliterated, the side of every war that the hosts of little people have to endure so the unscarred, well-fed leaders can proudly proclaim victory and take control.

Reports began to detail the cost of war that is not figured in dollars spent but in blood spilled. But they gave no scale, offered no cup to measure. The nameless eyewitnesses could begin to tell. But they were not much heard and soon forgotten. History would allow them scant testimony. It was more intent on recording wins and losses and which general counted coup.

For a tormenting moment in '45, the human tragedy shone through. One commentator relayed the report of an Imperial Japanese officer who had been sent to Hiroshima to investigate the damage.

"I saw women," he reported, "all their hair burned off, skin hanging in shreds, bodies raw like pieces of butchered meat, lips too burned to form words.

"I saw two children, clothes burned off, open sores oozing all over their bodies. They were huddled on a pile of rubble, both blinded by the explosion. Their eye sockets were hollow, dirty pus running down their cheeks. They were crying and holding up their fried arms, begging for someone, anyone, to help them.

"I saw part of a brick wall that stood through the blast, and on it was the light-colored shadow of a twisted human body that had been blown against the wall and instantly evaporated, leaving a print like a picture negative as their memorial. I became sick and had to turn away."

The Oster families heard the devastating words tumbling out of Fred's radio and shuddered. At every breath the announcer took, they could only mutter a mute "Ei, yei, yei."

Their minds told them that their sandwiches and nectar were good, but the sickening words morphed the taste into bitter gall. The sandwiches smelled of burnt meat.

"It looks like we might have won the war," GP reflected, taking a bite of tasteless food, "but what a price the whole world had to pay."

"And for what?" Bertha added.

"For a few twisted big shots who want to control the world!" Fred spat out in disgust. "And make us all their slaves."

"I know it was terrible, really terrible," Selma ventured timidly, "but maybe now the world is safer again with those two big *doobles*, dumbheads, gone."

All Tuesday, radio reports were full of rumors. One minute, Hirohito had surrendered. The next, he was talking about it. One minute the Imperial War Ministry voted to give up. The next they vowed never to dishonor the ancestors and the fatherland by giving up the fight like gutless cowards and voted to defend the homeland to the death of every man, woman, and child in all Japan.

Toward evening, when GP, Bertha, and Eddie were shocking wheat in the far corner of the old Gottfried land, Fred's car suddenly came bouncing across the stubble field, with a white dish towel wildly waving out of the passenger window.

"Dear God, this time, let it be," GP said as he stopped and watched the car careening between rows of shocks.

The car had not quite come to a stop when Selma bolted out, shouting, "It's over! Can you believe it, the president just announced that Hirohito finally surrendered!"

She flew into Bertha's arms, and for a long time they hugged and cried. When they stepped apart, both blew their noses.

Eddie and the two cousins took hands and wheeled a merry-go-round dance in the stubbles. Their laughter sounded the trumpet of innocence.

"Thank God," GP said softly, adding, "maybe we should thank him right now."

In a moment the two families had taken hands and knelt in the stubbles as GP led them in a soulful prayer of thanksgiving to God for bringing the dreadful war to a close. When the children sneaked a look at the adults' faces during the prayer and saw tears streaming down each face, they knew this was indeed something really big and important and meaningful, because tears were uncommon water on the prairies.

"Come over tonight," Selma said as they got back in the car, "and we'll listen some more."

All during the evening hours, every radio station Fred could tune in dropped their regular programming and broadcast further developments, along with frenzied celebrations in every major American city.

"This afternoon it was just crazy," Selma told them. "First they said Hirohito wanted to surrender. Then they said the army rebelled and organized a coup and overthrew him. Then word was that some special forces were going around executing all the American prisoners-of-war in the camps. You didn't know what to believe anymore."

"Anyway, it's done," Bertha said, relieved but suddenly feeling weary from a war that weighed down the soul without one realizing it. She was glad her own son was too young to be involved in it, beyond wearing the little sailor suit they bought for him when he was only six.

"Yeah," Selma replied, "around four thirty the president announced that Japan surrendered, and it's finished."

Later, they finally heard the news that President Truman had proclaimed Sunday, September 2, nearly three weeks hence, as

Official V-J Day, when the Allies and Japan would sign the final surrender documents and the world could celebrate freedom and, finally, an end to the awful war.

Newspapers headlined V-J Day, Victory over Japan, with the biggest letters they had ever used. Parties broke out across the Allied world. In the Valley, celebration was tempered with worry over loved ones left behind in the old country and not heard from since the beginning of the war.

Still, on Saturday night Beulah came alive with hundreds of area farm-and-ranch families coming in to celebrate. The men headed for the Mirror Bar, or Jim's or Goetz's Bar, and all were shoulder to shoulder as round after round was ordered and downed by enthusiastic, thankful revelers. Beer breath hung heavy in the crowded, poorly ventilated saloons.

Women gathered in the Sweet Shop, the Five and Dime, or in the aisles of the SuperValu or bathed in the delight of splurging to have their hair done at Hildebrandt's Beauty Shop, which was always open on Saturday nights. The Dreamland Pavilion hurriedly scheduled a special Victory Dance, which was packed with sweaty bodies whirling round and round in ecstasy not felt during all the years of the terrible war.

In the Valley, the most heartfelt celebration happened on Sunday morning.

Sunday, the second of September, V-J Day resounded with songs of thanksgiving as the rafters of Peace Lutheran rang with "*Lobe den Herren,* Praise to the Lord . . . who doth shelter thee under his wings, yea, so gently sustaineth."

Not only were they thankful for war's end but also for all their men being protected. Several were wounded, but not one of the Valley sons was killed in action. Every mother in church that day silently poured out her heart in tearful gratitude to God for his hand of mercy resting over them.

"We truly rejoice this day," the pastor proclaimed in the sermon, "but verily, the valley of the shadow is a lonesome walk indeed, dark and filled with bitter pain." Little did his people know.

After church was over, GP asked Pastor Grossmann, "Have you heard anything from any of your family in Dresden?"

"Nothing. And I've prayed so much, so much." Then, after a long pause, Reverend Grossmann looked down at the ground and added, so softly that GP had to strain to hear, "Golgotha, during the crucifixion, was God's biggest silence. Maybe this is my Golgotha."

"I'm sorry, Reverend."

"Thank you."

"Bertha and I are keeping you and them all in our prayers."

"Thank you again. You're so kind."

"Our pastor is so worried," GP told Bertha on the way home. "He just seems all worn out to me."

The war was over. But, for them as for millions in war-torn lands, it was far from done.

Chapter 27

How Do You Live Without War?

In the next weeks, nearly every woman who came into the SuperValu Store picked up some item and ended up asking the clerks, "You mean that's not rationed anymore?" They hardly knew how to shop without their ration books in hand. Of course, for months, it didn't make a great difference, since many products were still not available.

Men went to buy tires to replace their patched rubber, but sadly there were none available for months as well, except a few on the black market—if they wanted to pay the high price.

Soon factories were busy converting from war production back to consumer goods; as an article in the *Beulah Independent* put it, "from shell casings to kettles, from jeeps to Chevrolets, from army camouflage to ruffled blouses." People were hungry for a return to normal, but they had almost forgotten what normal was.

For Bertha, it also meant scouring through war surplus supplies in a catalogue the government sent out. Finally she spotted surplus white nylon parachutes and ordered one. Before long, she had her Singer treadle machine humming and sewed several fancy blouses for herself, along with a few slips and a stylish junior cowboy shirt for Eddie.

"Don't you look snazzy," she chuckled when he tried it on, proud of her own handiwork and proud of the handsome young man her son was growing into.

****

While Eddie was reading the school Weekly Reader's articles about factories retooling and new businesses burgeoning across the country, he noticed a small blurb about the *Grit* newspaper looking for delivery boys across the country.

"Mom," he came home all excited, "I could start selling the *Grit* newspaper. I'd make four cents a week for every one I sell. I'll bet lots of our neighbors would buy it."

"I don't know what that thing is," she replied. "You better ask Dad."

When GP reluctantly agreed, they sent for a sample, and before long they received the current forty-four-page issue of *Grit* filled with news, fashions, recipes, stories, even convenient household hints for daily living.

"Wow, Mom," Eddie shouted, flipping the pages, "look, this has all kinds of funnies. They even got the *Lone Ranger*."

GP and Bertha glanced through the paper and soon noticed that it had a large variety of articles that looked interesting. "Funny," GP said after he read through a good portion of the issue, "but I just feel kinda good after reading this thing." Little did he or Bertha realize that *Grit* was precisely aimed at rural America and geared to produce good feelings in the readers.

They agreed to let Eddie send in his name as a carrier and ordered ten copies a week.

About the same time, Uncle Adam had seen an advertisement looking for mechanically inclined progressive men to sell army surplus jeeps across rural America and responded as well.

Several weeks later, he and his two boys came driving into GP's yard with the topless army-brown machine, and he shouted, "Come on, GP. You and Eddie jump in, and we'll take a ride." Within minutes they were roaring up the steepest prairie hills and down the backsides, bouncing over rocks and through buffalo wallows. On the steepest hills, Adam shifted the jeep into four-wheel drive and they growled up inclines at angles that made them afraid of rolling over backward.

"Hang on," Adam shouted, laughing as he stepped on the gas.

Soon they were sitting on top of a big hill, and Adam turned off the engine.

"You know," he said, patting the steering wheel, "I hooked this thing up to my two-bottom plow, and it pulls 'er better'n my tractor does." He looked across the valley and envisioned jeeps plowing on every farm that eyes could see.

When GP nodded, Adam quickly added, "And faster too."

But despite all their fond hopes, Adam never sold a jeep, and Eddie only got two customers for his *Grit* enterprise—and those two lasted only until the bitter cold and deep snows of winter brought his walking deliveries to an abrupt stop. Almost as quickly as they began, the entrepreneurial dreams in both houses came to an unhappy end.

****

Threshing that fall felt more relaxed, the result both of good crop yields and the end of the war. For GP, it triggered memories of past days, and he spent lunch times regaling the threshing crew with stories of Teddy Roosevelt and exploits from his own time at the Elkhorn Ranch. The threshing crew learned to appreciate TR even more and laughed themselves to tears at the events on the big ranch, which GP brought right to their eyes. Of course the snakes got bigger, the storms more fierce, the mountain oysters juicier. It turned into a memorable season of joy without worry for the Valley men. For the women it was a carefree joy they had forgotten, now knowing that their men were safe once more.

In school, Eddie, now in sixth grade, found himself climbing the ladder of the eight-grade student herd, halfway between the big bulls and the young heifers. Testosterone hung heavy at times in the entry-coat room. School, in Wittenberg #2, was definitely not just about books and dry history. "Boy, we got some nice girls in our school," Eddie told his cousin Leonard one day. Leonard didn't catch the excitement in his words, and the conversation died.

But while Eddie noticed some exciting features of physique in the older girls, he was careful to avoid stepping on the turf of the seventh- and eighth-grade boys who saw the girls as their domain for young romance. A wrong move could prove big trouble outside after the school day was over.

At the same time, Eddie found himself growing faster afoot, able to swing a decent bat and make a good catch. Now during the serious games of kitten ball at recess time, the big captains who chose sides after stacking hands on the bat to see who picked first began picking Eddie sooner rather than later. *"Hey, this feels kinda good,"* flashed across Eddie's mind as he ran with a new swagger to his captain's side. The captain's grin put Eddie on a high for the rest of the day.

After Eddie walked home from school one afternoon, he wolfed down a sandwich and asked Bertha, "Mom, can me'n Cuddy go hunt frogs over at the old Gottfried place?"

"Ja, but get home before the sun goes down," Bertha replied, "you got chores to do, you know."

"Mamma, who was old Gottfried again?"

"Well, he was your Grandpa John's brother, and they came here together from the old country."

"That was in the old days, huh!"

"I guess you'd say so. Before I was born too."

Eddie wiped his hands on his bib overalls, slapped his cap on, and bounded down the three-quarter-mile trail across the prairie. Arms flying, he ran and skipped the dance of youth, with Cuddy's exuberant barks and leaps encircling him, to the old Gottfried homestead place. The solid old sod house was still standing, doors and windows now all gone, sky showing through holes in the roof, the old dirt floor manure-strewn from cattle. The walls still held a fading soft blue, which Grand Uncle Gottfried and Grand Aunt Mina lovingly applied many years ago. Swallows, irritated by the intrusion, darted at dog and boy as they explored the musty rooms. Eddie saw Indians and cowboys chasing each other, heard shots ricocheting off the walls, smelled the sweat of their horses.

Down the hill from the sod house, Eddie worked the old water pump, which still pulled up water, and held his hand over the spout to trap water. Loosening the palm of his hand just a crack, he released a stream of wonderfully cool water for Cuddy and himself, and they were on their way to the old stock pond with its croaking army of frogs.

Walking along the soft bottom of the ravine, they passed under a small grove of poplar trees. The strong south winds of fall made the sinewy poplars sway like dancing harem girls around Salome's seven silky veils. Eddie's ears were raptured by millions of golden leaves hymning an antiphon of farewell to each other as many floated a final good-bye and huddled together on the cooling earth below.

To his dismay, the stock pond was overgrown with green stuff that smelled rotten, and the frogs were nowhere to be found. "Oh well," Eddie told Cuddy as they started for home, "we had fun anyway," and took Cuddy's bark to mean *"We sure did."*

Before they knew it, summer was over and November's savage winds came roaring over the treeless prairies from the frigid north—strong enough that the honking *V*s of late-flying geese could almost set their wings and coast. The sky was the color of wet mud, and the riled-up water on the stock pond took on the shade of Bauer's face leading his mule out after a long day in the mine. The scudding clouds and cold nights had one sure message: "get ready."

GP spent long days hauling home stacks of hay from the pastures and straw from the threshing stacks in the fields. "I sure like raising our cattle," GP told Bertha over coffee between loads, "and if I want to keep our herd growing, I better take care of them over the winter."

Loading the next rack, he couldn't help but think, *"Strange, but just saying that somehow makes the work a little easier."*

****

A buzz of excitement sent waves through the area when the RCU Store in Beulah ran an advertisement stating they were getting a supply of nylon stockings just before Christmas. Nearly every woman under grandmother age suddenly felt a new cluster of feminine urges. During the past four years, mafia dolls—like Al Capone's consorts—could dance in filmy nylons, but Valley dolls spent their war years in brown cottons.

When the nylons arrived at the RCU two Saturdays before Christmas, a mob scene developed. Over mild shrieks and pushing, with polite laughter, packaged pairs of nylons flew out of the RCU doors like bats out of Carlsbad Caverns at sundown. Of course, Valley men considered it spendthrift and highly wasteful to quit work and run into town early in the morning just for a silly pair of nylons, so by the time Valley families came into town on Saturday night, the nylons were long gone.

On Sunday morning, before church, the women gathered in their usual left-side pews and were commiserating together over their lot in life, with a few rather harsh words being spoken about niggardly, stubborn German men. But about that time, one of the young Renner women came waltzing into church and with soft giggles hoisted her dress above her knees, showing off her splendid, delicate new hose.

"Oohs" and "aahs" rose from every pew.

"Oh, they look so wonderful," came one voice.

"How did you ever manage to get them?" asked another.

"My sister lives in Beulah, and she got there early and got 'em," the excited young Mrs. Renner replied.

Moments later the pastor came in, followed by the men, and sober decorum was immediately established, with the women dreaming of what might have been. Perhaps not so strangely, very few women remembered what was said in the sermon that day.

****

One by one the Valley boys were discharged from the service and made their way home. Each one was greeted with a heartfelt "Welcome Home" party, bringing with them strange soldier-boy phrases like "hubba, hubba," and a deeper dependence on cigarettes, as well as mental horrors of things they went through and would never again talk about except for their screams in the night.

In early spring, cloud-banging south winds howled across the barren fields by day and around the eaves at night, moaning and hissing like the disembodied undead in Halloween movies. Yellow-bellied purple crocuses answered their whistling call, buffalo grass sprang up overnight; cows and sows, deer and coyotes lay down and gave birth. Barn swallows flitting on iridescent wings suddenly seemed driven to answer nature's call, mating in noisy fanfare and hauling a thousand beak-loads of mud from the dam. From first light on, they built nests under the barn eaves to get on with bringing in a new generation of mosquito hunters. When Eddie walked past their construction site, they dive-bombed his cap and give him a loud, twittered scolding.

Big-eyed frogs of every size came out of winter's mud in the stock pond to celebrate in a glad symphony of many-layered sound. Lazy hawks circled in the blue heavens, waiting for a careless mouse too much in love with warmth after somber hibernation. Almost overnight, this quiet world turned noisy with life.

Then one night, after the family was nestled into bed, a strong coyote began baying on the bluff above the house. His voice echoed with a force that sent shivers down the back of everything that possessed a spine. Bertha bolted up in bed. In a split second, GP followed. Eddie, in the next room, stopped breathing, afraid to look at the window, fearing the creature with yellow, devilish eyes was looking in at him. Cuddy, asleep on the haystack, raised his hackles, ready to defend the yard but not sure of the wisdom of barking back. The strength of that voice on the hill bespoke sharp teeth and an empty belly, all powered by a nasty temper.

Out in the chicken coop every head snapped up, all eyes on the door, their instincts listening for stealthy footsteps and snapping teeth.

Two more long baying howls followed and, in several seconds, a faint answer from somewhere across the valley but sounding more mournful than threatening. Then silence. Moments more and the silence became more frightful than the sound as all wondered what was coming next. Long minutes more and all hoped the lone hunter had moved on. After that, sleep was slow to return.

At first light of day, in the chicken coop Big Red, the senior feathered security guard had already turned impassioned chanticleer, heralding his master and his harem to the glorious joy of another day's labor. With that bright-feathered call, the terror of the night was forgotten, a new day at hand.

When the family gathered in the kitchen for breakfast, Eddie piped up, "Boy, that coyote sure sounded like he was right outside my window, kinda scary."

"Ja, it's kinda scary when they're that close," GP replied, "but as scary as they are, we need all those critters, because in this world they all depend on each other to keep alive. Everything is food for something else, so I guess we need coyotes too."

"But not mosquitoes, right?" Eddie wondered out loud.

As GP walked to the barn, fierce south winds continued to pour in from the faraway desert southwest. They made every creature with legs lean south to stay upright, and for all their pounding power, they still carried the faint, delicious smell of fresh growing grass that spoke of new life as well.

The warm winds soon birthed little rivulets of water that gurgled their way down every draw in the fields, every ravine on the prairies, channeling the final melt of harsh winter's snow from this quiet spot atop the States, down the Valley to the Knife, the Missouri, the Mississippi, finally to whisper into the great oceans of the world. There this quiet Dakota water would help feed shrimp and float the great iron behemoths of mankind across the seas.

A day later and everything was flooded. All the creeks coming down from the hills turned into running streams, and when they reached the Valley, they flooded the roads. The three families of Oster children couldn't walk to school, so GP hitched up the team and hauled them across the raging little streams to the Valley road. The lowest stretch of road was drowned in a hundred yards of moving water, and GP had no idea where the roadbed was, so he slacked up on the reins and let the sure-footed horses slowly walk their way through the cold water that ran belly high on the team.

The youngsters delighted in the near-boating experience, blissfully unaware that another three inches of water and it would have been high enough to sweep the wagon into the stream. They could hardly wait for the school day to be over, to "go boating" again, much to the envy of their schoolmates who wished they could ride along.

Three more days and the flood subsided, leaving all the young scholars to their regular daily mile-and-a-half walk, now with a narrow band of road across acres of water.

With the days warming up, Bertha got four young turkeys from a neighbor, three jennies and a jake, to begin raising her own flock. She also ordered two hundred baby chicks from the hatchery in Bismarck, and a week later the postman delivered them to the mailbox on the gravel road in two large, loudly cheeping cardboard boxes along with the rest of the mail. The chicken coop was still too cold at night, so she had to keep the boxes in the kitchen for a week—a little smelly but delightfully fun for the whole family to reach in and hold chicks in their hands.

"Oh, it tickles," Eddie laughed as he held the little yellow fuzz balls and let them nibble the finely ground wheat kernels in his hands. "They feel like little mice in your hand."

When Eddie went outside, two yellow-breasted meadowlarks, perched on sandstone outcroppings on the high hill behind the house, chanted an antiphon of praise back and forth, happy to be back in the land of their hatching. He couldn't help but smile.

With all this explosion of life, GP's juices turned him restless as well. He finished running last year's best wheat through the fanning mill to clean out all the weed seeds and chaff, bagged the seed, and stacked it in the shed, ready to pour into the drill. Then he started the

Farmall H, hauled out the last of winter's manure, put grease gun to zerk on plow, disc, and drill, ready to till the earth once more in this timeless cycle of life.

Out on the land, plowing furrows down the half-mile fields, his mind turned to his special Herefords. One by one his prized cows gave birth to beautiful white-faced, reddish-chocolate brown calves that were pictures of Hereford perfection. *"How blessed I am,"* he thought, *"that all the calves survived."* He pictured himself in the cattle-show arenas in Bismarck and Valley City, leading his prized bulls, holding the halter rope snug to keep their heads up high and stand at erect attention for judging. Using his shepherd's staff, he carefully prods their hocks to set their feet in perfect pairs with all the spit and polish of guards at the Tomb of the Unknown.

"With this special stock, I'm gonna make a mark in the cattle world with 'Oster & Son Herefords,'" he sang out over the steady throb of the tractor. "Sure feels good."

After the day's plowing, he finished supper with Bertha and Eddie and led them in prayer and reading a chapter from the Bible. While Mother did the dishes, he and Eddie lit the kerosene lantern and walked to the pig barn. Two Hampshire sows recently gave birth in a special farrowing pen filled with fresh straw, and eighteen little white piglets were crawling all over their mothers for supper. As soon as Eddie and GP sat down in the straw, the curious piglets grunted and bounced on them as well.

"This is really fun," Eddie giggled, "they're so soft, and they're even busier than the baby chicks."

"Don't you wish you could understand what they're saying," GP replied, "with all the grunts and squeals that come out of 'em?"

"Yeah, and their noses are so nice 'n' warm when they root around in my hands."

The two sows lay stretched out, two rows of faucets at the ready for feeding, occasionally grunting out low-pitched mother-pig talk about something they needed to share with their brood.

"See how they don't make any mess in the straw or any place in the pen?" GP asked. "They all poop over there in the corner."

"That's their toilet, huh?"

"Pigs are a lot neater than people think."

"Look here," Eddie whispered, pointing down to a little snuffler that rooted its way between his thighs, quietly resting its snout on his warm legs and closing its eyes. "I think he's going to sleep."

"Guess he likes you. Maybe he thinks you're his father." And both threw back their heads in laughter at the hilarity of it all.

Eddie grew pensive for a moment. "You think," he said softly, "maybe someday I can have pigs of my own?"

Chapter 28

Son Growing Up

During the summer, GP let Eddie drive the tractor, pulling the hayrack home from working in the fields. After supper, he told Eddie, "Start the tractor up and drive around the yard. I'll set up a couple blocks of wood, and you drive by 'em as close as you can, so you get used to judging the distance to where your wheels are running."

Then, when GP had the binder ready for harvest, one night at supper he told Bertha, "Tomorrow Eddie's gonna drive the tractor on the binder."

They both glanced at Eddie, who looked up wide eyed. His mouth dropped open, and breaths came short.

"He's ten now, and he can handle it," GP continued.

Eddie's mind reeled, *"Wow, I'm a man now."*

As soon as supper was finished, Eddie pushed his chair back and rushed out the door. With Cuddy bounding beside him, he raced up the bluff behind the house, over the hill, and down the other side, pumped his fists in the air, ran in jerky circles, and shouted until he was almost hoarse. Cuddy caught the excitement, jumping and matching him bark for shout. GP and Bertha could faintly hear the commotion, and Bertha said with a smile, "I think our son is happy."

"It's good to see him growing up."

"I'm glad we have somebody to take over the farm after we're gone."

****

A new school year just began when the family woke up one morning to fog so thick they couldn't see the barn from the house. The world outside had completely vanished.

GP made his way out to the barn, and when he came in from milking, he told Bertha, "You know, the old folks say when you get a heavy fog like this, ninety days from now you'll have rain or snow, depending on the season."

"Let's mark the calendar for December 14 and see if they were right."

After chores and breakfast, Bertha filled Eddie's lunch bucket; and with his school bag slung over his shoulder, he set out for school.

"Stay on the trail," Bertha admonished, tousling his cap when he stepped out the door.

"Boy, this feels like walking in a cloud," Eddie said to himself as the fog coalesced in clammy drops against his face. He stayed on the trail, but the world immediately turned scary strange. Neither hill nor ravine, buck-brush nor rock was visible, only the dew-covered grass at his feet. It was like walking in milk, except you could breathe.

While Mother worried that maybe she or Dad should have walked with him, Eddie's mind suddenly came alive with a big herd of long-horned Hereford cattle stampeding past him, chased by a crew of greasy cattle rustlers, shouting, snapping their long bull snake whips, screaming back and forth to each other. He couldn't quite make them out, of course, in the thick fog, but he could hear every sound as the pounding hooves went thundering by. In another instant, the Lone Ranger and Tonto came galloping by, pumping silver bullets and scaring the thieves away. Finally the herd was gone, but then he heard a frightening voice behind him. A gravelly woman's voice hissed, "I'll get you, my pretty. And your little dog too."

Several weeks ago, GP took the family to see *The Wizard of Oz* at the Roxy Theater, and it scared the shivers into Eddie. Now in the milky fog he heard the Wicked Witch shouting right behind him and started to run. The faster he ran, the louder were the pounding steps of Tin Man, clomping and banging just off his right shoulder. Cowardly Lion snapped his jaws and slobbered at him on the left, ready to claw his arm; Scarecrow blew fetid breath down his neck, making him gag. Toto circled him, barking just out of view, and all the while the Wicked Witch cackled something to Dorothy who was shrieking with high-pitched fear in the distance.

The hideous voices terrified Eddie to a level of fright he had never known, even in ghastly nightmares. The hair on his neck stood up, and his feet spun into a Bugs Bunny whirlwind. He had to pee so badly his bladder was near exploding, but he didn't dare stop or they'd overwhelm him and surely beat him to death. His legs were giving out, his side aching something awful, lungs bursting. He had to keep going.

His world was a moving ten-foot circle with absolutely nothing to see beyond that. Jagged yellow stones kept lurching at his high-top leather boots, bumping into his feet as he ran. The bewitched creatures were all around, and he swung his school bag blindly as he ran, trying to knock them away. It felt like he hit something, but he wasn't sure. He only knew they were grabbing at him from every side.

Suddenly he found himself at the end of the half-mile pasture trail from their farm and walked through the gate unto the gravel road. The one-mile sprint from there to school turned into a hundred miles and felt like a tortured fourteen hours!

When he finally arrived at school, he shot through the door, ready to collapse, saucer eyed and white as a ghost. He took one more step, rolled his eyes upward, and puked all over the rough board floor.

The shocked teacher, Miss Boeshans, ran to get the five-gallon pail in the corner and scooped out a dustpan full of sweeping compound to spread over the curdled, sour-smelling puddle while the other students turned their eyes away and held their hands over their mouths to lessen the awful stink they suddenly had to breathe.

"Oh, Eddie, are you all right? You don't look good," Miss Boeshans told him, pulling him behind her desk. She yanked off his cap and knelt down in front of him, holding her palm on his forehead. "You don't have a fever. Are you getting sick?"

"I-I don't think so. Ach, I heard some coyotes howling in the fog, and I thought they were chasing me," Eddie replied, "an' I got really scared."

The fog outside soon lifted, but in Eddie's young mind, it boiled on until recess.

For the next two days, the older boys sneered and called Eddie, "Hey, Coyote Man," until Miss Boeshans ordered, "Boys, that's enough. I don't want to hear that again, understand?"

"Yes, Miss Boeshans."

For days to come, whenever Eddie got into a small space, his stomach tightened and his heart began to pound. The witch's macabre face and taunting laugh echoed in his mind for weeks.

And sure enough, on December 14 it snowed.

"Would you believe that?" Bertha said with a smile. "The old folks weren't so dumb after all, were they."

****

In early spring, GP drove to Valley City for the Annual Winter Show. It was the state cattle show for the best cattle in every breed, and GP was looking to improve his herd. When the Reserve Champion Registered Hereford cow came up for sale, GP checked her pedigree and found that she came from excellent lines on both the dam and sire sides. Added to that, she had already been bred to a superior bull of the Domino line, one of the best among national Herefords, and GP saw an opportunity to make a mark in North Dakota Hereford breeding.

He entered the bidding, and it cost him a handsome price, but "Grand Dam Ione" would throw some excellent, high-quality calves, God willing, and open a new chapter with "Oster and Son Herefords" entering the showmanship ranks in cattle shows across the state.

The two-hundred-mile trip home seemed never to end, and "Ione" might have suffered sharp frostbite had GP not tied a blanket over her back and nailed tarps to the sides and across the top of the pickup rack. When he finally got home and unloaded her into a special pen in the cattle barn, she went wild, reared up on her hind legs, and kicked the boards, bellowing fiercely enough to put all the other cattle on edge.

"Why's she so wild?" Eddie wanted to know, edging close to GP and afraid she might come flying over the top of the six-foot-high pen, or maybe crash right through the sturdy boards that held her.

"Maybe she's afraid," answered GP, "maybe mad we took her away from her home. I don't know either, but after a day or so she'll be a lot better."

With Ione ornery and Eddie still nervous, GP suggested, "Let's let her settle down and go up to the house, and I'll tell you and Mother all about the Winter Show."

After canned-peach kuchen and coffee and stories, GP said, "Let's get back down to the barn. Eddie, you fork her some hay over the top of the pen."

When he was finished, GP said, "Now I'm going to unlatch the gate to her pen and pour some water in the trough. But listen good.

I want you to hold the gate, and if she comes after me, you swing it open real quick, just enough for me to get out and then bang it shut and latch it before she gets there. If you miss, we're both in trouble. Big trouble! *Verstescht du*, understand?"

"Ja," came the quick reply but a little too weak to be totally convincing.

The hay went over, GP slowly opened the gate and poured the water, wild-eyed Ione snorted once and took a stutter step toward him but quickly stopped, and all was well.

"Now, I want you to give her hay every day," Dad said, "so she gets used to it and trusts you, because after I get her going, I want you to lead her in the corral with her halter on."

"Ja," Eddie mumbled as he silently measured the size of Ione's horns. It didn't take much to picture himself dangling from one of them.

"She's gonna put our Herefords on the map."

"Ja."

It wasn't long until early one morning Dad come running back from the barn, shouting, "Eddie, quick get up. Ione had her calf!"

When all three got out to the barn, Bertha cooed, "Oh, isn't she just about the prettiest little thing around here? Like a little cow princess."

"Hey, 'Princess Ione,' that's a good name," GP added, bending over to study her from different angles. "She's got all the perfect Hereford markings."

"And look," Eddie laughed, "she's already bobbling against her mother looking for breakfast."

"You'll sure have fun training Princess for the ring," Dad said with his hand around Eddie's shoulder. "Let's finish chores, so I can get going on her papers."

After breakfast dishes were cleared, they gathered around the table as GP filled out the detailed registration papers for the new calf and, for the price of a three-cent stamp, sent them off to the American Hereford Association in Kansas City. There, in a filing cabinet at 300 Eleventh Street, "Princess Ione" was embedded into Hereford immortality.

****

As the next fall came, so did the relentless, driving south winds. For Eddie, again walking a mile and a half to school on stubby, little legs into the teeth of a thirty-mile-an-hour wind, it called for a daily dose of sheer guts. Time after time the miserable wind blew his cap off, and he had to chase it across the prairie or down into the ditch. He didn't want to swear, but after a while some of GP's favorite words of thunder scrolled in jagged waves across his brain.

He shortened the distance to school by throwing stones at fence posts along the road. "Ei, that felt good," he shouted out loud on those rare times when he hit one. Some mornings Cuddy came along part of the way, enjoying the excitement of flushing quail out of the ditch or barking at meadowlarks singing on the fence posts; he would gladly have gone to school each day as well had Eddie not shooed him home. "Ja, Cuddy, you're smart enough already," Eddie yelled, "now go on home."

Sometimes his cousins walked at the same time, and their meeting on the road usually brought on some boisterous jostling and often a quick challenge, "Race ya to th' big rock beside the fence." Their wild shouting even got the cows in the adjacent harvested field all excited, and they raced alongside, tails high and hooves flying. They seemed genuinely disappointed when it was over, staring at the youngsters and mooing for more.

On those windy days, Eddie's stomach growled through morning classes, hungry from the hard walk, and he could hardly wait.

There was no water to wash hands, and Eddie still had grit on his hands from picking up stones on the gravel road, but a quick wipe on the hips of his overalls and the hands were ready for lunch. He didn't like milk, so on warmer days Mother filled his thermos bottle with water, but now on cooler days she filled it with black coffee, which Eddie really enjoyed, and it hit the spot to energize him for playing softball after gulping down his quick lunch.

It wasn't long before the winds changed and came howling out of the frozen north. Heavy snows brought new schoolyard games: snowball fights, fox-and-goose tag in the hundred-foot rings they stomped out in the snow, and sliding on their backs down the tiny schoolyard hill. Their favorite was building snow forts for choosing armies and "conquering the king," where whoever was hit by a snowball was captured by the other side. Eddie and other younger players were often hit in the head as the snowball fights got serious, but soldiers quickly learned not to cry or they'd be labeled "yellow bellies."

****

Spring was a glorious time as the resting earth came back to life with green bursting out everywhere, like barium fireworks, and animals of every species bringing forth young. The new life all around them moved Fred to buy a new Schwinn bicycle for his two children.

Learning to drive it in the rough gravel yard, however, was a huge challenge that resulted in many a dose of painful iodine and strips of bandage tape. Gradually both cousins learned, and when Eddie came over, they offered him a turn. It didn't go well. He wanted so badly to cruise on a bike like his other cousins in town who were such smooth riders, but that would be a challenge.

At home he asked, "Dad, can I get a bike too, like Lorraine and Waldo?"

"A bike in the country is a dumb idea," was Dad's quick reply, and that chapter was closed.

With spring also came another profusion of purple crocuses, the honeyed scent of sweet clover along the roadways, and the mixed blessing of wild onions in the pastures. But bigger still, in the back of Valley minds, was the Annual Box Social at school coming up on the last Sunday afternoon before the end of the school year. Proceeds were dedicated to purchase library books and supplies for the school, so it was important event.

The unwritten rule was that every woman, married or single, would prepare a special picnic spread with some specialty of her own, including dessert, which was usually her best pie recipe. The entire meal was then carefully boxed and decorated into a beautiful art piece. Then at the social in school, the artistic culinary masterpieces were auctioned off to the men who then received the privilege of eating with the creator of the box.

Of course, the husbands knew which box their wife had made, and although there was often a tincture of good-natured bidding, for a dollar or two the husband got to eat with his wife and children.

Where the affair became exciting was over the boxes of the young, single women. Although the creator of each box was to be kept a strict secret, the young beauties were sure to make their boxes known to their boyfriends, who would be certain to win the bidding so they could share a few moments of not-so-private delight.

This time, GP, who also served as auctioneer, went to several neighbors and whispered,

"Let's have a little fun with young Hoffman."

"What are you thinking about?"

"Let's run up his bid and make him sweat to get his girl's box."

One by one they topped their young bachelor friend's bidding until they had him scrambling to borrow money. Sweat beaded on his brow, his hands shook, and finally he muttered in a growling stage-whisper, "You dumb suckers, get off my back!"

For twenty-five dollars, and months of terrible debt, he got to eat with his girl. As they spread out a blanket on the ground to eat, her hands were shaking so badly she couldn't handle the dishes, her face so deep a blushing red that tears welled up in her eyes.

"That was awful," she whispered.

"I know."

"As long as I live, I'll never stop thanking you, ever."

Now it was his turn to blush.

Then, several boxes later, scandal descended on the auction.

Benjamin and Mrs. Kreutzmann and their four small children also came. They had a hard time making a living, their clothes were disheveled and in need of cleaning, and Benjamin wasn't the sharpest knife in the drawer.

During the auction he took a sudden shine toward one of the young women, and when her box was auctioned he ran up the bid. With a satisfied smile, he handed over more money than the boyfriend could manage to scrabble together from all his friends.

When Mrs. Kreutzmann's box came up, she was mortified. Now alone with her stunned children, she raised her handkerchief to her face, shoulders silently shaking, until a Good Samaritan neighbor bid fifty cents for her box and invited her and the children to join his family.

The unfortunate young woman whose basket Kreutzmann bought was totally humiliated and never lifted her tear-filled eyes during her wordless meal with Benjamin. Meanwhile, he chewed noisily, in untroubled glee, needing no conversation, oblivious to all the clucking and *ei, yei, yei's* going on around them. Most of those around them were embarrassed.

The boyfriend got in his car, roared his engine, and sprayed gravel all the way out of the schoolyard. There were rumors of him beating up his girlfriend for making her basket too attractive, but no one had the courage to ask either of them about it.

The Kreutzmanns? Although everyone wondered, they still drove home together. No one ever heard what happened on the drive or at home. They noticed, however, that the Kreutzmanns did not go to Communion at church for the better part of a year.

On the way home from the social, GP's mind took quite a different turn. He couldn't help but reflect on coming to the social and sitting at the same desk he had occupied as a student years ago. The instant he sat down, an overpowering smell came whirling back into his brain. When he sat at this desk back then, the seat in front of him was occupied by a young lass just on the threshold of womanhood. She had not been well led into the paths of cleanliness, and at regular intervals there emanated from her the penetrating smell of blood-soaked cloth and uncleansed body parts—a smell GP never forgot. He never could share that memory with Bertha.

"Funny," he thought, almost driving off the road, *"how crazy stuff like that can come back so strong all over again, and so many years later."*

In Valley lore, that special school event was long and delightfully remembered as "Benny's Box Social."

Chapter 29

The Salt of Bitter Tears

"Bitte, bitte, Geliebten, kennen sie uns hilfen? Please, please, dear loved ones, could you help us?"

Those sad, startling words opened the letter that changed the Valley for years to come. It was from Germany and simply addressed:

Herr und Frau Gottfried Oster
Nord Dakotah, USA.

How the letter got to GP's rural mailbox forever remained a mystery.

"I guess somebody knew somebody," said GP, "who knew somebody somewhere."

"I say it was just plain a miracle," replied Bertha, "and God saw to it."

"Looks like it was written by an older person."

It was written in old German script, but fortunately, both GP and Bertha could read it from the training they received years ago in German Summer Bible School at church.

"Listen to this," Bertha said as she slowly made her way into it. "It says, *'We are relatives to you from Klostitz, and we remember you, Gottfried, and your father, Christian, and stories of your grandfather, Heinrich.'*"

"Guess they're talking about Uncle Gottfried," GP cut in, "but that's all right."

"Please, please, dear loved ones, could you help us? The terrible war has left us homeless and hungry. I hope the kind God will send angels to find you with this letter. We are so desperate. Please, if there is anything you can do, help us and we will be forever indebted to you. God bless you and watch over us all. Your relative, Frau Jakob Oster."

The next morning, GP and Bertha dropped everything and drove to Beulah, where they quickly picked up some nonperishable grocery items and packed them in a box. The grocer helped them wrap it for shipping, and they mailed it by air post to the return address on the letter. Bertha also included a brief letter of reply and promised to send more when they knew what was most desperately needed.

In the following days, Bertha mentioned the sad, pleading letter to Selma and to the women in church, who were also left wondering and waiting to learn more of this mysterious connection that suddenly sprang up, like a hand reaching out from the grave.

For two months, they heard nothing. Then one day Eddie rode out to get the mail, and when he saw a strange-looking letter, he tucked it in his shirt and galloped Barnie all the way home.

"Mamma," he shouted from a distance, "a letter, there's a letter."

Bertha told Eddie, "Run to the barn and get Daddy."

GP quickly came in, while Eddie stayed outside to play.

As soon as GP sat down, Bertha told him, "We got another letter," and she began reading:

Liebste Verwandte Familie Oster, Beloved relatives Family Oster,

Your package arrived safely and was truly a godsend. How can we begin to thank you for giving us a breath of hope in these dark, terrible days.

You asked what has happened to us. So often we thought our God had forgotten us.

We prayed and prayed, and there was only silence and more suffering. Precious relatives, we have lived through things more terrible than any words can ever lift out of us. It would take half a Bible to begin to tell, and it hurts too much to go back. But let me try to tell you just a few things. Before the war, Stalin's police rounded up all of us in Klostitz, like wild cattle, and shipped us and most of the other German dorfs far east to cruel Siberia. We suffered things there that I am trying to forget, and that you would never believe, but by the grace of our heavenly Father we stayed alive. My man and most of the men in our little Siberian dorf were shipped off to war, and we never saw them again.

What peace would flood my heart if I could just lay a flower on his grave, even now.

All our relatives are gone, either killed or starved, some frozen to death. My daughter, Marta, and I alone from our family made it through by the grace of God. How many nights I wake up sweaty from the terrible things I see in my dreams.

After the war, what our cruel masters called the Great Patriotic War, we fled from that place of horror in Siberia. *On that road of agony we hid under hay piles and in the brush under trees. We lived on roots and raw potatoes which our little boys had to steal and some chickens they caught, and we had to eat them raw because we couldn't make any fire, and other things I don't even want to remember. Many a night we ate the salt of bitter tears and nothing more. We were misused and beaten and robbed of the few things we had. We were sure we would die or be killed. Some days we even wished for that. Somehow, like Father Abraham going to the Promised Land, after long, long months we finally made it home to Klostitz. In all that time we had no change of clothes, no wash of hair. We felt so ugly, so animal foul. Yet, oh, we were so glad to finally be home again.*

But home was gone. Our beloved Klostitz was no more. The church was burned, most houses destroyed, Russians living in the few houses left standing. Before long some more hollow-eyed wanderers came by and said they were hoping to find a new life going west. We joined them, and for more months we were homeless gypsies again, living on the ground like so many rats. At least some towns and some farmers gave us a little food and often a barn to sleep in. They said we tramped through Rumanien and some other places I cannot remember, but we finally got to Germany, the West Zone they call it, away from the Russians.

There is no place to live, so we are many hundreds of souls packed in a bombed-out town. Sad to say, the American bombers did a complete job on this town. War is so hellish. It breaks my heart to find dolls and beautiful dishes and lace handkerchiefs from people's precious lives as we help move the rubble to rebuild this place. We are ten souls living in one small stone basement under a rubble pile of what they say was a four-story building. There are no windows, no lights, and it is always cold and damp. There is one well for water, and food only once a week that American army trucks bring in as they can. Sometimes they bring little tin cans of meat called SPAM. We can't tell what kind of meat it is, but it tastes good and dulls the hunger pangs for a few hours.

There are no stores to buy anything, and we have no money anyway. We are so worried, because soon it will be winter and we have no blankets, no shoes, no overcoats. We don't know how we will stay alive.

Dearest relatives, may God bless your hearts to help us in any way you can. Right now you are our only hope. We would stand forever in your debt and be debted to our Heavenly Father as well.

With all spiritual love,
Frau Jacob Oster

As the last words fell, GP and Bertha both sat stunned, silent for long minutes, tears welling up in their eyes.

"Dear God," GP finally whispered, eyes looking far away, "how can such things happen?"

"Those precious people, our own flesh and blood, having to go through that. What's keeping them alive?"

"Let's call Eddie in," GP said after a long silence. "He has to hear this."

When he sat down, Bertha slowly read the letter again, pausing several times to blow her nose. GP coughed but said nothing. Eddie couldn't understand some of the German words, nor feel the deep tragedy of it, but looking at their eyes, he sensed the pain it was causing both his parents, and he knew this was something terribly serious.

"Let's walk over to Fred's," GP suggested. "They have to hear this too."

Fred and Selma were as stunned about the horror these old country relatives were living through as were Bertha and GP. Finally Fred spoke up, "Let's take this to church on Sunday and read it for everybody to hear."

Before church, GP pulled Reverend Bergstaedt, their new pastor, aside and let him read the letter. The pastor also grew up and received his training in Germany and still had relatives there now in that immense army of suffering. "Yes, Gottfried," he said, looking down to hide his tears, "why don't you read the letter to the congregation, right after the sermon."

GP wasn't halfway through the letter when this stoic group began wiping their eyes, with a number blowing their noses.

After the letter, the pastor led in a heartfelt prayer, "Blessed Lord of all nations, especially sustain and provide for all thy children in devastated lands who are still suffering so bitterly from terrible bloodshed and war." Though these believers never spoke "amens" to prayers in church—that was the pastor's role in prayer—this day there were quiet "amens" whispered in several pews.

The Benediction was still reverberating in the little church when the women crowded around Bertha and the men surrounded GP outside.

"What can we do?"

"We have to do something."

Within minutes the little groups had come together and decided to send a care package each week, with four families taking turns each month and others helping those four. GP's and Fred's would each take a week, Pfennig's another. Then Mrs. Wiedeman took Bertha's arm and put in, "We'll take the fourth week every month." Quickly glancing at her husband, she added, "Won't we, Emil."

Helping some Osters was not up the highest rung on Big Emil's ladder, but how could he disagree with such need? "Ah-h, yes, yes, we will."

When they got home, Bertha quickly wrote Frau Oster, introducing herself, telling them that a package of goods would be on the way tomorrow and asking them for shoe and coat sizes.

Early Monday morning, GP and the family drove to Beulah to get supplies, bubbling over to tell the grocer what they were shopping for. He enthusiastically responded, "Great, I'll throw in the coffee and raisins."

With his help, it didn't take them long to gather bags of flour, sugar and salt, boxes of oatmeal, macaroni and raisins, tins of coffee, beef jerky, and peanut butter and pack it all in a padded wooden apple crate.

"Oh, I almost forgot," Bertha shouted from a back aisle, "here, they need candles and a box of matches, for sure."

"And here," Eddie piped from the front of the store, "I think they'd like these hard candies."

The grocer produced a heavy brown wrapping paper and twine to wrap it, Bertha printed the address on it, and they walked two blocks to the post office. By the time the package was stamped, they had bubbled the story again to the postmaster.

"That's just about the most meaningful thing I've ever done in my life," Bertha mentioned with a happy sigh as they walked to their car.

"All I hope is that it gets there," replied GP.

Every Sunday in church, the first question to Bertha and GP was "Have you heard back yet?"

"Nothing so far."

In coming weeks, every family in church brought something for the four families to add to their boxes, all anxious to hear whether the packages were getting there.

"You know," GP said one day, "their souls need feeding too." Working with the pastor, he gathered several German Bibles, hymnals, and catechisms. He also included *"Taegliche Andachten"* (Daily Devotions), a wall calendar with daily tear-off pages, which GP used for their family devotions every evening after supper, and he mailed these items as well.

Finally, after six weeks of anxious waiting, a second letter came.

Liebe Frau Oster und Gottfried, der Juengere, Dear
Mrs. Oster and Gottfried the Younger,

*We were overjoyed and thank God with all our
hearts and souls for letting our letter find you and
for the dear Lord Jesus answering our prayers with
your most welcome letter back to us. We cried and
hugged when we learned that we still have relatives
living. Now we know that our heavenly Father has
sent angels to the earth, and they are living in North
Dakota and are called Oster. I am sure God raised
you up to be our help and strength in trouble, just
like the Psalmist said. Your package came soon
after your letter, and, dear ones, it was to us like
the children of Israel finding manna in the desert.
Oh how blessed we are, and what gladness fills our
hearts to share with our whole house all the good
things you sent. When we opened the package, we
first lit the candles and got on our knees and sang
"Jesus Lead the Way."*

*It grieves us that before they shipped us off
to* Siberia, *all our Bibles and song books and
catechisms were burned. Now we only have pieces
that we can still remember, but though devils fill the
world, they will never get Jesus away from us.*

With greatest faith and love,
Your Oster Relatives

When GP read the new letter in church, the members sucked in
breaths and wanted to cheer. But of course, pioneer Dakota Lutherans
did no such thing.

After worship, they quickly decided to meet in the afternoon,
two weeks hence, and bring whatever they could for a Care Package
Sunday.

As the appointed time approached, they were surprised to see
cars fill the little churchyard. By now the word about Care Package
Sunday had spread, and people came from neighboring churches as

well, all moved by the plight of fellow humans swept up in the jaws of suffering and so desperate for any help they could find.

The August Little Soldiers and several other Native American families from the Reservation also came with boxes. Some of their sons fought in Europe and in the bloody Pacific Isles and knew firsthand the unbelievable devastation left behind when the awful fighting was done and the troops came home.

Soon cars were moved, blankets spread out on the grass, piles categorized, and boxes packed and wrapped for shipping. To GP's surprise, Big Emil Wiedeman came over and helped him pack items in a box. Neither man found handy words to say, but some ice was melted.

For people in ravaged lands who had absolutely nothing, the list of needs was long, and the Valley responded with dozens of necessities to help them survive and get back on their feet: bandage tape, undergarments and cotton stockings, sweaters, shirts, wool socks, and gloves. Aspirin, jack knives, work pants and cotton dresses, shoes of all sizes, cast-iron skillets and flatware for eating, combs, and tooth brushes and paste. Some women modestly slipped in packages of Kotex while others brought garden seeds. Families brought money for shipping, others packed boxes of their own to add. Heavy overcoats, blankets, and rubber overshoes would follow.

Thus was spent every second Sunday afternoon in the Valley for several years. In the meantime, other families in the Valley also received letters, some from relatives, some from strangers who had gotten names from relatives. All were answered, and all had packages sent.

The next letter from Frau Oster was particularly heartwarming.

Liebe Familie Oster,

You cannot imagine the depth of our joy when we opened your package and saw Bibles and song books. They shone brighter than diamonds and pearls. We called the neighbors in, and all sat down to hear the precious Word of God. We read the first chapter of St. John, then we sang hymns for a whole hour. When we lay down at night, it felt like our souls were on fire with a glowing flame.

Now every evening a group gathers in our little "cave" and we read the Daily Devotion page, several chapters from the Bible, and sing a hymn and pray, especially for you, our dear ones, that God may keep you and Peace Lutheran Church. Every week a few more people come. And every Sunday morning we gather outside for worship. One of the favorite songs is the old children's hymn,

Gott ist die Liebe, Laest mich erloesen.
Gott ist die Liebe, er liebt auch mich;

God loves me dearly, grants me salvation;
God loves me dearly, loves also me.

Even in the dark, we know that the blackest night is not dark to God, for his light brightens our path. He laid a heavy cross on our shoulders, but we rejoice in knowing that our Father found us worthy to suffer for Jesus our Lord. Our little hour of suffering is indeed nothing compared to Christ's. And suffering with Christ, we also trust that a crown awaits us, like unto his glorious crown.

Dear ones, you have fed us in hours of gnawing hunger, but you have fed our deepest hunger of all by giving our souls the sacred bread of life that is food eternal.

The Lord bless and keep you.
Frau Salomina Oster

"I'm so glad they still believe in God at all," Bertha stated, "after what they've been through. And it's not over yet."

"They are sure living through what we read in the Psalms, 'Thou hast fed them with the bread of tears. Thou hast given them tears to drink in full measure,'" GP replied.

"We aren't any better than they are, but oh, I hope the Lord never puts us through that."

In the following months, Reverend Bergstaedt heard from churches around the state, as well as South Dakota and Canada, that more letters were arriving with desperate cries for help.

In one of his next sermons, Reverend Bergstaedt talked about the help which these little churches across the Midwest were providing, telling the congregation, "The *Song of Solomon* puts it so well when it says, 'Many waters cannot quench love, neither can floods drown it.'"

Thousands of Care Packages flowed across the wide Atlantic to help keep countless anguished and homeless people alive. "It gives them hope," the pastor said, "just to know that they're not alone in this world."

Then for a long time the Osters heard nothing from Germany, nor were their letters answered. After more silent months, Bertha commented, "You know, we haven't heard from Tanta Salomina for a long time now. I wonder how come?"

Not long afterward, they received a letter from one of the housemates that she died. "We'll keep the packages going anyway," said GP.

The letters grew to a stream, flowing in both directions, and soon led to a new flow of people coming to America as well.

Chapter 30

DPs

The letter from Lutheran Refugee Services in New York looked urgent. It briefly described the desperate plight of millions of displaced persons—DPs—across the continent of Europe who were left homeless and starving by the terrible ravages of the recent World War. Now there was an urgent need to find homes for them, and LRS was trying to help.

It explained that one such refugee family, the Geists—Alex, Amelia, and son Albert—were relatives of Bertha's family and listed the Osters as potential sponsors for immigration to America.

Bertha checked with her parents, who told her that Mrs. Geist was her mother's cousin.

"Let's check with my brothers," Bertha said, "and see if they'll help."

"And maybe our people in church too," GP added.

All agreed to help get housing and a job lined up for them, and in several weeks the paperwork was done and returned to Lutheran Refugee Services.

In coming months, requests were received by other families throughout the area; and as forms were filled out and paperwork completed for government approval, soon people on both sides of the Atlantic began anxiously waiting to meet.

After nearly a year of waiting, the Geist family finally arrived. Bertha and her team had a house ready for them in town. People from the entire area appeared at the house with furniture, bedding, dishes, and stocks of food to fill the cupboards before they arrived. A local carpenter agreed to hire Alex to help build houses.

Since German was spoken nearly everywhere, the Geists had no trouble communicating.

The two areas of difficulty they had were the son's lack of English and his lack of interest for school; and the father, Alex, insisting that he should be able to drive a car since he knew how from driving in Germany.

"But you need a license," GP told him over and over.

"So help me get one," Geist insisted.

"We can't just get one. You have to pass a test, and you don't know English."

The Geists didn't like to talk in public, but in family gatherings they told of blood-curdling experiences they had to endure, both at the hands of the Nazis and then from the Russian army, and later in refugee camps where conditions were worse than in prison.

"We knew how the Prodigal Son felt," Amelia said one day. "We would have been glad to eat what the pigs ate, but we didn't even get that. Many days there was just nothing to eat. Oh, how my stomach ached so many nights until I cried myself to sleep."

Alex chimed in, "Twenty toilets for a thousand people."

"No baths, I felt dirtier than the pigs at home," Amelia rattled as feelings long pushed down suddenly gushed out of both like a dam bursting in the flood.

"The water was filthy, things floating in it."

"Three families to a tent, and those had holes that let the rain in," Amelia added.

"Shoes had holes in the soles, laces gone."

"Our animals at home never had to live like that," Amelia finally whispered, and her chin began to tremble, with tears rolling down her cheeks.

Alex felt her pain and sang out, "But thank God, we're alive and here now."

****

Months later, the women gathered for a sewing day. Out of nowhere, Amelia blurted out, "The ugly pigs!"

"What pigs, what do you mean?"

"The ugly Russian soldiers," she replied. A terrible bag of memories suddenly came slamming back into her mind, and she had to get it out. Immediately the rest stopped sewing.

After a long pause, studying her hands, suddenly not sure if she could share her awful secret with these women, she slowly began, her voice hardly above a whisper: "Our door was closed, but they busted in, and just like that, one twisted my left arm and they grabbed me."

Her voice began to rise: "Little Albert screamed and jumped at them, but they threw him outside and yelled, 'Don't you come back in or we'll kill you!'

"I fought and twisted, but I was no match for those beasts. They tore my clothes off and threw me in bed, and one after another they came on me, like mare-crazed stallions. They reeked of drink, and they stank. Oh, how terribly ugly they stank, like *scheiss*, like manure.

"One grabbed my head and twisted my face and pressed his lips on mine, the filthy swine. When I cried, he yelled, 'Oh Mamma, why do you cry? You know you like it.'" The agony washed back over her, making her voice tremble, and hot tears begin to flow. One of the women sitting close to her quickly produced a handkerchief from her bosom pocket and handed it to her.

"For an hour that seemed like a year, they used me, until I begged them to shoot me.

"They tore me so bad I bled for a couple days, and it hurt so bad I wanted to die.

"Finally they stumbled out, dumb laughing like crazies.

"I don't know how long I lay there, but finally Albert came and crawled into my arms and we both cried for a long time."

"When I finally got up, I went outside and puked until blood came up.

"At night I screamed at God until I fell asleep. If this was God, who needs him. I couldn't pray for a long time. Sometimes even today, I can't.

"Other women around us were put through the same torture. It was so awful, we couldn't even talk about it.

"I never told any of this to my man, I'm so ashamed. You won't tell anyone either, will you? Because I could never look at them again."

With those words, she covered her face and broke into great heart-wrenching sobs from so deep down that her whole body shivered.

As one, the women dropped their sewing and rushed to encircle her, holding her tight. Hearts pumped blood through the plasma of sisterhood that flowed between them until all felt the pain. Arms wrapped together, burning cheek to cheek wet with flowing tears, each added strength to calm the stinging anguish.

"Oh, dearest Amelia, we'll never leave you," poured out from one after another.

Under the hugs, Amelia's sobs turned to tortured wailing as she grieved the death of that other Amelia back on that godforsaken hellish day.

"Forgive me," she begged through staccato sobs, "I shouldn't have burdened you with all of this that God laid on me. I'm so ashamed, so ashamed."

The desperation of her broken soul reduced every heart to painful sobbing that filled the tiny room until they couldn't stop.

The terrible war tore wounds deep inside that would take long to heal.

Finally one of the women blew her nose and whispered, "Precious sister, God did not do this thing to you."

"No, no," several breathed.

"You have nothing to be ashamed of."

"You did nothing to make that happen."

"Nothing of this will ever pass our lips."

After long, long minutes of silence, they dried their tears, and with a final hug for Amelia, packed up their sewing and returned home, shaken to the core by sharing so painfully what this sister, their own flesh and blood, had endured. A few of the group had their own private anguish to deal with at home, and this shared suffering had not made it any easier.

Prayers that night were long and intense.

True to their word, that faithful band of sisters never betrayed their beloved DP sister until she was called from this life. Only then was her tortured story told.

****

When the Geists heard about Care Package Sunday at the church, they asked GP to pick them up and give them a ride to church. "It feels so wonderful to help my people that are still suffering so much back there," Amelia told the women.

Hearing her reaction, one of the women whispered, "I hope Amelia is starting to heal."

Before long, the trickle of arriving DPs turned to a river as thousands more were sponsored and arrived across the entire Midwest and finally across America and Canada as well.

Most experienced wonderful relief from the pain they had endured and enriched the communities in which they found a new home. A few, unfortunately, became virtual slaves to those who sponsored them with sordid aims in mind; and they moved to new locations as soon as they could break away.

Their shared experiences of flight and affliction, of untold misery in refugee centers, of unbelievable bestiality in concentration camps, brought many Americans in the communities where they came to count their blessings. Their very presence, sadly, also stood testimony to great evil in this world.

Chapter 31

Death of a Dream

"I don't know, but my throat sure hurts," GP told Bertha, "and my voice is all raspy." He just returned home from crying an auction sale with Fred and felt lousy.

"Why don't you gargle with Epsom salt and see if that helps."

It helped a little, but his throat was still sensitive for several days.

They cried several more auctions, and each time his throat felt raw, his voice became hoarse. Finally he talked with Fred, "You know, my throat can't seem to take that loud, steady lingo anymore."

"Yeah, I noticed you got hoarse toward the end, and you were coughing."

"I might have to give it up."

"Let's think about it and talk it over with the women."

A few days later Fred and Selma came to visit, and Fred brought it up, "You know, maybe we should give up auctioneering."

"I'm glad you feel that way," GP replied.

"Maybe it's time to move on."

"Don't think I could do it much longer."

"We've been at it quite a while anyway," said Fred.

"Ja, we had some good days and some rough ones," GP said. "It's been a long time since two scared prairie boys walked into the Reisch School in Austin."

"And a lot of days trying to outduel the howling wind to sell stuff."

"Ei, the memories."

"Well, then it's done," Fred replied with an unexpected catch in his throat. "Guess we better put the word out."

The time seemed right. They had given up their dance band a few years back. Fred was getting busier than ever with the West River Cooperative, trying to get rural telephone service established in the county; GP's Herefords were doing well in shows and sales, and he was selling and hauling more gravel from his pit. Crop and livestock prices were strong. The Oster children were getting deeper into 4-H activities—which called for steady parental involvement.

All of it seemed to point them in new directions.

GP built a show box for all his cattle-show equipment and had a sign painted: "Oster and Son Herefords, Beulah, North Dakota." The metal, two-by-four-foot sign, with fire-red print on white background, was attractive enough to hang over his prized Herefords in any competition, and he enjoyed training and entering his select cattle to shows around the state. With each show he gained more experience and knowledge of what the judges were looking for in award-winning Herefords.

In shows closer to home, Eddie was allowed to go along, and he enjoyed sleeping with GP on the piles of straw between the animals. The big ranchers spent nights in the hotels and had their hired hands sleep with the cattle, but the smaller operators could only afford to sleep in the barns.

Eddie's favorite show was Bismarck, because there they could walk to the nearby Greyhound bus depot for delicious lunch-counter hamburgers, fries, and pop.

Several times GP brought home the Reserve Grand Champion award, and one of his proudest moments was when Eddie won the Grand Champion award at the county fair with his Hereford steer, "Buddy." Father and son's long hours on the training halters and in the corrals at home, and the meticulous sessions of scrubbing, currying and trimming, were paying off.

Then one day when Eddie was in school, GP sat down at the table with Bertha. "You know, ever since Eddie was a little twerp, we've thought of him taking over the farm, like the Eisenbeiss and Keller boys."

"Ja, and?"

"And he's bringing home good report cards from school, but I've been noticing he can't seem to stand some stuff."

"Like what?"

"Like castration and stuff. When we're working the calves or pigs, he helps hold 'em, but he's looking the other way so he doesn't have to watch. And the other week when the guys came and we castrated the big stallion, I looked around and he'd disappeared."

"Reminds me, when we were butchering chickens, I noticed he turned away every time I chopped a head off. I didn't give it no never mind then."

"And when we unloaded his 4-H steer at the butchering plant, I looked over and saw he had tears in his eyes too."

"Well, who knows. There's plenty time. Maybe he'll get used to it."

****

There was no bigger day each year in Beulah than Labor Day. That was the time for the Annual Cowboys' Reunion, with a large parade on Friday evening and a sanctioned rodeo on Saturday and Sunday.

During the summer, Bertha mentioned to GP, "Wouldn't it be fun to get Eddie into the Junior Cowboy Section of the parade this year?" When he agreed, she quietly set to work.

Hauling out the remnants of her war surplus nylon parachute, she sewed a white nylon cowboy shirt with royal-blue embroidery and black buttons. Then she ordered a rose-tan gabardine, boy's cowboy suit from Sears, and found a boy's black Stetson hat and an agate string-necktie in town. To finish the outfit, he needed boots, but they were expensive. Luckily Dad had small feet, so with socks stuffed in the toes, his black cowboy dress boots were close enough to fitting that Eddie could wear them, with spurs, to finish off his cowboy ensemble.

Eddie polished his saddle and boot-blacked the bridle. Then he brushed Barnie's mane and tail, threw a coiled lariat over his saddle horn, and rode the parade. Barnie usually had a calm demeanor, but with all the horses and bands, the crowd noise and rumbling tractors, he pranced an edgy high-step, like a mini black Lipizzaner, the entire route. Eddie kept the reins snug in his right hand, left arm down, heels gently against Barnie's sides, and rode tall and easy in the saddle, rolling with Barnie's steady gait. In that heady, unpracticed moment, he felt like Roy Rogers riding in the Rose Parade, which he remembered from the movie newsreels.

When the judges awarded him the blue ribbon for "Best Dressed Junior Cowboy of the Reunion," Bertha had all she could do to curb her enthusiasm. "Gosh, I had to work to keep from letting out a yell," she laughed later when she hugged Eddie.

GP's truck had only a gravel box, with no stock rack, so the day before the parade, Eddie had ridden Barnie the thirteen miles to town. He was used to riding three miles to Bible School in church each summer, but this was a whole crow's flight further. So when GP suggested that he enter the pony race on Saturday, he wasn't sure. "Maybe he's tired from riding to town," he told Dad, "and besides, we haven't been training him at all."

"Well, anyway, let's leave Barnie in town overnight with your uncle," GP replied.

Eddie tossed in bed all night: should he or shouldn't he? Finally, when the first rooster crowed, he padded into his parents' bedroom. "Dad, let's try it."

The starting line at the pony race brought out six Shetland ponies from the area, all being ridden bareback by their young jockeys. One of the ponies was "Blackie," Barnie's half sister, who looked like his identical twin except for missing the white star on her forehead. She was still owned by the Oelkes, who bred Barnie, and was now ridden by their daughter, Dorothy.

When the starting gun sounded, a pony beside Barnie shot into the lead, but in the first turn he stumbled and tossed his rider. Barnie managed to jump around him, but by then he was more than a length behind Blackie, with two others ahead of him as well. Eddie noticed that Dorothy was riding high, so he lay flat against Barnie's mane and kicked his heels, yelling, "Go, Barnie, let's go."

By the third turn, Blackie was still in the lead, Barnie second, just behind her rump and gaining. Eddie slapped his pony's shoulder and yelled, "C'mon, Barnie, go, go,"

On the homestretch, as they neared the grandstand, the crowd was on their feet, screaming, going wild. Forty yards to the finish line and Barnie was behind by just a head, both ponies' flanks heaving and out of breath, mouths foaming, ears laid back and eyes wide, just trying to keep going. Eddie stayed low, giving Barnie full rein, and slapped his rump, "Move, Barnie, c'mon, go get 'er." Fifteen yards to the finish and they were in a dead heat, Dorothy screaming like a banshee, "Blackie, you gotta do it."

With three strides to go, Barnie pulled ahead and won by a nose and a half.

The finish was so close that the screaming crowd didn't know who won until the announcer got the word from the judges and yelled, "And the winner is . . . Barnie, ridden by Eddie Oster."

People in the stands who knew GP and Bertha clapped them on the head and nearly knocked them over with congratulations, shouting, "Wow, that was the best race we've seen in a long time!"

"Holy buckets," GP shouted back, "that was just about a pants wetter," and all laughed with relief.

Before they drove home, GP decided to stop at the SuperValu for a three-pound brick of marble *halvah* and a dozen sticks of St. John's bread, the "locusts" of John the Baptist, imported from the old country. The Cowboy's reunion had been a high time of exciting joy for the whole family, and he felt like a celebration was in order.

"Eddie, you sure done good today," GP said when they got into the car. Mother gave him a big hug with the biggest smile and a quick little kiss. Eddie looked around, hoping nobody saw it.

****

GP's pride continued to be his hardy Herefords. With every cattle show, Oster Herefords became better known; and as his stock improved, every prize he took made his herd more valuable.

His special joy was training the show stock in the corral. *"Ach, this feels good,"* he said to himself when he stopped the young prize bull he was leading, lifted the halter rope to raise his head high, prodded his feet with a long shepherd's cane to set them square, and gently nudged his belly to get his back perfectly straight. Holding him for a minute at show attention, he sighed again, *"That's good, Jupiter, you look good."*

The next summer, GP built a lean-to on the big barn to house the show bulls and told Eddie, "Your job every night after school from now on is to walk each of the bulls half a dozen times around the corral."

Eddie was less then totally enthused, "Aw, Dad, do I have to?"

"We have to get them really used to following you on the halter, so they do everything, every turn, every stop you tell 'em."

"Every single night?"

"And if they get ornery, clamp a nose ring on 'em and jerk it hard enough so they pay attention and follow you."

"I s'pose."

"Just remember, the better they behave, the more money they're worth."

Some of the bulls stood taller than Eddie, and he got some hard rides around the corral hanging on to the halter rope and bouncing along on his tailbone when they bolted. He soon learned the value of the nose ring, and on the next walks, with a few husky jerks, he calmed the orneriness of the feisty bulls until they obeyed him.

Eddie grew into handling headstrong bulls. But what he surely didn't like was having to fork manure out of the bull barn each Saturday.

"Dad, I feel so sick," he whined weakly when GP came to wake him for his job.

"You'll feel even worse if you can't go along to town tonight," GP replied, and soon Eddie was pitching hot manure.

****

More important than Herefords or any other matter was their continuing life of faith. And in centuries-old tradition, that meant, among other things, that matters in church were decided by the men. Women did not have a vote, nor did they speak or even attend church meetings. They were expected to follow St. Paul's biblical word, "Women should keep silence in the churches."

But heaven help the men if they decided important matters in church without first discussing them with the women at home. The first action on many a matter was "Well, let's think about it a while." That stood for "see what the Missus thinks, and then come back and vote on it."

But one matter the men reserved for themselves was voting on who would serve on the church board as elders and deacons who ran the church. Over some years, the men had long noted that although the Wiedemans and the Osters tolerated each other, they had no great love for one another. So the men of Peace Lutheran decided to take matters into their own hands. They elected GP and Big Emil Wiedeman both to the church board, where they would have to serve together.

The two were glad to serve but not thrilled to serve together. At first, they made sure they sat with plenty space between each other. Then, to their amazement, they discovered how much alike they thought on most issues that came before the board. GP's mind jumped from their first heated encounters of long ago to the first Sunday that church members met to pack Care Packages, and how Emil had come and worked beside him, with no words exchanged between them.

At the next council meeting, he sat down beside Emil and extended his hand. Emil looked down at the hand in front of him, somewhat taken aback, then up into GP's face. When their eyes met, here in the Lord's house, suddenly a higher grace overcame both hearts.

"*Nu, so gehts?* So, life is all right?" Emil quietly asked in time-honored exchange.

"*Alles gut.* Life is good," said GP in time-honored reply.

With those five simple words spoken into each other's eyes, a genuine bond of forgiveness was sealed, a massive brokenness healed, and three generations of distrust softly blown away.

For several moments, other business matters were lost on GP as his mind brought up an old Russian *Sprichwort,* proverb, that Father John used on occasion: *"All are not cooks that walk with long knives,"* meaning not all who look good on the outside are good on the inside, and not all who look homely are bad.

"Guess some of that old stuff is true all right," thought GP to himself.

A number of men exchanged glances. And that was that.

"God be praised," one of the other men quietly whispered on the way out to the cars.

****

GP was on the tractor, relaxed and chewing sunflower seeds, when it struck him. And a great shadow settled into his soul.

"You know," he told Bertha when he got home, "Eddie's doing so good in school, and that might mean the end of my dream."

"Dream?"

"Of building up a good operation to hand over to Eddie someday."

"Why can't you?"

"Well, if we're going to put him through high school, it's too far to drive every day, and there's no place to board him in town, so we might have to move to town."

"Hey, I sure don't like that idea," Bertha replied with a frown.

"I know. I don't either. It means selling everything."

"Everything?"

"The livestock, machinery, everything."

In the next few days Eddie noticed that his parents were strangely quiet, with not much talk happening between them. *"Maybe had a fight,"* he thought.

Little did he realize the consequences that an inquiring mind and a good report card from Wittenberg #2 could bring about.

GP and Bertha decided to visit Fred and Selma and talk about the whole situation.

"I kinda thought about the same stuff with our kids," Fred finally replied, "but I didn't want to say anything to Selma. Guess we'll have to pray some about it."

Chapter 32

She's a Really Big One

The winter of 1948–49 began early and never let up. Big snow drifts stretched across the fields, like billowing waves on the ocean, and licked into the ditches. Jack rabbits loved to borrow into the ditches with just their heads showing. In winter they turned white, making them almost invisible, but GP spotted them.

"How do you see them, Dad?" Eddie asked.

"You gotta look for their big black eyes."

GP carried his Winchester .22 Special when he drove the pickup, and when he saw those eyes, he coasted to a stop, cranked the window down, and picked the rabbit off. Sometimes when they were hit, their reflexes shot them several feet straight into the air and they came down in a ball of fur, making Eddie yell, "How can they jump when they're dead, Dad?"

"Don't know, but they sure do, don't they?" GP replied.

Eddie ran out to retrieve them and never got tired of seeing those big black eyes. When they got to town, Eddie sold them at the hide store and made candy money.

In January, a huge blizzard struck and buried everything in snow. The snowplows pushed up banks five feet high along the county roads. "Wow," Eddie said when they drove to town, "makes you feel like you're driving in a mountain tunnel."

Two weeks of icy, freezing temperatures and a second blizzard struck, bringing deep snow and fierce winds that leveled the banks, burying the roads under five feet of hard-packed snow. When everything ground to a halt, the governor called out the National Guard. They set up camp, brought in big war-time bulldozers, and cleared the roads, now pushing up twelve-foot high banks that felt like tunnels even to the adults.

As mile after mile was slowly cleared out, GP and other men walked from farmyards to the gravel roads where the guard picked them up in double-tandem four-by-four army trucks and took them to town to stock up on necessities. After the guard dropped them off, each man finished carrying his supplies home in heavy, bulging gunny sacks.

During days of hard blizzard, there was no school. But on days with less wind, Eddie and his cousins strapped on their skis to get to school, thrilled by this white leisure world that stretched as far as the eye could see.

The other students walked over the hard-packed snowbanks. Once there, they had a ball digging caves in the eight-foot drifts across the school yard and then connecting tunnels between the caves. The temperature was still below zero, so the teacher, Mr. Waltz, had to fire the old potbellied stove for all it was worth just to keep the ink in the ink wells from freezing, but in the caves it was eerily quiet and comfortable. Mr. Waltz used the experience to teach a unit on Eskimos and igloos, and the students developed a whole new appreciation of their far-north neighbors.

The snowbanks around the school were level with the outhouse roof, and several fathers helped dig a tunnel to the doors to clear the way for nature's calls. The students took to saying, "Gotta hit the igloo."

With the Valley road open, Mr. Schnaidt, the rural mail carrier, loaded up a week's worth of mail and quickly delivered it to all his customers. "Sure glad," he told GP, "that at least I don't have any Christmas catalogues to deliver."

"Or baby chicks," GP replied with a chuckle.

GP's house on the high plateau had little insulation in the walls, which meant keeping it warm during temperatures thirty degrees below zero with raging winds howling across two miles of open Valley was a constant struggle. Several times each night he got up and shoveled more coal into the groaning furnace.

"Sure glad I hauled in two extra loads of coal from Bauer last fall," he whispered to Bertha when he came back to bed in the dark, "or we'd be getting low by now."

Eddie lay in his little single bed at night enthralled by the howling winds swirling around the eves in a cacophony of sound. *"Ei,"* kept running through his mind in the dark, *"feels like scared ghosts crying to find a body."*

The National Guard worked from dawn to dark bucking snow to open the roads; and after a long, hard two weeks, they were finally finished and hauled their huge equipment back out.

The very next weekend, the third blizzard struck.

"She's a really big one this time," GP said when he got up and looked out the window.

For four days, they never saw the barns, nor anything else. Fortunately, the shrieking northwest winds were so strong that they blew the snow away from the front door, but GP only took several steps outside before he came back in, telling Bertha, "I'm almost scared to go out there. A guy could get turned around and end up out on the prairie someplace." He finally tied binder twine firmly to the door hinges, aimed for the water pump halfway between the house and the barn, wrapped it twice around the handle, and continued down the hill, unraveling it all the way to the barn. When he finally got inside the barn, he blew a huge sigh of relief: "Holy suffering cats, this is no fun," he told the cows.

The barn was warm from animal heat, and with plenty hay in the haymow, he climbed up the ladder and forked down enough for all the cattle and horses. But there was no way to get them to water. After he was done milking, he took a sturdy hay rope and, following his binder twine, ran it from the barn to the water pump. With two five-gallon buckets at a time, he carried enough water to give each animal a small drink.

When he was finished, he followed his binder twine once more and ran a stronger rope all the way to the house. "This storm is like nothing I ever saw before," he told Bertha.

A neighbor several farms away was not as fortunate. When he did not come back into the house, his wife thought he was being careful by staying in the barn. But when the storm abated, one of the older boys went out, and the father was not there. In a panic he returned and screamed, "I can't find Father anywhere."

The mother sent him to the neighbors to ask for help, and soon several dozen men and older boys battled through the snow on foot and joined in the hunt for their neighbor. Six days of looking in and around buildings, prodding snow banks with long sticks, scouring nearby hills and large rock formations all produced nothing.

During the storm, dozens of range cattle in the area got stuck in snowdrifts and froze to death; others walked over the hard drifts and kept going, ending up miles from home. Area newspapers helped by running free ads for farmers losing or finding stock.

When the horrific winds finally died down, the world stood transformed into an endless white rolling ocean. Just the roofs of the pig barn, chicken coop, and outhouse were visible; the rest of each building was buried in hardpacked snow. After breakfast, Bertha joined GP and Eddie, and they spent most of the day digging tunnels down to the doors to get in and carrying feed and water to the starved animals.

GP and Eddie then led the horses through the deep snow, breaking a path to the stock tank. The artesian spring kept the water open, but drifts were higher than the tank, so they had to shovel it out to keep cattle from falling into the icy water.

After supper, Eddie strapped on his skis and climbed the high hill behind the barns. The wind had laid one huge, sweet, three-hundred-yard-long snowbank down the hill, covering the fence at the bottom and level with the tall haystacks next to it.

"*Wow, this is skiing,*" Eddie said to himself. "*I can whip down the hill and shoot over the haystack and fly in the air like an eagle.*"

In the softening dusk, he surveyed his crystalline domain from the peak of the hill, took a deep breath, and pushed off on his ski poles. The cold hard snow shot him down the steep slope with the speed of a bullet, nearly blinding his eyes with tears. Over the fence, across the haystack, and in a split second, he was floating high in the air.

What Eddie had not checked was his landing space on the back side of the haystack. The strong winds had swirled between the rows of haystacks and blown all the snow away from the back side, leaving bare, hard-frozen ground. From the highest arc of his jump, Eddie looked down in horror at the bare ground, but it was too late.

When his eyes finally fluttered open, they came to rest on the Big Dipper in the Northern sky, sliding in and out of focus. "*Whoa, how come it's all blurry?*" he muttered, scared and shaking. He had no idea how long he'd been lying there, but by now everything around him was dark, and everything inside him was hurting.

His head was pounding, his right leg curled under his back, twisted in the ski. He moved his arms, then rolled over and slowly straightened his twisted leg. "Ouch," he murmured, "but thank you, God," when everything still moved. Every bone in his body ached, but he slid his foot out of the ski-strap, dragged himself to his hands and knees, then struggled to his feet and hobbled to the house.

"Where in the world have you been all this time?" Mother asked.

"Kinda crashed comin' down the big hill," he lied, thinking to himself, *"Well, I did."*

The next morning as he came out of his room, Mother noticed it was a real effort for him to walk. "You look kinda creaky," she said.

"Snow was hard. Guess I rolled pretty good."

"You better learn to be a little more careful. You coulda broke your legs up there."

"Ja, ja."

When he told his cousins about the adventure, he said, "Boy, I musta' been knocked out for a while, 'cause when I got my eyes open, it was all dark. For a while there, I thought I was dead."

****

For a week nothing moved. The roads were buried under twelve feet of snow, fences covered, drifts twice the height of a man in all directions. There was no school, no church, no commerce. Life revolved around shoveling snow. "We can't even walk over to the neighbors," Bertha lamented, feeling the effects of cabin fever. "We're cut off from the whole world."

The third week, with food getting low, GP walked to Fred's and they decided to take the sled to town, going across country, away from the roads. They would leave at dawn and take six horses—two to break trail, two on the sled, and two trailing at rest—changing every half mile or so.

Struggling in the deep snow, sometimes on top, sometimes breaking through, by noon both horses and men were exhausted. "Ei, I don't know if this was a smart idea," Fred puffed, fatigued and out of breath after leading the breaking team.

"Ja, and we've only gone a few miles."

A few miserable miles more and they met good news. Some other men decided to do the same thing and had broken a trail ahead of them. The rest of the way felt like a highway.

After buying groceries and picking up their mail at the post office, it was too late to start for home, so they stayed with relatives and wrestled their way back the next day.

Other farm people had not gotten mail for weeks and were going stir-crazy with no news, nothing to read. Finally Jess Thompson, rural mail carrier and WWII fighter pilot who now owned an airplane, put skis on his plane and loaded up neighborhood bags full of mail. He came over an area, flew several tight circles, dropped low, and dumped their canvas bag of mail into the snow banks. Neighbors scrambled to the spot as quickly as they could, and all got a shot of mail again.

The roads were not opened again until the welcome sun and warm south winds melted the snow down to a foot or two and the snowplows were able to break through once more.

GP hooked the pickup behind his Farmall tractor and dragged it through the shallower snowbanks out to the opened gravel road, and for the first time in six weeks Bertha got off the farm and into civilization.

"It's amazing how big our town is," she laughed when they drove in.

With the roads open, the mystery of the missing neighbor still hung over the Valley like a storm cloud, and the sheriff finally contacted the State Prison in Bismarck. They sent a team with a pack of bloodhounds, hunting far and wide for four long days, but found no trace of the missing man.

In the spring, a neighbor came to help the family by hauling in straw from a stack in the field. After forking half a load on his hayrack, he suddenly noticed the sole of an overshoe sticking out of the straw; and there, curled up in a ball, were the coyote-ravished remains of his neighbor.

The tragic funeral was the largest ever experienced in the area, and for long weeks naked grief hung over the Valley like a rain-soaked blanket.

Chapter 33

End of an Era

During the blizzard, GP spent long hours with his prize bulls. Few things brought more peace to his heart than rolling their names over his tongue while leading each for a few turns around the corral, brushing their luxurious reddish-brown coats, rubbing their foreheads, and scratching behind their ears. They loved it, more often than not licking his hands or his pants leg with their raspy tongues and softly lowing for more.

But sadly, after the next cattle show, some of the spark was gone. For all his hours of dedicated work, he earned no prize. He had been wrestling with some haunting thoughts recently and that sealed the decision for him. *"You cannot serve God and mammon,"* flashed across his mind on the way home. *"Ei, where in the world did that come from?"* he thought.

Over these weeks, Bertha and GP went through anguished times trying to decide whether to stay on the farm or quit, and they talked long into a string of nights. Eddie showed promise in school, and they dearly wanted him to have an education which they never got. But if that was going to happen, it would mean selling the farm and moving to town. Everything they dreamed about, everything they worked for since they got married was suddenly going to go up in smoke. Both developed headaches and couldn't eat. This decision was too big to handle, and they didn't know where to turn. Talking didn't help and settled nothing.

"Ei, I didn't sleep so good last night again," GP told Bertha when they woke up one morning.

"I haven't for the last week," she replied.

He finally noticed the rings under her eyes and the tired shuffle with which she walked.

"I've had the most gosh-awful nightmares," he continued. "Just don't know what to do."

"Ja, it's getting to me."

"If he starts high school in Beulah, it's too far for us to drive there twice a day," GP thought out loud.

"We don't want to load down the relatives in town, and I sure don't want him boarding with some strange family for four years," Bertha added.

They didn't want to lay guilt on Eddie, so they said nothing to him.

****

Eddie spent his last weeks at Wittenberg School #2 cramming with Mr. Waltz and getting ready for the state eighth-grade tests. He and two classmates had review books in the five major study areas and worked on them every day. After supper he and Mother worked long hours beside the kerosene lamp, answering page after page of questions in reading and spelling, arithmetic, geography, history, and health. "I don't think my brain is big enough," he told Bertha, "to remember everything I've ever learned my whole life in school."

Fortunately, he remembered enough to pass and was formally invited, along with almost a hundred other graduates from all the rural schools in the county, to attend the Mercer County Rural School Eighth-Grade Graduation Ceremony, which earned him a new suit and qualified him to begin high school in the fall.

It didn't take long to change clothes when they got home, and he asked Bertha, "Mom, is it all right if me 'n' Barnie go for a ride?" She barely opened her mouth when he had the bridle on Barnie to ride up to the Indian Mound on the high hill.

Sitting on the rock cairn, he recalled the neat stories Dad told him about Raven Feather, the Charging Bears, and the Indians of old. In the stillness, he could almost feel them running close by him, laughing. The breeze carried the faint smell of the rising Missouri, and the wide horizons stretching out to the four winds made for wonderful healing from the recent stress. "Boy, those lucky ducks," he told Cuddy, sitting expectantly at his feet, "at least those Indian kids never had to pass all those lousy exams."

His brain, unfortunately, had precious little time for vacation. The next week he had to begin the month-long German Bible School session, preparing for confirmation. It meant riding Barnie three miles to church every morning for day-long classes in Bible History and memorizing thirty-five pages of the catechism. Add fifty Bible verses and three hymns and it filled his brain to the cork.

Dad and Mom drilled him every night at home, and Reverend Gevers made the great Bible stories come wonderfully alive. Eddie could feel the stark terror of the children of Israel as they raced through the holding tunnel of Red Sea water, hear the smack of David's smooth stone on Goliath's forehead, feel the thunder in that short man's heart when the Lord said, "Zacchaeus, you come down." He felt the pain of the Crucifixion and stood in awe of an empty tomb. Somehow he got into a rhythm, and even the memorizing became almost enjoyable.

But the most fun in Bible School was during lunch. The elderly Reverend Gevers took a nap each noon in the parsonage next door, and that gave time for the nine girls in the class to put on gobs of sweet cherry Five and Dime lipstick, like Jane Russell, and ganging up, chase the two boys until they caught them, and covered their faces and necks with red-lipped kisses. Hormones ran high as the two boys tried to escape, but with nine juiced-up thirteen-year-old girls chasing them, how could they break free?

All the girls giggled when Eddie got up after being captured and kissed and called out to the other boy, "Ei, that hurt really good."

One of the girls put on a perfume so rich that Eddie thought, *"Almost makes me wish my whole body were a nose,"* and went on to bigger fantasies.

On the high holy day of Confirmation, the tension was agonizing. For each of the class, the thought of having to stand up in front of the whole congregation, including many of their relatives, to answer the pastor's long list of memory questions brought up feelings just short of terror. "I'm afraid I'm gonna have to go to the toilet during the middle of church," Eddie lamented on the way to church. Several of the girls cried, and one threw up before church. But the pastor by now knew their abilities and mercifully gauged his questions accordingly.

After a few minor hiccups and some gentle hinting by the pastor, all the confirmands in their white dresses and new suits over perspiring bodies did well, and the mothers breathed a huge sigh of relief at not being put to shame. Their thoughts turned to the big dinner waiting at home, and, unfortunately, Reverend Gevers's carefully chosen words in the sermon landed at the bottom of the ash heap of memory as soon as he sat down in his ornate clergy chair.

Strangely, in succeeding weeks the confirmands experienced a feeling of deep disappointment: the days of intense struggle together had drawn them into a closeness which they didn't recognize until it was over, and they missed each other. For this prairie eleven, in the weeks to come, sly winks across the aisle during worship in church instantly raised pulses, and worship would long carry the aroma of sweet cherry lipstick.

****

When all the excitement finally settled down, GP and Bertha visited Fred's again. Fred and Selma were also wrestling with the decision about their future. As soon as the children went outside, the four swung into conversation about what they should do.

"We've talked, and we're getting nowhere," Bertha said.

"And we prayed and prayed and there's no answer," GP added.

"Ja, I know," Fred put in. "Same with us."

"I always hoped Eddie could take over the farm someday," GP said.

"Us too, but all the kids are good in school," Selma said, "and it would sure be nice if they could make something of themselves besides farming, don't you think?"

The more they talked, the more confusing everything became. There were good things and bad things as well, no matter which direction they chose.

"I don't know if I can ever be happy living in town," Bertha said, shaking her head.

GP's lower lip trembled, and he looked at the floor. It was just too painful, but he had to get it out: "They're only animals, and I know we shouldn't get that close to them, but giving up my Herefords feels like losing our baby all over again."

"Is it all really worth it?" Fred asked. "What if our kids end up not liking school and they quit. Then what?"

A long silence followed. No one knew what to say.

"Ei, my stomach hurts," Selma blurted out and got up to get some lunch ready.

"I know, I haven't slept for days," Bertha added.

The next week brought more sleepless nights and bitter worry. But finally Fred's came to visit GP's and things seemed calmer.

"We have to get off the pot and decide," Fred said to start the discussion.

"Well, I don't know, but I guess it's time we made some changes," GP replied. "We have to think more about our kids than about what we want ourselves."

"Looks like we sell out," Fred finally added, and a long silence followed, with uncomfortable coughing. Selma and Bertha got up and hugged with tears flowing. The men sat in stunned silence, trying to make sense of what they had maybe just decided.

"I guess the Herefords gotta go," GP stammered and couldn't hold back the rolling tears. He got out his red handkerchief and coughed. "Ei, that hurts so bad I can't take it." Fred got up to step outside, and GP followed him.

"Guess that's it," Fred choked and walked off by himself for a while. When he came back, he told GP, "Suppose we gotta start putting some things together."

Arrangements became a little easier when Fred got a telephone installed, the very first in the area. With Fred on the Rural Telephone Board, he received priority treatment. Their new phone was not grandmother's wall phone with a crank but the sleek, ultra-modern, black desk phone with a rotary dial and no need for the operator to put you through.

Eddie asked, "Dad, aren't we getting a phone?" But GP had a policy of paying cash for any purchase they made, and they owed no bills. He replied, "I'm not going to get tied down with a darn telephone bill every month for the rest of my life."

Fortunately, Fred used his new phone to call the North Dakota Hereford Association in Bismarck, who came out, gathered all the registration forms, took pictures of the top sires and dams, and printed a booklet under the title "Oster Brothers Hereford Dispersion Sale." They distributed the booklets along with sale bills across five states, and the die was cast.

The sale meant trucking all the livestock to Mandan, site of the largest sales ring in the area. All of this would be expensive. "I guess you wanna make money, you gotta spend money," GP told Bertha with no enthusiasm in his voice.

Seeing his prize bulls, each one a friend with a name, sold and led out of the ring, nearly broke GP's heart and brought grieving that dogged his soul for weeks to come. But there was scant time for self-pity. They had to find a house in Beulah and schedule an auction sale for the farm. Within two weeks, they accomplished both.

"We'll keep the land and rent it out. And we'll sell off everything else," GP said across the supper table.

"Ja, I suppose," Bertha replied. Eddie noticed a strange sadness in her voice.

"Mom, are you all right?"

"I guess it just kinda hurts," she replied as a sudden tear ran down her cheek, and she quickly wiped it with the back of her hand.

They decided to keep the car, the big truck, and the household furniture, along with faithful Cuddy and GP's tools for the move to town. Cattle, horses, pigs, chickens, all the machinery, diamond-willow fence posts, the kerosene refrigerator, all the things they had built up over two decades of hard work would be sold at auction.

With all the stressful things swirling around them, GP decided they had enough money from selling the Herefords to get a new car. He drove the old '35 Chevy to town and picked out a pale, sea-green, tudor '49 Ford sedan. "Did you work out a loan at the bank?" the dealer asked him.

"Don't need to," GP quietly replied. "Got cash."

Eddie liked the slick, push-button radio best of all on the new car. GP would trade it all back in a heartbeat to have his Domino Herefords back again.

After Labor Day, Eddie started high school in Beulah, scared and alone, knowing only two people in the whole school: cousin Ronald and neighbor girl Elsie Keller, both several grades ahead of him. GP had arranged for Eddie to board with a family they knew in town, but there too he was a stranger, and nights were long and lonesome.

The day of the auction brought a big crowd to the farm. With his years of auctioneering experience, GP was disappointed that the auctioneer didn't get higher prices for a number of things, but what could he do?

Bertha did fine with the auction until the milk cows were sold. "I know each one's name," she told Selma with tears welling up, "and how many hours did I spend sitting under each one, morning and night, milkin' her." Letting them go, along with her chickens, was a stab in her heart.

For GP, the milk cows were a relief. But when his team of work horses, Black Shorty and Brown Shorty, came up, a lump closed his throat, and he couldn't even talk loud enough to tell the auctioneer their names until Nephew Gilbert yelled them out. For so many years, they were his right arm. They were never sick; on the grass mower, the hayrack, the bundle wagon at threshing, he never had to use the reins; a word and they knew exactly what to do and did it. His jaw muscles worked, his chin trembled, fists clenched.

"Oh, dear God, this is almost too much," he breathed. *"What'll happen to them now?"* Fred, standing beside him, saw his reaction and whispered, "It's all right. I know the guy that bought 'em, good man."

Eddie skipped school the day of the auction and really couldn't quite understand the strong emotional reaction of his parents. But then Barnie came up for sale. The auctioneer asked Eddie to jump on Barnie's back and ride around the little circle a few times to show how well trained he was. Some wag in the crowd yelled out, "Think he can still beat Oelke's pony?"

Eddie smiled and circled his thumb and index finger, signing "yes," and handed the reins to the auctioneer. But when the bidding began, he choked and had to walk away. When he got clear of the crowd, he broke into sobs and raced to the house.

After supper, the whole place was ghostly silent, and they suddenly felt like strangers on their own farm. Dad led them in devotions in that haunting silence, and then it was time to take Eddie back to town for school the next day. The drive was silent, both in mourning. GP and Eddie both felt a heavy weight on their chest but neither could talk about it.

Bertha couldn't sleep and spent most of the night crying. The next morning, there was no rooster crowing to wake them, no pigs grunting, no cows to milk; and with no sounds outside, she felt even worse. She sat at the table, coffee cup in hand, and sobbed.

GP quietly left the silent house and walked up to his old refuge on the high hill. Sitting on the stone cairn, he reflected on how different his life might have been had his parents given him to the gentle Charging Bears who so desperately wanted him. *"The Indians here had dreams, and our people so cruelly shattered them. Just like I had dreams, and they're gone too,"* he reflected. *"And if Eddie doesn't make it in school, is all this for nothing?"* The peace he always experienced up here eluded him now. *"What's gonna happen to us yet?"* Suddenly he felt old and tired and worn out. *"Somebody said there's peace in the valley, but there's no peace in my soul."*

All three of the family, each in their own way, grieved for days over precious things that were torn out of their lives and would never again be part of them.

Eddie spent the next few days of high school in a daze. He kept hoping that someone would call his name and walk down the hallways with him. No one did. During the long nights in bed, he thought of Barnie, dreamed of Barnie, bolted upright in bed from terrifying nightmares about awful things happening to Barnie. *"I wish I'da flunked those tests and stayed on the farm,"* he thought over and over. *"Mom and Dad sure woulda been happier too."*

The new house in town had both good and bad things about it. The good part: it was located only three blocks from school, and it was cheap. The bad: it had no bathroom, a rubble stone basement with a dirt floor, no central heating, bad windows, and no garage. When the full impact of all the work that needed to be done on it struck GP, he suddenly felt like giving up. "I think we been screwed with that good deal we got," he remarked to Bertha.

With help from relatives and a hired plumber, they spent the next weeks remodeling, patching, and painting. Soon they were ready to move their meager furniture in and bring Eddie "home." The house still needed a lot of work, but it was home. Against their better judgment, they even had a telephone installed and added a portable radio in the dining room.

Cuddy moped a lot, not thrilled to be a town dog. A rabbit hunter with no rabbits to hunt, no mice to chase, no cats to pester. And nobody thought of taking him for a walk. Sitting by the door waiting for people to come home was not a dog's life for a country dog.

Within a week, GP was offered a job helping a carpenter build and repair houses, where at least he could be outside, and life was bearable again.

Eddie soon found himself at the edge of enjoying school. So many pretty girls, and so many books in the library. And chorus, where church music stood him in good stead, gave him the joy to open up and trill like a meadowlark on a fence post.

He took up playing trumpet and went out for football. With town kids a year, or even three or four, ahead of him, he faced an immense challenge in both, trying to catch up with skills they had learned years earlier. But teachers and coaches were patient, and he had a good ear and fast feet. With a lot of grit, he soon was at least past the embarrassment of the first beginnings. And the girls kept him on his toes.

"The cutest thing in skirts," he thought was Delores Hoover, a year behind him. He wanted to ask her for a date, but he was yet entirely too bashful. Instead he scribbled a note, "Will you go to the movie with me Friday night?" He signed it, folded it up, put her name on the outside, and passed it down the rows to where she sat in study hall. Luckily the note passers were all careful, and the study hall teacher didn't see it being passed.

He saw Delores get the note and read it, and then she didn't move. *"I'm sunk,"* flew across his mind. Finally, after what felt like hours, she slowly turned toward him and nodded, with the slightest of smiles that totally unglued him.

"I think I'm really gonna like this school thing," he told Cuddy when he came home walking on air, "especially with that cutie around."

Eddie also discovered two new Wulff cousins in school, that he never knew he had, and they soon grew to be good friends. Dennis, the same age, was good in band; Jerry, a year older, was a good football player. Both were good students, and both nurtured him in this new way of life—how to dress for different stuff, girls, some people to stay away from, what to leave or not in the unlocked homeroom desk, parties, bullies who wanted to fight, a whole lot of things he needed to know and about which he was country-naive.

Returning home from school one day, Eddie noticed that Cuddy didn't meet him at the door. Cuddy always met him at the door! "Where's Cuddy?" he sang out. "Have to ask Dad," Bertha replied and busied herself in the kitchen.

When GP walked in the door, Eddie met him, "Hey, Dad, where's Cuddy?"

"Well, you know how much he's had trouble walking lately."

"Yeah? So?"

"And he hasn't been eating much of anything?"

"What'r you saying?"

"Well, I had to take him out and put him out of his misery."

"Dad, you didn't!"

"It was no good for him anymore, poor old buddy."

"And you didn't even let me say good-bye to him?"

"I didn't want to make it any tougher on you."

Eddie spun on his heels and ran up the stairs to his room. "I hate you for doing that. I hate you!" he screamed over his shoulder. GP looked at Bertha, and neither said anything. Eddie felt like his best friend had died and for a time wasn't sure he could trust his dad.

When GP volunteered to take his car to haul some football players to the next out-of-town game—since there was no team bus—Eddie saw the easy banter between his teammates and his father and how they enjoyed him. He saw Dad in a softer light again, and their relationship quietly began to grow back.

****

In these years Eddie was busy with studies and school events. A small school meant he was involved with everything: sports, music, plays, and parties; and he enjoyed it to the full. Along with dozens of friends, he was into roller skating, ice skating, and sledding down the icy street behind the school all the way down to Main Street. The local constable warned the students several times, "Kids, you know you're crossing several streets of traffic when you go flying down that hill on your sleds."

"Yeah, we know," they all chorused back. "We'll be careful." And when his patrol car was down the hill and gone, they went back to sledding down the street.

Maybe it was destiny, maybe extra careful drivers, but no sledders were run over by cars during those winter nights of exciting entertainment.

Through all those memorable growing-up days, one of Eddie's favorite times continued to be dating girls, sometimes alone, sometimes in groups, on hayrides, youth activities in church, movies, whatever. Growing up without sisters, he was enthralled by the alluring mysteries of femininity.

"Girls sure are different, aren't they," he told Cousin Dennis one evening when they were riding in Dennis's grocery-delivery car.

"But hey, nice difference, right?" Dennis replied.

At basketball games, one of the cheerleaders was Delores Hoover. She had a rhythm and a smile that drew him like a bear to honey, and he loved watching her perform. Though they had only dated a few times and then broken up in his freshman year, he often admired her perkiness, her bright personality, and her attractiveness in succeeding years. At the beginning of his senior year, she broke up with her boyfriend, and Eddie again asked her out. A month of dating and he gave her his class ring and letter sweater, and they were a pair for all the events from then on. Never had he been happier.

With Little Mike, one of the players on the football team, however, it was a different story. At six-foot-three and two-hundred-forty pounds, he was still "Little Mike," simply because his father was "Big Mike" to everyone. Little Mike had designs on Delores as well and asked her for a date. When she turned him down and later went with Eddie instead, Little Mike took it as an insult. He waited outside the school after football practice, and when Eddie came out, he snarled, "Hey, cowboy, think you're pretty good, don't ya," and shoved him in the chest, looking for a fight. With Little Mike's size and coming from the tough side of the tracks, he knew how to fight. Eddie knew nothing about street fighting and quickly realized this would end up badly.

"Just drop it," he stammered with a sudden knot in his stomach, turned, and walked away.

"Chicken liver," Little Mike yelled after him, "yellow belly." And things yet more descriptive as Eddie walked on, half fearing an attack from the back.

The next afternoon in football practice, playing defense, Little Mike stretched out to make a tackle on the runner, and Eddie blindsided him with a block, putting a shoulder into his ribs so hard that it knocked Little Mike out of breath, and he lay on the ground with a look of fear in his eyes. That freed up dating Delores.

These were busy days for the family. GP worked, Bertha volunteered to help with old people and in church activities, and they never missed any of Eddie's football games. They had trouble understanding all the strange rules of the game, but they could easily tell if the Beulah Miners were doing well or poorly.

In the spring, they drove Eddie to all his track meets. Although several other boys occasionally ran with Eddie, no other boys were interested in track, and he turned out to be a one-man Beulah track team, running the mile and the half mile. His lazy track coach registered him for meets and told him, "Good luck, Eddie," but never bothered to go along, so GP became his meet manager and substitute coach, and the whole family enjoyed track.

Eddie's senior year went well, and he won every race he ran. GP grinned and patted Eddie's back, and he knew Dad was proud. Bertha usually said, "You did pretty good out there," and she was so proud that several times she almost told Eddie.

After graduation, Eddie got a job with a company laying a pipeline across the area.

"What do you do?" Delores asked.

"I'm a welder's assistant," he told her. "I steel brush all the welds on the pipe joints."

"Doesn't sound like lot of fun."

"And sometimes when we're in the hills and the water truck can't get in, we all have to pee on the pipes to get 'em clean."

"Oh, quit," she replied, turning away, "that gives me the *eggles*."

Eddie couldn't help but laugh at the hilarity of the scene he just painted.

It was a dirty job, often on his back at the bottom of the pipes, often down in deep trenches, with biting flies, mud, mosquitoes, and stifling heat. But the pay was good.

"Hey, Mom, I'm really learning a lot of new language from those guys," Eddie teased when he got home after a day's work.

"Just you be careful," she fired back, "and don't you be using any of that kinda talk around here, understand?"

By Labor Day, he, Cousin Dennis, and another friend were off to Wartburg College in Waverly, Iowa, seven hundred miles from home. All three were thinking of becoming pastors, and Reverend

Kammerer said, "If you want to be a pastor, that's where you ought to go."

Going to college in Iowa meant leaving Delores, and it was a bitter experience. Telephone was entirely too expensive, trips home out of the question. Staying close meant writing letters, and they both did, five nights a week. Letters were wonderful, but the lonesomeness was almost overwhelming. "My Dearest Sweetheart," Eddie wrote, "I can taste your kisses, smell your heavenly perfume, feel the wonder of you curled up tight in my arms, but I'm so lonesome without you that I'm ready to quit school and come home."

The next year, when Delores graduated from high school, she went off to Minot State Teacher's College. Now she and Eddie were nine hundred miles and more hundreds of letters apart.

The following summers, Eddie found work driving a huge Euclid earth-moving truck, hauling dirt at the massive Garrison Dam being built on the Missouri River. The monstrous earth-moving trucks with immense power and huge payloads were a delight for young bushy tails to operate.

"Mom," he said after several days hauling dirt, "those heavy-equipment guys make the pipeline guys sound like Sunday school teachers."

At $1.95 an hour, the pay was better than anything around, and Eddie was home dating Delores every night. The only problem was mornings. After late dates, he still had to be up at 4:00 a.m. and on the road to work.

"I really think you should stay home some nights," Mother said, "and get more sleep. You're gonna have an accident yet."

"Oh, Mom." To himself, he thought, *I guess she just doesn't remember being young.*

Too soon, it was time to return to college, while GP also got a job at the Garrison Dam, billed as the largest earthen dam in the world. They were not among the wealthy, not even by small-town standards, but as GP said, "Somehow we got enough to eat, and we're healthy, and we're putting our kid through school."

"I'm so thankful," GP mentioned later to Bertha in bed, "Eddie's been a good kid, and we've really had no big troubles in our life."

"The Lord's blessed us pretty good," she replied, nestling against him in thankful comfort.

Chapter 34

Ave Atque Vale

Eddie couldn't wait to get home from college for Christmas. He had an engagement ring in his pocket and was hoping his beloved Delores would accept his proposal of marriage. And his parents had written with great excitement about plans to move back to the farm in the spring. They all had much to talk about and futures to form.

The first morning home, GP took Eddie out to the farm, and they made plans to begin renovations in the spring. In the afternoon, GP had a physical exam at the clinic before the carpal tunnel surgery he was to have on his hand after Christmas. And in the evening, after they attended Christmas Eve services in church, Eddie drove Delores out to a secluded parking spot at the edge of town and nervously fumbled with the little box that held the ring.

She was wonderfully surprised but not shocked since they had discussed marriage for several years. After long hugs and kisses to seal the moment, they drove back to tell the news to both sets of parents.

The parents were shocked. Eddie was nineteen, a sophomore in college; Delores, eighteen, and a freshman.

"Wonderful. But you're way too young," were the first words from both sets of parents.

"Well, don't worry. We're not getting married yet," Eddie replied. "We hope in a year and a half, when Delores is done with school and starts teaching, and I'll be in my last year."

Christmas Day was hazy, with the young in a cloud of ecstasy, the elders in a bigger cloud of uncertainty.

Breakfast the next day brought new reality. The phone rang asking GP to bring Bertha along and come to the clinic. "That doesn't sound like Christmas cheer," GP said, cradling the phone.

"Your blood work showed some abnormalities," Dr. Levi told them at the clinic. "I'm afraid it might be something kind of serious."

"Uh-oh," GP replied, looking at Bertha, whose eyes were suddenly wide with fear.

"I'd like to send you to a specialist in Bismarck to check it further."

The tests were scheduled for the following week. Eddie had to return to college and didn't want to go back, but GP and Bertha both assured him they'd call if anything drastic turned up.

A battery of tests confirmed the diagnosis as cancer, and the doctors recommended exploratory surgery to see if they might find where the cancer was centered and how to attack it.

"We might as well get on it right away," GP agreed.

After GP had recovered from surgery, the doctor came to the room. "Surgery went OK," he said, "but what we found, I'm afraid, isn't the best news."

"Bad?"

"Well, it's metastasized."

"Meaning what?"

"Meaning the cancer has spread over all your vital organs. We tried to take some of the globs of tumorous mass out, but everything is all grown together in one big knot."

"So is there any medicine," Bertha pleaded, "any place we can go for help?"

"Not really. It's too far developed."

"So how long do I have?" GP asked in a whisper.

"Of course we never know with any certainty, but I'd say maybe six weeks to a few months?"

The room was filled to the ceiling with stunned silence.

"I'm sorry," the doctor answered, rubbing GP's arm, and slowly walked out.

Bertha called Eddie at college, "I think you'd better come home. Dad isn't doing well."

A week and half of recovery at the hospital and they returned home.

The next weeks they rushed around trying to get some things in order, but GP was so weak that he could do very little.

Reverend Kammerer came and prayed, but GP grew steadily weaker, with increasingly more pain.

"I think we better get him back to the hospital in Bismarck," Bertha told Eddie. "He's so sick, and I hope they still might be able to do something."

Relatives and neighbors heard about GP's condition and dropped by his room for farewells, but GP's pain grew intense, and visiting was more burden than cheer. "I think we better call Reverend Kammerer for Communion," Eddie said.

After Communion was finished, there was a soft knock on the door, and in walked big Emil Wiedeman and his wife. Emil quietly stepped to GP's bed and held out his hand. That big catcher's-mitt hand swallowed up GP's weakened one, and to Bertha it looked like the hand of God himself enfolding her husband. For long moments, the two men simply looked deep into each other's eyes without a word passing between them. The silence grew so long that Bertha and Mrs. Wiedeman both began to fidget, wondering if ghosts of feuds past would circle the bed.

They need not have worried. Old streams of antagonism had been thoroughly washed away, and now a deep river of caring flowed silently between the two old warriors of the prairie. Suddenly, as their eyes held each other, big tears welled up in the eyes of both men. Bertha quickly glanced at Wiedeman and noticed his lower lip trembling as he said in a soft, low, rumbling voice, "You have been my brother."

GP's mellow baritone was all gone now, and with a strange high voice, he quietly replied, "And you mine." Nothing more was said. Eight quiet words bespoke redemption and forgiveness and a bond stronger than the flooding Missouri. They pumped each other's hand once more; and Wiedeman quietly turned, ran his sleeve over his nose, took his wife's arm, and walked silently out of the room. GP wiped his eyes with his sleeve and said no more.

Several more days and GP's condition grew steadily worse. As the pain increased, the doctors injected more morphine. But with more morphine, more delirium swept over him.

"Ei, those ugly birds keep flying at me," GP complained hoarsely, waving his arms to beat them off. "They've got such terrible claws. Get 'em outta here!" He grew so agitated that he had to be restrained with cloth bands in bed, and that irritated him even more. Bertha and Eddie sat by his bed, rubbing his arms, stroking his cheeks, speaking gentle words of endearment. "It's OK," Bertha softly whispered, "we love you. You can go to sleep."

"I'll shoo the birds away, Dad, you'll be all right," Eddie added, with a smile that wouldn't work. But terrible things kept attacking GP's mind, making him wild eyed and stressed out.

Eddie wanted to talk with his Dad and tell him so many things, but conversation, like eating, was past. No words could even make him turn his eyes in acknowledgment. Eddie prayed, Mother prayed, some silent, some out loud. All prayers seemed to bounce off the ceiling and evaporate. GP's wide eyes darted around the room, unseeing, in drugged-up fear.

Bertha walked out into the hall for a breather when Eddie came running. "Mom, Dad's getting worse." They took hands, and Eddie led in a desperate prayer. GP's breathing grew irregular, and Bertha recognized the death rattle that vibrated each breath like a slow-idling Harley. A few agonizing minutes more, one final gasp, and GP's struggle was over. Bertha grasped his head with both hands and laid her shoulders on top of him, sobbing bitter tears, while Eddie walked out into the hall, heartbroken and hurting, bitterly angry at God. When he came back into the room, Bertha stood up and swept him into her arms.

"Now you have no more father," she cried, sobbing on his neck. "He's gone, Eddie, he's gone!"

"I'm so sorry, Mom," was all he could say.

After a long silent hug, Eddie turned and softly closed his father's eyes and gaping mouth.

"Oh, Dad," he murmured, "I don't want to be doing this," and broke into heart-wrenching sobs.

The nurses and doctors asked them to step out while they quickly straightened up the bed and the body. When they came back into the room, GP was cleaned up and looked amazingly at peace.

"Now he's home," Bertha blurted through tears. "And I'm a widow."

"Some April Fools' Day this is," Eddie replied.

"Forty-nine is too young to die, way too young."

Before long, the funeral directors came; and Bertha, moved to tears at the terrible reality of their presence, stammered, "G-guess we've got a funeral to put together, huh."

After the funeral, committal, and lunch at church, dozens of friends and relatives gathered at Bertha's house. Eddie lost track of how many drew him aside and quietly offered him well-intentioned comfort. Invariably, they began, "Remember, Eddie . . .," and already he knew what was coming: another Bible verse aimed right between his eyes. He wanted so badly to snap, "Stick your Bible verses. I just want my dad back." Instead he smiled and answered with a wan "Thank you." After a while, he sneaked down into the basement coal bin all by himself and let the tears roll for long minutes.

Several more days at home, an evening with Delores in which neither knew what to say and the only comfort was in silently wrapping their arms around each other, a long tear-filled hug with Mom the next morning, and it was time to return to college. Before he left, he drove out and climbed the long hill to Raven Feather's grave.

No sooner had he sat down on the rock cairn than tears began to roll. "Why, God, why did you have to take him?" burst out of his lungs. After long minutes, the tears stopped, and a strange peace fell over him. *"Feels like two fathers got their hands on my shoulders,"* he thought and walked away at peace, at least for the moment.

When he got back to college, Eddie was fortunate to have a religion professor that took him under his wings and saw him through days of grief that nearly immobilized him at times.

In world literature class, Eddie read the Roman poet Gaius Catullus who wrote an immortal tribute to his fallen brother: "Ave Atque Vale." Hail and Farewell.

Those words moved Eddie to write a tribute to his father for another class:

Spring 1955

Dear Dad,

I thought I knew you, and as a child, I did. But I am so sad that we never really got to know each other as adults.

You shaped my life in more ways than you will ever know and taught me so much. Most of all, you and Mom set my feet on the pathway of faith. Thank you with all my heart. You will be an inspiration to me until they close my eyes as I closed yours on that terrible day when the Lord called you home.

Forgive me, Father, for so often not doing what you told me to do, for yelling at you when you didn't give me the car to go out, but most of all, Dad, forgive me for taking away your dreams so you and Mom could fulfill my dream of serving the Lord.

I know where you are it's a never-ending green, with no drought or tumbleweeds burning, and your final pain is all gone. Now you're singing with the angels, and I'm so glad for you, but I miss you so much and wish that just once more I could tell you how much you mean to me and how much I love you and always will. Somehow we never said that to each other, and now it's too late.

Dad, you were taken away from me far too soon and left my heart awash in tears. But in these few years you nourished my soul more than I could ever tell you and filled my cup to overflowing. We still had so many times to share and things to do, and now they'll never be, and I'll miss that for the rest of my life. Since you're gone, there is such a terrible hole inside me. Right now my heart is broken.

I only hope that one day I can make you proud that you had a son, and you taught him well. And I hope I don't have to come see you for quite a while, but I'll do my best to round up some people to come to God ahead of me.

As a famous poet wrote long ago, "Ave Atque Vale." Hail and Farewell, dear Father, Hail and Farewell.

Dad, I love you more than words can tell.

Your Son Always,
Eddie

Acknowledgements

Where does one begin to express gratitude that stretches beyond anything that words can deliver, to people that stretch around the globe, across time that stretches over so much history?

I am hugely indebted to:

-Delores, lifetime helpmate, organizer, for her patience when she was more single than married during my surges of writing.

-faithful friends, teachers, authors, mentors, at every age of my life, some degreed, some "wisdomed," who sculpted my whole being.

-the Mercer County (ND) and the Freeborn County (MN) Historical Museum staffs (especially Linda Evenson) who provided invaluable information of so many kinds about people and days gone by.

-Paul Goodnature, Dr. Wm. Buege, Catherine Ost, Deb Durand and Bill Hobson, Susan Carlson, and the Park Avenue Writer's Group: editors, shoulders, voices of correction and encouragement who helped shape thoughts into readability.

-Gerhard and Irmgard Kleih for indispensable German language assistance.

-the entire staff of Xlibris who provided expertise in turning raw script into a finished book.

-Dagnis and Olesja Dreimanis, Riga, Latvia, dear translator/guides in travels to Russia.

-the host of precious tantas, grandmothers, across two continents, whose hands I held as they shared a treasure-trove of memories. They suffered much, and their holy tears and blessed laughter are seared into my heart and woven into the fabric of these pages so the world will know the story.

-that Holy Source beyond all knowing, for gifts beyond telling, the Author whose story goes on….

Author Blurb

Milt Ost is a retired minister, who now resides with his wife, Delores, in Albert Lea, Minnesota.